DOWN OUR STREET

Also by Joan Jonker

When One Door Closes
Man Of The House
Home Is Where The Heart Is
Stay In Your Own Back Yard
Last Tram To Lime Street
Sweet Rosie O'Grady
The Pride Of Polly Perkins
Sadie Was A Lady
Walking My Baby Back Home
Try A Little Tenderness
Stay As Sweet As You Are

DOWN OUR STREET

Joan Jonker

HEADLINE

First published in 1999
by HEADLINE BOOK PUBLISHING

10 9 8 7 6 5 4 3 2 1

British Library Cataloguing in Publication Data

Jonker, Joan
    Down our street
    I.Title
    823.9'14[F]
    ISBN 0 7472 7441X

Typeset by
Letterpart Limited, Reigate, Surrey

Printed and bound in Great Britain by
Clays Ltd, St Ives plc

HEADLINE BOOK PUBLISHING
A division of the Hodder Headline Group
338 Euston Road
London NW1 3BH
www.headline.co.uk
www.hodderheadline.com

With love to my family, Edna, Elsie, Enid, Joseph,Griff and Vincent.

And to friends who were so supportive of my charity work:
Margie and staff at Lucy In The Sky cafe in Cavern Walks.
Alfie and customers at The White Star pub in Rainford Gardens, Matthew Street.
Pat, John and Josie of Solitaire Fashion House.
June Lornie at the Liverpool Academy of Art.

A friendly greeting to the readers.

This book has been written in response to the many requests from readers who were eager for more news on the Bennet families. Molly and Nellie certainly captured peoples hearts, as they did mine. If I have made any slip-ups on ages, etc, I crave your indulgence as I have written five more books since I said farewell to Molly and Nellie in SWEET ROSIE O'GRADY.
Enjoy DOWN OUR STREET as much as I enjoyed writing it.
I guarantee you many hours of laughter.
Take care.
Love

Joan

Chapter One

Molly Bennett threw the sheet on the draining board and looked down at her hands which were red raw with wringing the washing out. One of the nuts on the mangle had worked itself loose and the handle wouldn't turn properly, so rather than wait until her husband came in from work, she'd decided to wring the clothes out by hand. 'Serves yer blinking well right,' she said to the empty room. 'Yer should have waited until Jack came in.' Then she answered herself. 'It would have meant leaving the dolly tub in the middle of the kitchen all day, and there's not enough room to move as it is.'

A knock on the front door had her wiping her hands on a corner of her pinny before picking her purse up from the sideboard and making for the door. 'This should be Tucker. I hope he's got some decent coal on for a change.'

'Good day to yer, Molly.' White teeth shone from the face blackened with coal dust. 'Have yer recovered from yer hangover yet?'

'I have, Tucker, but me ruddy mangle hasn't. The damn thing's conked out on me.' Molly poked her head out of the door and gazed up and down the street which was still festooned with coloured bunting left up from the street party they'd had last week to celebrate the end of the war in Japan. 'I still can't believe it's all over, can you?'

'It takes some getting used to after nearly five years of war, Molly. We won in the end, thank God, but paid a very heavy price for the victory.'

'I know. I've prayed that much, I'm sure God must be fed-up listening to me. Prayed for our lads that got killed, the ones who'll come home wounded and the lucky ones, like my Tommy. By the time he got called up, the worst of the fighting was over. I count me blessings, Tucker, I know how lucky I am.'

When Molly saw a smile come to the coalman's face, she turned her head to see a neighbour, three doors up, step into the street. Nellie McDonough, all eighteen stone of her, folded her arms under her mountainous bosom, hitched it up and swayed towards

1

them. 'I'll tell yer what, girl, yer can't half talk.' She nodded to the horse standing between the shafts of the coalcart and tutted. 'The poor bloody horse got so fed-up with the sound of yer voice he's gone to sleep on his feet.'

'Oh, ye're there, are yer?' Molly tried to keep a smile back, but it was impossible. She only had to look at her best mate and her face took it upon itself to widen into a smile. Nellie was better than a dose of medicine any day. 'I bet yer've been peeping through yer curtains, dying to know what me and Tucker were talking about.'

'Well, I didn't see Tucker doing much talking, unless he's a bloody ventriloquist. I could tell he wasn't able to get a word in edgeways with yer, so I came to put him out of his misery.'

'That's very thoughtful of yer, Nellie,' Tucker said. 'But I've only been here a few minutes.'

'Six minutes by my clock.' Nellie nodded her head and the sharp movement sent her layers of chins flying in all directions, and the turban she wore over her thin, straggly mousy hair, fell down to cover her eyes. She'd worn the turban all through the war, ever since she heard the women in factories making munitions had to wear them. If anyone asked her why, she said it was her contribution to the war effort. Pushing it out of the way now, she said, 'And it doesn't take six minutes to say yer want a bag of coal. Unless me mate's been complaining about the muck yer've been giving us. All ruddy slate it was last week, Tucker, and I'm telling yer straight to yer face that if I hadn't used it I'd be giving it back to yer and asking for a refund.'

'Yer've been getting the same coal as all me customers, Nellie, and yer were lucky to get any at all. All the best stuff has been going to help the war effort.'

'Well, the war's over now, lad, so yer can throw me a bag of nuts in.'

'The war might be over, but it'll be a year or two before rationing is over. Things are not going to be back to normal for quite a while.'

'Take no notice of her, Tucker, she's having yer on,' Molly said. 'We were only saying this morning when we were having our elevenses that it would be ages before rationing was finished.'

'It was you what said that, girl, not me. And if yer'd been paying attention yer would have noticed I didn't say I agreed with yer. I'm living in hope that this time next week I'll be able to walk in the Maypole and ask for a pound of streaky bacon and a dozen eggs.'

'Wishful thinking, sunshine,' Molly said. 'Mind you, there's nothing to stop yer walking into the Maypole today and asking for a pound of streaky bacon and a dozen eggs. Yer won't get it, like, but there's no harm in asking. And yer'd give them all a good laugh.'

'If I thought yer were being funny, girl, I'd clock yer one.'

'Ladies, I hate to break this up, but I do have work to do.' Tucker looked from one to the other. 'Can I take it that yer both want a bag of the muck I've got on me cart?'

'Yes, please, Tucker.' Molly opened her purse and passed over two half-crowns. 'Give us some copper in the change, for the gas.' She took her change, dropped it in her purse and gave him a big smile. 'And I want to thank yer for doing yer best for us while the war was on, I really appreciate it. It can't have been easy having hundreds of women moaning at yer every day, as though it was your fault.'

Nellie gasped. 'Well, you polished bugger! D'yer know, Tucker, she's been calling yer fit to burn for the last five years! Some of the names she called yer had me blushing.'

'At least I had you on my side, though, Nellie. I bet you never called me names.'

'What! I wouldn't dream of it, Tucker! Anyway, yer know I'm not one for swearing. It's not ladylike.' When Nellie's body started to shake, Molly waited for the laughter to erupt. 'There are exceptions, though,' the big woman spluttered. 'If I've got to spend an hour coaxing that ruddy coal to light, I'll call yer every name I can lay me tongue to.'

'I'll try and be out of the street by then.' The coalman whistled softly and the horse moved up to stop by the side entry. It had been doing the same round for so many years it really didn't need Tucker, only to carry the sacks. 'Can I have yer money, Nellie?'

'I haven't got me purse on me. You pay him, girl, and I'll give it to yer later.'

'Sod off, Nellie McDonough!' Molly's eyes rolled. 'Yer did that to me once before and I'm still waiting for me money back.'

'In the name of God, that was ages ago!' Nellie looked put out. 'Yer've got a ruddy good memory, girl, I'll grant yer that.'

'Yes, I've got a good memory, sunshine, but what I haven't got is me money back.'

'Can yer hear that, Tucker? We've just got one war over and me mate here wants to start another! All over a couple of bob!'

'Nellie, go home and get yer purse, the man hasn't got all day.'

'I don't want to go home, girl, I want to come in yours. I've got something very important to tell yer.'

'I'm not falling for that, sunshine! Yer haven't been over the door since yer left here earlier, so unless yer ceiling's fallen in on yer, nothing important could have happened. Anyway, ye're not

3

getting in here 'cos me flamin' mangle conked out and I've got clothes dripping all over the place.'

A crafty gleam came to Nellie's eyes. 'There's nowt wrong with my mangle, girl, it's in good nick. So if you pay Tucker, I'll come in yours and have a natter, then we'll take yer washing to my house and put it through me mangle. Now yer can't say that's not fair.'

Molly saw the coalman's chest heave in a sigh, and she felt sorry for him. If he spent this long at all his calls he'd be working until midnight. She opened her purse and counted out the correct money. 'This is nothing but barefaced bribery, and I'm only doing it so Tucker can go about his business.'

Nellie grinned and her cheeks moved upwards to cover her eyes. 'See yer next week, Tucker.' With that she pushed Molly aside and entered the house. 'I'll stick the kettle on, girl, and we can have a cuppa while we're talking.'

'Don't mind me, sunshine, you just make yerself at home.' Molly followed her mate into the kitchen. 'It doesn't matter that I'm up to me neck in work. Nor, I might add, can I afford to be making yer two lots of tea in one day. Me caddy's nearly empty now, and it's got to last me until next week.'

'Me heart bleeds for yer, girl, it really does.' Nellie was grinning as she struck a match under the kettle. 'In fact, it's bleeding that much I've got to do something to stop it before it's running all over yer kitchen floor. So I'm going to say something that will shock yer, so hang on to the sink for support in case yer feel faint.' Her eyes full of mischief, she laid a chubby hand on Molly's arm. 'When we take these clothes into mine to mangle, I'll give yer the coal money, plus a couple of spoonfuls of tea to help yer out. Now, that's a bit of good news, isn't it, girl?'

Molly cupped her chin in her hand and looked thoughtful. 'By my reckoning, sunshine, yer've had over a thousand cups of tea in this house since rationing started. That's only the elevenses. If I take into account the times yer've been here to a party, well, that's another couple of hundred.'

Nellie tried to look suitably impressed. 'Ay, aren't you good at sums, girl? Just wait until I tell George that yer've counted every cup of tea I've had – he won't believe me. I don't suppose yer know how many mouthfuls that is, do yer, so I can tell him that as well?'

Molly went back to looking thoughtful. 'Well, seeing as yer can drink half a cup in one go, all yer need do is double the number.'

The kettle began to whistle and Nellie moved away from the stove. 'Yer've put me off now. I could no more drink a cup of tea off yer than fly.'

4

'I wouldn't worry about that, sunshine, 'cos it's going to be so weak yer won't know what ye're drinking.'

'Oh, that's all right, then.' Nellie leaned to look into her friend's face. 'I'll go and sit down because I couldn't stand the excitement of watching yer count each tea-leaf.'

Molly was grinning as she carried two steaming cups through. 'I did warn yer! It's warm, wet and very weak.' She put Nellie's cup in front of her. 'I've been trying to get a little stock put by for us when the boys come home. Don't forget, there'll be a couple of weddings to worry about in the very near future.'

Nellie sipped on the tea and pulled a face. 'I was going to say it tastes like maiden's water, but I know yer'd only get a cob on so I won't say it.' She put the cup down and leaned her elbows on the table. 'That's what I wanted to talk to yer about.'

'What! Yer said it was something important!'

'Well, isn't my son marrying your daughter important?'

'Nellie, we've talked about Jill and Steve getting married for God knows how long. We even talked about it this morning!'

'Keep yer hair on, girl, don't be taking off on me.' Nellie sighed and her bosom rocked the table, causing the tea to spill over. But a little thing like that didn't worry her, she wasn't as houseproud as Molly. 'I can't stand being in the house on me own, that's the truth of it, girl. I can't wait for me sons to come home. I haven't seen our Steve for nearly two years, and Paul for eighteen months. When I see them standing in front of me, and know they've not been injured or anything, then I'll be as right as rain. It's the waiting and not knowing I can't stand.'

'I know, sunshine, I feel the same about our Tommy. But at least we know they're alive, that's more than some poor families can say.'

'Well, can we talk about the wedding, to cheer me up? Remember yer said years ago that yer were going to buy the biggest hat in Liverpool for Steve and Jill's wedding? Yer haven't changed yer mind, have yer?'

Molly shook her head. 'The biggest hat that Lewis's have got. I'm going to be dressed to the nines the day they get married. We've waited long enough for it, haven't we, sunshine?'

'My George said I'd look a right nit in a big hat.' Nellie looked dejected. 'And I don't want to let me son down by making a show of meself.'

'There's a happy medium, Nellie. Buy a hat that's in between. Not too big but not so small it would look like a pimple on a mountain. Tell your George to keep his flamin' nose out, anyway! We women know what's best for us.' Molly glanced at the clock. 'I'm sorry, sunshine, but I'm going to have to put a move on. I want to get the sheets on the washing line so they'll be dry for ironing in the morning.'

Molly held her breath when Nellie pushed her chair back and it creaked in protest. Never a day went by that Molly didn't expect the chair to collapse and her mate to end up on the floor. And she couldn't make up her mind whether she'd be more worried about the chair being broken, or having to try and lift her eighteen-stone neighbour off the floor. 'We can talk while we're doing the mangling. I'll feed the sheets in and turn the handle, and you can catch them the other side. Is that OK, sunshine?'

Nellie grinned. 'How much is it worth?'

'It'll pay for that cup of tea yer've just had, yer cheeky article.'

'What cup of tea, girl?'

Molly pointed to the empty cup. 'That one!'

'That was never tea was it? Well, I'd never have known. It just goes to show, girl, that yer learn something new every day.'

The postman knocked on Molly's door the next morning with a huge grin on his face. He handed over two letters. 'One for you, Molly, and one for Jill.'

Molly was so delighted she couldn't resist planting a kiss on his cheek. 'Oh, you lovely man, yer've made me day.' She closed the door and gazed down at the envelopes. Her heart began to race when she recognised her son's handwriting on one, and Steve's on the other. Clasping the precious letters to her heart, she walked back to the living room where her two daughters were having breakfast. Jill, her eldest girl, was twenty-one and Doreen a year younger. The sisters were very alike in looks, having inherited their mother's long blonde hair and bright blue eyes. But where Molly had put weight on over the years, the girls had slim, shapely figures. 'Jill, there's a letter for yer, sunshine, from Steve.'

With a shriek of delight, Jill dropped the piece of toast she was eating and reached out for the letter. 'Please, please, please say he's coming home.' Her hands shaking with excitement, she tore the envelope open and took out a two-page letter. As her eyes moved quickly over the lines, her smile grew wider. 'He's coming home, Mam! He's being demobbed and is hoping to be home next week!'

Doreen left her chair to give her sister a hug. 'That's marvellous news, our kid, I'm really made up for yer. Isn't that great, Mam?' Then she noticed her mother was standing with a letter pressed to her lips. 'Is that from our Tommy, Mam?'

Molly's voice was choked. 'I know I'm daft, but I'm going to cry. And when ye're a mother yerself yer'll understand.'

'I understand now, Mam,' Doreen said. 'I feel like crying

meself. Would yer like me to read it to yer?'

Sniffing loudly, Molly said, 'Not ruddy likely! I want to be the first one to know when he'll be home, safe and sound.'

'Well, hurry up and open it, then! Me and our Jill have got to go to work.'

Jill, having devoured every word of her boyfriend's letter three times, put it back in the envelope and turned her attention to her mother. 'Come on, Mam, open up.'

'Give our Ruthie a shout for us, will yer, while I read what Tommy's got to say. I don't want her to be late for school.'

Jill was standing at the bottom of the stairs when she heard her mother's cry of delight. 'He's back in England! He wrote this letter on the ship and says by the time I receive it he'll be back on English soil. Oh, thank God for that! He hopes everyone is well and sends his love.' Her eyes wet with tears of happiness, Molly read on. 'He can't wait to see us all, he's missed us so much.'

'Ruthie,' Jill shouted. 'Hurry up, me Mam's had a letter from our Tommy.'

The loud clatter from above had Molly shaking her head. 'She'll probably jump down the flaming stairs and break her neck.'

The baby of the family entered the room like a whirlwind. 'When's he coming home, Mam?' Ruthie had been a surprise addition to the family, coming along seven years after Tommy was born. It was a time when Molly was having a struggle to make ends meet with three children to clothe and feed on the low wages her husband earned. Another mouth to feed wasn't exactly welcome. But from the time the baby had been put in her arms by the midwife, she'd been cherished not only by her parents, but also her sisters and brother. 'Does he mention me in the letter?'

'No, sunshine, he doesn't mention anyone by name. He just sends his love to everyone and says he can't wait to see us all.'

'I've had a letter from Steve,' Jill said. 'And he's coming home next week.'

'Go 'way!' Twelve-year-old Ruthie was the spitting image of her two sisters. The same blonde hair, blue eyes and slightly turned-up nose. 'If Steve's coming home next week, Mam, why isn't our Tommy?'

'He is, sunshine! He doesn't know exactly when, but he's going to write again as soon as he finds out.' Molly pointed to the clock. 'Jill, Doreen, yer'd better get cracking or yer'll be late clocking in.'

Jill slipped her arms into her coat. 'I wonder if Auntie Nellie's had a letter from Steve?'

'She's bound to have had. Anyway, I'll be giving her a knock as soon as I get Ruthie off to school. Then I'm going to me ma's to see if they've heard from Tommy.' Molly wagged her shoulders and bottom. 'Isn't this just a beautiful day?'

Jill gave her a kiss. 'Yer can say that again, Mam. There were times when I thought this day would never come.'

Doreen followed with a kiss. 'Yer'll soon have all yer chicks around yer, Mam, like a mother hen.'

'Until yer all start leaving the nest.' Molly smiled. 'When yer were young I was wishing yer'd grow up, now I wish yer were youngsters again.'

The two sisters stood framed in the doorway. 'Yer won't get rid of me that easy, Mam,' Doreen said. 'When me and Phil get married we'll only be living over the road.'

'And me and Steve won't be moving far away from yer.' Jill's gentle smile brought a lump to Molly's throat. 'We'd be lost without you and Auntie Nellie.'

Molly followed them to the door. 'Wait until yer Dad knows, he'll be over the moon. I bet him and George go for a pint tonight to celebrate.'

'Me dad deserves it, the hours he's been putting in at work.' Jill linked arms with her sister. 'Me and Doreen will mug him to a few pints.'

'I'll see yer tonight. Ta-ra.' Molly waved them off and went back into the living room to find Ruthie reading Tommy's letter. 'Ay, buggerlugs! Out in the kitchen and get yerself washed while I make yer some toast. And in future, don't read letters that aren't addressed to yer.'

Ruthie's grin was cheeky. 'I looked at the envelope, Mam, and it said to Mr and Mrs Bennett and family. That means me.'

Molly held her arms wide and the girl walked into them. Rocking her gently, Molly said, 'Oh, sunshine, I must be the luckiest woman alive. I've got a lot to thank God for. A marvellous husband and four lovely children. And He's kept us all safe through the war. I'll never complain again as long as I live.' She patted her daughter's bottom. 'Go on, sunshine, get yerself washed or yer'll be late for school.'

Ruthie was eating her toast when she heard her mother talking to herself in the kitchen. 'Just look at that pile of ironing I've got to do. And I hate ruddy ironing.'

'I knew yer wouldn't keep it up, Mam!'

Molly popped her head around the door. 'Keep what up, sunshine?'

'Yer said yer'd never complain again as long as yer lived. Five minutes later ye're complaining about the ironing!'

Molly stopped the chuckle from leaving her mouth. Standing with her hands on her hips she said, 'Listen to me, Miss Nosy

8

Poke, I was having a private conversation with meself, if yer don't mind. And I can't complain to meself about meself, can I? Now if I'd said to you that I had a stack of ironing to do and I hated ironing, then that would be complaining. Can yer see the difference?'

'Not really, Mam! But seeing as it's a special day, I'll let yer off.'

'Gee, thanks, kid!' Molly retreated, thinking that when she was young, children were seen and not heard. The war had a lot to answer for.

Nellie opened the front door, folded her arms and came to stand on the edge of the top step. 'You're late, aren't yer?'

Molly looked up with surprise. 'What d'yer mean, I'm late? I'm not supposed to be here, so how can I be late?'

Nellie delved into the pocket of her pinny, brought out a letter and waved it in her friend's face. 'This came two hours ago, the same time as yours.'

'How did yer know I got a letter?'

'I asked the postman, of course, soft girl.' Nellie jerked her head back and tutted. 'It wouldn't have done me any good asking the blinking milkman, would it?'

Ooh, I'll get you for that, Molly thought, chuckling inside. 'That's very perspicacious of yer, sunshine! Ye're nobody's fool, are yer?'

Nellie narrowed her eyes and clamped her lips together. That was a very long word, that was, and she hadn't a clue what it meant. She might have done if she hadn't sagged school so often, but it was thirty years too late to worry about that now. So, not wanting to be beaten, she decided that two could play at that game and she'd bluff her way out. 'Ye're right there, girl! I'm nobody's fool and it's nice of yer to say so.' She stepped aside and made a sweeping movement with her hand. 'Come in and tell me all yer news.'

She's a crafty minx, Molly told herself as she turned sideways and took a deep breath before squeezing past her mate's enormous tummy. But she's too nosy to let it drop. I bet she'll ask me what the word means before I leave. 'I won't stay long, sunshine, 'cos I want to slip round to me ma's to see if they've heard from Tommy.'

'What did he have to say in his letter, girl?'

Molly feigned surprise. 'Oh, didn't the postman tell yer?'

Nellie's face was deadpan. 'I did ask him, but he said although he could see the writing, the envelope was too thick to make out the words. So I've had to wait two hours for you to come and tell me. I hope it's been worth the wait.'

9

Molly couldn't keep it in any longer. 'He's coming home next week, same as Steve.'

'Oh, that's the gear, girl!' Their two hands met across the table and they gripped each other tight. 'D'yer know, I've done nothing but cry since the blinking postman came. George said he couldn't make me out, that I should be dancing for joy.'

'They're tears of relief, sunshine, and I've shed a few of them meself. My Jack doesn't know yet, he'd left for work before the post came.' Molly had a thought. 'Oh, I haven't asked yer about your Paul! Have yer heard from him?'

Nellie shook her head. Paul was her youngest child, and although he was now twenty he was still her baby. 'George said it'll take weeks to get the lads home from all the different countries, so I'll have to be patient. It's all right for him to talk, though, isn't it, girl? Men don't have the same feelings as us women. Before he went out, he said Paul was alive and well and that was the main thing. But I won't rest until I've seen him with me own eyes and hugged him to pieces.'

Molly looked with fondness at the woman who'd been her best mate for nearly twenty-five years. Many of them had been lean years, when the children were little and it was a case of robbing Peter to pay Paul. But they'd always shared what little they had with each other. 'I'd never have got through the war without you, Helen Theresa McDonough. Yer kept me sane when I was nearly out of me mind with worry, and yer made me laugh when I was down in the dumps. Ye're the best mate anyone could have.'

Nellie's chubby face lit up. 'And I'm clever, as well, aren't I, girl?'

Molly puckered her lips before saying, 'I think crafty is the word for you.'

'Oh no, I like that other word better. It sounds more posh.'

'Which word was that, sunshine?'

'Don't come that with me, Molly Bennett, yer know damn well what the word is. What yer said I was for not asking the milkman.'

'Oh, yer mean perspicacious? It's a good word, isn't it, sunshine? I wonder what it means?'

'Don't tell me a clever bugger like you doesn't know what it means?' Nellie was trying to think fast so her mate wouldn't get one over on her, and she came up with what she thought was a beauty. 'I'll tell yer what, girl, save yer racking yer brains, just write it down and I'll ask George what it means when he comes in. My feller's very clever with words.'

Not to be outdone, Molly raised her brows. 'Have yer got a

pencil and a piece of paper? I'll print it in case he can't understand me writing.'

Like a little girl who's been caught out in a game of rounders, Nellie made her way to the sideboard and opened a drawer. She slapped a piece of paper and a stub of a pencil down on the table. 'I bet yer can't spell it.'

'Of course I can!' Molly sounded more confident than she felt. She'd come across the word in a dictionary and had kept it in her mind until the time came to use it on Nellie. But she hadn't taken any notice of the way it was spelt. Still, George wouldn't know, either. So, licking the tend of the pencil, she wrote down what she thought was near enough. Handing it to her mate, she said, 'I know what it means, too! It means understanding clearly.'

'Well, why the bloody hell didn't yer say that in the first place?'

'It's no good knowing big words if ye're not going to use them, sunshine.'

'And by the same token, girl, it's no good using them if no one can ruddywell understand them!' Nellie gazed down at the scrap of paper. 'There's thirteen letters in that word. Six I can manage, thirteen I wouldn't even attempt.'

'Well, I'm going to attempt to get away now, sunshine. If me ma's had a letter she'll be expecting me.'

'Can I come with yer? Me nerves are too shattered to stay in the house.' Before Molly had time to refuse, Nellie reminded her, 'Don't forget, yer'd never have got through the war without me.'

Molly knew when she was beat. 'Are yer respectable enough to go straight from there to the shops?'

Nellie looked highly indignant. 'Of course I am! I've got no holes in the heels of me stockings, the elastic hasn't snapped in the leg of me knickers and I haven't got no tidemark.' She leaned her weight on the table and lifting her leg she rubbed the front of her shoe over the back of her stocking, then changed foot for the other one. 'And me shoes have been polished.'

Molly was looking at her with an amused expression on her face. 'How come yer can get up and down on your chairs without a creak from them, but when yer sit on mine they creak that much I think they're going to collapse?'

'Ah, well, yer see, girl, I take yours by surprise. Mine are used to me, and when they see me coming they brace themselves for the onslaught.'

Shaking with laughter, Molly folded her arms on the table and laid her head on them. And Nellie, happy that she'd made her friend laugh, sat down and followed suit. And there wasn't a peep of protest from the chair.

★ ★ ★

Bridie Jackson was always pleased to see her daughter but this morning her smile was wider and her eyes sparkling with excitement. 'I knew yer'd be round, me darlin', so I did.' She cupped Molly's face and kissed her soundly. 'Sure, isn't it the best news we've had in years?'

'Yer knew we'd had a letter then, Ma?'

'Didn't Tommy tell us that he'd written to yer as well? And wouldn't he be wanting his mother to know before anyone else?' Bridie stepped aside to let her visitors pass. She smiled at Nellie and kissed a chubby cheek. 'Top of the morning to yer, Nellie, me darlin'. Come along in and sit yerselves down.'

Bob Jackson was sitting in his favourite chair at the side of the fireplace and he lifted his cheek for a kiss. 'Marvellous news, isn't it, love?'

'It certainly is, Da! I was that happy this morning I even kissed the postman!'

Nellie's jaw dropped as she gave her friend a dig. 'Yer didn't kiss him, did yer?'

Molly nodded. 'He must have thought I'd lost the run of me senses.'

'He never told me that!'

'Well, he wouldn't, would he? He knows what ye're like for gossiping, and it would have been round the street like wildfire. He'd told yer about me getting two letters and probably thought yer'd wangled enough out of him for one day.'

'Did yer get two letters, then, love?' Bob asked.

'I got one from Tommy, and I'm going to let me mate tell yer about the other one.'

This pleased Nellie no end. 'Me and Jill got one from Steve.' She paused as an actor would before delivering a dramatic line. 'He's coming home next week.'

'Oh, thanks be to God!' Bridie put a hand to each of her cheeks and rocked gently. 'Yer'll soon have all yer children around yer again. It's happy I am for yer, and for Jill.'

'I haven't heard from our Paul, yet, though,' Nellie said. 'Still, I'll probably get a letter any day now.'

'Yes, yer will, Nellie,' Bob told her, knowing that for all her joking and fooling around, she was as sensitive as anyone. 'They'll get the lads home as fast as they can.'

'Ma, did Rosie get a letter from Tommy?' Molly slipped her coat off and draped it over the arm of the couch. 'Or did he write to everyone in general?'

'She got her own letter, me darlin', and wasn't the girl altogether over the moon? Sure, when she left this morning she was walking on air, so she was. I'd like to bet she got to work

12

without her feet even touching the ground.' It was nearly fifty years since Bridie had left her home in Ireland but her voice still had that lovely lilt to it. Her accent was mixed now with a Liverpool one, but when she was excited she reverted right back to the thick Irish brogue. 'I'll put the kettle on and yerselves can have a cup of tea with one of the fairy cakes I made this morning. Light as a feather they are, and that's the truth of it, so it is.'

Molly watched her mother walk through to the kitchen and her heart was filled with love. Bridie was in her late sixties now, but she was as slim as a young girl, her back was ramrod straight and she held her head proudly. Her white hair was combed back into a bun, away from a face that still held traces of the beauty she'd once been.

Molly turned now to her father. 'Some excitement in the house this morning, then, Da?'

'That's putting it mildly, love.' Bob was only a shell of the man he'd been before he had a heart attack eight years previously. His thinning hair was snow-white and his face lined. But he always looked immaculate, Bridie saw to that. From the day he'd come home from hospital she'd waited on him hand and foot. 'I don't get up early these days, as yer know, and I was half asleep when I heard yer ma and Rosie laughing and crying. When I came downstairs it was to see Rosie waltzing Bridie around the room. I'm not ashamed to say I cried with them. It was such a lovely feeling, Molly, to know we'd soon be seeing Tommy again.'

'There's nothing wrong with a man crying, Da! I know another man who'll be shedding a few tears tonight.'

'Oh, who's that, girl?' Nellie asked.

'Jack, of course, soft girl! Who d'yer think?'

'I knew it wouldn't be my George, he never cries.' Nellie folded her arms across the top of her bosom but didn't feel comfortable. So she hitched herself up and her arms disappeared from view beneath the mountain of flesh. 'No, I tell a lie. He cried when our Steve was born. When Lily came along twelve months after, he went to the pub to wet the baby's head. But when Paul was born twelve months after that, he said if it was going to be a regular thing every twelve months there was no point in celebrating because the novelty had worn off.'

Bob chuckled. This woman had given them so many laughs over the years, she deserved a medal. But how she managed to keep a straight face he'd never know. 'It's a good job we know your husband, Nellie, or yer'd have us believing yer.'

'It's the truth, Bob! I mean, I've proved it, haven't I? I never had no more children after our Paul, 'cos I thought if me husband wasn't even going to notice there was another addition to the family there was no point in going to all that trouble.'

Bridie bustled in carrying a tray with china cups and saucers set out on a lace cloth. 'See to the tea, Molly, me darlin', while I fetch the cakes.'

'I'm glad I came with yer, girl,' Nellie said 'I'd have missed the tea-party if I hadn't.'

'Nellie, sit still on that chair, will yer? Yer've got me heart in me mouth.'

'All right, Miss! And I won't spill no crumbs, Miss, honest! Will it be all right if I breathe, Miss?'

'As long as yer do it quietly and gently.'

'My God, this daughter of yours has an answer for everything, Bridie!' Nellie took one of the small fairy cakes in her chubby hand and devoured half of it in one go. 'Has she told yer she's going to buy the biggest hat in Lewis's for Steve and Jill's wedding? I can't have a big one, though, in case I steal the limelight.' Nellie put on a woebegone expression. 'I can only have a middling one.'

'Well, now, won't that be altogether different, me darlin'? Yer'll be the only one at the wedding wearing a middling hat, and that's a fact. Sure, it must be the latest fashion because meself has never even heard of it.'

'Don't tell them any more, sunshine. Wait until the day and give everyone the surprise of their lives.' Molly smiled at her friend before turning to her mother. 'Yer'll be able to get rid of this now, Ma.' She tapped the huge table which took up nearly all the room. Under the cloth which Bridie kept it covered with, was a Morrison air-raid shelter. Molly had got it for her parents when the air raids started so they wouldn't have to be trekking up to the big shelter in the park every time the sirens went. It was a big ugly thing, but it had served its purpose and given the family peace of mind. 'I bet yer won't be sorry to see the back of it, eh?'

'That I'll not, me darlin'. Sure, I can't wait for the day when I'm able to have me room back to normal.'

'I can ask for yer, Ma, but God knows when they'll get round to picking them up.' Molly could see the disappointment on her mother's face and knew she'd been hoping to get rid of the monstrosity before her beloved grandson came home. 'I'll tell yer what though. It was brought in in pieces and assembled inside, so I'll ask Jack if there's any chance of it being dismantled and left in the yard until the men from the Corporation pick it up.'

Bob shook his head, doubt showing on his face. 'Jack would never manage that, lass, it's solid iron! It took three men to put it together!'

14

'Then I'll get three men to take it apart, Da! Where there's a will, there's a way. I'll ask George and Phil to give Jack a hand.'

'Ay, hang on a minute!' Nellie's chins did a quickstep. 'My feller could do himself an injury lifting this ruddy thing!'

'Nellie, is your mind yer bedroom again?'

'Well, I've got to protect me interests, girl! And it's in my interest to make sure my feller doesn't strain his—'

Molly moved quickly to put a hand across her friend's mouth. 'All right, sunshine, we get the message, yer don't have to spell it out for us. It's the table that's under discussion, not the antics you get up to in yer bedroom.'

Nellie removed Molly's hand with a look of disdain on her face. 'Molly Bennett, yer've got a mind like a muck midden. What I was going to say, before I was so rudely interrupted, was that I wouldn't like my George to strain his—er—his wrist.' She stuck her tongue out before saying, 'So there, clever clogs.'

Bob was shaking with laughter, Bridie smiling behind her hand, while Molly told herself to give it up as a bad job. 'Come on, let's go down to the shops.' She pushed her chair back ready for the off. 'I'll see if I can get yer table sorted out, Ma, I won't forget. If yer ask Rosie to come to ours tonight I might be able to tell her if Jack thinks it can be done.'

Nellie was quite comfortable and didn't want to move. The longer she stayed here the less time she'd have to sit in her own house on her lonesome. Not that she couldn't find work to do because the fluff underneath all the beds was thick. But she couldn't manage to get down on her knees and shift it, so it could wait until the weekend when Lily was off. 'Ay, Bridie, remember when yer got that letter from yer great-niece in Ireland, asking her if yer'd take a fifteen-year-old girl in 'cos there was no work for her over there? I bet yer never dreamt that girl would end up courting yer grandson?'

'No, I never did, Nellie, me darlin'. But didn't Rosie take one look at Tommy and tell us he was the lad for her? Both only fifteen, and Tommy of an age when he thought girls were nothing but a nuisance. It took Rosie a full year to convince him that she was the one for him, and sure, aren't Bob and meself delighted with the outcome?' She smiled across at her beloved husband. 'Taking Rosie O'Grady in was the best thing that could have happened to us. She's given us four years of love and laughter.'

'She's given us all four years of love and laughter, Ma,' Molly said, remembering how she'd been against her parents taking a young girl in, thinking they were too old to have a teenager in the house. But, thank God, they hadn't listened to her. 'As you say, she's the best thing that could have happened, not only to you, but all of us.' She glanced at her mate. 'I can see yer mind working, sunshine, but we'll have no more delaying tactics. Get your backside off that chair and we'll be on our way.'

Chapter Two

'What are yer getting for the dinner, girl?' Nellie linked her friend's arm as they walked towards the main road. 'I don't know what the hell to get 'cos I haven't got enough coupons to make a decent meal.'

'Neither have I, sunshine, so it'll have to be a pan of pot luck.' Molly felt herself being pushed towards the kerb as Nellie's swaying hips edged her sideways. 'Move back to the middle of the pavement, will yer? One of these days I'll end up in the road and get knocked down by a tram or a bus.'

'Nah, it couldn't happen, girl!'

'Why couldn't it happen?'

'Because yer don't get no trams or buses coming down this street.'

'Not this street, no! But when we turn the corner into the main road there's one passes every few minutes. And I don't fancy lying under one.'

Nellie gave this the careful consideration she thought it was worth. 'I'd always come and visit yer in hospital, girl, yer know that.'

'Oh, aye, I can just see it! You sitting on the side of me bed eating all me grapes.'

'What grapes are they, girl?'

'The grapes that yer intended to buy me but forgot until yer were walking up the path to the hospital.' That should give her something to think about, Molly thought. It might keep her quiet for a few minutes.

But Nellie had it figured out. 'They must be the grapes Jack brought yer in, then.'

They were outside the butcher's shop by the time and Molly was chuckling as she walked ahead of her friend. She might have known Nellie would have the last word. 'Hi, Tony! And you, Ellen! How's tricks?'

Tony Reynolds's grin stretched from ear to ear. These two were guaranteed to brighten up what had been, up to now, a very dull day. 'Have yer got yer list written out, Molly? Is it a leg of mutton

17

and two pounds of stewing steak?'

'In me dreams, Tony! I've just got enough coupons for half a pound of mince. And I was going to ask if yer had any scrag ends yer could let me have to make a pan of broth?'

Nellie had been standing by, her face that of an innocent cherub. She wagged a finger at the butcher, inviting him to lean closer. 'And you, Ellen, come and listen.'

Tony's assistant, Ellen, was Molly's next-door neighbour and well used to the shenanigans of the two women. But she also knew the other side to them, and she owed them a debt of gratitude she'd never be able to repay. 'What is it, Nellie?'

Nellie's acting skills came to the fore. With a finger over her lips, her eyes rolled from side to side to make sure there were no spies in the shop. Then she said softly, 'If she mentioned grapes, humour her.'

'What's grapes got to do with anything?' Ellen asked, while Tony's eyes twinkled with merriment. He could tell by the big woman's face they were in for a laugh.

'That's what I want to know!' Nellie's eyes were as wide as she could stretch them. 'Five minutes ago, she had me sitting on her bed in the hospital eating her grapes! Now I ask yer, Tony, what d'yer make of that?' She tapped a podgy finger on her temple. 'She's me best mate, but I've got to say I don't think she's all there on top.'

'She can't be,' Tony said, his face dead-pan. 'Yer haven't been able to buy grapes for love nor money for the last four years.'

Nellie put her basket on the floor and folded her arms before facing her friend. 'There yer are, girl, straight from the horse's mouth. How could I have brought yer grapes when the flaming shops haven't had any in for four years?'

'Ah, but you said Jack brought them, not you.' Molly just managed to get the words out before doubling up. Leaning over the side counter, she breathed in deeply. 'Yer wouldn't believe it, would yer, Tony? It started off by me telling me mate not to push me into the road, then it went on to me getting knocked down by a bus and ending up in hospital!'

'No, it ruddywell didn't!' Nellie feigned indignation. 'Don't you be trying to make out that I'm the one what's doolally. I never mentioned buses, hospital or grapes, Molly Bennett, so don't be saying I did. And that's the last time I'll offer to visit yer in hospital. Let someone else eat yer grapes for all I care.' Her shaking head was moving so fast it left her layers of chins wondering which way to go. 'I wouldn't care, but I hate the ruddy things 'cos the pips get stuck in me teeth.'

'Ah, yer poor thing! Ye're badly done to, aren't yer sunshine?'

Molly patted a chubby cheek. 'Never mind, we'll call into the corner shop on the way home and see if we can wangle some biscuits off Maisie to have with a cup of tea.'

'Are we having a cup of tea in your house, girl?'

'Well, we certainly won't be having it in yours, will we? The day you invite me in for a cuppa I'll think ye're sickening for something and send for the flaming doctor.' Molly winked at the butcher who was highly amused. 'Half of mince, Tony, and anything yer can find that I can make a pan of broth with.'

'I've got a couple of scrag ends, Molly, but there's no meat on them.'

'Beggars can't be choosers, Tony. Anyway, the bones will add flavour if nothing else.'

Tony was walking out to the cold room when Nellie called, 'I'll have the same, lad!'

The butcher held out his hands. 'Yer'll have to fight it out between yerselves, ladies – there's not enough for two. I wish I had a magic wand, but I haven't.'

'Just do what yer can, sunshine, and we'll sort it out. If it comes to the push I'll make one ruddy big pan and we'll share it between the two families.'

A look of rapture covered Nellie's face. Her mate could make the best broth in Liverpool. She'd often shared a pan with them when they'd run out of meat coupons. George always licked his lips after enjoying a plate of Molly's broth. Not that he knew who'd made it 'cos Nellie wasn't daft enough to tell him.

Ellen glanced out to the back of the shop to make sure her boss was busy, then came to lean her elbows on the counter. A few years younger than her neighbours, she was small and slim with mousy-coloured hair and had a very quiet disposition. 'Mary Watson was in before, Molly, and she said Miss Clegg had told her Tommy and Steve were due home next week.'

'Yeah, it's great news, isn't it? I can't wait for my feller to come home to tell him.'

'I'm having a Welcome Home sign made to go across the front of the house,' Nellie said. 'With our Steve's name in great big letters.'

'When did yer decide that, sunshine? Yer never mentioned it before.'

'Well, I only got the letter this morning, girl, so yer can't say I've been slow. I might have mentioned it before but yer were too busy sitting up in the hospital bed watching me eating the grapes that your Jack brought in.'

Molly roared with laughter. 'Helen Theresa McDonough, ye're a bloody smasher, yer really are. And yer deserve a pat on the

19

back for thinking of a nice big Welcome Home banner – it's a cracking idea. Whoever yer get to make yours, yer can ask them to make me one for our Tommy.'

'Have you got an old sheet we can cut up, girl?'

'All me sheets are old, sunshine, but I'll find something. Who have yer got in mind to paint them, anyway?'

A crafty look came to Nellie's eyes. 'Well, I was going to ask you to paint them, girl, but if ye're giving the material it would be cheeky of me to ask. Mind you, if yer volunteered of yer own free will I'd think it was very magnificent of yer.'

'Nellie, yer mean magnanimous of me.'

'There yer are, I knew yer'd do it! Did yer hear that, Ellen? I bet yer wish you had a mate as generous as mine. And clever with big words, too!'

Tony was chuckling as he came in from the back, having heard every word. 'Nellie, I think yer go through life getting everything yer want by acting daft. That was one of the smartest tricks I've come across.'

Nellie beamed. 'Thanks, Tony. I'm glad someone appreciates me.'

'I hope yer family appreciate yer when they find they're having bones for their dinner.' Tony smiled ruefully as he held out a piece of paper with the scrag ends on. 'There's the odd bit of meat attached to them, but yer'd need a magnifying glass to see it.'

'I can make a meal out of them, Tony,' Molly said. 'I'll boil them for an hour to get the flavour out, then add all the veg and pearl barley. It'll have plenty of goodness in and will put a lining on their tummies.'

'I'll give yer a hand with the veg, girl.' Nellie nodded her head and with each nod her turban slipped further down her forehead. 'It's the least I can do.'

'Not on your life, sunshine!' Molly huffed. 'The last time yer offered to help I gave yer a ruddy big carrot to peel thinking even you couldn't make a mess of that. But I was wrong, wasn't I? The carrot yer handed back to me was ten times smaller than the one I'd given yer 'cos yer'd cut the peel an inch thick!'

As Nellie pushed her turban up, she winked at the two behind the counter. 'I can't help being heavy-handed, girl, can I? I mean, we've all got faults. If me memory serves me right, doesn't it say in the Bible, "Let he who is without fault, peel the first carrot"?'

There were guffaws from behind the counter but Molly managed to keep a straight face. 'Nellie McDonough, I hope ye're not expecting to go to heaven when yer die 'cos there's nothing down for yer.'

Nellie's mouth formed a childish pout and she stared down at

20

the floor for a second. Then, with her lips trembling and a sob in her voice, she said, 'I've always known I wouldn't go to heaven, girl, 'cos they wouldn't have wings big enough to fit me. Besides which, I can't play a harp, either.'

'Ah, diddums do it?' Molly used the voice she reserved for baby talk. 'Don't cry, darling, I'll pick yer dummy up.'

'Yeth pleathe, Auntie Molly,' Nellie lisped. Then her eyes narrowed. 'You bend down, girl, and I'll give yer such a kick up the backside yer feet won't touch the ground until ye're outside your house.'

'That would have its good points and its bad points,' Molly said. 'On the one hand it would save me shoe leather, but on the other I'd only have to come back for yer to help yer across the main road. Yer know how hopeless yer are, dodging in and out of the traffic. If I wasn't with yer, yer'd walk into the first car what came along.'

When Nellie's body began to shake with laughter, the floorboards creaked loudly in protest. 'We're back where we started, girl! Only this time it's me sitting up in the hospital bed and you, yer greedy thing, are lording it in the chair, eating all me grapes.' With her vivid imagination she could see the scene in her mind. Holding out a hand, palm upwards, she said, 'Just look at that, Tony, the flamin' bag's empty! She's eaten the bloody lot!'

'Ah, that's mean, that, Molly.' The butcher was having difficulty keeping a straight face. 'Fancy stealing from someone in a sickbed.'

'I'm getting paid back for it, Tony, 'cos the ruddy pips are stuck in between me teeth. And it's worse for me 'cos I haven't got false ones, like me mate.'

Nellie's jaw dropped. 'I haven't got no false teeth, girl!'

'Yer'll soon be needing them, sunshine, if yer don't keep yer trap shut. Now stand there and don't move.' Molly laid her purse on the counter. 'How much is that, Tony?' She felt Nellie pulling on her coat and turned. 'I'll pay for yours and yer can settle with me later.'

'It's not that, girl! Yer told me not to move and I want to know if that includes blinking? Me eyes are sore keeping them open, yer see, and I'm frightened of getting stuck like that. So is it all right if I blink?'

'Holy suffering ducks! What am I going to do with yer, Nellie McDonough? So help me, ye're more trouble to me than any of me kids. And I'm warning yer now that if yer mention grapes in the greengrocer's, I won't be responsible for me actions.' Molly passed over a two-bob piece. 'That's the right money, Tony, a shilling each.'

21

Ellen leaned over the counter. 'I'm glad yer've heard from Tommy and Steve. It's a big worry off yer minds.'

'Ye're not kidding, Ellen, me and Nellie are over the moon. We'll be having a knees-up jars-out party for them.' Molly linked her arm through Nellie's and squeezed. 'But we won't have it until Paul's home, eh, sunshine?'

'I'm glad yer said that, girl, 'cos I wouldn't like my Paul to be left out.' Nellie smiled at her mate before turning to Ellen. 'What about you? Have yer any idea when Corker's ship's due in?'

Ellen shook her head. 'No, but now the war's over I don't need to lie awake every night worrying.' Jimmy Corkhill had been a merchant seaman since he was seventeen. At six foot five, he was a giant of a man, a colourful character who was popular with everyone in the neighbourhood. He was Ellen's second husband and had changed her life, and that of her four children, from one of poverty and squalor to one of perfect happiness. He was the complete opposite of her first husband, Nobby Clarke. A man of extreme violence, he spent his wages on drink, cigarettes and horses, while his family starved. And he got his pleasure from beating Ellen and the children. But since his death, four years ago, Ellen had never once spoken ill of the man who had stolen her heart during a quick-step at the Grafton ballroom, then broke it within weeks of their wedding. 'It would be nice if he was home to welcome the lads – he'd really like that.'

'He'd better be home for this party to end all parties,' Molly said. 'It wouldn't be the same without Corker.' She turned her mate around towards the door. 'Now, let's see if we can get the rest of the shopping in without any messing. See yer, Tony! Ta-ra, Ellen!'

They were on the pavement when Nellie jerked her arm free and poked her head back in the shop. 'She never did pick me dummy up, Tony. So if yer find it when ye're brushing up, put it to one side for us. Yer see, I have trouble dropping off to sleep without it.'

Molly and her three daughters were waiting with mounting excitement for Jack to come home from work. And when he walked through the door, he looked so tired Molly's heart went out to him. He'd been working all the hours God sent during the last five years and it had taken its toll. His shoulders seemed to be more stooped, his black hair was peppered with white strands and there were lines on his handsome face.

'Would yer like yer dinner first, love, or the news?'

Jack sighed heavily as he slipped his jacket off. 'I'm not very hungry, so if it's good news I'll have that first. If it's bad news, don't bother, I'll go straight up to bed.'

Molly crossed the room and put her arms around his waist. 'Oh, I think yer'll want to hear this news. Tommy and Steve will be home next week.'

It was only a matter of seconds before the smile broke, but in that short space of time Molly could see the moisture build up in his eyes. She pulled his head down and kissed him soundly. 'How about that, then, Mr Bennett?'

Holding her close, Jack said, 'The best present yer could give me, Mrs Bennett.'

Jill left her chair to put her arms around her parents, followed closely by Doreen and Ruthie. This was a moment all the family wanted to share, and they clung together as the tears of joy flowed. Molly was the first to break away. 'You show yer dad the letters, Jill, while I get his dinner out of the oven. I've got a feeling his appetite will have returned.'

Out in the kitchen, Molly wiped her eyes on the corner of her pinny. She could hear the girls chattering to their dad, each one trying to outdo the other. And there was laughter in Jack's voice, something that had been missing since the day his son walked out of the house in his soldier's uniform. His going had affected Jack badly. Well, it had all the family, but it was worse for him because he carried a burden of guilt. As a father, he thought it was his duty to protect his children, his home and his country. Instead his son was called to war before his young life had even started. And as father and son worked for the same firm, Tommy as an apprentice, Jack missed travelling to work with him every morning and watching with pride as the gangling fourteen-year-old boy grew into a confident, hardworking young man.

'Come to the table, love, and get this while it's hot.' Molly put the plate down and sat opposite her husband. The other chairs were quickly taken by the three girls who didn't want to miss a second of this feeling of togetherness. The difference in their dad since he heard the news was unbelievable. He looked years younger with a wide smile on his face and in his eyes. It was as though someone had lifted a heavy burden from his shoulders.

'Tuck in, love, while I'm telling yer about me day.' Molly let out a hearty chuckle. 'As yer might know, me mate was up to her usual antics.' She went from the postman to the visit to her parents, then the saga of the grapes and the Welcome Home banners they were going to make. 'At least *I'm* going to make, because Nellie said she can't spell "welcome".'

There was much laughter around the table and it felt so good. And it would be even better next week, Molly told herself, when she would see her son sitting in his usual chair.

23

'I'll ask the boss tomorrow about Tommy getting his job back,' Jack said, pushing his empty plate away. 'There shouldn't be any reason why not, 'cos he was a good little grafter. They took a lot of older men on when the young ones got called up, and I've heard a few of them saying they'll be glad to retire.'

'I've been thinking about that,' Molly told him. 'He's missed part of his apprenticeship, so does that mean he'll never be qualified as a skilled worker?'

'I couldn't tell yer, love, but it would be unfair if he was punished for serving his country.'

'Mam, I could get the banners done in work for yer.' Doreen worked in a factory where they made parachutes and barrage balloons. 'Some of the women have already started making them for their husbands and boyfriends coming home. So don't you worry, I'll get that sorted out.'

'That's good, sunshine, 'cos I wouldn't know where to start. I'd have a go, like, but it wouldn't look very professional.' Molly rubbed a finger down the side of her nose. 'Can I be cheeky and ask yer to get one made for Paul? I know Nellie's worried 'cos she hasn't heard from him yet, but she's bound to get a letter soon.'

'Of course I will,' Doreen nodded, sending her blonde hair swinging around her face. 'I wouldn't leave Paul out for the world.'

'Auntie Nellie worries a lot more than people think,' Jill said of the woman who would soon be her mother-in-law and whom she adored. 'Because she's always laughing and making jokes, folk think she doesn't give a continental about anything. But deep down she's very caring and worries about a lot of things.'

'Yer don't have to tell me that, sunshine, I know yer Auntie Nellie inside out. She's a real softie at heart but doesn't let anyone see that side of her. I wouldn't hear a wrong word said against her 'cos she's kept me going over the years.'

'Me and George often talk about you two,' Jack said before holding a match to his Woodbine. 'All these years yer've been mates and never once had a row.'

'Oh, I wouldn't say that, love, 'cos it wouldn't be true.' Molly laced her fingers and laid her arms flat on the table. 'When the kids were little and they were fighting in the street, neither me nor Nellie would have it that it was one of ours that started the fight. We used to shout at each other, roll our sleeves up and before yer knew it there'd be skin and hair flying. But it always ended up with us having a damn good laugh at ourselves and saying we were worse than the kids. We never, ever, fell out. And if I had a penny for the number of times I've thanked God for giving me Nellie McDonough as a neighbour, I'd be a rich woman.'

'I love me Auntie Nellie, 'cos she always cheers yer up when ye're feeling miserable,' Ruthie said. 'D'yer remember when me granda was in hospital, Mam and yer left me with Auntie Nellie while yer went with me nan to visit him? I was only little, and yer gave her me storybook and asked her to read me one of the fairy tales. Well, she said she didn't need no book 'cos she knew all the stories off by heart. And she began with Little Red Riding Hood walking through the forest. Only instead of meeting the Big Bad Wolf, she was met by the Three Bears who shouted at her for eating their porridge.' Ruthie joined in the laughter before going on. 'I told Auntie Nellie Red Riding Hood was going to visit her grandma's with a basket of fruit, and d'yer know what she said? "Oh no, girl, that was the day after. But don't worry, 'cos the Three Little Piggies happened to pass by on their way to the market, and they chased the bears away. So Red Riding Hood was able to keep walking through the woods, and very soon she was safe and sound in her grandma's cottage, eating an apple in front of a roaring fire".'

'Yer can't complain over that,' Molly chuckled. 'Yer got three stories for the price of one.'

'I almost got four!' Ruthie said. It was five years ago now, but she could see the scene as if it were happening right now. 'Yer know how me Auntie Nellie screws her eyes up tight when she's thinking? Well, she did this for a minute, then said, "I don't know whether I've got me facts mixed up, girl, but I'm sure some flamer had poisoned that ruddy apple".'

Jack banged a fist on the table as he roared with laughter. 'She's a bloody hero, that woman. I wonder if she knows how funny she is?'

'What? She makes a career out of it!' Molly was using the back of her hand to dry her eyes. 'There isn't a shopkeeper for miles around who doesn't smile as soon as she walks in the door. And that's before she opens her mouth! But she's crafty with it. While they're laughing their heads off she cadges an extra half ounce of tea or sugar off them.'

'Steve adores his mam,' Jill said softly, wishing she could go to sleep until the day her beloved was coming home. 'He says he's never once heard her complain, even when yer can see she's not feeling well.'

'Ye're lucky to be marrying into that family, sunshine,' Molly said. 'They don't come like that very often.'

'I know how lucky I am, Mam. I've got the best mother in the world, and soon I'll have the best mother-in-law in the world.'

'Well, go along and see her and yer can both be happy together. She'll be dying to show yer Steve's letter.'

25

'I'm going over the road to see Phil,' Doreen said, 'but we're not going out so I won't be late in.'

'I'll come with yer for ten minutes.' Molly picked up Jack's plate and carried it through to the kitchen. 'I usually call every day to see how Victoria is, but with one thing and another I haven't had the chance.' She kissed her husband's cheek. 'I won't be long, love, because me ma was going to ask Rosie to come round. She'll be part of the family one day in the not too distant future, and I'd like her to share in the excitement and happiness.'

'I'll keep her company until yer get back, so don't worry.' Jack moved to his chair at the side of the fireplace with the *Echo* tucked under his arm. 'I was going to say give my regards to Miss Clegg, but it's a day for more than regards, so give her a big kiss from me.'

'Will do, love. And Ruthie will make yer a nice cup of tea, won't yer, sunshine?'

'I'll make him a cup of tea, but I can't guarantee it'll be nice.'

'The way yer dad feels tonight, I don't think he'll notice what it's like.' Molly made her way to the front door followed by her two older daughters. Once outside, Jill turned to the left to go to the McDonoughs' while Molly and Doreen crossed the cobbled street to a house on the opposite side.

The door was opened by Doreen's boyfriend, Phil Bradley. He was tall and well-built, with blond hair and vivid blue eyes. A handsome lad by any standards. 'I'm really happy for yer, Mrs B.' His smile for Molly was wide. 'I can imagine what it's been like in your house today.'

Molly kissed him as she passed. 'Laughter and tears all day, sunshine.'

When her mother was safely in the living room, Doreen walked into Phil's arms and their lips met. 'I love you,' she whispered.

'And I love you.' He released her and they walked into the room holding hands like the young sweethearts they were.

Molly was kneeling down at the side of a fireside chair, her hands holding those of a frail elderly lady, whose sparse hair was snow-white and her face lined with age. 'Well, Miss Victoria Clegg, the day we've all been waiting for has finally arrived. This time next week I'll have all me family around me and I'll be the happiest woman in Liverpool.'

Victoria's faded eyes were moist with tears. In four weeks she would be ninety years of age, and she was alive now because of the kindness of three women in the street. Twice they had nursed her back from the brink of death. The woman kneeling beside her chair was one of them, Nellie McDonough another and Mary Watson, her next-door neighbour. A spinster, she had no family or relatives of her own, and these three women had made her part of their families. She owed them so much she could never repay them. She had shared their heartaches through the war and was overjoyed that now she could share their happiness. And she would like to think that her prayers every night for the safe return of the boys had been heard by God. 'I can't wait to see Tommy and Steve. I know it's been worse for you and Nellie, because they're your own flesh and blood. But I have missed them and worried about them.'

'I know yer have, sunshine. And although yer might not be our flesh and blood, ye're still part of our families. We adopted yer, didn't we?'

Phil, who was standing by the sideboard with his arm around Doreen's waist, said softly, 'Like you adopted me, Aunt Vickie. We're not flesh and blood, but we love each other.'

Molly turned her head to look at the young man whom Victoria had offered a bed to one night five years ago, and who was now like a son to her. Molly had been dead against the old lady taking him in because he came from a bad family who had moved into the street and had stolen everything they could lay their hands on. None of the neighbours had ever seen Phil, who went to work every day, using the back door to come and go because he was ashamed of the family his mother had married into. He was only waiting for the day when he earned enough money to get away from them. Then one night he'd caught his stepbrother, Brian, climbing over Miss Clegg's back wall intending to break into her house and rob her. He'd pulled Brian down and was giving him a good hiding when the noise brought the neighbours out. It meant Phil couldn't go home that night because he'd have got a leathering off his stepdad who made a living out of thieving. Miss Clegg had taken pity and offered him a bed for the night. She ignored Molly's advice about taking him in, and he'd been there ever since. He was the family she'd never had and she adored him. He in turn had paid her back a thousandfold and idolised her.

All of this flashed through Molly's mind in seconds. She'd been wrong about her ma and da taking Rosie in, and she'd certainly been wrong about Phil. Not only had he given Victoria something to live for, be he'd brought about a change in her daughter she never expected to see. Doreen had always been the wayward one of the family, with her quick tongue and cocky attitude. But since she'd fallen head over heels in love with the blond, handsome Phil, she was kind and caring and more thoughtful for others.

Molly smiled at the lad whom she'd be happy to have as a son-in-law. 'Yeah, I think you two got a real bargain when yer adopted each other.'

'They'll be getting a bigger bargain when they get me,' Doreen said. 'This twosome will soon be a threesome.'

'Well, God granted me this extra time on earth to see the lads safely home.' Victoria pushed a wisp of hair from her eyes. 'I hope He'll also allow me to stay long enough to see you two married and settled in the house that has been my home for fifty years.'

'Ah, ay, Victoria Clegg, don't be getting so maudlin!' Molly struggled to her feet. 'I flatly refuse to be anything but happy today.'

'Then I'll put the kettle on, shall I, Aunt Vickie?' Phil asked.

'Yes, please, sweetheart. And I'm sure Doreen would love to give yer a hand.'

Molly watched Phil limp into the kitchen, and once again her mind went back in time. Phil had joined the army before he was called up because he was afraid that while he was living with the woman he now called Aunt Vickie, she was in danger from his family. They'd been driven from the street by angry neighbours, but Tom Bradley, his stepfather, had returned to demand money with threats. So the boy had joined up and within weeks was sent overseas. He was one of the thousands of soldiers stranded on the beach at Dunkirk who had the sea behind them and nowhere to run. His leg had been shattered by shrapnel from an exploding bomb dropped by one of the hundreds of German planes whose mission it was to kill as many allied soldiers as possible. Phil had been lucky, he was picked up by one of the armada of small boats which had set sail from England to try and rescue as many of their countrymen as they could – many risking their own lives to do so. Phil had had several operations on his leg but they hadn't been able to remove all the shrapnel and he'd been left with a permanent limp. He'd gone back to work but it had taken a year for the haunted look to leave his eyes. And he had never talked about the horrors he'd seen.

Molly shook herself mentally. 'D'yer know, Victoria, I can't stop me mind from going back over the last few years. If you and me ma had taken my advice, neither Rosie O'Grady or Phil would be part of our lives. It's a good job yer didn't take any notice of me 'cos I'm a lousy one to be giving advice.'

'You were acting in our interests, Molly, me and Bridie understood that.' A mischievous glint appeared in Victoria's eyes. 'Just put it down to the extra years me and yer ma have had. They've given us the wisdom to judge people and also the right to be stubborn when we want.'

'Ye're right there, sunshine! My ma can be as stubborn as a mule. Once she sets her mind on anything she'll not be budged.' Molly pulled one of the wooden dining chairs over and sat down.

'Me and the girls have inherited that from her; we've all got a stubborn streak.'

'Tea up!' Phil called, coming through with a tray set with cups and saucers. 'The maid is bringing the teapot in.'

'Hey, we'll have less of that!' Doreen put a wooden stand down and placed the teapot on it. 'I'm going to have to take you in hand, Phil Bradley, ye're getting too big for yer flaming boots. Don't think I'm going to be a skivvy when we get married.'

'Oh, and when is that likely to be?' Molly asked, her brows raised.

'We haven't set a date yet, have we, Phil?' The message of love in Doreen's eyes was there for all to see. 'We didn't want to make any plans before our Tommy and Steve came home. I couldn't get married without me kid brother being there.'

Phil looked up from pouring out the tea. 'There's another reason, Mrs. B. Your Jill has been courting Steve for a long time, we wouldn't want to upstage them by getting married first.'

Doreen leaned across the table, her eyes alive with excitement and happiness. 'Since Phil went on full pay, we've been saving up like mad, Mam. We've got enough money for the wedding and I've got stacks of things for me bottom drawer. But as Phil said, we wanted to wait and see what Jill and Steve were going to do. I thought it would be nice if we could have a double wedding.'

There was doubt on Molly's face as she took the cup from Phil. 'Ooh, I don't know about that, sunshine. Our Jill's been saving up, but don't forget they won't have a house to walk into. Getting the house won't be a problem because I've already asked the landlord. He said he often has an empty property and would be more than willing to give Jill and Steve first offer. But a house needs to be furnished, and that would take a lot more money than they'll have.'

Doreen pulled a face. 'Trust me not to think of that! I've got fresh air where me brains should be. I've been selfish, I can see that now. The number of times I've bragged to our Jill about how much we've got saved, and never once did it enter me stupid head that I might have been upsetting her. Because I wouldn't knowingly upset her, Mam, honest!'

'I know yer wouldn't, sunshine, and so does Jill. She wouldn't think yer were bragging, she'd be glad for yer. You know yer sister hasn't got a selfish bone in her body.'

'A double wedding would be lovely, though, Molly, wouldn't it?' Victoria had a faraway look in her eyes. 'Two pretty princesses and two handsome princes. It would be quite a sight to see.'

'That's true, Victoria, but I'm afraid it's not going to happen. Don't forget Steve's been in the army for two years, he won't have been able to save on the few bob soldiers get. Oh, we could all rally round and give them bits and pieces of furniture to start them off, but yer know what our Jill's like for having everything just right. She wouldn't want to start married life with a couple of chairs, a table and a bed. And I certainly wouldn't want it for her, or Steve. They've been sweethearts since they left school; they deserve nothing but the best when they get married, and that includes a decent house to live in.' Molly handed her empty cup to Phil. 'Perhaps we should leave talk of weddings until we see the lay of the land, eh?'

'You're right, Mrs B.,' Phil said, putting the cup on the tray before reaching for Doreen's hand. 'Let's look forward to welcoming the boys home and leave the serious talk until they've settled back into civvie street.'

'Yeah, let's do that, Mam. I won't say anything to our Jill unless she mentions it herself.' Doreen hid her disappointment behind a smile. She couldn't wait to marry the boy who'd stolen her heart the minute she'd clapped eyes on him. But her mother was right. Her sister and Steve didn't have the luxury of a fully furnished house to move into, like her and Phil. So she should be grateful and count her blessings, instead of bragging.

Molly stood up and pushed her chair back under the table. 'I'll have to scarper because Rosie's coming round. And d'yer know what, Victoria, I can't wait to see the smile on that lovely face of hers.' She bent down to cup the lined face in her hands. 'I'll see yer tomorrow, sunshine, and I'll tell yer what Rosie has to say. And it'll be in me best Irish brogue.' As she straightened up Molly chuckled. 'But if she says one word about her and our Tommy getting married, so help me I'll flatten her. Two in the family is enough to be going on with.'

'Rosie can just get in the queue,' Doreen laughed. 'It should be our Jill first, me second and then our Tommy. After all, they're both only nineteen.'

'If I said that to Rosie, I know what her answer would be. "Now, Auntie Molly, me darlin', surely yer'll not be forgetting that it's meself that's nineteen years, two months and five days?".' Molly had the Irish lilt off pat. But then hadn't she been hearing it all her life? 'And after a quick calculation in her head, she'd say, "And that lovely son of yours, who's me everloving boyfriend, sure isn't he is a month and two days older than I am?".'

'Mam, if I closed me eyes I'd think it was Rosie talking,' Doreen said. 'Yer sound just like her.'

'Yes,' Molly laughed as she walked to the hallway, 'and if I don't get going won't herself be nineteen years, two months and six days, so she will.'

30

Chapter Three

Molly barely had time to put her foot in the door before she was being smothered with kisses and hugged so tightly she could hardly breathe. 'Auntie Molly, I've never been so happy in me life, and that's the truth of it. Sure, haven't I spent the day laughing and crying with the joy that's inside of me?'

'Rosie, ye're nearly choking me, sunshine,' Molly croaked. 'If yer don't let go, I won't live long enough to welcome me son home!' She felt the grip relaxing and stepped back to smile into a pair of deep blue eyes that were set in a face as pretty as a picture and framed by a mass of tumbling, rich black curls. 'It's certainly a day for laughing and crying, and also a day for rejoicing.'

'And for prayers, Auntie Molly. As me mammy would say, "Never take without giving something back". And as the good Lord has looked after Tommy and Steve for us, sure 'tis only right we give our thanks in return. So on Sunday me and Auntie Bridget are going to church, so we are, to light candles.'

'Me and the girls will come with yer,' Molly said. 'I might not be the best living Catholic in the world, but I'm no heathen, either.' She looked across at Ruthie. 'Have yer offered our visitor a cup of tea, sunshine?'

'The kettle's on a low light, Mam. I thought I'd wait until you came home, otherwise the tea would be stiff.'

'Well, be an angel and see to it for us, there's a good girl.' Molly was smiling inside. Rosie worked in a shoe shop and she loved her job because it gave her the chance to meet people. But how did she cope today with her head being in the clouds? 'How many customers did yer sell two left shoes to, sunshine?'

Rosie's infectious chuckle brought a smile to Jack's face. It was easy to see why his son had fallen for this girl, she was a treasure. 'It sounds as though yer Auntie Molly's hit the nail on the head, eh, love?'

'No, I'll not be saying that, Uncle Jack. The truth of it is I didn't sell anyone two left shoes. It was two right ones, and didn't the woman hot foot it back to the shop just before closing time? And not a cross word passed her lips, either! She told me boss it

31

was perfectly understandable that I would have me mind on other things when I'd just heard me boyfriend was coming back from the war. She was a darling woman, right enough, and didn't I give her a big kiss and tell her so.'

'So yer told all yer customers that Tommy was coming home, did yer?' Molly asked, although she knew what the answer would be.

'That I did, Auntie Molly! And I told the people in all the shops on the block, too! As me mammy used to say, yer should never keep happiness to yerself, yer should share it with others.' There was a sparkle in her eyes. 'I showed them all the letter and told them what was in it, but I wouldn't be after letting them read it. All those kisses Tommy sent were meant for me, and even me mammy wouldn't expect me to share them.'

'No, kisses are very special, sunshine, and yer don't share them. I suppose he told yer he'd be writing again as soon as he knew the date he was being discharged?'

Rosie nodded. 'I can't wait to see him, Auntie Molly, me whole inside is shaking and me heart is thumping like mad. Me head is telling me to be patient, that the time will soon pass. But me heart is very stubborn, so it is, and it won't take a blind bit of notice of what me head is telling it. I don't think I'll last the week out, Auntie Molly, and that's the truth of it.'

'Of course yer will. There's so much to do the time will fly over.' Molly told her about having the banners made and how preparations would soon be in hand for a Welcome Home party. 'It'll be a party and a half, sunshine, you mark my words.'

Rosie was clapping her hands with joy. 'I'll not be going to work the day he's due home. Me boss said it would be perfectly reasonable for me to take that day off because me mind wouldn't be on the job and he didn't want a queue of customers bringing back the odd-sized shoes I'd sold them.'

Molly smiled, Ruthie giggled and Jack let out a loud guffaw. 'I'd say your boss had his head screwed on the right way, love.'

'He has that, Uncle Jack! He has his eye to business, all right. Every night he checks the till and the money's dead on, never a penny out.'

'That's because he has an honest staff,' Molly said, handing out the cups of tea Ruthie had poured. 'Now, let's put our heads together and discuss where we're going to scrounge enough food from for this gigantic party. I'll have a go at Maisie and Alec in the corner shop, and Nellie can work her charms on the bloke in the Maypole. Any other suggestions over the next few days will be welcome.'

★ ★ ★

32

On the Monday morning Molly sighed with disappointment when she popped her head into the hall for the umpteenth time to find there was no letter lying on the floor. 'The postman will have been by now,' she told her daughters, 'so there'll be no news today.'

'There's still the afternoon post,' Jill said. 'One could come then.'

'Have a little patience, Mam.' Doreen pushed a crumb from her lips into her mouth. 'Don't be worrying so much or yer'll be a nervous wreck by the time the boys come home.'

'I know, sunshine! I gave meself a good talking to yesterday and told meself to fill me days with work so they don't seem so long. So as soon as Ruthie's gone to school I'm going to give Tommy's room a ruddy good clean. The windows and woodwork are going to get such a good washdown they'll think it's their birthday. That's after I've mopped the lino, like, and before I polish what bit of furniture he's got. Then tomorrow I'll do the landing and stairs.'

'I was going to say leave it until the weekend and we'll give yer a hand,' Jill said. 'But they might be home before then.'

'If this house isn't shining in every nook and cranny by Wednesday, sunshine, then I will be a nervous wreck! And I feel sorry for any speck of dust that dares to land anywhere after that, 'cos I'll marmalise it.'

The two sisters were going out of the door as Ruthie came down the stairs rubbing sleep from her eyes. 'Mam, why didn't yer marry a millionaire? Then I could stay in bed as long as I liked and even have the maid bring me breakfast up.'

'Get a load of you, Lady Muck! If yer want to be waited on hand and foot, I suggest yer look for a man with pots of money when yer grow up. Young Billy Brennan from the next street won't be able to keep yer in luxury.' Molly smiled when she saw the blush cover her daughter's face. 'I've seen yer giving each other the eye.' She ruffled the tousled hair. 'I'm only pulling yer leg, sunshine, don't take it to heart. But remember, I married a man who gave me much more than money. He gave me love, warmth and happiness. And best of all, he gave me four of the most beautiful, adorable children in the world.'

Ruthie gave her a hug. 'And he gave us the best mam in the whole world.'

'There yer are, then, sunshine, we're all satisfied with our lot.' Molly patted her daughter's bottom. 'Go and get a swill while I make yer toast.'

Half-an-hour later, after seeing Ruthie off to school, Molly made straight for the kitchen. She was bending down to get a bucket from under the sink when the knocker sounded. 'Oh Lord, who can this be?' she said aloud. 'Talk about no rest for the flippin' wicked!'

Her eyes flew open when she saw Ruthie standing outside, with her friend Bella Watson from the house opposite. 'Have yer forgotten something, sunshine?'

'Auntie Nellie wants to see yer.' The two young girls were giggling. 'She said she'd come down here but she's not decent. But as you're never anything else but decent, will you honour her with yer presence.'

Molly didn't know whether to laugh or cry. All her great plans would go for a burton now. If Nellie had her way, they'd be sitting talking for hours. 'OK, girls, you poppy off now or yer'll be late for school.' She watched them walk away, arm in arm, then went inside to stand in the middle of the living room to have a conversation with herself. 'Why couldn't she have left it for an hour and I'd have had the windows and woodwork washed? I've a good mind to get on with it and make her wait a while.' Then in her mind's eye she could see Nellie's chubby face peeping through the curtains, waiting for her, and she let out a long sigh. 'It's no use, I'll have to go. Otherwise I'd be worrying meself sick in case there's something wrong.'

She picked up the front-door key from the glass bowl on the sideboard. And as she walked the short distance to her mate's, she was muttering, 'I'm not staying, though. I'll get our Tommy's room done today if it kills me.'

When Nellie opened the door with a smile on her face, Molly felt like clocking her one. 'The had better be important, sunshine, 'cos I've got a stack of work to do.'

'It is important, girl, so come on in.' Nellie pressed herself back against the wall to make room. 'I'd have come to you, but I look a sight.'

As Molly followed the swaying figure into the living room, all thoughts of Tommy's room evaporated and were replaced by a surge of affection for her best friend. Nellie was wearing a skirt that was far too tight and was riding high on her ample hips, showing an expanse of bare leg above the rolled-down stockings being kept up with a piece of knotted elastic. 'Is it good news, sunshine?'

'A bit of both, girl, a bit of both.' Nellie sat down and pointed to a chair on the opposite side of the table. 'Park yer carcase and hold on tight. I'll have yer gripping the edge of yer seat with excitement.' She scratched her head with the fingers of both hands. 'Don't worry, I haven't got fleas. I enjoy a good scratch first thing in the morning, it wakes me up. It's only a habit, so take that look off yer face.'

34

'Nellie, will yer get on with it, please! What did yer ask me to come for?'

'D'yer want the good news first, girl, or the bad news?'

'The good news, please. Yer can keep the bad news to yerself.'

'I had a letter from our Paul this morning. He's in a demob centre down South, and as soon as he's been kitted out with civilian clothes, he'll be home.'

'Oh, that's marvellous news, sunshine! I'm so happy for yer, I really am. But what d'yer mean about being kitted out in civilian clothes?'

'Haven't yer heard, girl?' Nellie looked surprised. 'All the lads are getting demob suits, shirt, shoes, the lot! I thought yer knew! It's been on the wireless.'

'I haven't been listening to the wireless, not since the war ended. That's a nice surprise, that is. Our Tommy's probably outgrown the clothes he was wearing before he went away.' Molly was beginning to feel glad she'd come. 'If the suits are any good, it might do your Steve to get married in.'

'Yeah, it could come in handy.' Nellie tilted her head. 'D'yer want to hear the bad news?'

'Only if it doesn't affect me or me family.'

'Our Lily got a letter this morning, too. From that feller she was going out with.'

'That's not bad news, it's good news.'

Nellie's head shook so vigorously, her chins couldn't keep up with her. 'I don't like him, girl, I just can't take to him.'

'It's not you courting him, though, is it, sunshine? If your Lily's happy with him, that's all that counts.'

'Yer wouldn't say that if one of yours was going out with someone you didn't like, would yer? Yer'd be singing a different tune, then.'

'I don't understand yer,' Molly said. 'What have yer got against the lad?'

'He's shifty. Little piggy eyes set too close together, and he never looks yer straight in the face when ye're talking to him. Not that we've had much in the way of conversation with him 'cos he's got very little to say for himself. I wouldn't trust him as far as I could throw him, and if our Lily sets her mind on marrying him, it would break my heart.'

'I don't know what to say, sunshine, 'cos I've only seen the bloke a couple of times. And then it's only been more or less in passing. I don't even know his name.'

'That's what worries me! We hardly know anything about him. Our Lily calls him Len, but what his second name is, only God knows. She always meets him outside, and I'm sure it's because he

35

doesn't want to come here.' Nellie looked sad. 'She's a good kid and could do a damn sight better than him.'

'What does George say?'

'He doesn't like him either. Says there's something fishy about him. Our Steve's never met him 'cos he was called up before she started going out with him. And Paul only met him once or twice before he went in the army. And yer know what our Paul was like, out with a different girl every night. He was too busy enjoying himself to notice who his sister was going out with. They were both called up about the same time, and I've been hoping our Lily would meet someone else while he was away. But no such luck. She thinks the sun shines out of his backside and won't hear a word against him.'

'Oh dear, I had no idea yer felt this strongly about him. It's a shame because every mother wants what's best for her children. Particularly when it comes to them getting married. Having a son-in-law yer don't like doesn't make for harmony in the family, does it?'

'No, it doesn't girl! And I'm going to be straight with yer and tell yer I intend doing all I can to put a stop to it. When our Steve and Paul are home, I'm going to ask them to find out a bit more about him. They always looked after Lily when they were younger, her being the only girl in the family, and they wouldn't want her involved with someone who was no good.'

'Where does this bloke live, Nellie?'

'That's just it, girl, we don't know! When I asked Lily, she just tossed her head and said Walton. That's all I could get out of her. And that's not a bit like her. She's usually so open, says exactly what she thinks. But the queer feller seems to be able to wrap her around his little finger, worse luck.'

'Don't be downhearted, sunshine.' Molly had never known her friend look so miserable. 'Something will turn up. Your Lily's not soft, she wouldn't marry someone if she wasn't sure he would make a good husband. She hasn't seen him for a long time and her feelings might change when he comes home.'

'Aye, and pigs might fly! If she wasn't serious about him she'd have been out enjoying herself while he's been away. I know she's had plenty of chances.' Nellie looked thoughtful as she pinched the fat around her elbow. 'I've been thinking about that fly turn in number sixteen. She certainly didn't let being married stop her from going out with anything in trousers. Her husband's been away over four years, a prisoner of war for three. How's the poor bugger going to feel when he gets home and finds she's got a twelve-month-old baby? It's enough to send him around the bend after what he's been through.'

36

'I have heard that the American this Mavis had the baby with wants to take the child back to the States. He's a married man, and apparently his wife, for some reason, can't have children of her own.'

Nellie was open-mouthed and wide-eyed. 'Who the hell told yer all this? I'm the gossipmonger in this street, not you! Where was I when yer were told this?'

'I just happened to be in the corner shop when the woman in number eighteen was telling Maisie. I couldn't help but overhear.'

Nellie banged a curled fist on the table and her face took on a ferocious look. 'I've got two bones to pick with you, Missus! First, how come yer went to the shop without me? Yer know damn well that's not allowed. And secondly, do yer realise the harm yer've done to my reputation as the know-all of this street? I'll never live it down.'

'Does that mean yer don't want to know the rest of what I heard?'

Nellie pretended to give this careful consideration. 'Go on, I might as well. There must be someone I can pass it on to.'

'It isn't to be passed on, Nellie, that's the thing. The fewer people who know, the better. Yer know what some of the women are like, they'd take great delight in telling the husband.'

'He's bound to find out she had a baby! That's not something yer can keep quiet!'

'After what he's been through, it would have to be a very cruel person to tell him. We've heard what some of the prisoner-of-war camps were like, so God knows what state the poor man will be in when he gets home. They're still clearing the camps out, so although she's heard he's alive, she doesn't know whether he's sick or injured.' Molly looked at the clock and groaned. 'I'm going to tell yer this quick, sunshine, 'cos I've got loads of work to do. And if yer repeat it, I'll never talk to yer again.' She took a deep breath. 'The American's name went on the birth certificate as the father of the baby, so although there'll be a lot of legal work to do, he will be allowed to take the child to America. It seems he's not short of money so he's paying a woman to care for the child until everything is settled. That means there'll be no baby in the house when the husband comes home.'

Nellie shook her head. 'I don't get it! Yer mean that Mavis is going to give the child up? How can she do such a thing?'

'To try and save her marriage.'

'For crying out loud, girl, she's a bit late thinking of that, isn't she? She's been out with every nationality under the sun, even had them in her house when her three kids were there. And d'yer mean to tell me those kids won't miss the baby, or talk about it?'

'Nellie, it's not for you or me to say. It's their problem, not ours.' Molly pushed her chair back. 'And now, sunshine, I'm off to do the work I would have had finished if you hadn't asked me to honour yer with me presence.'

'Ah, ay, girl, don't be going home with a miserable gob on yer! Let me think of something to make yer laugh, so yer go out of here with a smile.'

'No need to think of anything to make me laugh, sunshine, just walk in front of me to the front door.'

Nellie screwed her eyes up. 'What d'yer mean, Molly Bennett?'

'Well, that skirt doesn't leave anything to the imagination, sunshine! On the way in, I saw the top of yer stockings and yer garters. Plus yer bare legs up to your backside. In fact, if yer'd bent down, I'd have seen what yer had for breakfast.'

'No yer wouldn't, clever clogs. Yer see, I haven't had me breakfast yet.'

'Haven't had yer breakfast? Nellie, it's nearly ten o'clock!'

'Well, yer see, girl, when I got our Paul's letter me tummy went all of a flutter and I didn't feel like eating. Then you came down and yer've kept me gabbing for nearly an hour. I thought yer might take the hint when me tummy started rumbling with hunger, but yer were that busy listening to the sound of yer own voice, yer didn't hear. I didn't want to tell yer to shut up 'cos I knew yer'd get a cob on and take the huff.'

Molly's shoulders shook with laughter. 'Nellie McDonough, ye're a case, yer really are. I don't know what I'm going to do with yer.'

'Yer could take me home with yer and make me something to eat.'

'Not on your flaming life, sunshine! I'm going home to work like the clappers until twelve o'clock, when it's time for us to go to the shops. By then our Tommy's room will be shining like a new pin.'

'Like my boys' bedroom?'

'Oh, ye're going upstairs to do theirs now, are yer?'

Her face that of an angelic cherub, Nellie shook her head. 'I was up with the larks this morning, girl! I knew what you were going to do and I wasn't having yer get one up on me. So I turned the fingers of the clock forward twenty minutes, called George and Lily, gave them their breakfast and watched them hurrying down the street thinking they were late for work. That's when the postman came with the two letters. Lily hasn't seen hers yet, it's up on the mantelpiece. I read Paul's letter and was so happy I felt like doing cartwheels down the street. And I would have done, girl, only I'm not built for it. So instead I got cracking on the bedroom and was finished just as your Ruthie crossed the street.' She folded her arms and hitched up her bosom. 'That's my story and I'm sticking to it.'

Molly gaped. 'Yer altered the time and let George and Lily think they were late? They'll kill yer when they get in!'

'They won't know unless you snitch on me. I've put the clock back to the right time and if they say anything I'll just act daft. Yer see, I'm not as quick with the elbow grease as you, girl, and I needed that bit of extra time.'

Molly shook her head. 'But I haven't even started mine!'

'I know! Ye're a lazy bitch, Molly Bennett. Sitting here gabbing yer head off and yer house is like a pigsty.'

'I'm going before I strangle yer.' Molly hurried to the front door. 'Twelve o'clock and not a minute before.'

'Ta-ra, girl! It's been nice listening to yer.'

Molly stood at the door of her son's bedroom and nodded her head in satisfaction. It looked a treat, everything cleaned and polished. There was a smell of the Parr's Aunt Sally she'd used in the water to mop the floor, but she had the window open and the smell would soon go. She gazed at the bed and said, 'All that's missing now is Tommy, and please God he'll be home before the week is out.'

There was a loud knocking on the front door and she grimaced. Surely this wasn't Nellie already! She wasn't ready to go to the shops yet, she needed a good wash and a change of clothes before she could venture out. Her hand running down the banister as she descended the stairs, she muttered, 'She'll just have to sit and wait for me, that's all.'

But when Molly opened the door it wasn't her friend standing there, it was Maisie from the corner shop and she looked full of excitement. 'Molly, I've just had a phone call from your Tommy. He said to tell yer he was travelling home on Thursday and his train should get into Lime Street Station about four o'clock.'

Molly's hand went to her mouth. 'Oh, my God, I've gone all faint. Oh, that's marvellous news, Maisie, I could kiss yer.'

'I'd rather yer didn't faint on me, Molly, or kiss me, if yer don't mind. Me and Alec were over the moon when the call came and I've left him with a shop full of customers so I could come down and tell yer.'

'Did Tommy have anything else to say? Is he all right?'

'He said there was a queue waiting to use the phone so he had to be quick. He did say not to meet the train because with so many lads being demobbed, it could be full and he'd have to wait for the next one. But come what may, he'll be home Thursday even if he has to walk the two hundred odd miles. And, Molly, he sounded in very high spirits.'

'Maisie, ye're an angel and I'll love yer for ever more.'

'My husband's mind will be running along different lines right this minute. I won't be getting called an angel, but a crafty so-and-so for dashing off and leaving him to cope on his own. So I'll buzz, Molly, and see yer later. Ta-ra for now.'

'Ta-ra, Maisie, and thanks for being the bearer of good news.' Molly closed the front door and leaned against it. She didn't know whether to slump down on the floor and cry with relief, or go out in the street and shout with happiness. And fancy Tommy keeping that scrap of paper she'd slipped in his pocket with the corner shop's number on it! She thought he'd have lost that by now.

There came a rapping on the front window and the sound of glass shaking in the frame. 'So help me, she'll put that window in one of these days. Why the hell she can't use the knocker like everyone else, I don't know.' Molly turned and opened the door. 'If I wasn't delirious with happiness, Nellie McDonough, I'd break yer flamin' neck for knocking on me window like that.'

'If ye're delirious with happiness, girl, how come yer've got a gob on yer that would stop the clock and turn the milk sour?'

'Seeing as the clock's in the living room and the milk's in the kitchen, sunshine, it would be impossible for them both to see me face at the same time, wouldn't it?'

'It would be for people with one face, girl, I'll grant yer that. But seeing as ye're a real two-faced article, you wouldn't have no trouble.'

'I'll let yer off with that, Nellie, 'cos I refuse to get into a slanging match with yer. I'll not let yer ruffle me feathers on this day of all days.'

As Nellie squeezed past she eyed her friend with suspicion. 'I don't know what yer've had to drink since yer left our house, but whatever it is I'll have a drop of the same.'

Molly was so excited she didn't even hold her breath when Nellie plonked herself on a protesting chair. 'I haven't had nothing to drink, sunshine, so ye're out of luck. What I have had is a visit from Maisie.'

'Oh, aye, girl, what did she want? I bet it wasn't the loan of a few bob because her and Alec must have a long stocking stashed away by now. Their shop's a little goldmine, and they've no family to spend it on.'

'They deserve every penny they've got 'cos they work damned hard for it. The shop's open seven days a week from early morning until late at night. And I bet they'd give everything they've got to have children of their own.'

'Don't bite me head off, girl, I didn't mean no harm!'

'I know yer didn't! Anyway, as far as I'm concerned, today is a day of goodwill towards all men.' Molly leaned across the table and smiled into her friend's face. 'Maisie came down to say our Tommy had phoned the shop. He'll be home on Thursday, about teatime if he gets the train he's aiming for.'

Nellie's chubby cheeks moved upwards as a smile lit up her face. 'Oh, that's the gear, girl! He's the first, our Steve and Paul shouldn't be far behind.' Then she frowned. 'How come your Tommy had Maisie's phone number?'

'I wrote it on a piece of paper and put it in his pocket. I thought he'd have lost it by now with all the moving around he's done, but apparently he's hung on to it.'

'I never thought of giving it to mine.' Nellie looked dejected. 'But I wouldn't, would I, being as thick as two short planks?'

'Listen, sunshine, yer may be many things, but as thick as two short planks you are not. Yer pretend to be daft, and yer've got it down to a fine art. But in actual fact ye're as crafty as a boxload of monkeys and yer could leave me standing any day.'

Nellie clapped her hands. 'A compliment! I knew if I waited long enough I'd get one! And I've got Maisie and your Tommy to thank for it. Just wait until I tell George yer've finally admitted that I'm more cleverer than you.'

'More clever, sunshine, there's no such word as cleverer.'

'Yes there is, Miss Know-All, I've just said it.'

'Because you've said it doesn't mean . . .' Molly threw her hands in the air. 'I give in, I can't win with you. Besides, we've got no time to be sitting here discussing your vocabulary, we've got loads to do.'

'Such as, girl!'

'First I want to go over and tell Victoria the good news before we go to the shops. We won't be there long, just a quick in and out. Then when we go to the shops I'll work on Tony to see if I can scrounge something to have a decent meal for Tommy on Thursday. And your job, sunshine, is to work yer charms on the bloke in the Maypole and see about getting a little extra tea and sugar to put by for when we have the party. I want yer to put yer heart and soul into it and play on his sympathy. Put a sob in your voice when yer tell him there's three soldiers coming back from the war and everyone should rally round to give them a big welcome.' Without realising she was doing it, Molly spoke with a sob while dabbing her eyes with an imaginary hankie. 'Say it's only what they deserve after fighting for us.'

It would have been hard to put a name to the expression on

Nellie's face. 'Ay, girl, yer'd be better doing it yerself. Yer were so convincing then, I could feel meself filling up and I nearly offered to give yer me next week's sugar and tea ration!'

'Yer nearly offered, but yer didn't, did yer? Which means I'm not as good at cadging as you are. So have a hankie in yer hand, and a tear in yer eye when yer put yer Bette Davis act on for the bloke in the Maypole. And I'll have a go at Tony and Maisie.'

'Corker always brings some food home from the ship. If he docks before the boys come we'll be laughing sacks.'

'We can't rely on that, sunshine, so don't be trying to wriggle out of it. Yer don't want your Steve and Paul to celebrate their homecoming with a round of bread and dripping, do yer?'

Nellie cast her eyes towards the ceiling and muttered, 'She's a proper bloody slave driver, this one. All she's short of is a ruddy whip!' Then she smiled sweetly at Molly. 'Have yer got a clean hankie for me, girl? If yer want me to cry I may as well do the job properly.'

'I'm going upstairs to get changed so I'll find something for yer.' Molly was laughing as she turned at the door. 'Would yer like a pretty white hankie with a lace border, or would a piece of old sheet do?'

'I don't want no fiddling little thing that I can't blow me nose on. And yer know I always blow me nose when I'm crying. So I'll settle for a piece of yer old sheet.'

'Behave yerself while I'm upstairs, please. Don't be shuffling yer backside on the chair 'cos it won't stand up to it.'

'No problem, girl, 'cos I've no intention of sitting on me backside twiddling me thumbs. I'll be off this chair before ye're halfway up the stairs. To pass the time, I'm going to have a good root through yer sideboard drawers and cupboards. But it's nothing for yer to worry about, yer won't even know I've done it. I'll be really sly and put everything back the way I found it.'

Molly's eyes darted from left to right. Would Nellie have the nerve? Nah, she was only pulling her leg. 'If yer find anything interesting, sunshine, let's know, won't yer?'

'Go 'way!' Jack and the three girls had their eyes fastened on Molly. 'Yer didn't, did yer?'

'Cross my heart and hope to die.' Molly could hardly contain herself. 'Nellie was absolutely brilliant! We got to the Maypole just a few minutes before they closed for dinner and there were no customers in the shop. Nellie nabbed the manager and as soon as she started talking the three girl assistants came over because they knew they were sure of a laugh. And they got one, too! According to my mate, if it hadn't been for Steve, Tommy and Paul, we wouldn't have won the war. Everyone in this country would be going around doing the goose-step, giving the Nazi salute and shouting "Heil Hitler!". And all the time she's talking, she's dabbing her eyes with this piece of old sheet. Honest to God, Jack, if I hadn't been there to see it with me own eyes, I would never have believed it.'

'The manager didn't swallow all that, did he, Mam?' Ruthie asked. 'If he did, he must have a screw loose.'

'Of course he didn't, yer soft nit! He said she could have two ounces of tea and half a pound of sugar because she deserved it for the best acting he'd seen in years. And apart from that, he was hungry for his dinner and knew Nellie wouldn't give up until she got something off him. I was over the moon when he said that, and had made up me mind to give her a big kiss when we got outside. But me mate hadn't finished with the poor man. Still dabbing her eyes and her voice choked, she pointed to me and said "What about me friend? Yer wouldn't leave her out, would yer? Not a kind man like you. Don't forget, her Tommy's been doing his bit for his country, as well." I thought she'd gone too far, and yer could have knocked me over with a feather when he told one of the girls to give Mrs McDonough a quarter of tea and a pound of sugar that she could share with her friend. And in case the girls got any ideas, he said he would bring his own ration book in tomorrow and hand over the coupons.'

'I can't see him doing that, love,' Jack said.

'Neither can I, but I won't lose any sleep over it. I didn't do badly meself with the butcher. I'm getting some stew off him on Thursday to make a dinner for Tommy, and he's promised to let me have some brawn when we have the party. And I blackmailed Maisie and Alec. I said they would be invited to the do if they helped out with the eats.'

'You and Nellie have got more nerve than me – I couldn't do it,' Jack said. 'Still, it's all in a good cause, isn't it?'

'Don't put me in the same class as Nellie; I'm not in the meg specks compared to her. She gets away with murder! The staff at the Maypole were in stitches at the way she was carrying on, and while they're doubled up, she manages to fiddle two weeks' rations off them! After being her mate for all these years, she still never ceases to amaze me.'

'Ye're good together, Mam,' Doreen said. 'I've watched yer, and yer just seem to bounce off each other. You start the joke, and Auntie Nellie comes in at the end with the punch line.'

'Yeah, I've noticed that.' There was a smile on Jill's pretty face. 'One without the other would be like Laurel without Hardy.'

Molly screwed her eyes up, hitched her bosom and did a very

passable imitation of Nellie. 'Is that an insult, girl? If it is I'll clock yer one.'

Doreen began to collect the dirty plates. 'If ye're going up to see Uncle Corker's mother, yer don't want to leave it too late, Mam, because she'll be frightened to open the door in the dark. Me and our Jill will wash up for yer.'

'Ah, I was going to say I'd go with me mam to see Mrs Corkhill,' Jill said, pulling a face. 'I haven't been up there for a while.'

'Oh, go on, me and Ruthie will do the dishes.' Doreen winked at her young sister. 'It's you and me, babe! I'll wash and you can dry.'

'Let's go while the going's good, Jill.' Molly stood up and looked in the mirror over the mantelpiece. Patting her hair, she said, 'If a bloke picked me up in the dark he'd soon drop me in the daylight, I look such a mess. Still, I'm not proud.' She bent to kiss her husband's cheek. 'Half an hour, love, that's all we'll be.'

Molly was standing on the pavement as Jill pulled the door shut behind her, when she spotted Lily McDonough coming out of their house. 'Hello, Lily, off gallivanting, are yer?'

'I'm going to the pictures with one of me mates from work.' Lily had inherited Nellie's mousy-coloured hair and hazel eyes, but there the resemblance ended. She was tall and slim with a nipped-in waist and very shapely legs. And while she was a pleasant girl, she lacked her mother's quick humour.

'Oh, aye!' Molly was thinking of what Nellie had said about Lily's boyfriend. 'Is it a male workmate, or a female?'

'It's a girlfriend. I go out with her once or twice a week for company.'

'I'm surprised yer haven't got a boyfriend,' Molly said, telling herself she was being nosy and underhanded. But it would be worth it if she was told something that would stop Nellie from worrying. 'Yer look very smart tonight, a real treat.'

'I've got a boyfriend, Auntie Molly, he's in the army. At least he was in the army – he's being demobbed this week.'

'Oh, is it anyone I know?'

'I think yer met him last year before he was called up. Yer probably don't remember 'cos yer only saw him for a few minutes.'

'I remember him,' Jill said. 'His name's Len, isn't it?'

Lily nodded. 'I had a letter from him saying he'd be home one day this week.'

Trying not to sound too interested, Molly asked, 'Is he a local lad?'

'No, he lives in Walton.'

'Yer'll have to bring him to the Welcome Home party we're

44

having, then we can all meet him. That's if ye're going out with him serious, like.'

'Oh, yes, we're serious.' Lily sounded very definite. 'But I don't know about him coming to the party. He's a bit shy, yer see.'

'Well, yer can ask him, anyway. Tell him he'll be welcome.' Molly linked her arm through Jill's. 'We'll let yer get on yer way, sunshine, yer don't want to keep yer mate waiting. Ta-ra for now.'

'Ta-ra, Auntie Molly, and you, Jill.'

Walking arm in arm up the street, Molly asked casually, 'So yer know Lily's boyfriend, do yer?'

'I wouldn't say I know him, I've only met him briefly.'

'And what d'yer think of him? Is he a nice bloke?'

Jill was silent for a few seconds. 'He's all right, I suppose. He's not my type, but then we all have different tastes, don't we? It wouldn't do for us all to fall for the same bloke.'

'Yer don't sound very keen.' Molly squeezed her daughter's arm. 'Come on, sunshine, tell me what yer really think of him. And then I'll tell yer why I'm being so nosy. And whatever we say is just between the two of us.'

'I didn't like him at all, Mam! I thought he was miserable, sullen and not a bit friendly. He's not someone I'd trust. I don't know what Lily sees in him. But then again, as I said, I reallly don't know him well. Perhaps he's not bad when yer get to know him. But to tell yer the truth, Mam, I wouldn't want to get to know him. He gave me the creeps.'

They slowed down when they neared Mrs Corkhill's house so they could finish their conversation without being overheard. 'Nellie can't stand him, sunshine, and she's worried sick about Lily wanting to marry him. She thinks there's something shifty about him and said she doesn't trust him. So what we've heard and talked about tonight is not to be repeated to her. Perhaps when Steve and Paul are home they can find out a bit more about him. All Nellie knows is that his name's Len. She doesn't know his surname or where he lives. And anyone with any sense can see that's not right when her daughter's talking about marrying him. I'd be worried sick, too, if I was in her shoes.'

'Don't worry, Mam, Steve and Paul won't let their sister marry someone who isn't good enough for her. They'll get to the bottom of him.'

'I hope so, sunshine, I hope so. Now, let's go and see Corker's mother and keep her company for half-an-hour.'

Chapter Four

Steve McDonough was weary as he stepped off the train at Lime Street Station and turned to pull his haversack from the compartment. He'd been standing for five solid hours because the train was overcrowded with servicemen returning home. Packed in like sardines, they were, with every seat taken and every inch of floorspace covered with sprawling bodies. He certainly wouldn't like to do that journey again in a hurry, it had been a nightmare. He'd been so excited at six o'clock this morning when he and the lads in his unit had climbed aboard the army lorry that was to take them to the railway station. In his mind, every turn of the wheel was taking him nearer to his family and loved ones. But when they'd arrived at the station the train was already full, and he'd been split from his army friends in the mad scramble, rushing from compartment to compartment to find enough room to squeeze in. And now he felt weary and scruffy. The platform was a mass of swaying bodies and the hiss of a shunting steam train filled the air. The sooner he was off here the better. He'd try the station toilets and see if he could at least swill his face and comb his hair to look a bit respectable when he walked down his street for the first time in two years.

'Hey, Steve! Steve McDonough!'

Steve turned around and scanned the sea of faces. Then he saw two arms waving in the air and made his way towards them. 'Tommy! Tommy Bennett!' The two lads dropped their haversacks and flung their arms around each other. 'It's good to see yer, Tommy.'

'And you, Steve.' They were being pushed and shoved from all sides and were forced to break apart. 'Yer've lost some weight, mate!'

'I'm lucky that's all I've lost.' Steve didn't want to be reminded of the last two years, so he put it from his mind and smiled. 'You've sprouted up, haven't yer?'

'Yeah, I'm six foot two now. They didn't have a demob suit to fit me so they're going to send one on to me. I've got the shirt and

47

shoes, though, and I'm just hoping they fit.' Tommy grinned. 'I can't get over yer being on the same train as me! Where've yer come from?'

'Our regiment came back from Germany last week, and although we were officially demobbed then, we were sent to Chatham to be issued with civilian clothes. Otherwise I'd have been home nearly a week earlier.'

'Well, I'll be blowed.' Tommy shook his head in disbelief. 'Our lot came back from Germany last week, too. *And* we were sent to Chatham. Fancy both being there and not seeing each other!'

'Tommy, there were thousands there. It would have been like finding a needle in a haystack. But I've been luckier than you, I've got all me demob clothes.' The dimples in Steve's face deepened. Seeing Tommy's familiar face was easing away his tiredness and he could feel his excitement rising. 'It certainly wasn't like going to Burton's and trying things on for size and style. Half the men in Liverpool will be walking around in navy-blue suits with a narrow grey pinstripe. Still, I suppose we should be grateful 'cos the army have got a job on their hands trying to kit everyone out.' He pointed to his haversack. 'Everything's in there 'cos I wanted to go home in me uniform.'

'Is anyone meeting yer?'

Steve shook his head. 'I told them not to in case I didn't manage to get on this train and they had to hang around for a couple of hours.'

'Yeah, same here.' Tommy looked with envy at the many couples who were kissing and embracing. Mothers, wives and girlfriends, separated from their loved ones for so long were crying with happiness at having their men home safe and sound. 'I'm sorry I did now, 'cos I'm dying to see me mam and the family, and a kiss from Rosie would go down very well right now.' He bent and picked up his haversack. 'Come on, Steve, let's get out of here and hope we can catch a tram without waiting in a ruddy queue.'

'I was hoping to freshen up,' Steve said. 'I feel sticky and grubby.'

'To hell with that, I just want to get home.'

There was a spring in Steve's step as they walked from the station into Lime Street. With a bit of luck they'd be home in twenty minutes. His dad and Lily wouldn't be home from work yet, but his mam would be there, and Mrs Bennett. And then it wouldn't be long before Jill came home. The thought of her was enough to set his heart pounding. All the time he'd been away he'd felt as though part of him was missing. She was in his mind the whole time, even when his unit was in the midst of heavy fighting. He'd never be parted from her again, he vowed, not for anything or anybody.

They were sitting on the tram when Tommy said, 'I didn't see much fighting. We were stationed in Belgium for a few months, just to help with the mopping up. Then when we got sent to Germany it was all over bar the shouting. How about you?'

Steve sighed and stared out of the window for a few seconds. 'I was in the thick of the fighting before Germany surrendered. We were on the offensive, though, thank God, because our lads had them on the run. Then after the peace treaty was signed, we were sent into the war camps to liberate the prisoners. That's when I found out exactly what the war had cost some of our lads. Some camps were worse than others, with men walking around looking like skeletons without any flesh on their bones. They'd been beaten, starved and treated like animals. As long as I live I'll never forget the sights I saw, Tommy. I would never have believed it possible that there were human beings who could so cruelly degrade another human being. And from what I've heard, those camps were nothing compared to the internment camps where people were gassed because of their race or creed. What I saw was bad enough, so God help our lads who had to go into those camps.'

'I know, I heard a couple of the older men talking about it and it turned me tummy. It must have been terrible and doesn't bear thinking about.'

'I don't want to think about it, Tommy, and I don't walk to talk about it when we get home. I might tell me dad in time, but I'll never tell the girls. And I don't think you should either. They'll be all excited and happy that we're coming home, don't let's spoil it for them or ourselves.'

Tommy pointed out of the window. 'This is our stop. Home Sweet Home, here we come.'

Ruthie moved away from the wall when she saw two soldiers step down from the tram. She'd been watching out for Tommy and was surprised to see his companion was Steve. With a cry of delight, she took to her heels and ran like the wind.

'Mam, Dad, they're here! Our Tommy's just got off the tram and Steve's with him!'

'Run up and tell Auntie Nellie, quick. We'll all go outside and give them a rousing reception.' Molly put a hand on her heart as it pounded inside of her. 'Jack, I feel sick. Please God don't let me be sick now.'

The small living room was full. Jack had taken the day off, so had Jill and Doreen. And Bridie and Bob were there, with Rosie.

49

'Calm down, love,' Jack said. 'I want yer to welcome our son home with a smile on yer face.'

Ruthie came running into the room followed quickly by Nellie, George and Lily. 'They're just by the bottom entry, Mam.'

Nellie looked flustered. 'I'm all of a dither, there isn't a part of me that isn't shaking.'

George put an arm across her shoulders. 'No, now, love, pull yerself together. Yer son hasn't seen yer for two years, don't let him see yer upset.'

'I've just been telling Molly the same thing,' Jack said. 'Now come on everyone, let's go outside to meet them, Bridie, let me give yer a hand.'

'I'll do that, Uncle Jack.' Rosie was already helping Bridie and Bob to their feet. 'You see to Auntie Molly.'

Jill was sitting at the table and made no attempt to move. Her face was as white as a sheet and she was nervously picking at her nails. Doreen took one look at her and pulled on her arm. 'Come on, our kid, don't yer want to see yer brother and yer sweetheart?' She gave her sister no chance to argue and dragged her off the chair and out into the street.

The boys had seen them and quickened their steps. 'I'm going to cry, girl,' Nellie said with a catch in her voice.

'Don't you dare, Nellie McDonough, or I'll flamingwell throttle yer.' Molly was so full of emotion herself she thought her head would burst. The sight of her son, and the boy who would soon be her son-in-law, was too much to take. She broke away from the crowd and ran towards them, followed closely by Nellie. Her arms outstretched, she said, 'Oh, sunshine, yer'll never know how happy I feel right at this moment.'

'I feel pretty good meself, Mam.' Tommy held her close, his cheek pressed against hers. Over her shoulder he saw Steve wrap his arms around Auntie Nellie and suddenly the last few years faded away. They were home now and all was right with the world.

Molly pressed him from her. 'My God, son, yer must be as tall as Corker!'

'Not quite, Mam, he's about three inches taller than me. Mind you, I might still have some growing to do.'

'Yer dad will have to look up to yer.' Molly cupped his face and gazed into his eyes. 'I haven't half missed yer, sunshine. So have yer dad and yer sisters.' She gave him another kiss before calling to Nellie, 'Let's swap over, sunshine, so I can say hello to Steve before the crowd get to him.'

The first thing Steve asked when he was being smothered to death by Molly was, 'Is Jill all right, Mrs B.?'

'She's as nervous as a kitten right now, but one of your kisses should cure that.'

'She'll be getting plenty of those, Mrs B. I intend to make up for lost time.' Steve's dimples appeared. 'Not all in one go, like, 'cos I don't want her to have sore lips. I'll double up every night for the next two years.'

Molly looked to where Nellie had her arms around Tommy's waist. 'Will yer put Tommy down, sunshine, and let the rest of the family have a turn?'

'Put him down did yer say, girl?' Nellie's eyes were on a level with the buttons on Tommy's uniform. 'Have yer seen the ruddy size of him? I've got a kink in me neck looking up at him! I can't remember him being this big when I used to change his nappies.'

Steve was laughing as he bent to pick up his haversack. His mam was still the same old mam, she hadn't changed at all, thank God. Then as he straightened up, his eyes met Jill's and a smile full of love and longing lit up his face. But before he could move, his father was in front of him. George put his hands on his son's shoulders and gazed into his face before pulling him towards him and embracing him in a bearlike hug. 'Welcome home, son!'

Then Lily came to stand beside them and stood on tiptoe to kiss her brother's cheek. 'It's good to see yer, our Steve. The house hasn't been the same without you and our Paul.'

'I haven't been the same without our house! I'll never go away again, not even as far as New Brighton.'

'There's a certain pretty girl been waiting patiently,' George whispered in his son's ear. 'Don't make her wait any longer.'

Steve didn't need telling twice. The haversack was flung on the floor and as he passed Bridie and Bob, he asked, 'I hope yer don't mind if I say hello to me girlfriend first? She looks more beautiful than ever and I haven't held her in me arms for two years.'

'We've got all the time in the world, me darlin', so we have,' Bridie said. 'And wouldn't any man with red blood in his veins be wanting to hold such a beauty?'

Bob and Rosie were watching Tommy being kissed, hugged and slapped on the back by Jack, Doreen and Ruthie. Bob had tears in his eyes for the grandson he idolised, while Rosie was waiting with mounting impatience to get near the boy she adored.

Tommy caught Rosie's eyes and grinned. 'Hello, Rosie O'Grady.'

'Sure, yer were a foine figure of a lad when I fell for yer, Tommy Bennett, so yer were. And I'd not be telling lies if I said yer were now the finest figure of a man I've seen in the whole of me life.' When laughter erupted, Rosie's face lit up. 'If yerself is not too tired after fighting the war, would yer not be coming over to kiss yer nan and yer granda? After that yer can get down to the serious business of giving yer girlfriend a different kind of kiss than the one yer give yer nan. And if yer've forgotten the difference, sure aren't I just the one to teach yer how it's done?'

Tommy's head dropped back and he roared with laughter. At fifteen he'd been terrified of Rosie's outspoken compliments and avoided her like the plague. At sixteen he was smitten, at seventeen head over heels in love, and when he'd joined the army just before his eighteenth birthday, they became unofficially engaged. It had to be unofficial because Tommy was only earning an apprentice's wage and couldn't afford a ring. But Rosie didn't let a little thing like a ring worry her. She'd got the boy of her dreams and her cup of happiness was overflowing.

Bob put a hand on his wife's elbow and led her forward. 'Come on, sweetheart, we've waited a long time for this.'

Tommy held his arms out and put one around each of the grandparents he adored. They seemed to have become more frail since he went away, and he was careful not to hold them too close. The lump in his throat was becoming bigger and he knew if he spoke he wouldn't be able to keep the tears back. He rocked them gently and whispered in a choked voice, 'I love yer very much.'

Rosie, who watched over Bridie and Bob like a mother hen, was afraid the emotion brought on by seeing their grandson after such a long time, might be too much for them. 'Now Auntie Bridget and Uncle Bob, will yer not be having a thought for Rosie O'Grady? I've been very patient, so I have, but me lips have been puckered for a kiss since me beloved walked through the door.'

Molly, who was shedding a few tears herself, said a silent thank you to Rosie for making light of the situation. If it carried on like that everyone would be crying buckets. 'Tommy, will yer give the girl a kiss, please?'

'Mam, I've been savouring this moment for eighteen months and I'm weak at the knees in anticipation.'

'If it's too weak yer are, Tommy Bennett, then it's meself that'll make the long journey across these two paving stones.' With a twinkle in her deep blue eyes, Rosie walked into arms that eagerly awaited her. But before their lips met, and to the amusement of everyone, she said, 'I'll be expecting an extra two kisses every night, so I will, until yer've made up what I've missed for the last eighteen months.'

Nellie sidled up to her friend. 'Ay, girl, they haven't even noticed the flipping banners after us going to all that trouble.'

'They haven't had a chance, sunshine, they've had people hanging around their necks since they arrived. I don't think they've even seen daylight, yet.'

'Why can't we tell them to look at them now?'

'Holy suffering ducks, Nellie, ye're worse than a child! They're both busy right now – look!' Molly pointed to where Steve was talking to his dad and Lily, his arm tightly around Jill's slim waist. And Tommy couldn't hold Rosie any closer as they engaged in animated conversation with Bridie and Bob. 'Just give them a chance.'

But Nellie wasn't happy with that. 'They're Welcome Home signs, Molly Bennett, and I don't see any point in welcoming them home when they've been home and done all their kissing and talking! That's doing things arse about, that is.'

Molly gave a pretend sigh of exasperation. 'See these white hairs in me head? Well, it was you what put them there.'

The families had stopped talking now and were listening with grins on their faces. Particularly Steve and Tommy. Oh, how they'd missed these hilarious exchanges between their mothers. And nobody had seen doors on both sides of the street open as neighbours came to join in welcoming home two very popular lads.

'Don't yer be blaming me for turning yer hair white, Molly Bennett.' Nellie squared her shoulders and hitched her bosom. 'Yer worry too much, that's what done it. Yer dropped a crumb on the floor one day, and before me very eyes, two hairs on yer head turned white.'

Molly's shoulders began to shake. 'Yer have a very convenient memory, sunshine. Yer only remember what suits yer. So I'll remind yer that the day I dropped the crumb, it was because you'd spilt a full cup of tea all over me good chenille tablecloth.'

'Don't be changing the subject, girl, and making excuses. Are yer denying that yer dropped that crumb?'

Molly lifted her hands in surrender. Glancing around the smiling faces, she said, 'Yer'll never believe what started all this off. It's those blinking banners she's on about. She's doing her nut because two certain people haven't noticed them.'

'I noticed them, Mam,' Tommy said. 'I've just been telling Rosie and me nan and granda how made up I am. They look great and I'm dead chuffed.'

'They were the first thing I saw,' Steve said. 'I got a lump in me throat when I saw them. Another thing I've seen is Miss Clegg. She's got her curtain drawn back and is waving to us.'

'She's been back and forward to the window for the last couple of hours.' Mary Watson had joined the crowd with her daughter, Bella. 'She was determined not to miss this homecoming for the world.'

Molly stuck her tongue out at Nellie. 'Are yer satisfied now, sunshine?'

The crowd had swelled to about thirty, and Tommy and Steve looked very happy to be surrounded by their loved ones and neighbours they'd known all their lives. Nellie was well satisfied, thinking it was no more than the boys deserved. 'Yes, everything's under control now, girl, so why don't yer go in and put the kettle on. The lads must be dying for a bite to eat and a drink.'

'Sod off, Nellie McDonough! I'm not slaving away in the kitchen while you're out here playing queen of the castle. If yer want a drink, then yer can ruddywell help me make it.'

But the drink was to wait for a while because Mrs Robinson, from three doors down, started to sing 'Roll Out the Barrel', and within seconds the street was ringing with happy voices. The Bennetts and McDonoughs were well liked in the street and the neighbours wanted them to know they shared their joy at having their sons home. Molly and Nellie were delighted, it couldn't have turned out better if they'd planned it. So they were in high spirits when Mrs Robinson began to belt out 'Tipperary', and they looked at each other and grinned.

'Come on, girl, let's shake a leg.'

'You lead, sunshine, and I'll follow.'

Several of the women joined in, and those who were too old to be kicking their legs in the air, supplied the singing. And their antics gave Steve and Tommy a chance to get their emotions in check. Surrounded by their families and with their girlfriends in their arms, it was all happening so quickly they were finding it hard to take it in. The Welcome Home banners had brought a lump to their throats. Then the neighbours turning out in force, clearly happy to see them – well, it really pulled on the heart-strings. They hadn't expected such a rousing reception and were overwhelmed. It would have been easy to give way to tears, but nineteen- and twenty-two-year-old men didn't cry. Especially when they were wearing a soldier's uniform.

'Me mam's in good form, Dad,' Doreen said, as her father and George clapped in time to the jigs. 'I wonder how long she can keep that up? She's got more energy than me.'

'It won't be long now,' Jack laughed. 'Nellie's sweating cobs and yer mam's beginning to flag.'

'I'm just nipping down the yard, I won't be long.' Doreen disappeared into the house, but was out again within seconds. 'Mam!' She touched her mother's arm. 'D'yer know yer told us yer had to get down on yer knees and beg the butcher for that pound of stew? Well, yer lowered yer dignity for nothing, 'cos it's boiled dry and the bottom of the pan is burnt.'

'Holy suffering ducks! I'd forgotten all about it!' Molly fled, leaving Nellie floundering without the support of her arm. Steve saw his mother about to keel over and reached her just in time to prevent her falling on her backside.

Nellie screwed up her face. 'Where the hell's she gone? I'll flatten her when I get me hands on her. I nearly ended up on the ground, showing all I've got.'

'Mam, yer were doing that while yer were dancing. Everyone in the street knows yer've got yer pink ones on today.' Steve grinned down at the woman who had given him so much love and happiness since the day he was born. 'I think I heard Doreen say the dinner was burnt.'

'Oh, bloody hell!' Nellie moved fast for her size. She reached the kitchen to see Molly taking a pan down from the shelf. 'Is it ruined, girl?'

'Not far from it! It's dried-up and stuck to the bottom of the pan. I'm just going to see if I can salvage some of it. If not, Tommy's first meal at home for eighteen months will be a bag of chips from the chippy.'

'What were yer thinking of to let that happen, girl?'

Molly's face was a study as she eyed her friend. 'What was I thinking of? Well, now, let me see. I know it was daft of me, but I was thinking of showing me son how happy I was to see him. I mean, like, it's been eighteen months, not eighteen ruddy days! I could hardly shake his hand and say, "Hello, son, yer dinner won't be long".' Molly began to spoon the stew from the burnt pan to the clean one. 'Anyway, shouldn't yer be worried about yer own dinner? While ye're standing there watching me, the backside could be burning out of yer own pan.'

'No, it won't, girl, I'm not that daft! Yer see, with George and Lily being off, we had our dinner at one o'clock.'

'Steve didn't though, did he? Surely yer've got something on the go for him? He's probably starving with hunger.'

Nellie did something she very seldom did, she blushed. 'Well, it's like this, yer see, girl. I thought Jill wouldn't want to let Steve out of her sight, not with him being away for two years. So I thought the least yer could do would be to let him have some dinner with you.'

Molly couldn't express her feelings with a pan in her hand, so she put it on the stove before facing her friend. With her hands on her hips and her nostrils flared, she said, 'Nellie McDonough! You are one scheming, cunning, conniving, hard-faced article! I don't know how yer've got the nerve to stand there, with that innocent look on yer face, and say what yer've just said! When it comes to cheek, sunshine, you really take the biscuit.'

Nellie's whole body quivered as she got on her high horse. 'I don't know why ye're taking off like that on me for! I've hardly opened me flaming mouth! It's you what's been doing all the talking. Instead of you getting a cob on with me, I'd be well within me rights to tell yer off for spoiling me son's dinner! But have yer heard me complain? No, I haven't said a dickie bird! Now let's be fair about it.'

'Let's be fair about it? I'm abso-bloody-lutely flabbergasted!' Molly feigned indignation while inside her whole being was chuckling. 'Anyway, I'm surprised yer don't want yer son to be with you and George on his first night home.'

'Oh, we do, girl! I'm not letting Steve out of me sight for one minute!'

The chuckling inside of Molly slowed down. She might be able to salvage most of the stew because it wasn't as bad as she'd first feared. If she added some water and Bisto, it shouldn't be too bad and there'd be enough for Steve if the helpings weren't too big. But it certainly wouldn't stretch to Nellie, George and Lily. 'I know what ye're thinking, sunshine, but yer can forget it. I'll be glad to have Steve for his dinner, but I ain't feeding the five thousand.'

'Lily's going out, so there's only me and my feller. And we'd be quite happy sitting on yer couch with a bag of chips in our hand. We understand that Steve will want to spend every minute with Jill, but we want to know where he's been the last two years and everything he's done and seen. The letters we've had told us nothing, thanks to the bloody feller who censored them. And I bet you wouldn't be very happy if Tommy went round to yer ma's tonight, to be with Rosie, would yer?'

'No, I wouldn't. But Rosie's taking me ma and da home for their tea, then coming back later. Why can't you do the same?'

'Waste of shoe leather. Beside, I want to reserve a good speck for the night.'

Molly gave it up as a bad job and turned back to the stove. If Nellie said she was going to sit on the couch with a bag of chips in her hand, then that's what Nellie would do. Talking to her would be like talking to the wall. 'It's going to be a full house, right enough. What with your three, me ma's three and my six! And Phil is bound to come over to see the lads, and be with Doreen, of course. How many does that make?'

'I dunno, girl, I ran out of fingers when I got to ten. But yer were near enough when yer said a houseful.'

The families started to troop back in and Jack came straight through to the kitchen. 'Was the dinner ruined, love?'

'The bottom had caught, but it'll be all right with a bit of doctoring.' Molly glanced through to the living room to see Tommy smiling down into Rosie's upturned face, and suddenly the stew didn't seem important. The boys were home and that's what really mattered. And she vowed that never again would they go away to war. If another Hitler came along in her lifetime, she would personally see he was hung, drawn and quartered. She would have to take Nellie with her, of course, 'cos she couldn't do it alone.

'It was good of the neighbours to come out, wasn't it?' Molly asked. 'They knew yer were coming home today, but we couldn't tell them what time because we didn't know ourselves. They must have been watching out.'

'I never expected a welcome like that, Mam,' Tommy said. 'It was a real surprise. I thought me dad and the girls would be at work.'

'Yeah, me too.' Steve speared a potato. 'Never in a million years did I expect that sort of reception. I had a lump in me throat half the time.'

'Yer should have been here when Ruthie came running in and said yer'd just got off the tram!' George said, from his seat on the couch. 'Molly and yer mam were nervous wrecks and I thought we'd be needing a bottle of smelling salts to bring them round. And Jill's face was as white as a sheet. She couldn't even get off the chair. Doreen had to drag her out in the end.'

Jack chuckled. 'Yeah, I thought yer were going to come home to find all the women laid out on the floor. Still, it all turned out well in the end, and the neighbours joining in made yer welcome home a bit more special, something to remember.'

Molly was watching their faces anxiously. She'd been afraid the stew might have a slight taste of burning, but everyone was tucking in with gusto so she laid her fears to rest. 'I was surprised at Mrs Robinson, it's not often she lets herself go.'

'She brought back a few memories for me,' Steve said, his grin wide, his dimples deep. 'I was remembering the times she used to chase me and me mates when we were playing footie in the street. "Go and annoy someone else," she used to shout. Or, "Go and play outside yer own house and see how yer mam likes it".'

Tommy's broad shoulders were shaking. 'I used to be terrified of her. She once wagged her finger at me and said, "If I see yer playing footie outside here again, I'll put yer over me knee and tan yer backside for yer". I kept well away from her house after that.'

'She'd have a job to do that now, son, with the size of yer.' Molly's cup of happiness was overflowing now Tommy was back in his chair at the table. Mealtimes hadn't been the same for the last eighteen months because the empty chair had been a constant reminder of him. Not one night had gone by that she hadn't wondered where he was and if he was all right. But he was back in the fold now and her heart could be at peace. 'If yer grow any taller yer won't be able to get in the door.'

'I've had strict instructions from Rosie that I'm not to grow any more. She's threatened to hit me on the head with the frying pan every night, to stunt me growth.'

'Someone would have to lift her up to do it,' Ruthie said. She had given her chair up to Steve and was sitting on a fireside chair with a plate on her knee. 'Unless yer were daft enough to bend down so she could hit yer.'

'I did tell Rosie she'd have a problem, but as usual she had an answer. "Sure, I'll not be letting yer get the better of me, Tommy Bennett, that I'll not. I reckon if I stood on the third stair I could manage it right enough".'

'She's a case, that girl.' Nellie screwed up her chip paper and was about to throw it on the hearth when she caught Molly's eye and thought better of it. 'Yer'll definitely have yer hands full with her.'

'And me arms, Auntie Nellie, I'm pleased to say. I can't think of nothing I'd like better than to have me hands and arms full of Rosie O'Grady.'

Doreen looked at the empty plates. 'Ma, I'll do the dishes then go over and see Miss Clegg. And Phil will be coming back with me to see Steve and Tommy.'

'I'd like to go, as well,' Steve said. 'If yer think Miss Clegg's up to it.'

'Me too!' Tommy piped up. 'I'd love to see her.'

'She'd be made up to see yer. But don't stay too long or get her excited. Remember, she's ninety.' Molly pushed her chair back. 'Go on, the four of yer. Me and Nellie will do the washing up.'

There was loud laughter when Nellie threw the chip paper and caught Molly on the nose.

'Yer can sod off, Molly Bennett! Me and George weren't good enough to have any of yer dinner, so I'm ruddywell not going to wash the dishes what you greedy buggers had yer dinner off! Me and my feller had to sit on yer couch and eat chips out of the paper, like two naughty children. And, to add insult to injury, I had to pay for the ruddy chips meself! So don't be expecting any favours from me 'cos yer've no chance.'

Molly had the plates stacked up in front of her. Without raising an eyebrow or turning a hair, she asked, 'Shall I wash and you dry? Or would you rather wash?'

Nellie dug her curled fists into the couch and pushed herself up. 'I'll dry, girl, 'cos I don't want to get me hands chapped.

George doesn't like it when me hands are rough.'

Steve, Tommy, Jill and Doreen were still laughing when Phil opened the door of Miss Clegg's house. And within minutes they had the old lady in stitches. The tears of emotion that had sprung to her eyes at the sight of the two young soldiers, were quickly turned to tears of laughter. And conversation during the half-hour visit was kept light. When Victoria asked questions about the war, either Steve or Tommy would relate a funny incident rather than the reality. So that when the old lady they all adored went to bed, she would go to sleep with a smile on her face.

Chapter Five

When Rosie came back alone, it was to say that Bridie and Bob were looking tired and she'd suggested they stay in and have an early night. 'Sure, wasn't herself up at seven this morning? She couldn't sleep with the excitement of it all. And while Uncle Bob didn't get up so early, he hadn't had a good night's sleep. So I've told them to go to bed early and they'd see their beloved grandson tomorrow.' Rosie's bonny face had a smile for everyone. But she reserved her special one for Tommy. 'It's palpitations we've all had for the last week, Tommy Bennett, so it is. And it's meself that's wondering if yer appreciate the worry yer've put us through?'

'I didn't put yer through any worry, it was some bloke called Hitler.' Tommy winked broadly. 'Come and give us a kiss, Rosie, I haven't had one for two hours.' He was sat at the table with Jill and Steve, and Doreen and Phil. Patting the empty chair next to him, he said, 'Come on, I've saved yer a seat.'

'Auntie Molly, since yer son put on that soldier's uniform, he's become very forward, so he has. And bossy with it.'

'We'll make allowances for him, sunshine. For the next week we'll pamper him and give him all his own way. Then it's back to normal.'

'So yer think I should give him a kiss, do yer, Auntie Molly?'

'Most definitely, sunshine!'

There was a twinkle in Rosie's deep blue Irish eyes as she walked around the table. 'Me mammy used to always say that I should have respect for me elders. So I'm giving yer a kiss, Tommy Bennett, 'cos yer mam said I should.'

Nellie, from her speck on the couch, said, 'For heaven's sake get on with it, girl, before he dies from the want of.'

Tommy jumped up, his pulses racing at the mere sight of the girl he adored. 'I don't enjoy a kiss sitting down. Let's do the job properly.' And when he pulled Rosie into his arms his kiss was not only proper, but a real humdinger.

Steve leaned towards Jill, and in a loud whisper said, 'While all the eyes are on Tommy, d'yer think we could steal a kiss?'

'I was just thinking the same thing,' Phil said. 'How about it, Doreen?'

Nellie watched the three couples, with their arms entwined and their lips meeting, and when she thought they'd had enough, she called, 'Okay, break it up! If yer carry on, I'll be dragging me feller upstairs.'

Molly gasped. 'Nellie McDonough! Will yer be careful what yer say? Honest to God, I don't know where to put me face sometimes! No matter what we're talking about, we always manage to end up in your bedroom!'

Nellie pulled her tongue out. 'Ye're wrong there, girl. It wasn't my bedroom I was talking about, it was yours! What's the use of us running home while you've got a perfectly good bed upstairs? Besides, by the time we'd got to ours, George would have lost interest.'

'I give up,' Molly said, her mind smiling while her head wagged from side to side. 'I don't know how yer put up with her, George.'

'With great difficulty, Molly, with great difficulty.'

'Go 'way, Dad, yer'd be lost without her.' Steve sat down and pulled Jill on to his knee. 'Yer life would be very dull.'

Nellie wasn't as demonstrative as Molly, but her love for her children was just as deep. And while she resorted to humour now, as she looked at her son her devotion to him could be seen in her eyes. 'Oh, yer've come up for air, have yer? Well, now yer've got yer breath back, perhaps yer'll tell us a bit more about where yer've been for the last two years, eh? We got no news in yer letters 'cos most of the words had ruddy big blue lines through. That feller who read the letters before censoring them had a good job, didn't he? I bet his hair used to stand on end reading the passionate ones.'

'You should have applied for that job, Nellie,' Jack said. 'Yer'd have been good at it.'

'Nah, I'm no good at words with more than six letters in. Mind you, I could have taken me dictionary with me.'

Molly laughed. 'Yer haven't got a dictionary!'

'Yes, I have, smart arse.' Nellie tried a look of disdain, but as she was sitting down it wasn't very effective. 'I've got you, haven't I? I could have took you with me.'

'Yer mean yer could have taken me, sunshine, not took me. That's very bad grammar, that is.'

Nellie bit on her bottom lip in an attempt to keep her face straight. 'Yer don't half get me mixed up, girl, and I'll swear yer do it on purpose. What's me grandma got to do with it?'

George touched her arm. 'I would very much like to hear about the war, and I'd like to hear it before the next one starts.'

As quick as a snap of the fingers, Nellie's whole attitude changed and she became the docile housewife. 'Yes, love! Anything yer say, love! Steve, you heard what yer dad said. Don't be sitting there like a love-struck giraffe, tell him what he wants to know.'

'I've already told yer most of it.' Steve had given a very watered-down version of his time overseas. It had been such a joyous homecoming, he didn't want to put a damper on it. He'd tell his dad the truth when they were on their own one day, but to do so now would only upset the women. But all eyes were on him and he had to say something. 'If yer think Liverpool was badly hit by bombs, it's nothing compared to the hammering Hamburg got. It was razed to the ground. Even when the Germans surrendered, our soldiers were on orders not to let anybody into the city because it was too dangerous. People weren't allowed to go back to their homes, and even though I hate Hitler and his cronies, I couldn't help feeling sorry for the civilians. Particularly the elderly and very young who were walking around bewildered and homeless. They probably didn't want the war any more than we did.'

'Somebody should have stopped Hitler before he got so powerful,' George said. 'The top brass in the German army must have known from the very beginning what he was up to, and yer can't tell me they all agreed with him. So why didn't they knock him down to size?'

'Dad, anyone who disagreed with Hitler didn't live long enough to tell the tale. He was ruthless. His one aim was to rule the whole of Europe, and anyone who raised their voice in opposition was quietly disposed of.'

'We passed through Holland on our way to Belgium,' Tommy said. 'And there were women and young girls walking round with their heads shaved. When I mentioned it to one of the lads, he said the Dutch people did that to anyone who fraternised with the enemy. Some of the girls had made friends with the Germans, probably to get food off them, but the Dutch people didn't take kindly to them and shaved their heads to shame them, so everyone would know what they were.'

'Yeah, we saw that on the *Pathé News*,' Molly said. 'I can understand the Dutch people wanting to shame them because they were eating potato peelings while these girls were well fed. But I have to admit I asked meself if I wouldn't have done the same thing if me family were starving. It's easy for us to criticise, but we don't know what we'd have done in the circumstances.'

'One of me mates, Hooter, said he heard some of the girls had babies to the German soldiers stationed there, but I don't know whether that's true or not. Hooter was always pulling our legs and we never knew when he was having us on.'

'Hooter!' Nellie said. 'What sort of a name is that when it's out? The poor lad wasn't lumbered with a name like that, was he?'

'No, his real name is Archibald Higgins.' Tommy's chuckle turned into a fullblown laugh. 'Hooter was a nickname we gave him because of his nose. Honest to God, he had the biggest conk I've ever seen in me life.'

'That wasn't very kind of yer, Tommy Bennett,' Rosie said. 'Sure, the poor lad can't help the way the good Lord made him.'

Nellie's shaking body had the floorboards creaking. 'Perhaps not, Rosie, but his mother didn't help by giving him a name like Archibald. She was either thick or had a bloody good sense of humour. I can just imagine it when he was a kid out playing and his mother coming to the door to call him in. "Archibald, yer dinner's ready!" The poor lad must have had his leg pulled something rotten.'

'I doubt it, Auntie Nellie, 'cos he's a big lad and knows how to handle himself. He can give me a couple of inches, easy. Anyway, yer'll be meeting him one of these days because we're keeping in touch. He only lives in Hawthorne Road and we'll be getting together with a couple of other lads in a week or two.'

'He doesn't live near the gasworks, does he?' Nellie asked. 'The smell from there is terrible, and if he's got as big a nose as yer say, he'll get the smell twice as bad as anyone else.'

Molly tutted. 'Nellie, will yer leave the poor lad alone!'

'I don't mean no harm, girl. In fact, I'll look forward to meeting this Archibald, and his hooter.'

'Ye're in for a surprise, Auntie Nellie, 'cos he could lift you up and toss yer in the air as though yer were a rag doll.'

Nellie shuffled to the edge of the couch, her eyes wide with anticipation. 'Ooh, d'yer think he will, Tommy?'

'He will if he thinks ye're asking for it.'

'Ooh, I wouldn't ask for it, lad, that would look brazen. But there's nothing to stop you putting in a good word for me.'

'That's enough, Nellie McDonough!' Molly slapped a hand on the arm of her chair. 'Wherever he is, the poor lad's ears must be burning.'

But Nellie had to have the last word. 'Well, if there's anything burning, girl, he's got the right equipment to smell it.'

Molly turned to her son. 'Tommy, why did yer have to mention yer mate? Nellie will worry it like a dog with a bone.'

There was a hint of devilment in Tommy's smile. 'Mam, Archie does have a large nose, that's the truth. And we nicknamed him Hooter. But he's one of the most handsome men ye're likely to meet in a month of Sundays. And the nicest.'

'He wouldn't happen to be about forty, would he?' Nellie asked. 'Yer see, I could do with trading my George in for another model.'

'Sorry, Auntie Nellie, he's only twenty-one.'

'Isn't that just my luck?' Nellie let her shoulders slump and the corners of her mouth turned down. Then she spotted a smiling Ruthie sitting on the floor next to her mother's chair. 'He's too young for me, and too old for you, queen. So we've both missed out. Mind you, he'd be just right for our Lily.'

Steve leaned forward. 'Lily said she had a date tonight. Mam, is she courting?'

Nellie felt George dig her sharply in the ribs and she chose her words carefully. 'I don't know, son. She was going out with a bloke for a while, then he got called up. That's about all me and yer dad know.'

'She said she had a date, so he must have been demobbed. Unless, of course, she's found someone else while he was away.'

No such luck, Nellie was thinking as she answered. 'I honestly couldn't tell yer, Steve. With all the excitement of you and Tommy coming home, I've had so much on me mind. And then not knowing when Paul will be home, that's been a worry.'

'At least yer've had a letter from him, so yer know he's in England. I wouldn't worry, Mam, he'll walk in as large as life any day now.'

'Of course he will,' Molly said. 'And then we'll have a real Welcome Home party. I hope Corker's ship docks before then 'cos it wouldn't be a party without Corker.'

'He should be home soon,' Jack said. 'He's been away about four months now.'

'D'yer know what I've been looking forward to all the time I've been away?' Steve gave Jill's hand a squeeze. 'Apart from wanting to be with you, sweetheart, and me family and friends. Well, it's walking into the corner pub for the first time in me life, with me dad, Uncle Jack and Uncle Corker. It's a few years ago now, but I can remember one night when the three of yer were going for a pint and I must have looked dead jealous. Uncle Corker ruffled me hair and said not to worry, the time would come when I'd be old enough to go with them. So when I have me first pint, standing at that bar, I want those three men with me. Then I'll know I am well and truly a man.'

Jill, the shy and gentle one, wasn't going to let that pass. 'Yer don't need a pint to become a man, Steve. In my eyes, yer've always been one.'

'And so has my Phil.' Doreen gave her boyfriend a quick peck on the cheek. 'From the second I clapped eyes on yer at Barlow's

Lane Dance Hall, yer've always been my man.'

Molly's eyes were filling up. *Oh God, I'm going to cry.* Then she heard Rosie's lovely lilting voice, which was like music to her ears.

'I'll not be leaving you out, Tommy Bennett, indeed I'll not! Sure yer were fifteen when I met yer, but I knew even then that yer were the man for me. I had a bit of trouble convincing yer, that's the truth of it, but sure didn't yer come round to my way of thinking eventually? And I'll be telling yer this. Neither age, a soldier's uniform nor a pint of beer, make the man. Yer are what the good Lord made yer, and He made you a man, Tommy Bennett.'

'I'm glad he did, Rosie, and that's the truth of it.' Tommy's attempt at an Irish accent did him credit. ''Cos if He'd made me a woman, wouldn't I be after asking yer to get off me knee right this minute?'

'If yer were a woman, Tommy, I wouldn't be on yer knee in the first place! But seeing as ye're not, would yer kindly keep yer knees still and stop bobbing me up and down?'

'Come here, wench, I want to whisper in yer ear.' Tommy whispered so low nobody could hear him. But the smile on Rosie's face told them that whatever he'd said had found favour with her.

'Auntie Molly, Tommy wants to know if it would be all right if he walked me home now? He'd like me to himself for an hour, and it's meself that's saying it would be altogether fine by me.'

Amidst the laughter, Jack scratched his head and said, 'Now I can't for the life of me imagine what he wants to get yer on yer own for.'

George, his hands clasped between his knees, chuckled. What a bonny girl this Irish lass was. As pretty as a picture with a smile that would melt a heart of stone. 'Whatever it is, it's got Tommy blushing.'

'I don't know why I bothered whispering, Mr McDonough! I might have known Rosie would blurt it out. And this blush yer see on me face – well, that's me getting in practice. I've got a feeling I'll be doing a lot of blushing in me life. Rosie doesn't believe in beating about the bush. If she thinks it, she says it.'

'There's nothing wrong with that, as long as yer don't hurt anybody,' Molly said. 'Rosie told me once that if the good Lord hadn't wanted her to think, He wouldn't have given her a brain. And if He hadn't wanted her to talk, He wouldn't have given her a mouth.'

'And isn't that the truth, Auntie Molly? So yer son had better get used to me using both me brain and me mouth.'

'Will yer get yer coat, Rosie, and I'll walk yer home.' Tommy gave a broad wink behind her back. 'And when we get there, leave yer brain on the hallstand 'cos yer'll not be needing it. Just bring those ruby red lips in with yer.'

'I'd better be going, too,' Phil said. 'I want to make sure Aunt Vickie got herself to bed all right. I don't like her going up those stairs on her own, but yer know how stubborn and independent she can be.'

'I'll come over with yer for half-an-hour.' When Doreen stood up and looked down into his handsome face, her heart flipped. This was the man she couldn't wait to marry and spend the rest of her life with. 'Yer don't have to worry about a brain with me, 'cos I haven't got one. But my lips are in good form.'

After seeing the two couples out, with strict instructions to be careful not to wake the old folk, Molly went back into the living room rubbing her hands. 'Now, Ruthie, it's way past yer bedtime. Lay yer school clothes out ready for tomorrow.'

'Ah, ay, Mam! Just another half hour! And why can't I have the day off tomorrow? I won't get into trouble, not with me brother just coming home from the army.'

'Yer've had today off, sunshine, yer can't have another one or the School Board will be after me. Now be a good girl and get yourself ready for bed.'

Jack saw rebellion in his youngest daughter's face and stepped in before she had time to answer back. 'Do as yer mam told yer, Ruthie. Yer've been very good today, helping out, so don't go and blot yer copybook now.'

The young girl knew when she was beat and scrambled to her feet with a sigh. 'I can't wait to leave school.'

'Don't be wishing yer life away, girl,' Nellie said. 'When yer get to our age yer'll be wishing yerself back in a gymslip.'

There was mischief in Ruthie's smile. 'Ah, but think of the fun I'll have getting to your age, Auntie Nellie.'

'Fun! Who said I've had fun!' Even Nellie's chins danced in indignation. 'I've had a ruddy hard life, believe me! It's been no joke being married to a man who cracks the whip if his slippers aren't in the hearth when he comes in from work, or his egg is either too hard or too runny. And if his porridge is lumpy . . . well, I have to make a run for it 'cos all hell breaks loose.'

There was a stitch in Molly's side with laughing, and she was pressing her hand into it as she looked at George. He was a big man with a deep voice. There were few men who would dare to clash with him, but he was as soft as putty with the wife he adored. He never raised his voice to her in anger and would never, ever raise a hand. 'Ye're a terrible man, George, giving yer poor wife a dog's life. I don't know how she's put up with yer all these years.'

'I know, Molly, I don't know what gets into me sometimes.' George wasn't as funny or outgoing as his wife, but he wasn't without humour. 'I'm always sorry after I've belted her, though. I usually go upstairs and sit on me bed 'cos I can't stand the sight of the bruises starting to show around her eyes. And I swear to meself that I'll never hit her again. The trouble is, I can't abide cold slippers or a runny egg!'

Molly happened to turn her head and noticed Jill and Steve staring into each other's eyes. They hadn't had a minute to themselves all day. Right now they were probably thinking Rosie would be in Tommy's arms and Doreen in Phil's. And they were stuck with the two sets of parents. 'Ruthie, off yer pop, right this minute. Auntie Nellie and Uncle George will be going soon 'cos it's been a long day and we're all tired.'

'I'm not tired, girl!' Nellie said.

'Oh, yes yer are,' Molly answered, while willing her friend to follow her eyes to where the two sweethearts were sitting. 'Yer might be thinking ye're not, but yer are really.'

It didn't take long for Nellie to twig. 'D'yer know, I think ye're right! I could have sworn I wasn't tired, but I can feel me eyelids drooping. It just goes to show, girl, that you know more about me than I do meself.'

George hadn't failed to notice the eye-contact between the two women, and when he saw his wife struggling to get off the couch, he stood up and held out both hands. 'Come on, light of my life, let me give yer a lift up.' With his arm across her shoulders, he led her to the door. 'I'll see yer tomorrow when I get home from work, son. No doubt yer'll be having a good lie-in.'

'I will that, Dad! I can't wait to get back in me own bed.' Steve blew a kiss to his mother. 'I'll see yer in the morning, Mam. Give us a shout when me breakfast's ready.'

After they'd gone, and Ruthie was in bed, Molly looked at Jack and yawned. 'I'm all in, I think I'll hit the hay. Are yer coming up, love?'

The message in his wife's eyes was loud and clear. 'Yeah, I'm tired meself. And it's back to the grind tomorrow.'

Molly waited for Jack to follow her out of the room, then she turned to close the door behind them. And a smile crossed her face when she heard Steve say, 'I thought I was never going to get yer on yer own. Come and let's sit on the couch so I can kiss yer properly and tell yer how much I love yer.'

As soon as George and Lily left for work the next morning, Nellie set to with a vengeance. It was Steve's first morning home in two years and she was determined to have the place warm, comfortable and shining. The fire was raked out and ashes taken down the yard to the bin, the fireplace polished until yer could see yer face in it, then paper, wood and coal was laid in the grate ready to put a match to. Although there was no rush because Steve wouldn't expect to be called before nine, Nellie worked like the clappers. The room was dusted before she washed the dishes, then the hot water left in the kettle was used to give herself a wash down. All the time she had her ear cocked for any sound from above that would tell her her son was up and about. She'd go mad if he came down before she was ready for him.

By a quarter to nine, dressed in a clean pinny, stockings without a ladder or hole in, Nellie was all ready except for her hair. She'd slept in dinky curlers all night, and after she'd taken them out she gave her scalp a gentle rub. 'They're bloody murder to sleep in.' She spoke to the empty room as she put the curlers into the sideboard drawer. 'What we women will go through just to get a blinking curl! I wouldn't care, but with the hair I've got, it'll go dead straight as soon as it sees the ruddy comb!'

It was nine o'clock when Nellie stood on tiptoe to look in the mirror hanging over the mantelpiece. 'I'll have to do! If I spend all day titivating meself up, I still wouldn't look like Jean Harlow.' She gazed around the room and gave a sigh of satisfaction. The kettle was on a low light on the stove and the bread had been sliced ready for toasting. All that was missing now was her son. She was halfway across the room when she hesitated. Perhaps he'd like another hour after the long day he'd had yesterday. She hadn't heard him coming in last night so God knows what time he got to bed. But her tummy was rumbling with hunger because she'd put off having her breakfast so she could eat with Steve. So while he might enjoy an extra hour in bed, her tummy wouldn't wait that long.

Standing at the bottom of the stairs, Nellie shouted, 'Steve! Come on, lad, yer breakfast is ready!'

It was a few seconds before a sleepy voice answered, 'I've been awake for a while, Mam, but I hear yer've got visitors.'

'I haven't got no visitors! It was me talking to meself, soft lad! Just throw something on and come down because I'm famished.'

Nellie was buttering the toast when Steve came through to the kitchen. His hair was tousled and his dimples deep in a smiling face. He made straight for her and wrapped his arms tightly around her waist. After several kisses, he said, 'Oh mam, yer've no idea how good it is to be home. I've missed everyone so much.'

'It's good to have yer home, son, back where yer belong. All I need now is to hear from our Paul and all me worries will be over.'

She removed his arms from her waist and her chubby face creased. 'Have a quick swill, then we'll have a good old natter while we're eating our breakfast.'

'That toast brings back memories, Mam.' Steve pulled out a chair and sat down. 'Nice golden brown with the butter soaked in. It was never like that in the army.'

'It's not butter, son, it's marge. And I've been generous because I scrounged some off Maisie. In fact, me and Molly have done nothing but scrounge for the last four years. It's been hard going with the mingy rations we're allowed. Still, with a bit of luck things should start getting a bit easier now with the war over.' Nellie wiped a hand across her chin, where the margarine had trickled. 'I bet yer were happy to see Jill again, eh?'

'Yer've no idea, Mam. I had to keep pinching meself to make sure I wasn't dreaming. I'll never be parted from her again, not for anything.' Steve grinned. 'I'd have stayed there all night, just holding her, but I don't think Mrs B. would have approved.'

'What time did yer get in? I must have been dead to the world 'cos I never heard yer.'

'It was after midnight. I lay awake for a while because me head was buzzing, and I was just dropping off when I heard our Lily come in. I hope she didn't walk home on her own at that time of night. Did she say if her boyfriend was home?'

'She didn't say, son, and I didn't ask her.' Nellie curled her hands around her cup. 'To tell yer the truth, she doesn't tell us anything about him. If she is courting him, it's the funniest courtship I've ever known. The few times she's brought him here, we couldn't get a word out of him.'

Steve raised his brows. 'Why do I get the feeling yer don't like him?'

'Perhaps it's because I don't! Neither does yer dad. All we know about him is that his name's Len, and he lives in Walton. Now, yer'd expect to know a bit more about the feller yer daughter was going out with, wouldn't yer? I think he's underhanded. He never says anything unless we ask him, then he looks down at the floor instead of facing yer. He never smiles and can't get out of here quick enough.'

'Haven't yer asked our Lily about him? Perhaps it's just that the lad's shy.'

Nellie shook her head. 'No, Steve, there's more to it than that. I've given up asking Lily because yer can't get a thing out of her. Just that his name's Len and he lives in Walton. She must like him 'cos she's never been out with any other boy while he's been away, but there's something not right about the whole thing.' Nellie put her cup back in the saucer. 'Figure it out for yerself. If he has

70

been demobbed, and is home, why didn't she say anything? Why didn't she bring him here to meet you?'

'Perhaps he wanted to be with his family. There'd be nothing wrong with that. She'll probably bring him to see yer tonight or tomorrow.' Steve studied his mother's face. It wasn't like her to take a dislike to anyone unless there was good reason. And she was usually a pretty good judge of character. 'Are yer really worried about this bloke?'

'Me and yer dad are worried sick, Steve. Now, yer know how easygoing yer father is – well, he tried to make the bloke feel welcome. And he put it down to shyness the first time. But after a while he gave up because he couldn't get any response at all. It was as clear as the nose on yer face that this Len didn't want to be here. He never called for her, like most boys call for their girlfriend, she used to meet him outside.'

'I'll have a word with her,' Steve said. 'I won't let on that yer've talked to me about him, I'll just bring it up in conversation. And I'll ask her to bring him along one night, then I can see for meself what he's like.'

'We're having a party when Paul gets home, all the usual gang. So yer can tell her to invite him to it. I'll bet a pound to a pinch of snuff she makes an excuse for him not coming, but it's worth a try.'

'Well, I'm not going to let it spoil me homecoming, that's a cert! When things calm down and we're back to normal, I'll suss this bloke out.' Steve reached for the teapot to refill his cup. 'Now let's have some news from the street. How are Ellen and the kids?'

'Ellen's fine. She hasn't half come out of her shell. Like all of us with men away, she's been worried sick about Corker. Especially when it was on the wireless every day about how many ships the German submarines had sunk. But the smile's back on her face again now. And yer won't recognise the kids when yer see them. Yer wouldn't believe they were the same kids that used to walk around filthy dirty, with rags on their backs and fleas in their hair. Thin as rakes the poor buggers were with not getting enough to eat, and often sporting bruises from that villain Ellen was married to. The best thing she ever did, for herself and the kids, was to marry Corker.'

'They won't be little kids any more, will they? Phoebe must be about fifteen now.'

'Phoebe's seventeen, and she's grown into a very pretty girl. Dorothy is fifteen and the spitting image of Nobby Clarke. If yer can remember that far back, he was a nice-looking bloke when him and Ellen moved into the street. The pity was, he was nice on the outside and a devil inside. Anyway, the girls are both working,

71

and Gordon leaves school in a couple of months. That only leaves young Peter.'

'Time flies over, doesn't it, Mam? It doesn't seem any time since I was kneeling in the gutter playing ollies. Or hanging around hoping Jill would come out to play.'

Nellie jumped when there was a loud ran-tan on the door. 'Who the heck can this be? It won't be Molly, 'cos she'll be busy with Tommy. And the rent man's not due, or the coalman.'

'Mam, wouldn't it be easier and quicker to open the door, instead of trying to guess?'

It was with great reluctance that Nellie stood up. 'I was hoping to have yer to meself for a couple of hours, so whoever it is can just sling their hook.' She swayed towards the front door, shouting, 'Whatever it is ye're selling, we don't want none.'

'If that's the way yer feel, Mam, I'll go and join the army again.'

Nellie was open-mouthed as she stared in surprise at her youngest son. When she'd waved him off after his last leave before being sent overseas, although he was dressed in a soldier's uniform, he was still a boy in her eyes. And that's how she expected to see him now. But standing before her, in a dark fawn suit, white shirt and brown tie, was a man. She was so stunned she couldn't speak.

'Mam, if yer don't move out of the way, I'm going to have to climb over yer.' Paul McDonough could see the tears building up as his mother stepped back. 'Mam, ye're not allowed to cry, and ye're not allowed to laugh at me new suit.'

Steve heard his brother's voice and pushed his chair back with such force it toppled over. He reached the hall to see his mother being held close as the tears flowed down her chubby face. 'What have yer done to make me mam cry, our Paul?'

Over his mother's head, Paul returned his smile. 'I only knocked on the door, honest!'

Nellie moved away from his arms, wiping her eyes with the back of her hand. And as usual she resorted to humour. 'I thought it was me club woman and I was going to tell her to leave me until next week 'cos I'm skint.'

'That's more like it, Mam! Now you go and put the kettle on while I say hello to me big brother.'

Nellie turned at the door of the living room to see the two brothers fling their arms around each other. Then she fled to the kitchen where she shed enough tears to fill the kettle.

'Me mam's been expecting a letter from yer,' Steve said, as the two brothers faced each other across the table, with the sound of their mother pottering about in the kitchen. 'Why didn't yer write and tell her yer were coming home today?'

'I didn't have time!' Paul's eyes travelled the familiar room. When he'd joined the army he didn't realise how much he was going to miss his home and his family. But he'd missed them so much he'd prayed for the day when he'd be back again. And now he was so happy to see his mam and Steve. And the room was just as he remembered it. Except the aspidistra plant looked twice the size. 'I was in a camp down South when I wrote to her, then one day we were bundled into lorries, with no notice, and brought up to Ashton-in-Makerfield. It was no good writing from there because I knew I'd be home before the letter arrived.'

Nellie came bustling in with a fresh pot of tea and a plate of toast. 'Where's this Ashton-in-Makerfield when it's out?'

'It's not far from here, only about forty miles. I heard one of the drivers saying he was passing through Liverpool today so I cadged a lift. Then it was only a couple of stops on the tram.' Paul stood up and fingered the knot in his tie. 'How d'yer like the demob suit? Not bad for nothing, eh?'

'It looks better than mine,' Steve said. 'I came home in me uniform yesterday and haven't had a chance to try the suit on yet. But what put me off was seeing everyone being issued with the same navy-blue pinstripe. There was no selection, it was a case of take it or leave it.'

'The demob centre we were in down South, they ran out of suits. That's why we were sent to Ashton-in-Makerfield.'

'Tommy Bennett didn't get a suit. They didn't have one to fit him so they're sending it on.' Steve chuckled. 'Ay, yer want to see the size of him. Six foot two he is, in his stocking feet!'

Nellie glanced from one to the other. She couldn't remember being as happy or as proud as she was now. 'Don't say yer got the suit for nothing, Paul, 'cos yer more than paid for it with eighteen months of yer life. This country owes yer a damn sight more than a ruddy suit that yer could have got from Burton's for fifty bob!'

'Yeah, but it's better than a kick in the teeth, isn't it?' Paul picked up a slice of toast and folded it over. He didn't want to get grease on his suit the first day on. 'How's me dad and our Lily?'

'They were fine when they left for work this morning. I can't wait to see their faces when they come home and find you sitting here. Yer dad will be as pleased as Punch.'

'We'll take him out for a pint, eh, Steve? First time in a pub with our dad! Unless, of course, yer've got a heavy date with Jill? I suppose she's still your girl?'

'Need you ask? It goes without saying that I'll be seeing her tonight, but I think she'll spare me half-an-hour to go for a pint with me dad. We could ask Mr Bennett as well, he'd like that.' Steve tilted his head and raised his brows. 'What about you, anyway? Have you got a special girl in yer life?'

'No, I'm as free as a bird. There were plenty of girls before I went in the army, but not one I could fall flat on me face for. Anyway, I was only eighteen, too young to tie meself down. So I'll be out playing the field, in me new demob suit, as soon as I've sorted a few things out. Like going to see me old boss to ask whether I can have me job back.' Paul and Steve were very alike in looks. They had the same thick mop of black hair and deep brown eyes. But Paul's dimples weren't as deep and he was about two inches shorter than his brother. He was the most carefree of Nellie's children, and she often said he wouldn't worry if his backside was on fire. With mischief dancing in his eyes, he winked at Steve. 'I can't play the field if I've no money to put on the horses.'

Nellie poked him on the arm. 'Ay, buggerlugs, don't you be classing girls as horses.'

'Come on now, Mam. Even you must admit that all females are nags.'

'That does it!' Nellie's chins quivered to show they agreed with her. 'Yer'll not be coming to me party now, so there!'

'What party's that, then, Mam?'

'It's a Welcome Home party me and Molly are having. But yer wouldn't enjoy it, 'cos there'll be a lot of nags there.'

'Ah, let him come, Mam!' Steve said. 'Go on, don't be mean.'

Paul put his hands together and begged, 'Can I come if I bring a peace offering?'

Nellie shuffled her bottom on the chair, her face alight. 'Oh, yes! What will yer bring?'

'A nosebag of hay!'

Mother and sons doubled up with laughter. 'Mam,' Steve said, 'it's good to be home.'

Paul nodded. 'No place on earth like it. And no mother could compare with you, Mam, ye're a smasher.'

Nellie smiled, happy and contented. 'My life is complete now you two are home. And because me and Molly always share good things, I'm going down to give her the news and make arrangements for the party.' She stood up and wagged a stiffened finger. 'Now behave yerselves, d'yer hear? I don't want none of yer army cursing and swearing in this house while I'm not here, and definitely no dirty jokes.' At the door she turned and grinned. 'Save them for when I get back.'

Chapter Six

There was much noisy chatter and laughter around the McDonough table that night. George was so happy now that both his sons were home. They were boys to be proud of, and he was like a dog with two tails. He fired question after question at them, wanting to know everywhere they'd been and everything they'd done since he last set eyes on them. 'I can't get over how yer've grown! Steve is the same height as me now, if not taller, and Paul's not far behind! Yer old clothes won't be a ha'porth of good to yer now.'

'I know,' Paul chuckled. 'I tried a pair of me old trousers on, 'cos I don't want to get this suit ruined, but the trousers were at half mast. I'll have to get down to TJ's tomorrow and buy a cheap pair.'

'I've got the same trouble,' Steve said. 'I can just about get into me overalls because they were always too big for me. But the rest can go in the bin.'

'They will not,' Nellie said on a high note. 'The bin indeed! There's plenty of men would be made up to have any of yer old clothes. Don't forget, we've had clothes rationing for five years now, and none of us are particularly well dressed.'

'I wouldn't say that, Mam,' Steve said. 'You had a nice dress on yesterday and yer've got another one on today. I thought yer must have come into money.'

George set his knife and fork down on his empty plate. Then, with a loud chuckle, he pointed to his wife. 'Tell them how yer got the dresses, love.'

Nellie gave him daggers. 'I'm sure they're not interested in where I got me flaming dresses from, George McDonough! Men don't want to know that sort of thing.'

'I'm interested, Mam.' Paul knew by his mother's face that there was a story behind the dress she was wearing. 'Where did yer get them from?'

Nellie's head and chins quivered. 'If yer must know, Doreen made them for me. She's a wizard on the sewing machine, that girl, and can run a dress up in a day.'

75

'Even Doreen's not clever enough to make a dress without material, Mam.' Lily was trying to hide a smile. 'Tell the boys about the friends yer've got that let yer have things without coupons.'

'This is a set-up!' Nellie said. 'Ye're all ganging up on me, so I'm keeping me trap shut. It's four against one, but I'm more than a match for the lot of yer put together.'

'Oh, I'm on your side, Mam.' Steve nodded for emphasis.

'Me too,' Paul said. 'A man should never go against his mother.'

'That's my boys!' When Nellie tried to lean forward, the table got in the way of her bosom. For a few seconds there was a fight for supremacy between wood and flesh. But the table never stood a chance and in the end gave it up as a bad job and move a few inches. Then, feeling more comfortable, Nellie beckoned to her sons to come closer. 'I'll let yer into me little secret, but don't tell these two miserable buggers because they don't appreciate my bargaining skills.' Her eyes darted around the room. 'Yer can't be too careful, 'cos yer never know who's listening. Anyway, it's like this. Me and Molly made a friend of a feller in the market, and he lets us have things without coupons.'

Steve lifted his hands and feigned horror. 'Mam, don't tell me yer've been buying things from a spiv on the black market?'

'No, not the black market, son. Great Homer Street market!'

Despite himself, Steve couldn't help smiling. But he had strong views about people making money on the black market and couldn't hold them back. 'Yer shouldn't buy off those blokes, Mam, it's not right! Spivs have been lining their pockets all through the war, while the likes of me and our kid have been away fighting, and being paid a couple of bob a week. They'll be rolling in it, while we've come home with nothing and will be lucky to get our jobs back.'

'I've been telling yer mam that,' George said, 'but she doesn't take a blind bit of notice of me.'

'Blimey! Anyone would think me and Molly had spent a fortune getting things from under the counter, but we haven't. A few fiddling little things, that's all. No one would make a fortune on what we spent.' Nellie's nostrils were flared when she glared at her husband. 'See what yer've done now, George McDonough? We were all laughing and happy before you put yer twopenny-worth in, now everyone's as miserable as sin. I hope ye're satisfied.'

'I'm not miserable, Mam,' Steve said. 'In fact, I've never been so happy and content in all me life.'

'That goes for me, too.' Paul looked down the table to where Nellie was sitting, looking really down in the mouth. 'I haven't

76

stopped loving yer, Mam, even if yer have been keeping some spiv in the lap of luxury.'

Nellie looked decidedly more cheerful. 'I've got something to tell yer that will please yer, but first there's two points I want to make. First, I promise I won't buy no more black market stuff. Secondly, d'yer see that shirt yer dad's wearing? Well, that came out of the battered case Mr Spiv used to keep his stuff in. He had to be on the move all the time, yer see, in case the police nabbed him.'

George's heavy frame shook with laughter. 'I should have known yer'd bring that up. I've never been able to get the better of yer yet, Nellie, and I don't know why I bother.'

'Oh, you have yer moments, love! And don't stop bothering, 'cos I like it when yer get the better of me.'

Steve lowered his head to hide a smile. He was thinking if Mrs B. was here she'd say his mam was talking about bedroom activities. So, as Molly would have done, he steered her away from the subject. 'Mam? Did this bloke in the market wear a long raincoat and a trilby hat pulled low over his eyes?'

Nellie looked surprised. 'How did yer know that, son?'

'Because that's how all spivs dress. Yer can tell them a mile away.'

'Go 'way! Well, yer learn something new every day, don't yer? I bet if I live to be a hundred, I'll be using words with thirteen letters in, like me mate.'

Paul's curiosity finally got the better of him. 'Yer said yer had something to tell us that would please us, Mam, so what is it?'

When the lads had been called up, Nellie had made herself a promise. There'd been times when she nearly broke that promise, but right now she was glad she'd resisted the temptation. 'Yer said before that the pair of yer had come home with nothing. Well, perhaps yer have come home with nothing. But neither of yer are completely skint, 'cos the few bob a week army allowance yer left me, I've never used. Every week, without fail, it went into the post office. There's a savings book for each of yer in the sideboard drawer, and while it's not a fortune, it'll be enough to buy whatever clothes yer need.' Her two sons were looking at her as if they didn't know whether to believe her or not because she was always pulling someone's leg. But she wouldn't pull their legs over something like this. She leaned towards them, rubbing her hands and beaming. 'Honest, it's the truth! So that's a few bob Mr Spiv didn't get his black-market hands on.'

'Mam, that's brilliant!' Steve was elated. There'd been a nagging at the back of his mind since he found none of his clothes fitted him. All he had to his name was an old pair of overalls and his demob suit. 'I'll be able to get meself some gear, now. Thanks, Mam!'

'Yeah, thanks a million, Mam!' Paul said, thinking he'd be walking tall with money in his pockets. 'I wasn't expecting anything like that.'

'Well, it's not a fortune, but it's better than nothing,' Nellie said. 'I think you've got about twelve or thirteen pounds, Steve, and Paul's got about nine.'

Steve's spirits were high. 'I can't tell yer how grateful I am, Mam. But I hope yer didn't leave yerself short by doing it.'

'Of course I didn't! I've had yer dad's wages coming in every week, and Lily's. I'm better off for money than I've ever been in me life. So buy yerself some new gear and enjoy yerself.'

Steve thought it was his birthday and Christmas all rolled into one. His mother had certainly come up trumps. 'Any money over I'll give to Jill. She's been saving up all the time I've been away and it'll be nice to give her something towards it. We'd like to get married, but it won't be this year 'cos we'll not have enough money. I just hope to God I can get me old job back so I can start saving in earnest.'

George struck a match, lit his cigarette and took a long draw on it. 'I went to see Mr Hargreaves today, and yer can have yer old job back. Ye're to go and see him in the morning at ten o'clock, just to sort a few things out.'

Steve shook his head in disbelief. 'That's another thing I didn't expect, Dad. You and me mam are full of surprises, and I hope yer realise how grateful I am. I can't take it all in at once, but I'll definitely be at Mr Hargreaves's office at ten in the morning.'

'D'yer think yer heart will take another surprise?' George asked, watching the smoke from his cigarette spiral towards the ceiling. 'Or would yer rather leave it so yer've got one to come tomorrow?'

'What! And lie awake all night wondering what it is?' Steve was imagining the look on Jill's pretty face when he told her all this. She'd stunned him when she told him she'd got nearly a hundred pounds saved up towards their wedding. He'd been thrilled to bits, but also a little sad that he hadn't any money to add to it. But he would soon be pulling his weight from the sound of things. 'Come on, Dad, out with it.'

'Well, I told Mr Hargreaves that yer were twenty-two now, and should be going on full money. I also mentioned that when yer were called up, yer were only eighteen months short of finishing yer apprenticeship, and it wouldn't be fair if fighting for yer country stopped yer from being classed as a skilled worker.'

'Good for you, Dad!' Paul said.

'I should damn well think so!' This was Nellie's firm opinion.

Steve was wide-eyed. Fancy his dad talking to the big boss like that! 'What did he say, Dad? Did he tell yer to get lost?'

George shook his head. 'No, he was very understanding. He'll tell yer all this himself in the morning, so don't let on I've jumped the gun. But from what I gathered, although yer'll be starting on full pay, it will only be on the same rate as the labourers. Then, after six months, he'll reconsider. If yer pass the test with flying colours, yer'll be classed as a skilled worker and will be paid the going rate.'

'I'm absolutely stunned! Ye're a hero, Dad, and so is me mam. And one day, I'll pay yer back for all yer've done, and that's a promise. I can't wait to tell Jill, she'll be dead chuffed.'

'I hope I can get me job back,' Paul said, with a grin. 'Would yer like to come down to the works with me Dad, and sort the boss out?'

'I would if I knew him, son, believe me! But I've got a feeling yer'll do very well without me holding yer hand.'

Lily had been listening very intently. She was touched that her parents had done so much to help her brothers, and felt mean that she hadn't contributed a thing to their homecoming. 'I'll buy yer a shirt each, as a little gift that says I'm proud of both of yer.'

'That's good of yer, Lily,' Steve said. 'I'd like that.'

'Yeah, that's great, our kid! If I have a choice, I'd like a beige one to go with me new suit.' Paul leaned his elbows on the table and laced his fingers together. 'Me and our Steve have been that busy nattering about ourselves, we've never even asked how you are. Yer haven't gone and got married while we've been away, have yer?'

'I'd hardly be sitting here having me dinner if I was married, yer daft nit!'

'Have yer got a feller, though? I mean, are yer courting?'

After a quick glance at her mother, Lily said, 'Yeah, I've got a boyfriend.'

'Well, come on, give us the low-down on him.' Paul had no idea the rest of the family were all sitting with their ears cocked. 'Is it serious? Like, is there a wedding in the offing?'

'He's been in the army for eighteen months, so give us a chance!' There was a flush to Lily's cheeks. 'He was only demob-bed yesterday.'

'What's his name?'

'Len Lofthouse.'

'Ye're not very forthcoming about this boyfriend of yours, are yer?' Paul grinned teasingly. 'I mean, how long have yer known him?'

Lily was wishing she'd gone out earlier and saved herself this grilling. It wasn't that she was ashamed of Len, but he was very shy and not good at mixing with people. She'd prefer him to be more outgoing, like her brothers, but as he said everybody wasn't alike, and he couldn't help the way he was. 'I was going out with him for about six months before he got his calling-up papers.'

Paul turned to Nellie. 'Yer didn't tell us our Lily was courting, Mam.'

'He's only been here a couple of times, son, so I can't say we know him. And our Lily doesn't tell us much. Tonight is the first time I've heard his name!'

'I've told yer he's shy with strangers, Mam. He goes all tongue-tied in company.'

'Well, he's got to meet us sometime if ye're courting him,' Steve said. 'And a good chance would be if he came to the party on Saturday night. Bring him along and he'll soon find out we're not going to eat him.'

Lily lowered her eyes. 'I'll ask him, but I don't think he'll come. As I've told yer, he's shy and feels uncomfortable with strangers.'

'We're not strangers, Lily, we're yer family. If he takes you on, he takes us on with yer, whether he likes it or not!' Steve was beginning to understand why his mother and father were worried. 'Yer can't go through life not meeting people just because he's shy. He'll never be any different if he doesn't make the effort. Invite him to the party and say your brothers want to meet him. If he thinks anything of yer he won't refuse.'

Lily made a move to get up from the table. 'As I said, I'll ask him. But if he says no I can hardly drag him along.' She pushed her chair back under the table. 'Can I leave yer with the dishes, Mam? I should be out by now.'

'Of course yer can, love, you just poppy off. I've got two big strapping men here who are just dying to wash up. Then they're going to make me and yer dad a nice pot of tea.'

It wasn't until the front door closed on his sister that Paul pulled a face. 'Sounds a queer sort of boyfriend to me. If he was shy when he went in the army, he most certainly wouldn't be shy when he came out!'

'Aye, well, it takes all sorts, son,' Nellie said. 'If he comes on Saturday we can judge for ourselves what he's like.'

'I'm surprised at our Lily giving in to him.' Steve could see his mother didn't want to elaborate on her daughter's courtship, so he didn't let on that both parents were concerned. 'She wants to start putting her foot down with him, otherwise life won't be worth living.'

'She'll come to her senses, don't worry.' In her mind, Nellie was giving this Len Lofthouse until Saturday. If he didn't show his face then, she'd be having sharp words with her daughter. 'Me throat's dry, boys, so how about making me and yer dad a cup of tea? That's after yer've washed the dishes, of course.'

Paul winked at Steve. 'Who won this war, anyway?'

'Ah, yeah, but Hitler was a doddle compared to me mam. Come on, before she takes me dad's belt to us.'

Lily was thoughtful as she made her way to the Astoria picture-house, where she was meeting Len. She could understand why her family found it strange that her boyfriend didn't call at the house for her, or that he wouldn't want to go to the celebration party. She'd thought it odd herself at first, until Len had explained that he hadn't had a happy childhood. His parents were very strict and used to beat him if they thought he'd been naughty. He wasn't allowed to play out or have friends, and was never given pocket money for sweets or to buy a comic. He'd been a lonely child, with no brothers or sisters, and that is why, now, he was ill at ease in the company of strangers.

Lily had never been invited to Len's house to meet his parents. This was because he had told her he was afraid she wouldn't be made welcome and didn't want to see her embarrassed. But there was a nagging doubt in her mind that this didn't seem normal. If he loved her, which he said he did, then surely the day would come when he'd ask her to marry him? And it would be a fine state of affairs if she hadn't met his parents before then and he wasn't familiar with her family.

Len stepped from a shop doorway when Lily appeared. There was no smile or happy greeting, just a surly, 'I thought yer weren't coming, I've been here for about twenty minutes.'

'Me brother Paul came home from the army today, and we sat talking. I hadn't seen him for eighteen months and I had to spend some time with him and our Steve.'

'I've been away for eighteen months, don't forget!'

'I know that! But I saw yer last night and knew I was seeing yer again tonight. And yer don't seem to be very happy to see me, either.'

'I don't like hanging around waiting for someone.' Len was tall and well-built, with mousy-coloured hair and blue eyes. He wouldn't be bad-looking if his thin lips weren't drooping in a permanent scowl. 'We've probably missed the start of the big picture now.'

'Can we skip the pictures tonight and go for a drink? I want to have a talk to yer.'

'What about?'

'For heaven's sake, Len, there's stacks of things I want to talk about! There's a pub over the road, let's go in there for a drink.' Lily didn't give him time to argue. She linked his arm and pulled him over to the kerb. As soon as the road was clear, she hurried him across.

The pub was quite busy, with many of the men still in army or navy uniforms. Lily spotted an empty table tucked away in a corner, and as she turned to tell Len, she noticed his eyes darting around the room as though afraid of seeing someone he didn't want to see. But as usual, she put it down to his nerves and told herself his parents had a lot to answer for. 'Come on, there's a speck over in the corner.'

'I'll get the drinks in now, save pushing me way through this lot again. What would yer like to drink?'

'A glass of port wine, please.'

While Lily waited on her own, she studied the noisy crowd. Everyone was laughing and joking, and she wished Len could be like that. Then she mentally scolded herself. He couldn't help the way he was, he'd had a lousy childhood. She'd have to be patient and try to coax him around slowly. The trouble was he seemed to be scared of people. The look on his face when they'd come in the pub showed how much he disliked being amongst strangers. Still, they loved each other and together they'd work things out.

Lily smiled when Len put the drinks on the table and sat down. He was wearing his army uniform and she thought how well it suited him. 'It's busy in here tonight,' she remarked. 'People still seem to be celebrating.'

'It's too crowded for my liking. I'd rather have gone to the flicks.'

'Yer can't talk in the pictures and we haven't had a really good conversation since before yer went away. Are yer parents happy to have yer home?'

'My parents are never happy. All they're interested in now is when I'm going to start work so I can hand most of me wages over.'

'They're not that bad, surely? I mean, ye're twenty-two now, they can't expect yer to hand most of yer wages over like a teenager. Pay for yer keep like I do, yes, but I only give my mam a pound a week.' Lily took a sip of her wine. 'Perhaps if yer took me home with yer, and they saw we were courting serious, they might be more understanding.'

Len shook his head. 'Out of the question, I've told yer before.'

'It's ridiculous! Yer won't take me to your house and yer won't come to mine! Yer'd get on well with my family, they're friendly and good fun. But yer won't give it a try, will yer?'

'I will! Just don't push me! I'll call for yer one night, when I'm more settled.'

'Yer'll meet them all on Saturday night.' Lily decided not to ask him to come, but *tell* him. 'There's a Welcome Home party for me two brothers and one of the neighbour's lads. Yer've been invited.'

'Some hope you've got, Lily, and I don't think! I'm not coming to no party and that's the end of it.' Len saw her face become set and quickly altered the tone of his voice. 'I'm sorry, love, but yer know how I hate strangers. I never know what to say to them.'

Lily remembered Steve's words and repeated them. 'These are not strangers, Len, they're my family. And I want yer to get to know them because if we stay together yer'll be seeing a lot of them.'

Len pursed his thin lips and shook his head. 'I'll call for yer one night, if that's what yer want. But I'm not coming to no party where there'll be gangs of people.'

'I want to go, Len, and I want yer to come with me. As me boyfriend.'

'Nah! We'll go to the flicks on Saturday night and sit on the back row holding hands.' His tone was wheedling. 'And I'll be able to steal kisses off yer in the dark, like I used to.'

'Yer wouldn't have to steal kisses in the back row of the pictures, or down an entry for that matter, if yer weren't so ruddy stubborn! I bet our Steve's never had to kiss his girlfriend down an entry. No, they were able to get all their kissing done in the comfort of Jill's own home. Either in the hallway, or on the couch if the family had gone to bed.' Lily conjured up a vision of her brother hugging and kissing Jill yesterday, openly, in front of everyone. That's how it should be when two people were in love. They shouldn't have to hide it! It was the feeling of injustice that brought the words to Lily's lips. 'I'm going to the party, Len, whether you go or not. It's for me two brothers whom I love dearly, and I'm not letting them down. If you would prefer to go to the flicks, then yer'll have to go on yer own.'

This was the first time Lily had gone against him, and from the expression on her face Len knew it was no use playing on her sympathy, like he'd been doing for the last two years. 'If yer feel that strong about it, I'll come, then. As long as yer don't expect me to be the life and soul of the party.'

Signs that his surrender was begrudged could be seen in his eyes and heard in his voice. But Lily was so happy she didn't notice anything amiss. All she could think of was that she wasn't going to have to make excuses for his absence. And once he got to know everyone he was bound to feel more relaxed and have no objection to calling for her every night. Then her mam and dad would find that under his shyness, he was really a nice bloke. 'Oh, I'm made up, Len! Yer'll get on well with me brothers, I know yer will. They both take after me mam, always laughing and full of fun. And there'll be plenty of pretty girls there, except yer better keep yer eyes off them or I'll clock yer one.'

Len picked up his glass and drank deeply of the bitter beer. He had his own views on Lily's mother but he'd be best keeping them to himself. She was certainly no barrel of laughs as far as he was concerned. And if he married her daughter, she wouldn't be visiting their house very often if he had anything to do with it. Not that she'd want to, 'cos for reasons of his own, he intended to move well away from Liverpool. That was something else he'd best keep to himself until he was more sure of Lily.

'D'yer want to sit down?' Jack asked. 'There's a few empty tables.'

Steve shook his head. 'No, I want to be standing at the bar for me first pint in this pub, like I've always imagined. And the first drink's on me.'

'No, son, put yer money away,' George said. 'Ye're not the only one that's had dreams over the last few years, yer know. I've been longing for the day when I could take me two sons out for a drink. So let me be the first one to do the honours.'

'I'll let yer get away with it, George, 'cos you've got two sons,' Jack said, with a smile and feeling ten feet tall. 'It's you three against me and our Tommy. But the next round is most definitely on me.'

'Right, ye're on.' George turned to lean on the bar. 'Five pints of bitter, Les, and seeing as it's a celebration, have one yerself.'

'Thanks, George.' The barman grinned as he pulled the handle of the pump. 'It's good to see all the lads back, isn't it? My trade should go up because they're all old enough to take a drink now.'

The chattering stopped and all heads turned when the door was pushed open with some force and in walked Jimmy Corkhill, a giant of a man. With his white moustache and beard, and his weatherbeaten complexion, he would stand out in any crowd. And the greetings that were called out, told of his popularity in the neighbourhood. He waved to the people he knew as he made his way to the bar, and the five men who had a place in his heart. 'I got home about five minutes ago and Ellen told me yer were here. She practically threw me out.' Each one was slapped on the back and shaken by the hand. And with hands like ham shanks, his handshake could bring tears to the eyes of grown men.

Corker's sudden appearance was the icing on the cake for Steve. This was how he'd always imagined it when the fighting in Germany got tough. Thinking of home kept him going. Jill was always uppermost in his thoughts, and his parents. But because he refused to think of anything bad happening to Paul, Tommy or Corker, he kept in his mind the night they would all be together in this pub. And now it was happening.

'I can't believe ye're here, Uncle Corker. The one missing link, and now yer've turned up. I wanted yer to be here when I had me first pint.'

Corker let out a loud guffaw. 'I pulled yer leg about it often enough, didn't I, lad? And have I missed yer first pint?'

'No, the glasses are all lined up on the bar.' Steve felt like throwing his arms around the gentle giant, who always brought out the best in people.

George called to the barman who had moved down the counter. 'Another one when ye're ready, Les!'

'Shall we find a seat?' Corker cast his eyes around the room. 'There's two tables over there we can pull together so we're not crowded.'

'Can we have the first pint standing here?' Steve asked. 'Yer see, Uncle Corker, I had this dream. And in the dream, the six of us were standing at this bar, just as we are now, with pint glasses in our hands. It was so real, I could even see the froth from the beer on yer moustache. So humour me, and let me live me dream out.'

Paul tapped Corker on the arm. 'Our kid's gone sentimental all of a sudden. I think it's best if we just go along with him.'

'There's nothing wrong with having dreams, lad,' the big man said. 'All the time I'm at sea, I have dreams. And if yer told me you didn't, I wouldn't believe yer.'

Paul grinned. 'Yer'd be right not to believe me. Never a day went by that I didn't dream of me mam's suet dumplings. And some days I got so hungry for them, me mouth used to water.'

'Same here!' Tommy said. 'But it wasn't dumplings I dreamed of. It was a toss-up between Rosie's deep blue eyes or me mam's apple pie.'

Corker's pint arrived and the six men lifted their glasses to each other. 'I don't know whether God approves of beer, but I think the first toast should be a thank you to Him for bringing us safely home.'

'Hear, hear!' Chorused George and Jack. Two men who would rather have been fighting by their sons' side on the battlefield, than wondering every day if they were still alive.

'I'll order the next round.' Corker waved away the protests. 'It's a drop of the hard stuff for me, George and Jack, and bitter for the lads, eh?'

'Me mam said if we go home drunk she'll take the rolling pin to us,' Paul said, with a twinkle in his eye. 'So me and Steve have decided to let me dad go in first.'

Corker's head dropped back and his loud guffaw rang out. 'I can just see Nellie, and the size of her, chasing you three down the street. Ooh, I can't wait to hear what her and Molly have been up to while I've been away.'

'How long have yer got, Corker?' Jack asked. 'Me and George live with them, but we can't keep up with their tricks.'

'I've got two weeks' leave. I'm owed a lot more, but there's so many countries crying out for food and materials I couldn't be spared for any longer.'

'Me and George will give yer a hand with the drinks, Corker, while the boys sort the tables out,' Jack said. 'We may as well take the weight off our feet.'

When they were settled with their drinks in front of them, Corker said, 'They're not boys any more, Jack. I can't get over how they've grown! Your Tommy will be catching me up before long if he keeps on at this rate.'

'No I won't, Uncle Corker,' Tommy said. 'Rosie's got that in hand. Every night when I go round there, she's going to hit me on the head with the frying pan. So what I gain during the day, I'll be losing at night.'

Corker's smile took them all in. 'Yer've no idea how glad I am to see yer all again. And I'm dying to see all the girls.'

'Yer'll be seeing the whole gang together on Saturday night, 'cos me mam and Auntie Nellie are throwing a party. And we were hoping yer'd be home for it.' Tommy was feeling all grown-up, sitting in a pub with a pint in front of him. 'Me mam said it wouldn't be like a party without you.'

'I'll look forward to that! Tell yer mam I'll help her out with a bit of food, and I'll see to the drinks.'

'We'll share the cost of the drinks, Corker,' George said. 'Me and Jack have been working a lot of overtime, so we're better off than in the old days.'

'Me dad saw the boss about me getting me job back, Uncle Corker, and I'm going to see him tomorrow.' Steve's smile was one of pride. 'I'll probably be starting on Monday.'

'I'm lucky too,' Tommy put in. 'I've got me old job back, thanks to me dad.'

'And I'm keeping me fingers crossed,' Paul laughed. 'If I don't get it, all won't be lost 'cos I can borrow off me big brother.'

'Some hope you've got, our Paul! Your big brother is going to be saving like mad to get married.'

'How is my princess?' Corker asked. 'Still as lovely as ever?'

Steve nodded. 'If it's possible, she's even more lovely.'

'And sweet Rosie O'Grady? Is she more lovely than ever?'

86

'I think she is,' Tommy chuckled. 'But then I'm biased.'

Corker raised his bushy eyebrows at Paul. 'And what about your fair young lady?'

'I don't know her name yet, 'cos I haven't met her. But I'm going to be working very hard on it, Uncle Corker. A pretty girlfriend is top of me list.'

The three older men exchanged glances which said that whatever happened in the lives of these young ones would fill their lives with interest and happiness. But although the older men were wiser, even they couldn't foresee the surprises in store for them.

Chapter Seven

'How many is that altogether?' Molly met her friend's eyes across the table. 'I get to so many, then I lose count.'

'Why don't yer write the names down, girl – then yer won't miss anyone out?' Nellie spread out one of her chubby hands and reeled off names as she pressed each of her fingers back. 'It's no good, I'd need four hands. And while I'm well endowed in some departments, I wasn't blessed with four hands.'

'I'll get a pencil and a piece of paper,' Molly said, getting to her feet. 'Otherwise we'll be here all day.' She rooted through one of the sideboard drawers and came up with a stub of pencil and an old envelope. 'This'll have to do, I've got no proper writing paper. We'll start with your lot first. There's five of you, and your Lily's boyfriend. Are you sure he's coming?'

'So she said, and she seemed quite definite.'

Molly wrote the names down. 'That's six from your house, and six from here. Then there's Phil, and Tommy's army friend, Hooter.' She looked up and grinned. 'Or should I say Archibald Higgins?'

'That's some name, that is! I don't think he'd like us calling him Hooter, 'cos that's making fun of him, really.' Nellie looked thoughtful as she tapped a finger on her cheek. 'I couldn't call him Archibald without laughing, so he'll have to make do with Archie.'

Molly counted the number of names she'd written down. 'That comes to fourteen and we haven't started yet. God knows where I'm going to put them all.'

'You'll manage, girl, yer always do.'

'You are bloody hilarious, Nellie McDonough! We're supposed to be having this party between us, but as usual I'm getting lumbered with having it in my house.'

'Now yer know I'd be more than happy to have it in my house if it wasn't for me having a bad heart. And don't you laugh, 'cos yer should never mock the afflicted.'

'Bad heart? You've never got a bad heart!'

When the table began to wobble, Molly knew Nellie was going

to come out with something funny. So, with the end of the pencil between her teeth, she waited to see what gem of information was on its way.

'I must have a bad heart, girl. If I had a good heart, I'd be having the party in my house to give yer a break.'

'Nellie, if the day ever came when yer invited me to a party in your house, I'd never make it because I'd die of ruddy shock!'

'There's no need to be sarcastic, girl, it doesn't become yer. Now get cracking on that list or the shops will be closed for dinner before we get out.' Nellie's chins did a tango when she shook her head and muttered, 'I dunno, I've never met anyone who could talk as much as this one. She'd talk till the cows came home if yer let her.'

'I'm not listening to yer any more, sunshine, I'm concentrating on me list.' Molly licked the end of the pencil and began to write. 'There's me ma, da and Rosie, and Maisie and Alec. That brings it up to nineteen.'

'Yer haven't got Corker and Ellen down, girl, and yer can't leave them out. Not when Corker gave us that four pound tin of ham, and butter, tea and sugar.'

'I have no intention of leaving Corker and Ellen out, soft girl! And I think we should invite young Phoebe. She's seventeen now and should be counted with our young ones. She's a nice kid, too.'

'That's a good idea. How many is that now?'

'Twenty-two!' Molly's laughter filled the room. 'Twenty-two people in here! We must be stark staring mad, sunshine, 'cos they'll never all get in!'

'Of course they will. Steve and Jill can be counted as one, because every time I see them they're standing so close together they look as though they're joined at the hip. And the same goes for Tommy and Rosie, and Doreen and Phil. They'll be made up if they're squashed in like sardines.' Nellie had a thought. 'I hate to add to yer worry, girl, but yer haven't got Corker's mother down, or Victoria Clegg.'

'They're not coming. Both Mrs Corkhill and Victoria said they're too old for parties now. So I'm having them for tea on Sunday. I'll keep some of the ham back for them.'

'Ah, that's nice, that is! Are me and George invited?' Before Molly could raise any objection, Nellie reminded her, 'Don't forget this party is between the two of us. So is that ruddy tin of ham! We'd only be eating out own flaming food if we come!'

'I love your logic, Nellie, it doesn't half stand yer in good stead. I think I'll try a little of it meself.' Molly ran her hands over the top of the table. 'D'yer see this?'

'If ye're talking about the table, girl, then I'd have a job not to see it! God knows, it's ruddywell big enough.'

'Well, yer'll be seeing a lot more of it, sunshine! Because, tomorrow morning, Steve and Tommy are carrying it up to your house.'

'Ah, hell's bells – no, not again! The last time yer did that we couldn't move in our house! I was black and blue all over with bumping into the ruddy thing!'

'I mustn't have heard yer properly before,' Molly said quietly. 'So will yer tell me again whose party this is?'

'It's between us, and you know it. Share and share alike.' Nellie could have bitten her tongue off when she realised she'd dropped herself in it. 'OK, but I bet you wouldn't like two ruddy tables in yer room.'

'I wouldn't mind. I'd rather that than have the worry of food and drink, and running around after twenty odd people all night.' Molly pushed a lock of wayward hair behind her ear. 'I'll tell yer what – you have the party and I'll have your table.'

Nellie now put on her angelic, butter-wouldn't-melt-in-her-mouth look. 'What time did yer say Steve and Tommy were carrying this up, girl?'

Molly chuckled. 'Now we've sorted that out to our mutual satisfaction, let's get out to the shops. I want to order the bread from Sayers for tomorrow, and ask Tony to have that pound of brawn he promised us ready to pick up. Then everything is under control. Me ma's baking some fairy cakes and Maisie has promised two large sponge sandwich cakes and a pound of assorted biscuits.'

'And the men are seeing to the drinks.'

'Yes, sunshine, the men are seeing to the drinks. All I'll have to do tomorrow is make a mountain of sandwiches.'

'I'll give yer a hand with them, girl, if yer like?'

Molly glanced through to her small kitchen, then at her friend. If Nellie got in that kitchen there'd be no room for anyone else. 'No thanks, Nellie, but I appreciate yer offering. I'll have Jill and Doreen to help me, we'll have them done in no time. And now, if yer can separate yer backside from my chair, we'll be on our way.'

'Mam, this is Hooter, the mate I was telling yer about.'

'Hello, son, I'm pleased to meet yer.' Molly tried to hide her surprise as she shook hands. After all the talk about this lad's big nose, it was only natural to be curious. And yes, it was on the large side. But the rest of him more than compensated. She had to crane her neck to look up into a face that was friendly and open. His hair was raven black, his eyes a melting brown and he had a perfect set of white teeth. As Tommy had said, he was a handsome lad, all right. 'I don't want to call yer Hooter, son, it doesn't suit yer. So what can I call yer?'

Molly felt herself being pushed aside, and before she knew what was happening, Nellie was standing fair and square in front of Tommy's friend.

'Hell, Archie, lad, I'm pleased to make your acquaintance.'

Tommy made the introductions. 'This is me Auntie Nellie.'

Archie's teeth flashed in a dazzling smile. 'I've heard all about you, Auntie Nellie, and the tricks you and Mrs Bennett get up to.'

Nellie preened with pleasure. 'Don't believe everything yer hear, Archie, only half of it. Me and Molly like a laugh, and we're best mates.'

'Yer wouldn't think so,' Molly said, 'the way I get pushed around in me own house.'

'Take no notice of her, Archie, she's not her usual self tonight. Yer see, she had to sell her table to help pay for tonight's party. She thought the world of that table and is inconsulate.'

Molly and Tommy were in stitches, but Archie didn't like to laugh in case Nellie thought he was rude. 'I'm really sorry about that.'

'My friend has a problem with words, Archie, I'm afraid, and she tells lies.' Molly wiped away the tear that was trickling down her cheek. 'She was trying to tell you I was inconsolable with grief over me table. But me table has been taken to her house to give us a bit more room here. So take everything she says with a pinch of salt.'

Tommy took his mate's arm. 'Come on, I'll introduce yer to everyone. Yer'll see plenty of me mam and Auntie Nellie after. They're the stars of the show.'

The two women watched as Tommy led Archie over to where his nan, grandad and Rosie were seated.

'He's a nice lad,' Molly said. 'Well-mannered and really good-looking.'

Nellie had the agreement of every layer of her chins when she nodded. 'Yer can say that again! I wish that feller of our Lily's was as pleasant. Just look at him standing there like a long string of misery.'

'Don't be so hard on the lad, Nellie! It's the first time he's set foot in this house, and he doesn't know a soul. He'll be all right when he's had a chance to get to know us all.'

'It's the first time Archie's set foot in the house, and he doesn't know a soul except your Tommy. But look at the smile on his face! He looked at home as soon as he walked in, and he's talking to yer ma and da as though he's really glad to be with them.'

'Let's see what the night brings, sunshine, instead of condemning Lily's boyfriend without giving the lad a fair chance.' Molly put her arm across Nellie's shoulders. 'If he's still got that sour look on his face at the end of the night, then I'll start to worry with yer, sunshine. But it's amazing what a few pints of beer will do.'

Corker arrived then with Ellen and a very shy Phoebe. The seventeen-year-old girl had never been to a grown-up party before and was obviously very nervous. 'Yer look very nice, sunshine,' Molly told her. 'Is that a new dress?'

'Yeah, I went into town this morning for it.' Phoebe's eyes went to where Tommy was introducing Len and Archie to Corker and Ellen. 'Me dad gave me the money for it.' There was pride in her voice when she referred to Corker as her father. She idolised the man who had transformed the fortunes of the Clarke family when he married her mother. 'I got a blue one 'cos he said it was the colour which suits me best.'

'He was right, sunshine, 'cos yer look very pretty.' Molly caught Jill's eye and called her over. 'You look after Phoebe, there's a good girl. She doesn't want to be stuck with the old ones all night, so take her around the young ones. And if yer think back to how shy you were at seventeen, it'll give yer an idea of how she feels right now.'

'Come on, Phoebe.' Jill linked her arm and led her across to where Steve, Archie, Paul and Phil were exchanging views on life in the army. 'Yer know these three, but this is Archie, a friend of Tommy's. Archie, meet Phoebe.'

Paul was staring wide-eyed as he watched the two shake hands. 'Ye're not telling me that this is little Phoebe Clarke, are yer?'

With her face the colour of beetroot, Phoebe replied, 'I'm not so little, Paul McDonough, and me name is Corkhill now.'

'Well, I'll be blowed! I wouldn't have recognised yer if we'd passed in the street.' Paul shook his head. 'Last time I saw yer, yer were a schoolgirl.'

'I was not! I've been working for the last three years.'

'Take no notice of Paul, he wouldn't have noticed if we'd all grown two heads,' Jill said, smiling at the boy who would one day be her brother-in-law and who she was very fond of. 'Before he got called up he was out every single night flying his kite. He'd have his dinner, get all dolled up and off he'd go to paint the town red. And he never went out with the same girl two nights running.'

'Ah, that's where ye're wrong,' Paul chuckled. 'There was one girl, her name escapes me now, but I went out with her twice. And she definitely didn't have two heads, Jill, 'cos I would have noticed that! She couldn't half dance though – she was as light as a feather on the dance floor.' He smiled down at Phoebe. 'So while I was tripping the light fantastic, yer went and got all growed up behind me back, eh?'

Phoebe had a very quiet disposition and was usually very shy. But she didn't want to appear stupid, so she said, 'I'm still growing, Paul, but I'll try not to grow two heads.'

'When me and Steve get married, Phoebe and her sister Dorothy are going to be our bridesmaids.' Jill saw Steve smile and nod his head in agreement. 'It must be five years or more since we asked them, so they've waited long enough.'

'And a pretty bridesmaid yer'll look too, Phoebe,' Archie said. 'I'll have to find out when the wedding is and come along and see yer in yer finery.'

Jill noticed Lily and Len standing in the hall. They hadn't made any attempt to mix, but Jill knew that wouldn't be Lily's fault. 'Come on, Phoebe, I'll introduce yer to Lily's boyfriend.'

As they walked away, Archie said, 'She's a nice little thing.'

'The whole family are nice,' Phil said, his eyes never leaving Doreen, who was talking to her nan. 'And they've got the best father in the world. Mr Corker is a real gentleman, one in a million.'

'Ye're right there,' Steve said. 'Ever since I can remember, he's been my hero.'

'Yeah, and mine,' Paul agreed. 'But yer could knock me over with a feather the way Phoebe's grown. She was always such a scrawny kid!'

Archie nudged his arm. 'Sometimes ye're better looking nearer home.'

'Nah! Nothing like that, she's not my type. It was just a surprise, that's all.'

Jill's attempt to bring Lily and her boyfriend into the company never even got off the ground. Lily was friendly enough, but Len didn't even offer to shake Phoebe's hand. So rather than embarrass the girl, Jill led her back to where Corker and Ellen were sitting.

Once she was amongst her own, Phoebe became a different person. Smiling and animated, she said, 'Jill still wants me and Dorothy to be her bridesmaids, Mam! She's never forgotten, after all this time.'

'That's nice, love,' Ellen said. 'It's something for yer to look forward to.'

'I'm dead excited, Mam, me tummy's turning over. Wait until I tell our Dorothy, she'll be cock-a-hoop.'

Corker pushed himself up from the chair and put an arm

across Jill's shoulders. 'And when is the big day going to be, princess?'

'I wish it was tomorrow, Uncle Corker, but I'm afraid it won't be for some time. Me and Steve have got enough saved for the wedding, and I've got bits in me bottom drawer, but we'll need a lot more to furnish a house.'

Corker put a hand under her chin and raised her face. He loved all the children, Ellen's, Molly's and Nellie's, and he would never admit to favouritism. But Jill had always been his little princess and he had a tender spot in his heart for her. 'It's early days, princess, Steve hasn't been home a week yet. Wait until he's back at work and things settle down. Then something might come along out of the blue and surprise yer.'

'Yeah, that's what me mam said. But our Doreen and Phil want to get married and they were hoping we could make it a double wedding. I'd like that meself, but I can't see it happening. They've already got a house and it wouldn't be fair to expect them to wait until me and Steve are ready.' Jill's pretty face smiled up at him. 'Still, I've got him home and that's the main thing. As long as he's here, I won't mind having to wait a bit to get married. After all, we've been courting since we were about six years of age, so another year won't hurt us.'

Jill turned when she heard her name called. 'Me mam wants me, I'd better go.' She stood on tip-toe and wrinkled her nose when her lips came into contact with the stiff whiskers. 'They always tickle me.' She glanced down at Ellen. 'If Uncle Corker had been twenty years younger, I'd have fought yer for him.'

Ellen smiled. 'Yer wouldn't have won, love! I might only be little, but I'd have fought yer tooth and nail for him.'

Corker was thoughtful as he watched Jill walk away. If it hadn't been for the flaming war, the two sweethearts would have been well married by now. He stroked his beard as an idea entered his head. It might not come off so he wouldn't mention it until he'd put the feelers out. But if it did, it would make a lot of people happy, including himself.

'I think it's time for the eats now, girl, don't you?' Nellie's arms were lost from sight, folded under her mountainous bosom. 'I mean, the party won't really start until we get the food out of the way.'

Molly grinned. 'And yer can't wait for it to start, can yer, sunshine? Are yer legs raring to throw themselves around while ye're doing the Charleston?'

'Well, the place wants livening up, doesn't it? All they're doing is standing around gassing! If we don't start soon, the whole flaming party will fall flat.'

'I can't see that happening with you around – it never has before. But if it makes yer any happier, we'll start dishing the food out.' Molly clapped her hands for a bit of hush. 'My co-hostess is feeling peckish, so we'll have something to eat now. If Rosie will give the plates out, Jill and Doreen will follow with the sandwiches.'

Maisie from the corner shop jumped to her feet. 'I'll give a hand. I'm not used to sitting on me backside for so long, I'd rather be on the go.'

Bridie pulled gently on the skirt of Maisie's dress. 'If yer've a mind to be making a cup of tea, Maisie, me and Bob would appreciate it.'

'Bridie, your wish is my command. Two cups of tea coming up.'

While the girls were giving the food out, Molly made her way to where Lily and Len were standing in the hallway, just outside the living-room door. 'Come on, you two! Yer can't be standing with a plate in one hand and a glass in the other. Step inside and make use of the sideboard. I've got it covered, so yer don't have to worry about putting yer glass down on it.' Still giving Len the benefit of the doubt about his unsmiling face, she took the plate from him and put it on the sideboard. 'There yer are, that's better. Now tuck into the food, and you make yerself at home, son.'

It wasn't a smile, but at least his lips curved upwards. 'Thanks, Mrs Bennett.'

'You look after him, Lily, and see he gets enough to eat. And when the singing starts, as it surely will, I want to hear your voices joining in.'

'Yer'll be sorry yer said that, Mrs Bennett,' Lily said. 'I've got a voice like a foghorn.'

'I'm not exactly a prima donna meself, Lily, but at least I'll have a go. Anyway, if yer want anything, all yer have to do is ask.' Molly gave them her brightest smile and turned away. The lad was heavy going, no doubt about that!

Nellie had been watching with narrowed eyes and a great deal of curiosity. And she wasted no time in manoeuvring her friend into the kitchen. 'Well, how did it go? What did he have to say for himself?'

Molly tapped the side of her nose. 'Ye're a nosy article, Nellie McDonough. But for your information, I had a long conversation with him.'

'Go 'way!' Nellie leaned back against the sink and folded her arms, ready to be told something of great importance. 'Go on, girl, what did he say?'

Molly's face was deadpan. ' "Thanks, Mrs Bennett".'

Nellie looked around to make sure there was no one else in the kitchen. 'Don't be acting the goat, Molly Bennett! Now, come on, out with it. What did the queer feller have to say for himself?'

'I've just told yer!'

'So help me, I'll clock yer one if yer don't stop buggering about!'

'I've told yer what he said. "Thanks, Mrs Bennett". Now if yer'd rather I made up some cock and bull story to feed yer appetite for gossip, it'll have to wait until tomorrow 'cos I've got guests to look after.'

'D'yer mean that's all he said, like? Just those three words?'

'Just those three words, sunshine, if I never move from this spot. Perhaps if you tried yer'd get a few more out of him. I don't think yer've even looked at the lad since he came in!'

Nellie got on her high horse. 'It's not my place to go up to him! I'm Lily's mother, so it's his place to come to me first.'

'Yer know, sometimes you can't see the woods for the ruddy trees! How d'yer think your Lily feels, when her mam and dad don't even acknowledge he's here? For her sake, yer could make the effort.' Molly put her hands on Nellie's shoulders and looked into her eyes. 'Yer might live to regret it, sunshine, and don't ever say I didn't warn yer. If he's the one Lily wants there's nothing yer can do about it. And through yer pigheadedness, yer could end up losing yer daughter. And for all yer puffing and blowing about him, I know if that happened it would break yer heart.'

'But I can't bring meself to like him! I've got this feeling in me bones that there's something fishy about him, and he's not to be trusted.'

Molly was half-inclined to agree, but knew that to say so could only make things worse between Nellie and her daughter. 'Even if ye're right, sunshine, ye're going about things in the wrong way. The more against Len you are, the more Lily will be for him. If there is something fishy about him, and he's not to be trusted, it'll come out sooner or later. Your daughter's not soft, Nellie, so just let things take their course and let her find out for herself.'

'But what if she marries him, then finds out he's a scoundrel? It'll be too ruddy late then, she'll be lumbered with him for life.'

'Nellie, take a bit of advice. Make friends with yer daughter, and if things do go wrong, she'll have your shoulder to cry on.'

'I know ye're right, girl, and I'm being a stubborn bugger. But I had such high hopes for all me kids. They were all going to fall in love, get married and live happily ever after. The trouble is, try as I may, I can't see Lily's happiness being with that Len.' Nellie squared her shoulders and sighed. 'Still, I'd better try, or I'll never hear the last of it from yer. So I'll have a go and see if I can get more than three words out of him.'

With determination in every step, Nellie walked from the kitchen. She didn't know it, but both her husband and eldest son, Steve, followed her every movement. 'Hello, Len, how are yer, lad?'

'I'm fine thanks, Mrs McDonough.'

Nellie waited for him to enlarge on that statement, but she waited in vain. In the end she turned to her daughter. 'How are you, love? Are yer getting enough to eat? There's plenty, so take as much as yer want.'

'We're all right, Mam, don't worry. Len doesn't eat much, but I'm making up for it by eating enough for the two of us.'

Watching from the sidelines, Steve could see his mother wasn't getting very far in trying to start a conversation. So he put his plate on the mantelpiece and made his way over. 'My sister seems to have forgotten her manners, so I'll introduce myself. I'm Steve, and I presume you are Len?' Steve stuck his hand out, making it impossible for his sister's boyfriend to ignore the greeting. He found the hand he shook to be limp and weak, and one of his pet hates was a weak handshake. But he didn't let his feelings show. If his mother was prepared to make the effort to be friendly, he'd help her out. 'I believe yer were demobbed the same day as me?'

The reply was a curt nod and few words. 'So Lily told me.'

Steve put his arm across his mother's shoulders and persevered. 'What regiment were yer with?'

'The Royal Engineers.' Len felt a sly dig in the back and knew Lily was asking him to be a little more forthcoming. He wasn't very keen. He didn't know these people and it wouldn't bother him if he never saw them again. But he needed to keep Lily sweet. 'What lot were you with, then?'

'The King's Regiment, Liverpool.' Steve was wondering what his sister saw in this bloke. He wasn't bad-looking, but he wasn't very pleasant or friendly. Nor was he trying to hide the fact that he didn't want to be here. 'D'yer live local, then?'

'Yeah, not far, in Walton.' The questions were getting too personal for Len's liking, so he took Lily's empty glass from her, saying, 'I'll get yer a refill.'

'I'm going to see if Molly needs a hand,' Nellie said. 'Otherwise she'll tell me I'm shirking on the job.'

'And I'm going to see if Uncle Corker wants any help with the drinks.' Steve squeezed his sister's shoulder. 'I'll bring Jill over after, kid, when the eats are out of the way.'

Nellie made straight for the kitchen and Molly. 'I did better than you, girl! I actually got five words out of him.' She ran the back of a hand across her brow. 'I'll tell yer what, though, he's hard bloody going! My corns talk more than he does.'

98

'Well, yer've made a start, sunshine, that's something. Have another go when he's had a few more drinks and yer might get six words out of him. Even if he doesn't appreciate it, your Lily will.'

Nellie's usual smile was missing as she shook her head. 'I'd feel easier in me mind if I knew a bit more about him. He didn't seem to like Steve asking him where he lived 'cos he made an excuse about getting Lily a drink. So, apart from him living somewhere in Walton, we're none the wiser.'

Molly chuckled. 'I'll tell yer what, sunshine, and this should cheer yer up. You and me will follow him one night and find out where he lives.'

A conversation from years ago came to Nellie's mind and she gripped hold of Molly's arm. 'Ay, girl, d'yer remember a few years back, when we were trying to find out where someone else lived? You said we should go into business together as two private detectives. I can hear it as plain as if it was yesterday. Partners, McDonough and Bennett. That's what yer said.'

'Like hell I did, yer crafty article! It's ruddy amazing how yer can remember things the way yer want to remember them! Let's just get this clear right now. If there's to be any partnership it'll be Bennett and McDonough, 'cos I'm the one what thought of it.'

'But I'm bigger than you, girl!'

'You are not! Yer might be wider, but I'm about six inches taller than yer! So put that in yer pipe and smoke it.'

'Oh, go on, if yer want to be childish about it. Yer'll be sucking yer thumb in a minute if yer don't get yer own way. And I don't really give a sod whose name goes first, as long as we're success- ful. So, are we going into partnership or not?'

Molly suppressed a grin when she studied her friend. Not for anything in the world would she say anything to upset her, but how the hell did Nellie think they could follow anybody and not be seen? Then Molly couldn't contain the laughter. 'I can just see us trailing someone, hopping in and out of doorways and trying to hide behind lamp-posts! We'd look like two of the Marx Brothers! In fact, we'd look a damn sight funnier than them!'

'I wouldn't mind looking daft if it brought results. I'm not proud, girl.'

Jill came into the kitchen followed closely by Doreen. 'That's all the sandwiches gone, Mam, and I think everyone's had enough.'

Doreen eyed the two women with curiosity. 'What are you two cooking up?'

'We've been discussing the price of fish, haven't we, Nellie? But we'll leave it for now and start collecting the dishes in. Then we'll get the party going and have a sing-song.'

Doreen pulled a face. 'Mam, yer make a lousy liar!'

'Well, I'm sure yer wouldn't want yer mam to be a good liar, would yer?' Nellie asked. 'Not like me, yer can't believe a word I say! I don't even believe meself half the time.'

'That's not true, Auntie Nellie.' Jill put her arms around her future mother-in-law. 'I know yer only tell fibs when yer want to make people laugh.'

'Come on, break it up, we've got guests to see to.' Molly put the plug in the sink before turning to take the boiling kettle off the stove. 'Bring all the dirty dishes out and I'll get cracking right away. There's nothing greasy so we should have them done in no time.'

Molly gazed around to make sure everyone's glass was full before asking, 'Right, who's going to give the first song?'

Rosie stepped forward. 'Is it all right with yerself, Auntie Molly, if me and Tommy go first?'

Molly looked flabbergasted. 'You and Tommy? Our Tommy can't sing for peanuts!'

'Well now, didn't we have a little practice last night, and the night before?' Rosie's bonny face was beaming. 'It's yerself that's in for a surprise, Auntie Molly.'

'I'll be more than surprised if yer even get him on the floor, sunshine, never mind sing!'

Rosie held out her hand. 'Come on, Tommy, me darling, let's show them how good we are together.'

Tommy was laughing as he got to his feet. 'Rosie reminds me of the sergeant I had in the army. One word from him and we all jumped.'

Molly sat on Jack's knee and whispered, 'I don't believe this!'

'I'm having difficulty meself, love. I never thought the day would come when our Tommy got to his feet, willingly, to sing a song. In fact. I didn't even know he could sing!'

But Tommy seemed to be enjoying himself and there was no sign of nerves. He was smiling down at Rosie as though she was the only person in the room. 'Ready, sweetheart?'

The attractive couple harmonised beautifully as they sang 'Girl of My Dreams'. And their obvious pleasure at being together brought a lump to more than one listener's throat. The applause when they'd finished was thunderous and well-deserved. 'Ye're a dark horse, Tommy!' Steve called. 'I didn't know yer could sing like that.'

'I didn't know meself,' Tommy chuckled. 'But Rosie can be very persuasive. She gave me an ultimatum. No singing, no kissing.' He looked towards Bridie and Bob. 'What did yer think of that, Nan and Grandad?'

100

'It was grand,' Bob said, his eyes moist. 'Really grand.'

'Sure, weren't we lying in bed listening to yer practising?' Bridie said. 'Little did we know yer'd be so quick to learn, me darling.'

'I had to, Nan. Like I said – no singing, no kisses! And I'd rather go without me dinner than forfeit one of Rosie's kisses.'

'Sensible man.' Corker said. 'But ye're going to be a hard act to follow. The only one I know with the guts to do so is Nellie!'

'Uh huh! They're not drunk enough to appreciate me, Corker. I like me audience to be paralytic. There's nothing worse for a performer of my standing than to be in the middle of a song and have a squashed tomato thrown in me face.'

'I know someone who can sing,' Tommy said. 'Come on, Archie, give the old vocal cords an airing.'

'No chance, mate.' Archie grinned. 'Unless one of the girls will sing with me.'

Jill moved even closer to Steve. 'Don't ask me. I can't sing, and I'd die of embarrassment anyway.'

'Our Tommy's represented the Bennett family, so it's the turn of the McDonoughs.' Doreen spotted Lily. 'I'll tell yer what, me and Lily will both sing with Archie.' Grabbing the unsuspecting girl by the arm, she dragged her into the empty spot in front of the fireplace. 'What's it to be, Archie?'

Lily looked anything but at ease when Archie put an arm around each of the girl's waists. 'I'm warning yer, I can't sing!'

'Don't worry about that. Just relax and enjoy yerself.' Archie whispered the title of the song and Doreen nodded, while Lily watched Len's face getting redder and redder as they all launched into 'Goodnight, Sweetheart'.

Archie, who had a good clear voice, was swaying from side to side in time with the tempo, and Lily began to enjoy herself. She loved music and dancing, and this was one of her favourite songs. It was a party after all, so there was no need for Len to get a cob on over her enjoying herself. So she swayed and sang in a voice that was passable.

Doreen caught Phil's eye and remembered the times they'd danced to this tune. So she broke away and walked straight into her boyfriend's arms to shuffle as best as they could in the crowded room.

There were calls for an encore when the song finished and Lily stayed, despite the dark looks coming her way from Len. To walk away now and leave Archie on his own would be churlish, and belittling to him.

The song was romantic and had a catchy melody. Bridie and Bob held hands and smiled at each other. Still so much in love after nearly fifty years of marriage. Molly had her arms around

Jack's neck and was crooning in his ear. Ellen was smiling as Corker serenaded her, while young Phoebe looked on, enthralled. Maisie and Alec were holding hands and singing at the top of their voices. Nellie was perched on the arm of George's chair and had joined in the singing. And Jill and Doreen were wrapped in their boyfriends' arms.

There were two men with no one to hold. But while Paul drank his beer, laughed and sang with the rest, Len stood stony-faced. In his mind, Lily had no right to make a fool of him by leaving his side to sing with some strange bloke. She wouldn't get the chance to do it again, he'd make sure of that.

'It's your turn now, Nellie,' Corker said when Archie returned to Paul's side and Lily was back with Len. 'Yer've got no excuse now.'

'I don't know why she needs all this coaxing,' Molly said. 'She's been waiting for her big moment for the last few hours. Come on, Nellie, sunshine, let's be having yer.'

Nellie gave a slight cough as she stood in front of the fireplace. Then she squared her shoulders and folded her hands across her tummy. 'Can we have a bit of hush for the first song, please? It's a classical one, as sung by Ivor Novello.' She saw the surprise and lifting of eyebrows, and her inside was gurgling with laughter. Looking down at her hands, she cleared her throat. Then the room erupted with the power of her voice as she belted out:

> 'Oh, Frankie and Johnny were lovers,
> My gawd, how they could love,
> Swore to be true to each other,
> True as the stars above:
> He was her man, but he done her wro-o-o-ng.'

Nellie's whole body swayed as she sang, egged on by the clapping and loud cheers. She always did a song justice, and 'Frankie and Johnny' had never been sung with such gusto. Every eye in the room was on her, except for Lily's and her very angry boyfriend.

'Don't yer ever make a fool of me like that again,' he hissed. 'I felt a right ruddy lemon standing here while me girlfriend cuddles up to another feller to make a fool of herself.'

Anger flared up in Lily, but she took a few deep breaths before speaking. She certainly didn't want a stand-up row in front of all these people, but she wasn't going to be spoken to like that. 'This is supposed to be a celebration party, and the whole idea is to enjoy ourselves. If everyone stood like statues with a frown on their faces, it would be a very poor do. My family have been friends with these neighbours since before I was born. And they're always there to help in time of trouble. And they like to have a sing-song and enjoy themselves. What harm is there in that?'

'Like yer mother? Just look at the state of her! I don't call that enjoyment.'

The worst thing he could have done was to criticise Nellie. Like her two brothers, Lily loved the bones of her mother. 'If ye're not enjoying yerself, and yer don't like the company, then I suggest yer go home.'

Len knew he'd gone too far and opened his mouth to wheedle his way back into her good books. But he was too late. Nellie had just finished singing and was bowing to the applause when Lily stepped forward to say, 'Len's got a bad headache so I've advised him to go home, take a couple of tablets and go to bed.'

Words of sympathy were offered, and Nellie said, 'It's a pity about that, lad, but Lily's right. Bed is the best place when yer've got a headache.'

In an effort to redeem himself, Len said, 'I had it when I came, but it's got worse now and me head is splitting.'

Without looking at him, Lily jerked her head. 'Come on, I'll see yer out. There's no point in putting a damper on the party.'

As he stepped into the street, Len tried to put things right. 'I'm sorry for what I said. But yer see, I really do have a headache. I didn't mean any of the things I said and I'm sorry I spoiled things for yer. But I'll make it up to yer tomorrow night, I promise.'

'I won't see yer tomorrow night. It'll be all hours when I get to bed so I intend having a lie-in in the morning. Then I'm going to wash me hair and have a lazy day.'

'I'll meet yer on Monday night then, eh? Then I can tell yer how I get on about me job.'

'If yer want to see me on Monday night, then you'll have to call for me.'

'I will, Lily, I'll call for yer about eight. Now, don't I get a goodnight kiss?'

Lily shook her head. 'It's funny, but I've just developed a splitting headache, too. I'm not going to let it spoil me enjoyment, though – it wouldn't be fair on me family and friends. So I'll get back in with them now and see if their friendliness and humour can cure me.' She began to close the door. 'Ta-ra.'

Chapter Eight

Molly yawned and stretched her arms over her head. 'It's a good job it's Sunday, I'd never have been capable of getting up at six this morning.'

'Yeah, that's the best of having a party on a Saturday.' Jack looked at his wife's tousled hair and eyes still heavy with sleep. 'Ay, it was some party, though, wasn't it? They all enjoyed themselves.'

'It was great! But then it always is when the gang get together.' Molly chuckled. 'I went to sleep thinking of Nellie strutting her stuff as Mae West. I had a stitch in me side and me voice was hoarse with laughing at her. They didn't make many like Nellie, she's one in a million.'

'It's George that tickles me. He's as funny as Nellie in his own way. I was watching his face when she was giving us her version of the Black Bottom, and it was a picture. He doesn't have much to say, but his expression speaks volumes. Like their children, he thinks the world of her.'

'That's only natural 'cos she's a good wife and mother.' Molly refrained from mentioning Len and his early departure. Jack didn't like talking about anyone behind their back, and if she was to say what was in her mind, he'd tell her it was none of her business. 'I was thinking last night, love, how lucky we are with our children. They've each chosen someone we love and get along with. It would be terrible if one of them was courting someone we didn't like, I couldn't bear it.'

'I couldn't see that happening, love, because you get along with anybody. But I agree, we are lucky with Steve, Phil and Rosie. To me they're like me own children.'

'I liked our Tommy's friend, Archie. I thought he was a smasher. He's a nice-looking bloke and has an open, honest face. When he said he didn't have a steady girlfriend, I asked him if he'd wait for our Ruthie to grow up, but he said eight years was a long time to wait.'

'I liked the way he mixed in with everybody, real friendly, like.'

Molly held her breath thinking he was bound to mention Len

105

now. He must have noticed the difference in the two men. But no, it wasn't to be. Jack went on to say, 'Anyone would think we'd known him for years.'

'I think we're going to see a lot of him, love! I hope so, anyway, 'cos I really took a shine to him. Tommy's already asked him to be his best man when he gets married. And Archie invited himself to Jill's wedding. He said he was coming to see Phoebe in all her finery.'

'She's a nice kid,' Jack said. 'She's too quiet and shy now, but she'll blossom over the next year or so.'

Molly looked at the clock. 'It's a wonder our Ruthie's not back from next door. They must be having a lie-in, as well.'

'I'm surprised she wanted to sleep there. I've never known her to miss a party.'

'Don't you breathe a word, but I think Gordon is the interest next door.'

Jack's jaw dropped. 'Molly, she's twelve years of age!'

'Seeing as I gave birth to her, sunshine, don't yer think I know that! But she's caught the bug off Rosie and tells her age in years and months now. If yer ask her how old she is, she'll tell yer, twelve years and six months. And Gordon is fourteen years and five months!'

'It's ridiculous! At her age she should be thinking of dolls, not boys.'

'She must take after me, then. Because I remember when I was at school I had a crush on a boy who I only ever saw through the playground railings. We used to smile at each other, and I thought I'd love him till the day I died. It didn't last, of course, and when I saw him after we'd left school I looked at his pimply face and wondered what I'd ever seen in him.'

Jack smiled. 'I thought I was yer first love?'

'You were my first real love, and it's a love that's lasted twenty-five years. But ye're not going to tell me you were never sweet on a girl when yer were at school?'

'Well now, let me think. There was a Primrose, a Daisy, an Ivy . . .'

Molly punched him on the arm. 'That's enough, soft lad.' She cocked an ear. 'I can hear the girls, I'd better see to their breakfast.' She was muttering as she walked through to the kitchen. 'Primrose, Daisy and Ivy, indeed! But no Buttercup – I wonder why?'

Nellie ran her fingers through her hair, making it stand up in spikes. 'Headache me foot! They must think we're deaf, dumb and blind! They had a row, and I'll bet I know what it was over. The bold laddo got a cob on because he didn't like to see our Lily enjoy herself.'

'Now yer don't know that for sure, Nellie, so be careful what yer say to Lily.' George had his own views on his daughter's boyfriend, but he was a thinker. He had to be sure he was right before he spoke or acted. And to agree with Nellie now would only inflame the situation. He had sympathy for Lily, because if she loved the bloke then she wouldn't see him as others saw him. 'Let it slide, love, and don't make a song and dance about it. Forget about last night and see how things go in future.'

'I just hope she finds out what he's like before it's too late. The thought of having him for a ruddy son-in-law is enough to drive me nuts.'

'Just skip it! Pretend last night didn't happen and try to put it out of yer mind. And don't discuss it with the lads, either. It wouldn't be fair on them or Lily.'

'I don't think Steve was impressed with him. Talk about getting the cold shoulder wasn't in it. Even when he took Jill over the queer feller didn't put himself out to be friendly. And, in case yer didn't notice, our Paul gave him a wide berth all night. So did Archie.'

'That's as may be, but leave things as they are for now. If yer stir things up it'll create a strained atmosphere in the house and that wouldn't be fair on the boys. After all, they've only just come home.'

'I won't say anything to Lily today, if that's what yer want. But I'll tell yer straight that by hook or by crook, I'm going to find out more about Len. After all, it's what any mother would do when her daughter's happiness is at stake. And if he ever hurts her, or brings trouble to our door, I'll break his bloody neck for him.'

'Promise me yer won't say anything when she comes down? If they've had a row, she'll probably feel bad enough without having you on her back.'

Nellie lifted her hands. 'OK, if that's what yer want I'll keep my mouth shut. There's no point in you and me falling out over it.'

'That's my girl!' George quickly changed the subject. 'It was a cracking night last night, wasn't it? You certainly excelled yerself, I must say.'

Nellie cheered up. 'Yeah, it's not very often I get the chance to show off me talents, so I was made up. The next party will be either Jill and Steve's wedding, or Doreen and Phil's. But as mother of the bridegroom I'll have to be on me best behaviour, I suppose. Especially when I'm wearing me big hat.'

'Yer won't suit a big hat, Nellie, I've told yer!'

Nellie's cheeky grin appeared. 'I told Molly what yer said, and she told me to tell yer to keep yer nose out, that we women know what's best for us.'

George chuckled. 'Then yer can tell Molly she can sit next to yer in the church. Ye're far too little to wear a ruddy big hat.'

Nellie went on the offensive. 'You want yer flaming eyes tested, George McDonough! Nobody could say I was little. Look at the ruddy size of me!'

'I'm not talking about the size of yer, I'm talking about yer height! Ye're four foot ten, Nellie, and everybody else towers above yer! Put a big hat on yer head and nobody will know who's under it.'

Nellie saw the funny side of that. 'Tommy Bennett's six foot two now, so him and Corker would have to get on their knees to me. And d'yer know, that's been the one ambition of me life – to bring a man to his knees.'

'Yer brought me to me knees over twenty-five years ago.' George's smile was one of tenderness for the woman whose heart was as big as her body. 'And in case yer haven't noticed, I'm still on me knees.'

Nellie scraped her chair back and rounded the table. She laid a hand on her husband's shoulder and said, 'Arise, Sir George. My knight in shining armour.' After giving him a kiss, she made her way to the kitchen. 'I'd better swill me face and comb me hair before the lads get up, otherwise they'll think their mother has turned into a witch.'

'So it was a good night, was it?' Lizzie Corkhill asked her son.

'Brilliant, Ma, as always. Molly certainly has a knack of throwing good parties. Me and Ellen didn't get to bed until two o'clock. And if Nellie had had her way, we'd still be there singing our heads off.'

'Then why didn't yer take the opportunity of having a lie-in?' Lizzie worried that when her son was home on leave he spent too much time with her. Not that she objected because she missed him living at home. Missed making him his favourite meals and baking the apple pies he loved so much. But he was married now and had a wife to consider. 'Yer didn't have to come up here so early.'

'Ellen's up to her neck in washing, I was glad to get from under her feet. With working, Sunday's the only day she has to get stuck into the housework.' Corker was a man with a mission, but he had to tread slowly and carefully. 'Am I too early for yer?'

'Good heavens, no! I've been up for hours. When yer get to my age yer don't need as much sleep.'

'D'yer ever get lonely, Ma?'

Lizzie averted her eyes. 'With you being away at sea so much, I got used to being on me own. I miss the excitement of yer coming home on leave, and making yer meals for yer. But I'm glad ye're married, son, and yer've got a good wife. I used to worry that if anything happened to me, yer wouldn't have a soul in the world.'

Corker leaned forward and rested his elbows on his knees. 'Have yer ever thought of taking in a lodger, Ma?'

'Certainly not! I don't want no stranger in me house! Besides, think of all the cooking and washing I'd have to do. No, I'm too old for that now.'

'What if it wasn't a stranger, Ma?' Corker stroked his beard and smiled at her. 'Say it was someone yer know very well? Not only know, but are very fond of.'

Lizzie tutted. 'Why don't yer just come out with what yer've got to say, son, instead of going all around the houses?'

'It's only a suggestion, Ma, I'm not trying to talk yer into anything. And nobody knows I'm asking yer this, so don't worry about refusing if that's what yer want. But I'd feel better if yer weren't in this house on yer own. I do love yer, yer know that, and I worry about yer when I'm away.'

'Who have yer got in mind, son?'

'Jill and Steve.'

Lizzie was silent for a while, disbelief in her eyes. 'Yer don't mean Jill Bennett and Steve McDonough, do yer?'

Corker smiled as he nodded. 'I don't know any other Jill and Steve! They want to get married but they haven't got enough money to buy furniture for a house of their own. And God knows they've waited long enough to get wed. I think their love began the day Steve picked up a doll Jill had thrown out of her pram.'

Interest flared in Lizzie's eyes. 'And would they want to come and live here, with an old woman like me?'

'Yer're not an old woman, Ma! Yer keep this house like a new pin, and yer take good care of yer own appearance. Better care than some women half yer age. Anyway, I haven't mentioned to a soul that I was going to ask yer. Not even Ellen. But ye're going down to the Bennetts' for tea tonight, so have a little think about it before then. I don't want to rush yer into anything, yer must make up yer own mind.'

'I don't need to think about it, Corker, I'd be over the moon to have them live with me. Before Steve was called up, they used to come and see me a couple of times a week. And there's not many young people that caring and thoughtful. I'm very fond of both of them and their parents. Salt of the earth, they are. I'd be delighted to have them here, but it might not be what they want.'

'Would yer like me to put it to them, Ma, or would yer rather do it yerself?'

'I'd rather you do it, son. If I suggest it they might not like to refuse and I'd hate to put them in an awkward position.'

'I'll call into Molly's before I go home, then.' Corker took a fobwatch from his waistcoat pocket. 'I think Molly should be presentable by this time, and Jill should be up and about.'

'What time are they expecting me for tea?'

'I heard Phil say he'd take Miss Clegg over about five o'clock. So I'll pick you up about ten to.'

'Yer've no need to pick me up! I can get down there under me own steam.'

'I've said I'll pick yer up, Ma, so don't argue.'

Molly's hand went to her mouth when she saw the big man framed in the doorway. 'In the name of God, Corker, fancy calling the morning after the night before! I look an absolute disgrace!'

Jack, who had answered the knock on the door, laughed. 'She told me whoever it was I wasn't to let them in.'

'Well, a woman's got some pride, yer know.' Molly searched frantically in the sideboard drawer for a comb. Then she saw the funny side. 'To hell with it! Yer've seen me now so it's too late to titivate meself up. But me false teeth are in a cup at the side of the bed, so run up and get them, Jack, please.' She laughed with the men, because she was very proud of her own set of strong white teeth. 'If it was true, Corker, I'd be down the yard hiding in the lavvy by now, waiting for yer to leave.'

Jack waved to a chair. 'Sit yerself down, Corker, and don't look at the mess because me and Molly were just relaxing before setting to and clearing away. Then we've got to get the table back from Nellie's.'

'I'll give yer a hand with that before I go.' Corker glanced towards the kitchen. 'Where's the children?'

'Ruthie isn't back from your house yet, Tommy is still in bed, Doreen has gone over the road to put Victoria's hair in curlers ready for tonight, and Jill's upstairs making her bed.'

'It was Jill I wanted to have a word with. And you two, of course.'

'Sounds very mysterious,' Molly said. 'I'll give her a shout.'

Jill's face lit up as it always did when she saw the gentle giant. 'Yer haven't come for another party, have yer, Uncle Corker?'

'It'll take me a few days to get over last night, princess.' Blue eyes smiled from a weatherbeaten face which was almost hidden by the huge white moustache and beard. 'I've come to have a little chat with you.'

Jill picked up one of the wooden dining chairs and placed it near him. 'It seems funny in here without the table to lean on. Anyway, Uncle Corker, I'm all ears.'

'What I'm going to say is only a suggestion. Something for you to think about. Whichever way it goes, there's no harm done.' As Corker stroked his beard he sought the right words. 'Yer were saying last night that you and Doreen would like a double wedding, but that you wouldn't be getting married for a while because yer haven't got enough money to furnish a house. Is that right?'

Jill nodded. 'Yeah. I'm going to tell our Doreen to go ahead and get married. It's no good waiting for me and Steve because it'll take ages to save the money we'll need.'

'Have yer thought about going into lodgings for a while?'

Jill looked horrified. 'Oh no, we wouldn't like that. We wouldn't want to live with strangers.'

'Would yer call Mrs Elizabeth Corkhill a stranger?'

Jill looked puzzled. She glanced at her mother and then back at Corker. 'I don't quite understand. Of course yer mother's not a stranger.'

'Well, why not have yer double wedding, then live with me ma while yer save up for a place of yer own?'

'Your mother wouldn't be very happy about that.'

'I've asked her, and she'd be very happy. Yer'd have yer own bedroom, could cook yer own meals and have the run of the house. With you and Steve both working, it wouldn't take yer long to save the money yer need. And it would mean yer wouldn't have to wait to get married.'

Jill's tummy began to turn over and her heartbeat raced. 'Can I go and get Steve, Uncle Corker, and yer can tell him what yer've told me?' Without waiting for an answer Jill fled from the room and within seconds was banging on the McDonoughs' door.

'What is it, Jill, is something wrong?' Steve asked as he was pulled down from the top step and was forced to run to keep up with her. 'Hang on a minute and tell me what's wrong.'

'There's nothing wrong, Steve. I just want Uncle Corker to tell you what he's told me.'

Steve could see there was nothing wrong when they ran into the Bennetts' living room. On the contrary, Mr and Mrs B. looked very happy.

'Grab a chair, sunshine and sit down,' Molly said. 'This is something that might interest you.'

While Corker was repeating everything he'd said, Jill went to stand behind her mother's chair and put her arms around Molly's shoulders. She was shaking inside and praying that Steve would feel the same way as she did. Just the thought that they could be married in months, rather than years, was making her dizzy with happiness. But she would abide by her loved one's decision.

Steve asked all the questions that Jill had asked and got the same answers. It was hard to tell what his reaction was going to be because he seemed to be having difficulty in taking it in. That is, until he turned to where Jill was standing behind her mother. And the excitement shining in her vivid blue eyes told him all he wanted to know. He smiled and held out a hand. 'Come and sit on me knee, love, because I think I'm going to fall off this chair.'

'Are you two happy with the offer?' Molly asked, while wondering how it was she always wanted to cry when something nice happened.

'I think the word happy is too mild, Mrs B. More like ecstatic or delirious. And if it weren't for Uncle Corker's beard, I'd kiss him.'

'I'll do that for yer.' Jill cupped the big man's face and kissed him. 'I couldn't love yer any more than I've always loved yer, 'cos that would be impossible. So I'll just thank yer for what yer've done for me and Steve.'

'So me ma's got herself two lodgers, has she?'

'If she'll have us, yes, definitely.'

'Thanks, Uncle Corker,' Steve said, his dimples as deep as they would go. 'I really appreciate yer doing this for us. Me and Jill will see yer mother and sort out the money arrangements. And we'll not let yer down. We'll take good care of her and try not to upset her life too much.'

'This is not all one-sided, yer know,' Corker said. 'My main reason for asking me ma was to help out two people who I love and admire. But yer'll be company for her, and I won't need to worry so much about her when I'm away, knowing you two will be there if she needs help. She never does need help, mind you, 'cos she's as fit as a fiddle and an independent so-and-so.'

'Can I get me twopennyworth in?' Molly asked, her own excitement knowing no bounds. 'Are we having a double wedding in the family?'

'It looks like it, Mrs B.' Steve couldn't wipe the smile off his face. Very soon the girl he'd loved for as long as he could remember, would be his wife. 'Yer'll be getting me for yer son-in-law sooner than yer thought.'

'It can't come soon enough for me, Steve! What do you say, Jack?'

'Molly, I'm lost for words. It's really marvellous news. Its very good of you and yer ma, Corker, and while I don't think it would be the done thing to kiss you, I'll be giving Lizzie the sloppiest kiss she's ever had.'

'Could we go up and see Mrs Corkhill?' Steve needed to know he wasn't dreaming. 'Would she mind?'

Corker was so happy he felt like he did when he was a lad and had won his mate's best ollie. 'Of course she wouldn't mind! She'd be chuffed to see yer.'

Jill couldn't keep still. 'Wait until I tell our Doreen and Phil. And yer mam, Steve, she'll be over the moon.'

'I'm going up to your house now, Steve, to give Jack a hand bringing the table back. So why don't you and Jill come with us and yer can tell her?'

'Not on your ruddy life!' Molly said with great indignation. 'I wouldn't miss seeing me mate's face for all the tea in China. I want to be there when she's told.'

'Then why don't we break eggs with a big stick and tell everyone at the same time?' Jack suggested. 'Ask Nellie to come down and bring Doreen and Phil across.'

'That's a very good idea,' Molly said, not wanting to miss anything. It wasn't the same getting news secondhand. 'But we'll need the table first. We can't have a conference in comfort without something to lean on.'

Corker's laugh was hearty. 'Come on, Jack, we'll go for the table and tell Nellie her mate wants to see her. And I'll give Ellen a knock as we pass, to ask her to keep the dinner back for an hour. I don't want to miss any of this.'

When the two men had left, Molly said, 'You go across and ask Doreen and Phil to come over, Jill. But don't tell her why. Not a word until everyone is here.'

'What the hell is all the mystery?' Nellie wanted to know. Her elbows were on the table and her hands cupped her chubby face. She narrowed her eyes as she looked at Molly. 'Ye're not pregnant, are yer, girl? 'Cos if yer are, I think yer should be ashamed of yerself at your age.'

The only one who didn't laugh was Molly. 'Trust you, Nellie McDonough! Is your mind ever anywhere else but in the bed-room?' Then she was sorry she'd spoken because her friend had an answer – as usual.

'The bedroom is not the only place yer can make a baby, girl! And if yer think it is, then all I can say is that yer've lived a miserable bloody life.'

'Nellie, if yer don't want to hear the news, why don't yer go back home?'

113

'Ooh, er!' Nellie's expression was comical as she scanned the faces around the table. 'She's narky today, isn't she? But she's probably tired after last night, so I'll make allowances for her.' The face she turned to Molly was one of total innocence. 'I want to hear yer news, girl! I'm waiting to hear yer news, girl! And when yer decide to bloodywell stop gabbing, I'll probably get to hear it! But if I go asleep in the meantime, yer'll have to excuse me.'

'Mam, it's me and Jill who have got something to tell yer,' Steve said. 'And it's the most marvellous news we could have been given.'

Nellie looked at her son, and then at Jill, who was sitting on his knee. Their faces told of the happiness they were waiting to share. 'What is it, son?'

'Mrs Corkhill has said we can go and live with her until we're able to get a place of our own. So we'll soon be setting the date for our wedding.'

The next few minutes were very noisy as everyone tried to speak at the same time. Doreen was laughing and crying as she hugged her sister. 'That means we can have a double wedding, kid!'

Jill smiled back into her face. 'Yes, isn't it wonderful? I'm so thrilled I don't know what to do with meself.'

Nellie nearly smothered her son with kisses. 'I'm so happy for yer both, son. They say good things come in threes – well, they have with you. Yer start work tomorrow, ye're marrying the girl of yer dreams and now yer have a place to live. And it couldn't have happened to a nicer couple. Just wait until yer dad, Lily and Paul find out, they'll be over the moon.'

'We've got Uncle Corker to thank for it.'

'Yes, I gathered that, son. I'll have a word with him.' Nellie swayed over and put her arms around Corker. 'It's easy to say thank you, it doesn't cost anything. But that all I can say, except that you are a good friend and one of life's gentlemen.'

'I was glad to help, Nellie, but I couldn't have done it if I didn't have the best mother in the whole wide world.'

'Yeah, I know that. I'll be seeing Lizzie tonight because I've invited meself to tea, so I'll tell her how happy she's made us all.'

Nellie went to stand by Jack, who was watching the four young ones with a smile on his face and pride in his heart. 'Just look at them, Nellie, doesn't it make yer feel good to see them so happy? I bet they're talking about a certain day that isn't as distant now as it was an hour ago.'

'What it is to be young and in love, eh, Jack? I'm really looking forward to their weddings, but I won't half miss our Steve when he leaves home. I'll probably cry me eyes out.'

'Me and Molly will be losing two, Nellie! But they'll both be living in our street so we'll be seeing a lot of them.'

'Yeah, it could be worse, couldn't it? Anyway, I'm going to have a talk to your one. You wouldn't be interested because it'll be about hats. Big hats!' Nellie was walking towards Molly when she thought, Sod it, it's a blinking celebration! So she lifted the front of her skirt and set her legs in motion. 'Come on, girl, let's be having yer!'

Molly followed suit. Lifting the front of her skirt she danced towards Nellie, singing, 'Oh, me name is McNamara, I'm the leader of the band.' The two women linked arms and spun around, singing at the top of their voices.

'Ay, Corker, take that ruddy table back to our house, will yer?' Nellie said, going red in the face and puffing. 'How d'yer expect us to dance with that thing in the way?'

'Why don't yer get on the table and dance, Mam,' Steve called. 'Yer'll have more room.'

'Like hell she will! That table is my pride and joy.' Molly noticed her youngest daughter standing just inside the living-room door. 'I thought yer'd left home, sunshine! I hope yer didn't outstay yer welcome next door?'

'No, Auntie Ellen said to tell yer I'd been no trouble.' Ruthie guessed there was something afoot by the smiling faces and the dancing. 'What's going on? It's not still the same party, is it?'

'No, sunshine, it's not a party, but a celebration nonetheless. I think yer sisters have got something nice to tell yer.'

'D'yer want to be me bridesmaid, Ruthie?' Jill asked.

'And mine?' Doreen added.

This sounds too good to be true, Ruthie thought. 'I knew you might be getting married soon, our Doreen, but Jill won't be getting married for ages.'

'It would have been ages,' Jill said. 'But Uncle Corker has made it possible for me and Doreen to have a double wedding.'

When she'd been told all the facts, the young girl was beside herself. 'When will the wedding be? What colour dress am I having?'

'Hang on, sunshine,' Molly laughed, 'there's nothing been arranged yet. Steve and Phil have a say in all this! So give them time to sit down with the girls and decide when, where and how.'

'Can I have a blue dress? Please say yes because blue is me favourite colour. Go on, don't be mean, say I can.'

'I think blue is a nice colour for bridesmaids,' Phil said. 'Don't you think so, Doreen?'

Doreen nodded. 'Yeah, the same blue as the sky on a summer's day.'

115

Jill smiled. She was so happy she wanted to share it with her kid sister. 'I like blue, too, and it would suit all the bridesmaids.'

'How many bridesmaids are yer having?' Nellie asked. 'If ye're short, I'll step in and help yer out. I'd do yer proud with flowers in me hair.'

'We're full up, Auntie Nellie,' Jill told her. 'There's Ruthie, Lily, Phoebe and Dorothy, and Doreen wants her friend Maureen to be one. So that's five.'

'And I can make the dresses,' Doreen said. 'Not the brides, of course, they've got to be really special. Something out of this world.'

'I hope I'm home to see it,' Corker said. 'This wedding is something I wouldn't want to miss.'

Ruthie's eyes widened as her hand flew to her mouth. 'Oh, strewth! I had a message for yer from Auntie Ellen and I forgot! She said to tell yer to get home quick, or the dinner won't be fit to eat.'

Corker winked at the young girl. 'Don't worry, sweetheart, I'm bigger than her. Although I might have to watch me manners in a few years with the boys growing up so fast.'

'Gordon said he wants to grow up to be just like you, Uncle Corker. He wants to be as tall as yer, and he's going to grow a beard and moustache.'

Molly saw Jack's expression and was sorry she'd told him about Ruthie having a crush on young Gordon. She'd have kept her mouth shut if she'd known he was going to turn it into a big issue. 'If I were you, Corker, I'd get going. There's nothing that upsets a woman more than spending hours making a dinner and then to see it ruined.'

When Corker left, it was with the thanks of four young people ringing in his ears. And he was delighted he'd been able to help. He knew where their heads and hearts would be now. They'd be on cloud nine, where his had been the day Ellen finally said she'd marry him.

'I think me and Steve should go and see Mrs Corkhill, Mam,' Jill said. 'I know she's coming to tea, but she won't want her affairs discussed in front of other people.'

'And I'd like to go and tell Aunt Vickie the news,' Phil said. 'She'll be on top of the world when she knows. But could we all meet tomorrow night to start the ball rolling? Like setting a date, which church, who to invite . . . you know, things like that.'

'Would Gordon be getting an invite?' Ruthie asked.

Jack leaned forward. 'Ruthie, just listen—'

Molly put a hand on his arm to silence him. 'Ruthie, did yer dad ever tell yer the story about the three girls called Primrose,

116

Daisy and Ivy? No, well perhaps he'll tell yer some time when we've nothing else on our minds. Right now there's more important things to discuss. So tomorrow night, Phil, we'll have a round table conference, eh? Is that all right with you, Nellie?'

'It's fine by me, girl, except it'll have to be a square table conference, seeing as yer haven't got a round one.'

'If ye're so fussy, sunshine, shall I get Jack to fetch his saw and round the corners of this table? Would yer be happy, then?' Molly tutted. 'I think you four should get going before Tilly Mint here thinks of something else to keep yer back. Go on, scarper.'

Molly waited until she heard the door close, then turned to her friend. With head jutting forward and hands on hips, she said, 'You can be on yer way, too, sunshine, so I can start on the dinner. And while that's on the go, me and Jack are going to give this room a thorough good going-over. Yer see, we had some friends in last night and they left the place like a ruddy pigsty.'

Nellie shook her head and clicked her tongue. 'Yer should be more fussy about who yer have for friends, girl, I'm fed-up telling yer! Me now, I'm very careful who I invite into me house 'cos yer never can tell.'

'Oh, ye're careful all right. So ruddy careful yer don't invite anyone! If I'd taken a leaf out of your book, sunshine, I wouldn't be left with this flaming mess!'

Jack was stretched out on his chair with Ruthie on his knee. They were both smiling, knowing the performance would end in laughter.

'I'm cut to the quick, girl, I really am. I don't know why yer say these terrible things to me when yer know how easily I get hurt.'

'I'm going to hurt yer even more, now, 'cos if yer don't leave of yer own free will, I'm going to throw yer out!'

Nellie folded her arms and stood her ground. 'I'll go if yer tell me the story about Primrose, Daisy and Ivy.'

Molly chuckled and turned her friend around to face the door. 'Some other time, when we're on our own.' She pushed the protesting Nellie out into the hall. 'On yer way, sunshine!'

'I'll see yer in the morning, girl, to go to the shops.'

'OK, sunshine! Ta-ra!'

Ruthie giggled. 'They're not half funny, aren't they, Dad?'

'They are that, pet,' Jack grinned. 'But they're clever as well. Haven't yer noticed that although they do it in a roundabout way, they always get what they want?'

Chapter Nine

Molly and Nellie were deep in conversation as they walked down the street on the Monday morning. They had so much to talk about, most of the time they were both talking at the same time. And on top of that, Molly was winning the fight to get her mate to walk in a straight line. 'The bedroom is furnished, so they don't need to buy a thing! It's Corker's old room, with the bed he used to sleep in. I thought our Jill mightn't like that, but she's so thrilled she wouldn't care what they slept in.'

'What about bedding, girl, are they all right for that?'

'Jill's got some in her bottom drawer, but Lizzie told them not to worry 'cos she's got plenty of everything.'

'They've hopped in lucky, no doubt about that. Our Steve was saying last night that he couldn't believe their luck. He'd reckoned the earliest they could get married would be a year, then this comes along out of the blue!'

Molly nudged Nellie when she spotted a woman stepping out of a house a few yards away. 'There's Mrs Patterson, I want a word with her.'

'What about, girl?'

'Never mind what about, put a move on!' Vera Patterson had seen them and waited until they came abreast. Molly smiled a greeting before saying, 'I was wondering how things were going next door.'

Vera glanced quickly at the window of number sixteen and gave a slight shake of her head. 'I'll walk down to the main road with yer.'

There wasn't a word spoken until the trio had turned the corner and were out of sight and earshot. 'I didn't want to say nothing 'cos yer never know who's listening.'

'It's safe here,' Molly said, 'and yer can trust me and Nellie not to say anything.'

'Well, the baby's gone! It's being looked after by a woman in Aintree until all the paperwork's been done. Mavis has been to the house and she said it's proper posh and the baby's getting the best of everything and wants for nothing. He's got every toy under the

119

sun, I believe, and Mavis says he'll have a much better life in America than she could give him. She can go and see him as often as she likes before his father takes him away, but she thinks it's better to make a clean break, so she's not going again.'

'Has she heard from her husband?'

'Yeah, that's another worry for her. He's in a hospital down South, and from the sound of things he's in a pretty bad way. The prisoner-of-war camp he was in was terrible by all accounts; the men were badly treated and nearly starved to death. Mavis has been informed that he'll be transferred to a hospital nearer home when he's strong enough to be moved.' Vera gave a deep sigh. 'Like everyone else in the street, I've called Mavis some names for the way she's carried on, but I can't help feeling sorry for her now. She did love the baby and she's broken-hearted at having to give it up. But, strange as it may seem from the way she's behaved, she really loves her husband.'

'Yer could have fooled me!' Nellie snorted. 'If she loves her husband so much, why didn't she stay true to the poor bugger, instead of sleeping with anything in trousers?'

'She's younger than us, Nellie, and some women can't do without a man,' Molly said. 'I'm not making excuses for her, and she's being punished for what she did. Having to give a baby up must be heartbreaking.'

'She did it because she said it would kill her husband if he came back and found she'd been playing around.' Vera gave a hollow laugh. 'But he's going to find out anyway, because there's a couple of women in the street that can't stand her, and they swear they're going to tell her husband as soon as he gets home.'

'I don't think they should do that,' Molly said. 'What good would it do? What's done can't be undone.'

But Nellie didn't agree. 'She deserves to be snitched on, girl! Her poor feller going through hell and she's out enjoying herself every night. She needs a bloody good hiding.'

'Yes, she does, sunshine, but don't yer think her husband's suffered enough? They'd be hurting him more than her. I'd be dead against anyone telling him, and I'd say that to their faces if I knew who they were.'

'Yer might know who it is, Molly,' Vera said. 'Fanny Kemp and Theresa Brown. Two nosy, miserable women who have nothing on their mind but to tell tales and cause trouble. I bet any money that as soon as Frank Sheild steps foot in the street they'll be over to him like a shot. Even if he was being carried in on a stretcher, it wouldn't stop them. I've no time for them, they're both wicked.'

'I should have guessed it would be them! The two of them spend most of their lives standing on their doorsteps pulling everyone to pieces. I wouldn't care if they were anything to write home about, but they're not! In all the years we've lived in the street I've never known either of them do a good turn.' Molly's mind flashed back to the time she'd gone with Doreen to visit Phil in hospital. Some of the lads in there were in a terrible state, with limbs missing, faces disfigured and minds destroyed. None of them deserved to have heartbreak added to their suffering, and neither did Frank Sheild. 'I'm going to have a word with Fanny and Theresa, whether they like it or not. I won't mention you've said anything, Vera, yer've no need to worry on that score.'

'Molly, I'm not the only one they've told, they've said the same thing to everyone down our end of the street.'

'And what did the other women say? Were they in agreement with them?'

Vera shook her head. 'No, they think the same as you and me, that the poor man should be left to get on with whatever life he has left.'

Nellie had been doing some thinking and in the process had changed her mind. Molly was right, and she was wrong. The fly turn in number sixteen had enjoyed the war years, with different men coming to the house regularly. But her husband shouldn't be the one to suffer for his wife's affairs. 'If ye're going to have words with Fanny and Theresa, girl, yer can count me in. I've already had a few con . . . confon . . .' Nellie scratched her head. 'What's the word I'm looking for?'

'Confrontations, sunshine.'

'That's it! I've had a few of those with them. Particularly that Fanny, she gets on me flaming wick. It wouldn't take much for me to clock her one.'

'There'll be no fisticuffs, Nellie, so yer can forget that.' Then Molly grinned. 'Mind you, queen, I'll take yer with me just in case they don't listen to reason.'

'Let me know when ye're going to have words with them, Molly,' Vera said. 'I think I'd find the conversation very interesting.'

'Let's see how things go first, Vera. We sometimes see them at the shops, so I'll just mention it casual like. It could be they're just full of hot air and when it comes to the crunch they may have second thoughts.' Molly linked her arm through Nellie's. 'We'll get on with our shopping, Vera, but thanks for the information. I'll let yer know if anything transpires.'

Vera pushed the handle of her basket into the crook of her arm. 'Ta-ra for now.'

Molly tried to steer her friend forward, but Nellie stood firm and wouldn't be shifted. 'Ay, girl, what is it ye're going to let Vera know?'

'How the heck do I know? I'm not one of these people who can see into the future.'

'But yer said yer'd let her know!'

'Yes! If anything happens!'

'Don't be raising yer voice and have people thinking I'm stone deaf! And don't be getting all het up, either. When I was young, me mam always used to say if yer don't ask, yer'll never find out. So I'm only doing what me mam told me. And yer didn't tell Vera yer'd let her know when anything happens, so what did yer tell her?'

Molly took a deep breath and blew out slowly. 'I said if anything transpires, sunshine, and that *means* if anything happens!'

'Yer know, girl, your brain must be on the go all the time, looking for words that yer know I won't understand. Yer do it on purpose.'

'Yer should thank me for it. I'm giving yer the education yer couldn't be bothered getting at school!' Molly gave a jerk which Nellie wasn't expecting and it forced her to move. 'Now, can we please get our shopping done?'

'Blimey! Listening to you anyone would think I was the one what's kept us back! It was you what wanted to talk to Vera, and that's only because ye're nosy. I get a name like a mad dog for talking too much, when it's really you what's the jangler.'

When they stepped into the butcher's shop, Tony and Ellen were standing behind the counter with grins on their faces. 'Me and Ellen have just been watching you two walking along having a real go at each other. I thought yer'd be all smiles today after what Ellen told me, not arguing the toss.'

Nellie put her basket on the floor so she could hitch up her bosom. She always felt more in command when her bosom was in the place it used to be many years ago. It didn't stay up for long, mind, because of the force of gravity. But by the time it had settled down again, she'd forgotten what she'd hitched it up for in the first place! 'Arguing? Now have yer ever known me and Molly to argue? Never in a month of Sundays! So it must have been two other women yer were watching what looked like us but wasn't.'

'Well, me eyesight must be getting bad, Nellie, 'cos I could have sworn it was you. Same colour coat and scarf, same walk. And what clinched it was the stockings around the ankles like a concertina! Dead giveaway, that is.'

Nellie rose to her full height. 'And what the hell were you doing looking at my legs? Have yer got nothing better to do, Tony Reynolds?' She turned to Molly and said in a loud whisper, 'When a man starts eyeing a woman's legs or bust, he's either sick in the head or he's not getting enough of what he fancies at home.'

'And by the same token, sunshine, any woman who thinks because a man looks at her legs he's after her body – well, she's either bad-minded or sex mad.'

'Sex mad, girl, that's me! Can't get enough of it!'

'You said it Nellie, not me!'

'Well, it's the truth. Best thing ever invented, was sex.' Nellie leaned back against the counter and folded her arms. 'Your Rosie's always saying God gave her a mouth to speak with and a brain to think with. She never goes any lower down than her chin. But He gave us a lot more than a mouth and brain! And I'm of the opinion that we should make full use of every part of our body. George isn't always of the same mind, like, and I sometimes wonder if he's frightened of wearing it out!'

Molly noticed that while Tony was grinning, Ellen was looking decidedly uncomfortable. Not everyone appreciated Nellie's outspoken views in mixed company. 'If yer can tear yerself away from yer bedroom, Nellie, I'll ask Tony what goodies he can suggest for our dinners.' She placed her ration book on the counter. 'I'm going down to see about our Tommy's ration book today, and with a bit of luck it'll have last week's coupons in as well. If it has I can go made and have meat twice in the week.'

'From what Ellen's told me, yer'll be gaining one ration book but losing two in the near future.'

'I don't want to think about losing them, Tony. I'm so happy for the kids I refuse to let me mind dwell on the thought of them leaving home for good. If I did that I'd spend me days crying me eyes out, and a fat lot of good that would do anyone. No, my two daughters are marrying good men who love them and will take good care of them. And it is my intention that they have a wedding day they'll remember all their lives.'

'All that me mate's just said goes for me too.' Nellie's chins gave their seal of approval by dancing up and down. 'We don't know when it'll be yet, but we're having a conflab about it tonight in Molly's. So next time we come in we'll let yer know more.'

'Our Phoebe and Dorothy are sick with excitement,' Ellen said. 'And if they're like this now, what are they going to be like on the day?'

'I only hope Corker's home for it,' Molly said. 'Our Jill would be very disappointed if he missed her big day.'

'He'll do his best to be here, yer can bet yer sweet life on that! Your Jill is special to Corker, he thinks the world of her. He was saying last night that as soon as the date is sorted out, he'll be looking to sign on a ship that's due home around that time.'

'If ye're hoping to have the reception somewhere, yer'd better be quick booking a place,' Tony said. 'Nearly all the men are home now, so as yer can imagine there's loads of weddings.'

'I hope to have the reception in a hall because there'll be too many people to fit in my small room. And with a bit of luck the money might run to having caterers to supply the meal. That would take a load of our minds, wouldn't it, Nellie? All we'd have to do would be to sit back and enjoy ourselves. To bask in the glory.'

'Sounds good to me, girl. I'll have sixpennyworth of that! And isn't it the way it should be for the mothers of bride and groom? I'm not getting meself all dolled up to the nines just to pass flaming sandwiches around.'

'I agree with yer, sunshine, but don't be sticking yer oar in tonight, please? Let the kids decide what they want for their big day, and we'll give them all the help we can.' Molly eyed the meat in the window. 'I'll have as much of that stewing meat as me ration book allows me to have.

'Same here, Tony,' Nellie said. 'When d'yer think this here rationing will be over? By Christmas, d'yer think?'

'Which Christmas, Nellie?' As Tony spoke, his razor-sharp knife was cutting the meat into small pieces. 'I've been talking to some wholesalers, and they're of the same opinion as meself. We've got another couple of years of rationing yet.'

'Oh, don't say that, Tony,' Molly groaned. 'I'm sick of it. Every day it's a headache wondering what to feed the family on. Whoever the feller is that said we could have four ounces of meat a week – well, he wants hanging. I bet he gets a damn sight more than that.'

'There's no shortage of anything for people with money.' Tony wrapped the meat and placed the two parcels on the counter. 'All the rich have to do is eat out every day! I bet they get fed on the best of everything at those big London hotels.'

'It's not fair, is it?' Molly put the parcels in her basket and took out her purse. 'It's always been the same for as long as I can remember. The rich live off the fat of the land while the poor have to struggle. And in most cases it's the poor working man who's putting the money into the rich man's coffers.'

'Yeah, but the rich don't know how to enjoy themselves as much as we do, girl,' Nellie said. 'And when ye're rich and have everything yer want, then there's no pleasure left in life, is there? I mean, like, if I get a new hearth rug I think it's marvellous and call me neighbours in to see it. But if I was loaded, it wouldn't mean nothing to me. See what I mean?'

124

'Yes I do, sunshine, and I think yer put that very well. I'll bet Lord and Lady Muck don't have half the fun we have.'

'They certainly don't have the fun that me and George do. They'd think they were too high and mighty for our shenanigans.'

'She's back to the bedroom, Tony! So will yer tell us what we owe and I'll get her out of yer shop before Ellen lays a duck egg?'

'Listen to me, girl. If Ellen could lay duck eggs I'd have her down in Great Homer Street Market next to them spiv fellers. Duck eggs could raise a lot of money these days and we'd be quids in.'

Molly passed two half-crowns over the counter. 'Take for Nellie's while ye're at it, Tony, then I can get her out of here. She can pay me later.'

'If yer keep on insulting me, I won't pay yer no money.'

'Suit yerself, sunshine! But I've got the meat in me basket so yer don't have much bargaining power.' Molly winked broadly. 'See yer, Tony. Ta-ra, Ellen!'

'Before yer go up for Corker and George, love, will yer bring the two wooden chairs down from the bedrooms?' Molly reached for the four corners of the tablecloth and brought them together ready for shaking in the yard. 'We'll all want to sit around the table, if possible.'

Jack grinned. 'Ye're enjoying every minute of this, aren't yer? Women are never happier than when they can complain about having too much on their mind, when all the time they're loving it.'

'Me two daughters getting married – of course I'm enjoying it! There's going to be a lot to do, and times when I get narky, but yer'll just have to put up with it. And I've found a way of stopping meself from crying. I keep reminding meself I'm not losing two daughters, I'm gaining two sons.' Molly nodded towards the door. 'Fetch the chairs, love, and then get going. The girls have nearly finished the dishes and I've only got to shake this cloth out. Then we're all ready for what Nellie calls the square table conference.'

'How long do yer want me out of the way for?'

'As long as it takes yer to drink three pints very slowly. We've got to count the pennies, don't forget. The bride's family always pay for the reception and lots of other things, so think on, sunshine, 'cos we want to give them the best.'

Jack slipped his arm around her waist and pulled her close. 'I love you, Molly Bennett.'

After a quick glance to the kitchen where the two girls were chatting away while doing the washing up, Molly kissed his lips lightly. 'And I'm crazy about you.'

'We could get married again and make it a triple wedding, yer know. I could take a couple of days off work and we could go on the honeymoon we never had first time around.'

'Jack Bennett, since the day I married you, my life has been one long honeymoon. I couldn't have loved yer more if yer'd whisked me off on a magic carpet to some far-flung exotic island and we lazed under palm trees all day.'

Jack chuckled. 'I was thinking more of two days in Blackpool! I, unfortunately, don't have the same vivid imagination as you.'

Molly pushed him gently away with one hand, while gripping the corners of the tablecloth with the other. 'Yer would have, sunshine, if yer had a mate like Nellie. With her, everything is believable and also more than likely to happen. But I can't stand here discussing me mate because she'll be down any minute with Steve, and Phil is expected.'

'I'm going, love! I'll bring the chairs down first, then call for Corker on me way to George's'

Lily McDonough had her ear cocked for a knock on the front door while feigning interest in what her mam was saying to make her father and his two drinking friends roar their heads off with laughter. She wasn't at all sure that Len would come after the row on Saturday, but she'd got herself ready to go out in case he did come. If he didn't show, it would mean he didn't want to see her again. She'd be sad if that happened because she had strong feelings towards him.

Her train of thought was interrupted when her mother tapped her on the shoulder. 'There's the door, Lily. It's probably for you 'cos I'm not expecting anyone.'

'If it is, I'll go straight out, Mam, but I won't be late in.' Lily picked her handbag off the sideboard and wagged a finger at the three men. 'No getting drunk, mind, or yer'll have the neighbours complaining.'

Corker's deep chuckle rumbled. 'In case yer hadn't noticed, Lily, we *are* the neighbours! If anyone complains, they've got three against them for a start!'

Lily was smiling when she opened the door, and when she saw Len standing there her heart smiled too. 'D'yer want to come in or shall we go straight to wherever we're going?'

'Let's go straight out and we can stop in a shop doorway so yer can give me two kisses.' They fell into step with Lily linking his arm. 'I saw me old boss today and I start work on Monday. That's worth a kiss, isn't it?'

126

'It certainly is! Good for you! That's one kiss, what's the other for?'

'To make up for the one I didn't get on Saturday night.'

'Yer didn't get one because yer didn't deserve one.'

'I had every right to get a cob on with yer! I was left standing like a right nit, while you were singing yer head off with another feller's arm around yer. If I'd have done that, yer wouldn't have been too happy, would yer?'

Lily groaned inwardly. It was only a couple of minutes since she'd left the house and here he was ready to bring up the argument again. She waited until they'd turned into the main road before pulling him to a halt. 'What's come over you, Len? Yer were never this miserable before yer went in the army. Yer weren't the easiest bloke in the world, but I made allowances for yer because of the life yer'd had at home. And at least we used to have a laugh and a joke together. Since yer came home I don't know where I am with yer!'

'It's the army that's made me like this. I saw some terrible sights, Lily, and they're not easy to forget.' And so Len began to lie, as he'd been lying to her since the day they met. He was a mechanic and had spent his time in the army maintaining the army vehicles. He hadn't seen any fighting and was never really in any danger. But he'd heard men talking in the demob camp and he put this knowledge to good use now. 'Seeing men with arms or legs blown off, it gets to yer. I've had nightmares every night since I came home.'

Lily fell for his lies, like she always had, even though one part of her mind was saying that her brothers had been in the army as long as Len, and so had Tommy Bennett, and it hadn't taken away their ability to laugh and be pleasant. But they'd had a loving family life, she reminded herself, where her boyfriend hadn't. 'Why didn't yer tell me this? I would have understood.'

'I didn't tell yer because I didn't want to upset yer. And I thought yer might think I was weak for letting it get to me.'

'Of course I wouldn't think that, soft lad! At least I'd have known the reason for yer being miserable and awkward to get on with.' She linked his arm and as they began walking she changed the subject. 'Me mam and our Steve are going to the Bennetts' tonight, to make plans for the weddings. It should be a lovely occasion, with Jill and Doreen getting married at the same time. They're so pretty, and our Steve and Phil so handsome, it should be a real fairytale double wedding.'

'I didn't think much of the girls meself. They're not my type.'

No one with eyes in their head could say the Bennett girls weren't beautiful, but Lily told herself not to answer in haste. So she counted to ten before saying, 'Go 'way, they're both lovely! But I'm glad they're not your type, otherwise I wouldn't be in the meg specks.'

She was smiling up into his face when she saw him flinch and felt his footsteps falter. She looked across the wide road where his eyes were directed, and saw two men standing on a street corner, deep in conversation. Then there was a girl passing a block of shops, and behind her two sailors. The scene flashed through her mind before she felt herself being dragged into the nearest shop doorway.

'What the hell d'yer think ye're doing?' Lily tried to pull her arm fee. 'Let go of me, ye're hurting.'

Len was facing her in the doorway, his back to the road. 'One of the blokes over there is an old workmate of mine and I don't want him to see me.'

'Why not? He can't eat yer!'

'I don't want him to see me, OK?' Len ground the words out and his face was set. He stood motionless for a short while, then ventured to turn his head. The men were still talking on the corner opposite, but the girl and sailors had passed on out of sight. Then he relaxed his grip on Lily and prepared to tell more lies. 'I'm sorry about that, love, but if he sees me I'll never get away from him. He'll be asking about the war and I don't want to be reminded.'

'And you nearly took the arm off me just for that! Why couldn't yer just have waved and walked on? If he's one of those blokes over there, we could be in this doorway all night 'cos they seem to have plenty to say to each other.'

'I was just thinking that meself. So we'll sneak out and hope he doesn't spot us.'

'I'm not sneaking anywhere, Len Lofthouse! And why the hell should I? If he sees us then we'll have a few words with him and be on our way. But don't ever ask me to sneak because that's not how I was brought up.'

'OK, I'm sorry! I don't seem to be able to do anything right, do I?' Len took her arm and rubbed his hand where he'd gripped her. 'Give me a kiss and tell me yer forgive me for hurting yer.'

After a passionate kiss, they left the shadow of the shop doorway. If Lily hadn't been in a dreamworld because Len had told her he loved her, she might have wondered why he didn't seem worried now whether the men opposite saw him or not. She wasn't to know he had no reason to worry because he'd never seen either of the men in his life before. Or that, as he walked with a jaunty air, her arm tucked into his, he was congratulating himself on a narrow escape.

But if Len had turned his head, he would have seen a figure step from a shop doorway a little higher up on the opposite side of the road, and his complacency would have turned to fear. He would have realised he *hadn't* had a lucky escape – he'd only been allowed a reprieve by the person whose eyes were ablaze with anger as they watched the couple walk away.

Chapter Ten

'Mam, can I sit on yer knee?' Ruthie was feeling left out because there wasn't a chair for her and she had to stand. 'I've a right to know what's going on, 'cos after all I am one of the bridesmaids.'

'Ye're too big to sit on me knee, sunshine. And ye're a ton weight!'

'Yer can have my chair – I'll sit on Steve's knee.' Jill was doing herself a favour as well as her kid sister. 'I'm not heavy, am I, love?'

'As light as a feather, sweetheart.' Steve saw his mother pulling a face and decided to pile it on and get her going. 'And me head goes as light as a feather when ye're near me and I can't think straight.'

It had the desired effect. Nellie banged a clenched fist on the table and huffed in disgust. 'Bloody hell! Doesn't it make yer want to puke? Will somebody split the two of them up, please, otherwise I won't be responsible if the dinner I had ends up on Molly's chenille tablecloth.'

'I know exactly how yer feel, Steve.' Phil's eyes were dancing with devilment. 'Doreen's only got to look at me and me mind goes blank while me heart races fifteen to the dozen.'

'That does it! No grooms allowed at any of the meetings!' Nellie's chins were wishing she wouldn't nod and shake her head at the same time. It left them at a disadvantage because they didn't know which way to sway. 'All they've got to do is turn up at the church on time. The women will see to the rest.'

'How the heck can we turn up at the church on time if we don't know the date?' Steve shook his head. 'No, Mam, I'm afraid yer won't get far without the grooms. But me and Phil promise to behave ourselves.'

'Thank goodness that's been sorted out,' Molly said. 'Now can we get on with the business in hand, please?'

Nellie's hand shot in the air. 'Excuse me!'

'D'yer want to go to the lavvy, sunshine?'

'No, I do not want to go to the lavvy!' Nellie looked highly insulted. 'What makes yer think I want to go to the lavvy? I mean,

131

I'm not jumping up and down or crossing me legs.'

'Because we used to put our hand up in school when we wanted to go.'

'Well, ye're wrong, yer see! I put me hand up because I have a request to make before the meeting starts.'

Molly waved her hand. 'Go ahead, sunshine, be my guest.'

'I wanted to ask Doreen if she'd make me a dress for the wedding? Remember, girl, yer made me one when Corker and Ellen got married? A nice dress with a little jacket to match. I can't buy anything nice, 'cos they don't make much in my size. And the one you made looked a real treat on me.'

Doreen puckered her lips and blew out. She was going to have her hands full as it was. Her mam had already put a request in, and although the old lady hadn't asked, she wanted to make a dress for Miss Clegg. Then there were the five bridesmaids. But how could she refuse this woman, for whom she had so much admiration and affection, and who was now waiting for her answer with bated breath. 'I'll do me best, Auntie Nellie. I've already got seven to make, but it depends on how long I've got to make them in.'

'Yer promised me yer'd pack in work when we got married,' Phil reminded her. 'But yer could always leave a week or two before and that would give yer loads of time.'

'Yer didn't tell me yer were packing in work, sunshine!' Molly sounded surprised.

'Everything has happened so quickly, Mam, I haven't had time.' Doreen worked in a factory making parachutes, and now the war was over they were laying people off. 'But I'd be out of a job soon anyway, 'cos the factory will be closing down.'

'It's the same in our place,' Jill said. She worked in the wages office of the Royal Ordnance factory in Kirkby. 'When the war in Europe was over, half the girls left because their husbands were coming home. And they weren't replaced. Now the war in Japan is over, there'll be no need for the factory and I think they'll wind it up soon. But I'm staying on as long as I can so me and Steve can save up.'

'Yer don't have to work, love, I've told yer.' Steve ran his fingers through her long blonde hair. 'I'll be earning enough to keep us and put some aside.'

'Look, can we get a move on?' Molly asked. 'The men will be back from the pub and we won't have even mentioned the weddings! Let's say that Nellie will be getting her dress made, Doreen will pack in work before the big day, and Jill will stay while there's still a job to go to. Now, can I ask the four people involved, when are yer hoping to get married?'

132

'We have been talking about it, Mam,' Jill said. 'And we thought we'd go together to see Father Kelly and fix a date. We were thinking of asking for a Saturday in two months' time, if possible. Would that be too soon for you?'

Molly kept the smile on her face but inside she was groaning. Two months wasn't long to save up the sort of money they'd need to spend. I hope Jack's enjoying his pints, she thought, because he won't be getting any more for a while. 'It's a bit short notice, sunshine, but I think it could be managed.'

'Me and Jill will help out with the money, Mam,' Doreen told her. 'We don't expect you to fork out for everything, it would be too much. One daughter getting married is bad enough, but two together – well, no one could afford that.'

'She's right, girl,' Nellie said. 'It's far too much in too short a time. I vote we all muck in together.'

'Nellie, they're our daughters and me and Jack want the very best for them. Once we have a date, I'll start looking for somewhere for the reception and a caterer to see to the food.' And a good moneylender, she added mentally. If I have to put meself in hock for the rest of me life, my daughters are going to have the best send-off me and Jack can give them.

'I suggest we see the priest first, get a definite date, then we can take it from there. If we all sit down and work out what's what, it'll be much easier,' Phil said. 'I don't know much about etiquette, but I believe the groom pays for the cars and drink. And they see the priest right. So me and Steve will take over the responsibility of seeing to them.' He gave a smile which was tinged with pride and a trace of sadness. 'Aunt Vickie has asked if you'd let her buy the flowers?'

'Certainly not!' Molly said. 'We couldn't let her do that.'

'She wants to, Mrs B., and she'll be upset if we say no. She said she can't get to the shops to buy us a present, and even if she could, she would much prefer to buy the flowers. As she said, giving flowers is a sign of love.'

'Oh Lord!' Molly screwed up her eyes. 'I thought this was one night I'd get through without crying.'

'Knock it off, girl!' Nellie said. 'Ye're going to have to stop this crying lark because every time you start to blubber, yer set me off.'

Molly was spared her tears when she heard the key turn in the front door. 'Here's Jack, so we'll bring the meeting to a close. You four go and see Father Kelly tomorrow night and we'll take it from there.'

Everyone had gone to bed and Molly and Jack were enjoying a last cup of tea before they too climbed the stairs. 'We're going to be hard put to find enough money if they're getting married in eight weeks.' Jack puffed on his Woodbine, a look of anxiety on his face. 'I'll get as much overtime in as I can, but even then we'll never make it.'

'Yes, we will, love, so don't start worrying until yer have to. Something will turn up, it always does.'

'I wish I shared your optimism, love, but for the life of me I can't see it. There's no way we're going to have enough money in eight weeks, it's an impossibility.'

'I thought that meself at first, Jack, but it's not going to be too bad. The cars, the priest and the drink, they're nothing to do with us. And Victoria insists on buying the flowers as her wedding present, so that's a load of our minds.'

'Molly, what about the clothes? Isn't the father supposed to buy the brides' dresses? And I haven't got a decent suit to me name. There's no way I'm going to walk down the aisle in the old one I've got – it's falling to pieces.'

'Let's wait and see, eh? I bet everything turns out fine, and yer'll be walking down the aisle looking a real toff.' Molly thought to take his mind off things or he wouldn't get a decent night's sleep. 'Ay, d'yer know that Fanny Kemp and Theresa Brown?'

Jack raised his brows. 'I wouldn't say I know them, only to wish them the time of day. Why d'yer ask?'

When Molly related what Vera Patterson had told her and Nellie, Jack shook his head in disgust. 'They wouldn't be so wicked, surely? I haven't got much time for the one in number sixteen meself, I don't suppose anybody in the street has. But I can't imagine anyone stooping so low as to tell her husband what she's been up to.'

'They don't come any lower than Fanny and Theresa. They love causing trouble and wouldn't think twice about telling the husband.' Molly knew Jack didn't like her getting involved in neighbours' squabbles, so she thought about it carefully before she told him. 'The poor man's been a prisoner of war for about three years, and Vera said he's in hospital in a bad state. I think he's had enough to put up with, without two meddling women adding to his misery. And the first chance I get I'm going to tell Fanny and Theresa what I think about them and warn them to keep their traps shut.'

'If it was anything else, I'd tell yer to keep out of it. But I agree with yer on this, I don't know how anyone can even think of being so cruel. Don't let it come to a boxing match, though, love, because in my eyes there's nothing worse than women fighting in the street.'

Molly grinned. 'I don't think they'd be soft enough to take

Nellie on, do you? If they did I would be referee and make sure me mate didn't batter the life out of them.' In her mind's eye she could see Nellie rolling up her sleeves ready for battle, and it brought forth a chuckle. 'I've just thought of a way of making money. I could sell tickets! There's not a woman in this street who wouldn't pay to see those two get their just deserts. Nobody likes them.'

Jack's imagination took over. 'I can see Nellie, the hero, with a huge grin on her face as she's carried shoulder high. She'd love every minute of it.'

'Yer might come home one night to find the pair of us laughing the other side of our faces, love. Nellie with her leg in plaster and me with two big black eyes.'

'If that happened, I wouldn't just sit back and do nothing. I'd give Corker a knock and take him with me to see the two husbands. One look at Corker and they'd die of fright.'

'D'yer know the husbands, then?'

'To say hello to, yes, but not to have a conversation with. I see them now and again in the pub, that's all.'

'That's worth bearing in mind. If me and Nellie don't get any joy out of the women, I'll ask you and Corker to have a word with their husbands. If that doesn't do the trick, nothing will!'

'I thought Nellie was suppose to be the crafty one? Ye're not exactly behind the door yerself.'

'How about yer saying I'm crafty in a good cause, eh?'

'And how about you saying that because it's your fault I'm wide awake now, yer'll tell me a bedtime story in bed?'

'Ah, yer poor little thing! What fairy story would yer like me to read to yer?'

'A love story. And I don't want yer to read it to me, I want yer to show me by doing the actions.'

'Oh, aye! And who's the crafty one now, eh?' Molly was smiling as she pushed herself to her feet. 'Come on, big boy, and I'll show yer a real love story.' She reached for his hand and led him towards the door. As she switched off the light, she said softly, 'If Nellie was here she'd say ye're not only a crafty bugger, but a sex mad one into the bargain.'

'Let's call at Victoria's first.' Molly pulled the door closed behind her and led her friend across the cobbles. 'Doreen said she made some sandwiches for her and Phil last night and there wasn't much bread left. I'd hate to think the old lady couldn't make herself something for her lunch.'

Victoria Clegg lifted her net curtain and nodded to say she'd heard the knock and was on her way. She moved very slowly these

135

days and it took her twice as long to get to the door as it used to. 'Good morning, ladies. Ye're out early today.'

Molly jerked her head towards Nellie. 'Me mate's usually late and I'm hanging around waiting for her. But she thought she'd catch me on the hop today and was knocking before I was ready. Bright and breezy she is, too.'

'She's never satisfied, girl. If I'm a few minutes late she gets a cob on, and if I'm early she still finds something to moan about.' Nellie's wink creased her chubby face. 'There's no pleasing some folk.'

Molly's jaw dropped. 'I didn't moan! I never said a dickie bird!'

'Yer don't have to say a word, the gob on yer is enough.'

'I can't help me face, sunshine, I was born with it. And it's funny that ye're the only one that ever complains about it.'

'Now yer heard that for yerself, Victoria. And honest to God, if I never move from this spot, I never complain about anything. My George said I must be the most easygoing person in the world.'

Molly huffed. 'Oh, aye! And when did he say that?'

'Just last night, clever clogs.' Nellie bit on the inside of her cheek, but she couldn't keep the smile back. 'After I'd burnt the egg which was his week's ration.' Her hands held out, she appealed to Victoria. 'It could happen to anyone, girl! I forgot I'd put the egg on to boil until I could smell burning. Of course it was too late then – the ruddy pan had boiled dry and the egg was as black as the hobs of hell.'

Nellie doubled up with laughter and couldn't speak. And although Molly and Victoria didn't know what was coming, they were laughing with her. 'Come on, sunshine, what happened next? Don't keep us in suspense.'

'Wait until I get me breath, girl, 'cos if I laugh much more I'll wet me knickers.'

'Not on my carpet yer won't!' Victoria's eyes were weeping with laughter. These two women had brightened her life for years now and she loved both of them dearly. 'Run down the yard to the lavatory, if yer must.'

Nellie had straightened up and was taking deep breaths. 'Some friend you are, Victoria Clegg, when yer won't even let me wet me knickers in your house! I mean, like, it's not as though I've asked to borrow your knickers to wet meself in.'

If she keeps this up, we'll all want to go down the yard, Molly thought. 'Will yer finish the tale about George's burnt egg, sunshine, please?'

Nellie wiped the back of her hand across her nose, then covered her mouth with it when she coughed. 'Did yer see that, girl? I

136

covered me mouth when I coughed, like the toffs do. So don't ever say I've got no manners.'

'Yes, I saw it, Nellie, and I also saw yer using the same hand to wipe yer nose. Now, I don't know any toffs, but I don't think I'd be wrong if I said that wasn't good manners.'

'Don't split hairs, Molly Bennett! And for being so sarcastic, I'm not going to tell yer what happened after I'd burnt that ruddy egg.'

'I'm afraid yer've got no choice in the matter! Yer don't set foot out of this house until me and Victoria have our curiosity satisfied.'

'Oh, all right, then, seeing as yer twisted me arm!' Nellie was chuckling again. Wild horses wouldn't have dragged her out of the house without her finishing the tale she thought was dead funny. She hadn't thought it funny at the time, like, but she did now. 'When I smelled the burning, I rushed into the kitchen, saw the state of the pan and the egg, and like a bloody fool I picked the pan off the gas ring. The handle was so hot I dropped the lot, pan and egg! I held me hand under the tap until it stopped stinging, then went to sit in the living room to nurse me wound.'

She glanced at Molly. 'Yer'd have been proud of me, girl, yer really would. I was only sorry there was no one in the house to appreciate me acting. Talk about drama queen wasn't in it! Me hand was killing me, but I bore the pain with dignity.' Nellie's bosom was hitched before she grinned. 'Did yer hear that, Molly Bennett? I bore the pain with dignity! That's as good as any of the lah-de-dah sayings you're always coming out with. I thought of it in bed last night and I've been saying it over and over so I wouldn't forget. So there!'

Molly felt like giving her a big hug, but instead she said, 'Nellie, the shops will be closing for dinner in three hours and I don't want to miss them. So hurry things along a bit, will yer?'

Nellie looked at Victoria and tutted. 'Yer'd think she'd paid to come in, wouldn't yer? A free laugh at my expense and she's still not satisfied. Still, if she doesn't get her own way she'll start bawling her eyes out, and we can't have her crying on yer carpet, can we? So here goes. When I remembered I had nothing in to give George for his dinner, I soon sobered up. I threw the pan and egg in the bin and sat wondering what story I could make up that he'd believe. I did think of lying on the couch and telling the family I wasn't well, but I couldn't do that because I was going down to your house for the meeting, wasn't I? And anyroad, I had the kids' dinner to see to. They were having eggs, but they'd all asked for them to be fried. It was only George who wanted his boiled. Anyway, to cut a long story short, I decided to tell the

137

truth. And while my husband was watching the kids eating egg on toast, he got this long tale about how I'd burnt me hand trying to save his dinner. He wasn't a happy man, I can tell yer. He said "I suppose yer were sitting on yer backside instead of keeping an eye on the pan?" I said, yes, I had been taking it easy while I had the house to meself. And that's when he said "Nellie, ye're always taking it easy! Ye're the easiest going ruddy person I know! If yer backside was on fire, yer wouldn't turn a hair".'

Molly nodded. 'He's got a point.'

'Ah, but I was ready for him, girl! I said if me backside was on fire it wouldn't be no good turning a hair, I'd be better turning a cheek!'

'I give up. I don't know how the poor man puts up with yer!' This was Molly's opinion. 'I think he deserves a medal.'

Victoria said, 'Either that, or he has a very good sense of humour and saw the funny side, as we do.'

'Ah, ay, Victoria, have a heart! One egg a week and I burn the bloody thing! My George can take a joke with the best, but I'm afraid he didn't see the funny side at all.' Nellie wagged her head. 'In fact, I'd go as far as to say he was very ratty about it!'

'Well, it didn't seem to have bothered you, yer were all right when yer came down to ours,' Molly said. 'And what did the poor man have to eat after all that?'

'I wasn't bothered, girl, 'cos we made it up before I left the house. I made a pan of chips and he had chips with a slice of the brawn I got for their carry-out. He was over the moon and tucked in like a man who hadn't seen food for a month.'

'Didn't that leave yer short for their carry-out?'

'Yeah, I had to cut corners, didn't I?'

'How d'yer mean, cut corners?'

Nellie's eyes were dancing with mischief. 'I only had enough meat for two, so I had to make it stretch to three. So half of their sandwiches have brawn in, and half are filled with fresh air.'

'The kids might let yer get away with that, but George won't,' Molly warned. 'Not after last night. There'll be no sweet talking him round when he gets in from work tonight, Nellie McDonough, you mark my words.'

'Have no fear, oh ye of little faith. George might come home in a bad temper, but when he sees me all bandaged up he'll be full of sympathy. I'll get waited on hand and foot, just you wait and see.'

Molly shook her head in exasperation. 'But yer hand isn't bandaged up!'

'It will be when we get back from the shops. I went to the corner shop, but Maisie didn't have any bandages, so I'll get one from the chemist's. That's if we ever get to the shops! If you don't stop talking so much, we'll get there just as they're closing.'

'I don't believe I'm hearing this! The older yer get, the worse yer get, Nellie McDonough. And I don't hold with yer telling George a barefaced lie.'

'It's not a lie, girl, I have got a sore hand.'

'Let's see it, then.'

When Nellie held out her right hand, palm upwards, Molly's hand went to her mouth. The flesh on the chubby palm was bright red, and there were at least six blisters. It really looked very sore. 'Oh, sunshine, I'm sorry! Why the heck didn't yer tell me? Just look at this, Victoria, and she never even mentioned it! Yer must have been in agony last night – why didn't yer say something?'

'Oh, aye! The kids were all happy and excited, making plans for their wedding, and yer expect me to hold me hand out and say, "Look what I've got!" No, girl, I wasn't going to spoil things for them. Me hand is sore, it's giving me gyp, but there's no point in making a song and dance about it.'

Victoria had left her chair and was holding Nellie's hand. 'A bandage on its own is no good. What yer want is some ointment on to soothe the pain, a piece of lint to cover it, and then a bandage. And don't leave it uncovered, because those blisters will burst soon and yer'll have to watch yer don't get dirt in.'

'I can't leave a bandage on all the time. How can I do me work and wash dishes with it on? But I will be careful, don't worry.'

'I'll make sure ye're ruddywell careful, sunshine, 'cos I don't trust yer! I'll wash up for yer during the day, then yer family can do it at night. And to hell with the housework, it'll be there when ye're dead and gone. Use yer good hand to give the place a quick dusting and let the rest go to pot.' Molly could see Nellie's brain was working and knew what she was thinking. 'I know what's going through that head of yours. Ye're thinking that when I'm not there yer'll please yerself. But yer can forget that, sunshine, 'cos I'm going to have a word with George and the kids. And I'm going to mark the bandage so I'll know if yer've taken it off. How about that, then?'

Nellie grinned. 'My old ma used to say that good often comes from bad, but I never believed her. I do now, though. I'm glad I burned that ruddy egg, it did me a favour. I'll have you looking after me during the day, and me family waiting on me at night. What more could anyone ask for? I'll be able to sit on me backside all day and get away with it. Oh, lucky, lucky old me.'

'Don't push yer luck, sunshine, and we'll get along fine. But right now we'd better get off to the shops. Which brings us to why we came over here in the first place. Our Doreen said yer were

139

short on bread, Victoria, so would yer like us to get yer a loaf?'

'Yes, please, Molly. A large tin if yer can.'

'I'll do me best, sunshine, but these days yer've got to take what they've got. We'll make the home-made shop our first stop, their bread's the best. And with a bit of luck they might just have some meat pies left. If they have, I'll get as many as I can wheedle out of them, and we'll share.'

Nellie licked her lips. 'Ooh, I don't half love their meat pies. Me mouth's watering at the thought of the gravy oozing out of the slits on the top. I could eat three of those meself.'

'Some hope you've got, sunshine! Yer know there's a long queue there every day, and they ration each customer to one small loaf and two pies. But if they know yer've got a big family, they give yer a bit extra if they can.' Molly kissed Miss Clegg's cheek. 'We'll be back with the spoils as quick as possible. This is one day we won't spend time jangling in every shop, 'cos I want to get me mate's hand cleaned and bandaged before she gets dirt in and it turns septic.'

Nellie followed her friend to the living-room door, and then she turned. Giving a wink that creased her whole face, she said, 'Oh, I'm not half going to enjoy this, Victoria! I've never had servants before, but I've seen them on the pictures. They wear a little white lace thing on their heads and a lace pinny that's not even big enough to wipe yer nose on. If my mate turns up tomorrow not wearing the proper outfit, I'll have to have words with her.'

Victoria's smile turned to a chuckle when Nellie suddenly disappeared from view and Molly could be heard saying, 'I've told yer, sunshine, just don't push yer luck.'

Vera Patterson turned her head and waved when she saw Molly and Nellie joining the end of the queue. 'I'll wait for yer! There's something I want to tell yer.'

Molly nodded before bending down to whisper in Nellie's ear. 'You keep me place, sunshine, while I have a quick word with Vera.'

'What d'yer want to do that for? She said she'll wait for us.'

'Yeah, but she'll be out of the shop by then and it'll be too late. I need to catch her before she gets served.' Molly kept her voice low. 'There's only Vera and her husband, so I'm going to ask if she can get a bit extra for us.'

'Ooh, nice thinking, girl! Yer've got a head on yer shoulders all right!'

If the people thought she was trying to jump the queue, there'd be murder. You took your turn, as they had done during the long years of the war, or it was woe-betide you. So for the benefit of those in front of her, Molly raised her voice. 'Keep me place, Nellie, while I have a quick word with Vera.'

She was only gone about half a minute, and when she came back she nodded to her mate. 'Keep yer fingers crossed.'

Vera passed them without a glance, a loaf of bread tucked under her arm and a cake bag in each hand. Molly didn't want to get her hopes up, but unless she was mistaken there were two pies in each of those bags. And with a bit of luck Vera wouldn't be wanting all four pies.

It was a family confectioners, very popular in the district for the high standard of their bread, pies and cakes. Tom Hanley worked in the bakery with son, Stan, while his wife Edna served in the shop with daughter Emily. It had been a thriving business before the war, but with the food shortages the Hanleys had had to cut right down. They were as fair as they could be with their customers, but as Tom said, he could only make as much as he had the ingredients to work with. So to be fair to each of their customers, they had started their own system of rationing. The shop only opened for half a day because they were always sold out by one o'clock.

Edna Hanley found time to smile when the two friends reached the counter. 'I could do with you two behind the counter raising a laugh. At least while they were calling me fit to burn for not giving them all they ask for, they'd have a smile on their faces.'

'Ay, we'd do that for yer willingly, Edna,' Nellie said. 'And we wouldn't want no money, for it, either. Yer could pay us in bread and pies.'

'Trust you, Nellie McDonough.' This came from Tilly Potter, a woman from their street who was behind them in the queue. 'Always got yer eye to the main chance, you have.'

'Yer know what they say about God loving a trier, Tilly. If yer don't try, then yer don't ruddywell deserve to get!'

Molly gave her friend a dig in the ribs to shut her up. 'There's a queue halfway down the road, Nellie, and this is no time for any of your shenanigans.' She smiled at the woman behind the counter. 'We both want a loaf and two pies, if we can, Edna. And I'm shopping for Miss Clegg, so if she can have the same I'd be grateful.' And so no one would think she was asking for more than her ration, she added, 'Yer know the old lady can't come out herself.'

'Pass yer basket over, Molly.' As she made the order up, Edna asked, 'How is Miss Clegg? She must be getting on now.'

'She'll be ninety-one in a few months. And a nicer woman never walked this earth. We all love the bones of her.' Molly opened her purse. 'I'll pay for the lot and me and Nellie can sort it out later. How much does it come to, Edna?'

'Seven and eightpence altogether.' The basket was passed back and a ten-shilling note changed hands. 'Tell the old lady I was asking about her and give her my love.'

'I'll do that, Edna. Me and Nellie would walk her down one day, slowly, like, but she'd never be able to stand in a queue.'

'I wouldn't let her stand outside.' Edna passed the change over. 'If anyone was miserable enough to complain about a ninety-year-old getting served first, they'd get short shrift from me.' She eyed the waiting customers. 'Aren't I right, ladies?'

Now no one wanted to be thought miserable, so they all voiced their agreement. And as they hadn't been served yet, they weren't taking a chance on being told the pies had now been rationed to one per customer.

'There's Vera, come on.' Molly carried the basket straight, afraid the juice from the pies would spill over. And that would be a tragedy because it was the juice that made the pies so mouth-watering. 'I wonder what she's got to tell us?'

Vera handed one of the bags over. 'Put these in yer basket, Molly, they're red hot. Edna let me have two extra because I said I was having visitors. It's the first time I've asked for extra so she didn't even pull a face. With there only being me and Bill, we don't have the same worries as women like you who have big families to feed.'

'Thanks very much, Vera, ye're an angel. Nellie will pay yer for them, seeing as I've got me hands full.'

This was one time Nellie didn't argue. Her mouth was already filling with saliva at the thought of sinking her teeth into one of the pies. 'Ye're a pal, Vera, and me and Molly will do the same for you one day.' She grinned. 'When you have a big family to feed.'

'The time for me having children passed over thirty years ago, Nellie. Me and Bill would have loved to have had children, but it wasn't to be. It was a bitter disappointment to both of us, but yer can't alter what life has in store for yer. And I tell meself that although we've got none to make us laugh, we've got none to make us cry.'

'That's the best way of looking at it, sunshine,' Molly said. 'Now, me and me mate are going to the butcher's – are yer walking that way?'

'Yeah, I'll walk that far with yer and tell yer the latest about next door as we go.' Vera waited until they'd fallen into step, then said, 'Mavis was sent a travel pass to go and see her husband. Apparently he's been fretting and asking to see her. They say he's not fit to be moved nearer home yet, but a visit from her may aid his recovery. That doesn't sound too good to me, what d'yer think?'

'It's hard to say, Vera,' Molly said, although she also thought it sounded none too good. 'Is Mavis going to see him?'

Vera nodded. 'She was worried about the kids at first, because although her family would have them, they live the other side of Liverpool and the kids wouldn't be able to go to school. Her nerves were shattered when she got the letter and the travel pass, and I felt sorry for her 'cos she really does want to see Frank. She's blaming herself for what's happened to him, says it's God's way of paying her back for her sins.'

'I'm glad her conscience is pricking her,' Nellie said. She saw the look on Molly's face and tutted. 'Don't be looking at me like that, girl, 'cos what I'm saying is true. She's been a selfish, bad bitch, and anyone who says otherwise is a hypocrite. But I agree with yer that her husband shouldn't be made to pay for her sins. And if he does come home, I'll help yer make sure no one digs up the past.'

'Anyway, I've said I'll have the three kids for the few days she's away,' Vera told them. 'There's only one bed in me spare room, but they can all snuggle up together, it won't do them no harm for two or three nights. And I can see they get fed and sent to school every day.'

'That's good of yer, Vera,' Molly said. 'I'd offer to help meself, but we're squashed in like sardines as it is.'

'Mavis was over the moon when I offered, said it was a load off her mind. So she's going to sees about train times today. The hospital is the other side of London, so she's got to take another train from there. It'll mean a whole day travelling, but she said she doesn't care as long as she sees Frank at the end of the journey. Then she can see for herself how he is, instead of worrying herself to death thinking things are worse than they are.'

'Tell her not to be upset by what she sees, Vera,' Molly said. 'She'll probably get a shock when she claps eyes on him, but she mustn't let him see that, no matter what. A smile on her face to show how happy she is to see him, will do him more good than sympathy or tears.'

'I'll tell her what yer said, Molly, and I think she's sensible enough to realise how right yer are. She's got more brains than most people give her credit for.'

Molly glanced along the row of shops and came to a halt outside a chemist's. 'I need some bandage, Vera, so we'll leave yer here. But if yer need any help with the kids, all yer've got to do is sing out.'

'I'll manage, Molly, but thanks all the same. They're not babies

143

any more, the oldest is ten, the youngest six. If I can't cope with them for a few days, I'll throw the towel in.' She turned to walk away. 'Ta-ra, Molly, and you, Nellie. I'll be seeing yer.'

There was a smile on Molly's face when she placed her basket on Victoria's table. 'Not a bad day, all in all, sunshine! We got eight meat pies, the bread we wanted, and I scrounged a couple of extra sausages off Tony the butcher. So you and Phil can have a pie and sausage for yer tea tonight, with mashed potato.'

Nellie was beaming. 'That leaves six pies, so can you and me have one with a round of bread for our lunch?'

'Nellie McDonough, you greedy so-and-so! My three pies are going to be cut in half so all the family can have a share. They'll enjoy that with sausage and mash, it makes a change. But if you're such a glutton yer must have one all to yerself, then yer can sod off to yer own house, 'cos ye're not eating it in mine!'

'Don't you take that tone of voice with me, Molly Bennett! It was us what had to stand in a queue for the ruddy things!'

Molly bent her head so their noses were almost touching. 'Ah, yes, we had to stand in a queue – but whose money paid for them, eh? Not ours, because we don't earn any money. It was Jack, George and the kids, out working all day, who paid for them'

'Bloody hell, girl, ye're too good to live, you are. And I wouldn't eat one of the flaming pies now if yer offered me ten bob! The ruddy thing would stick in me throat and choke me.'

'And that would be the price of yer, sunshine.' Molly moved back and grinned. 'So we'll have toast for lunch, eh, and both families share the pies tonight?'

'Yeah, go 'ed, girl, we'll do that. And I'll have all afternoon to look forward to me dinner.'

As Victoria crossed to the sideboard for her purse to pay for the messages, she was laughing softly. If a stranger had been in the room five minutes ago, they'd have thought the pair were going to knock spots off each other. But then they wouldn't know that these two women enjoyed winding each other up, and they'd never had a real argument in all of their twenty-five years of treasured friendship.

144

Chapter Eleven

Molly pushed her plate away, licked her lips and leaned her elbows on the table. 'Did yer all enjoy that?'

There were murmurs of approval all round. 'Yer can't beat a Hanley's meat pie,' Jack said, to nods from the children. 'I don't care what anyone says.'

'Did they taste all right to yer?' Molly asked. 'I mean, there wasn't a funny taste to them, as though the meat was off?'

There was puzzlement in the glances being exchanged. 'Tasted all right to me, love,' Jack said. 'There was nowt wrong with the meat.'

'Yer shouldn't have eaten it if yer thought it was off, Mam!' Tommy grinned. 'Yer should have passed it over to me because after the lousy food we got in the army, my tummy will accept anything I put down it.'

'Oh, I didn't think it tasted off.' Molly was dying to laugh as the events of the morning flashed through her mind. 'It's just that they were so begrudged I didn't expect them to taste as good as usual. And then there was the curse yer Auntie Nellie put on them.'

'Oh, aye, what's she been up to now?' When Jack leaned forward, the three girls and Tommy followed suit. 'Another of her mad capers, eh?'

Molly started with the early-morning visit to Miss Clegg's, then went right through to her parting with her neighbour. All she left out was the bit about the woman in number sixteen. That wasn't for young ears and would be told to Jack later, when they were alone. 'So when I left me mate, she was sitting in her fireside chair, looking very sorry for herself with her hand all wrapped in bandages.'

'Is it very sore, Mam?' Jill asked, concern written on her face.

'Yes it is, sunshine, she must be in pain. I can't understand why she didn't tell us last night, so I could have cleaned it up and covered it with a piece of sheet or something.'

'But you said she made a joke of it,' Ruthie said. 'How could she laugh if she was in pain?'

145

'Because that's the way she is! I'm convinced that even when she's on her deathbed, Nellie will still find something to laugh at. I told her that, and she said if she dies with a smile on her face, Saint Peter was bound to find her a seat on the front row. "They don't like miserable buggers in heaven, girl, they like happy souls". That's what she said.'

Tommy was convulsed with laughter. 'Oh, that's a smasher! I'll have to remember to tell Rosie that one.'

'I wouldn't tell yer nan, son,' Molly said. 'I've got a feeling she wouldn't appreciate the word bugger being used in the same sentence as Saint Peter.'

'How is Auntie Nellie going to manage the housework with her hand bandaged?' Doreen wanted to know. 'She won't be able to put it in water.'

'Nellie in pain is just as crafty as Nellie not in pain,' Molly chuckled. 'She's worked it out to a fine art. During the day, I do what she can't manage, then when the family come home they take over. I bet yer any money that right now she's sitting there like Lady Muck, nursing her hand while everyone waits on her.'

'Won't she be coming down tonight, then?' Jill asked. 'It won't be the same without her.'

'Of course she'll be down! She'll want to know how yer get on with Father Kelly, and she'd go mad if I was told the news five minutes before her.'

'Why don't we play a joke on her?' Jack asked. 'Me and Tommy could call for her and pretend we've come to carry her down between us.'

'Ooh, yeah!' Tommy was all for it. 'She'll see the funny side of that!'

'Don't kid yerself, son.' Molly sounded very definite. 'She'll tell yer to sod off.'

But Molly was wrong. For when Jack and his son arrived at the McDonoughs', and said they'd come to give her a chair-lift down to their house, Nellie didn't turn a hair. She knew it was a joke, and was bursting with laughter inside, but decided to play them at their own game. 'That's real thoughtful of yer, Jack. Don't yer think so, George?'

George was flummoxed. When he'd opened the front door, Jack had whispered that him and Tommy were going to play a joke on his wife. But they didn't know her as well as he did. And he was both amused and afraid that the joke was going to backfire. Very few people got the better of Nellie, and from where he stood, he reckoned Jack and Tommy were going to be taken up on their offer. Oh, this was something he had to see. 'I agree, love, that it's real thoughtful of them. I'd offer meself, but I don't want to put their noses out of joint.' No, thought George, finding the situation hilarious, but Nellie will probably put their backs out of joint. After all, at eighteen stone, she was no lightweight.

'How do yer intend carrying me, Jack?' Nellie asked. 'Are you making a chair with yer hands like we used to do when we were kids, or are yer going to carry me on one of the wooden chairs?'

Jack glanced at Tommy and raised his brows. He would have felt easier if Nellie had told them to sod off. Instead it appeared the joke was on them. But no, she wasn't serious, she couldn't be! She was just having them on. 'Whichever way yer want it, Nellie! Your wish is our command.'

After pretending to give it some consideration, Nellie then apparently came to a decision. 'I think I'd prefer yer to carry me. I wouldn't want the chair legs to get in yer way and trip yer up, 'cos then we'd have two invalids.' Using her good hand, she pushed herself up from the chair. 'I'm ready when you are.'

When Tommy saw the look of disbelief on his father's face he almost burst out laughing. Oh, how they'd had the tables turned on them. But it was their own fault, they should have known better. 'Here goes, Dad, give us yer hands.'

'Come on, love,' George said. 'I'll help yer so yer don't fall backwards.'

'I'm not going to fall backwards, light of my life, 'cos I'm going to put me arms around their necks.'

When Nellie lowered herself on to the cradle made by their hands, Jack thought his arms were being pulled out of their sockets. And when her arm went around his neck he waited to hear the sound of it snapping.

How Nellie contained her laughter she would never know. But contain it she did. 'D'yer know, it's really comfortable! Much softer than that couch of ours, with the springs sticking in yer backside.'

George decided to take on the role of supervisor. 'Will yer manage to get through the door, Jack?'

'We'll go out sideways,' Jack panted, knowing there was no going back now. They'd carry Nellie to their house even if he and Tommy got killed in the process. 'You lead the way, son.'

'I'll run and knock on yer door,' George said. "Cos you'll never manage it.'

They were in the hall when Lily came tripping down the stairs, dressed ready to go out. 'What on earth is going on?'

Her father gave her a broad wink. 'The lads offered to give yer mam a lift down to the Bennetts', seeing as she's got a bad hand.'

Lily's hand flew to her mouth to stop herself from laughing. I wouldn't miss this for the world, she thought, as she followed their slow and awkward progress. Len will just have to wait if I'm a few minutes late.

George gave a loud rat-tat on the knocker, then stepped back. Never in his life had he seen anything so funny. Nellie was sitting looking like a queen, enjoying every minute of it, while Jack and Tommy were red in the face, bent under her weight.

When Molly opened the door she doubled up. 'Oh, my God, will yer look at the state of them!' Between gasps, she stuttered, 'I did tell yer, but yer wouldn't take no notice of me.'

Molly's laughter brought Jill, Doreen and Ruthie to the door. And their shrieks of hilarity were joined by George and Lily's. The only one who had a straight face was Nellie. And the two men carrying her, of course. They couldn't have raised a smile to save their lives.

'Put me down, yer silly pair of buggers.' Nellie tapped each of them on the shoulder. And when she was lowered, and on firm ground, she shook her head at them. 'That'll teach yer to try and trick an old hand like me.' Then her face creased and her whole body shook as the pent-up laughter erupted.

'Come on in, ' Molly said, 'before the whole street is out to see what's going on.' She beckoned to Jack and Tommy. 'Will you two stop holding hands!'

Tommy squeezed his father's hand. 'We can't, Mam, they're numb.'

'Don't be acting the goat, come on in.'

'He's right, love,' Jack said. 'I've got no felling in me hands. Come down and massage them for us to get the circulation going.'

Before Molly could step down on to the pavement, Nellie drew her good arm back, and then, with all her weight behind it, swung it forward under the men's joined hands, separating them in a flash. 'There yer are, that's better than a massage any day. Much quicker and far less painful.'

'I wouldn't say it was less painful, Nellie.' Jack was beginning to feel better now he knew his arms were still in their sockets and his neck wasn't broken. 'Yer pack a powerful punch.'

'Yer asked for it, yer stupid articles. Massage, indeed! Numb, indeed! The only thing numb is yer ruddy brains! Fancy thinking yer could get away with teaching an old dog like me new tricks.'

'For crying out loud, will yer come into the house?' Molly was getting impatient. 'Or shall I bring the table and chairs out into the street?'

Nellie drew herself up to her full height. 'No need to get sarky, girl, just because your feller carried me in his arms. Jealousy gets yer nowhere.'

'Get in before I shut the door on yer.' Molly noticed Lily hugging her handbag to her chest and smiling. 'Are yer coming in, sunshine?'

'No, Mrs B. I'm meeting Len and I'm late as it is. But I wouldn't have missed that for a big clock. It was the funniest thing I've ever seen.'

'Life is never dull where yer mam is, Lily, yer should know that by now. I know I'd be lost without her.'

'We all would, Mrs B. No one's allowed to have a long face in our house when me mam's around. And our Steve and Paul take after her, so there's never a dull moment. Me and me dad are the quiet ones, we just sit back and let them entertain us.'

'Well, yer can't ask for more than that, can yer? Now you poppy off, sunshine, and don't keep yer boyfriend waiting. Are yer going to the flicks?'

'More than likely, there's not much else to do. Anyway, I'll see yer. Ta-ra for now.'

'Ta-ra, sunshine, enjoy yourself.'

Lily walked quickly, her high heels clicking on the paving stones. She thought about telling Len what had made her late, but dismissed the idea. He wouldn't see the funny side, and would say they were barmy. He certainly hadn't been blessed with a sense of humour, and besides, she knew there was no love lost between him and her mother. She had hoped that would change as he got to know her family better, but the way things were going he'd never get to know them. When he did call for her, he couldn't get out of the house quick enough. And when she suggested it was time she met his parents, he shied away from that, as well. She was going to have to be firm with him, otherwise she'd be walking down the aisle at her wedding a bent, frail, white-haired old lady.

Len moved away from the wall when he saw Lily hurrying towards him. 'Late again, Lily, it's getting to be a habit.'

She looked at him and noted his sulky expression. It's time to start putting my foot down right now, she thought. 'The Bennetts were playing a trick on me mam, and it was so funny I stayed to see how it ended.'

'That's a good excuse, I must say! It seems to me that all your family and friends do is play tricks on each other. They want to try growing up.'

'Not for my money they don't! I wouldn't want them any other way, I love them just as they are. I'd rather see someone with a smile on their face than a scowl.'

'Is that a dig at me?'

'If the cap fits, Len, then wear it! I'm getting a bit fed-up with

149

meeting outside, and that's the truth. Yer won't come to our house and yer won't take me to yours. I'm beginning to wonder whether we're courting for real, or just messing around.'

'I'm certainly not messing around! As far as I'm concerned, you're my girl. I wouldn't have written to yer every week while I was overseas if I wasn't serious, would I?'

'Then why won't yer take me to meet your parents?'

'I will take yer, but just give me more time. I've told yer what me parents are like, they're very strict and they don't like strangers. When I've been settled back at work for a while and have got some money in me pocket, I'll feel more secure and independent. Then I won't care what they say or think.'

'Do they even know yer've got a girlfriend?'

'They must do, seeing as I'm out nearly every night. But they're not the type yer can talk to, so I don't tell them much.' Len scanned the road on both sides then took her arm. 'Come on, let's go in or the big picture will have started.'

Lily pushed his hand away and stood in front of him. 'Yer said yer want more time – how much more time?'

'Another couple of months, that's all.' Len could tell he would have to offer something or he'd be getting his marching orders. 'Then when I'm able to start saving, we can talk about getting married, eh?'

A tiny voice in Lily's head told her she was a sucker for falling for it again. But she was in love with him and ignored the warning. 'OK, a couple of months, Len, but that's all.'

He paid her a lot of attention on the back row of the stalls, with his arm around her shoulders and a hand clasped in his. 'Give us a kiss.' When Lily lifted her head and kissed him briefly on the lips, he asked, 'What sort of a kiss d'yer call that?'

'I want to watch Franchot Tone, he's me very favourite film star. I'll give yer a proper kiss later.'

Len kept her to her word. They were passing an entry when he pulled her into the darkness. 'Yer promised me a proper kiss, so how about it?'

Lily put her arms around his neck. 'Yer can have two for being a good boy.'

The first kiss was warm with just a hint of passion, and Lily felt a thrill run down her spine. But when his lips claimed hers for the second kiss, they were hard and bruising, and his tongue came out to try and force her mouth open. And he moved his hands upwards from her waist to cup her breasts. Lily was startled and used all her strength to push him away. 'What the hell d'yer think ye're doing, Len Lofthouse!'

'I'm sorry, I couldn't help meself. I think about yer in bed every night, Lily, and I can't wait for the day when yer'll be mine. I love yer so much I want to possess yer.'

'What yer want and what yer'll get are two different things, Len! I'm not the sort of girl who is free with her favours, so don't ever dare try anything like that again.'

'I lost me head, Lily, and I've said I'm sorry! I'm crazy about yer, and if yer felt the same way about me, yer'd understand.'

'That's where ye're wrong, 'cos I don't think on the same lines as you. Even if I was madly in love with yer, yer wouldn't get what you're after. The first man that lays a hand on me will be the man who's put a wedding ring on me finger. And if you don't have enough will-power to respect me wishes, then you're not the man for me.'

'I am the man for you, Lily, I swear it! Ever since I laid eyes on yer at the dance in Blair Hall, I knew we were meant for each other. I lost control of meself before and I'm sorry, but it only happened because I love yer so much.'

'I'll let yer off this time, Len, but if it happens again I'll be telling yer to get on yer bike.'

'It won't happen again, I promise.' Len pulled her close and kissed her temple. 'As soon as I've bought meself some new clothes, I'll start saving to get married. Would yer like that?'

Lily believed him because she wanted to believe him. 'Yes, I'd like that very much.'

'We'll have a little house of our own and I'll have you to come home to every night.' In his mind he added, 'A little house as far away from Liverpool as possible.' He led her to the top of the entry, and on the pretext of straightening his tie stopped to glance quickly up and down the main road. Then, satisfied he saw no one he recognised, he took Lily's elbow and they began walking.

Len would have recognised the person who stepped from the darkness of the entry opposite. A person who had watched the couple going into the picture-house and had returned when they knew the second house would be letting out. It was someone with determination and patience, who, keeping close to the wall, followed them to the top of Lily's street. Then, satisfied that after many nights of keeping watch, their mission had finally been accomplished, they turned and walked back the way they'd come.

Molly's eyes and voice were eager. 'How did yer get on with Father Kelly?'

Doreen adopted a haughty air as she flounced towards the table. 'Your two daughters are to be married on the second Saturday in July, at two o'clock.'

'The banns will be read out a few weeks before then,' Jill said, her hand gripping Steve's. 'That's so anyone who knows of any reason why we can't get married, can come forward.' She giggled. 'Steve swears he's never been married before.'

Nellie had been doing some mental arithmetic and gave Molly a dig in the ribs. 'That's about ten weeks off, girl, so it gives yer a bit more breathing space.'

'Father Kelly couldn't fit us in before, 'cos they're fully booked for every Saturday until then. A Friday would have been fine, but that would mean everyone taking a day off work.'

'Yer couldn't expect them to do that, sunshine, not when they're counting their pennies.' Molly felt relieved. It meant they had an extra three weeks to get the money together. 'Now if I'm to look for a hall and caterers, I'll have to know how many people are coming. So as I've got me pencil and a piece of paper to hand, can we start on a list? Nellie, we'll start off with your lot first.'

'Ye know who my lot are, girl, so that's easy. And yer'd better put our Lily's feller down, 'cos I don't suppose we can leave him out.'

'Yer can hardly do that, seeing Lily's a bridesmaid! So altogether it's six for the McDonough family.'

'Don't forget Archie, Mrs B.,' Steve said. 'He invited himself, but I know Tommy would like him to have an official invitation.'

'He'll go down with our lot.' Molly was busy writing. 'With Maureen, that makes eight for the Bennetts, unless I hear otherwise. Oh, and me ma, da and Rosie, that's eleven.'

'There's another one for us, Mam,' Doreen said. 'I'd like Maureen's boyfriend, Sam, to come. After all, we've been friends for years.'

'OK, he's down. Now, there's you and Miss Clegg, Phil, so that's you done.'

'I was going to ask if I could invite one of me workmates, and his wife. I've been with him since the day I started as an apprentice, and he taught me everything I know. He's been like a father to me.'

Molly lifted her head to gaze with tenderness at the boy who had no family to call his own. He had Victoria, whom he idolised, and he'd been welcomed into the bosom of her family, the McDonoughs' and the Corkhills'. They all loved and respected him. But with the best will in the world, they weren't the same as having his own flesh and blood. 'Of course yer can, sunshine. It's your wedding day, isn't it?' Molly licked the end of her pencil. 'What's their names so I can write them down and make it official?'

'Jimmy Cookson, and his wife's name is Myrna. Yer'll like them, Mrs B., they're really nice people.'

'They better had be, lad!' Nellie's chins were aquiver as she shook her head. 'This is going to be a posh do, we don't want no riff-raff coming.'

Molly chuckled. 'Why didn't yer say that before I put your name down? I'm going to have to start me list all over again now.'

Nellie's eyes shot wide open, then slowly narrowed to slits. She couldn't let her mate get away with a crack like that! After all, reputations were at stake here. So squaring her shoulders, and thrusting her bosom forward, she feigned a look of what she thought was indignation. 'Well, the bloody cheek of you!' She raised a hand to bang on the table to emphasise how strongly she felt, and too late realised the hand crashing down was her sore one. Alas, it was too late to stop it and she yelped in pain. 'Damn, blast and bugger it!' Cradling her bandaged hand, and rocking back and forth, she glared at Molly. 'This is all your fault, Molly Bennett! If me hand wasn't so sore I'd clock yer one.'

'Seeing as how I haven't moved me backside an inch off the chair, how d'yer make out it's my fault? I never touched yer flaming hand!'

'Yer didn't have to move yer backside, did yer? It was that ruddy tongue of yours what did it. Wait until I tell my George yer said we were riff-raff! I've a good mind not to let me lovely son marry your daughter after all. I've said all along he was too good for this family.'

Molly noticed Nellie was no longer cradling her hand, and it was lying, forgotten and unloved, on her lap. That pain didn't last long, she thought. 'Ah, yer poor thing! Give me yer hand and let me kiss it better.'

'Yer can kiss my ruddy backside, Molly Bennett, that's what yer can do!'

'I won't if yer don't mind, sunshine.' Molly kept her face straight. 'Yer see, I don't think I could stomach it, not so soon after me dinner. But I don't want yer to think I don't appreciate the offer, 'cos it's a generous one.'

Nellie spluttered. 'Don't think yer can soft-soap me that easy, girl, 'cos you calling me riff-raff has cut me to the quick. It'll take more than a Sayers cream slice to get yer back in me good books.'

'I'm sorry to disappoint yer, sunshine, because me one ambition in life is to be in your good books. But, yer see, I don't happen to have a cream slice in the house.'

'I didn't expect yer would have, girl, I'm not that daft. But we'll be passing Sayers tomorrow when we're out shopping, and I'll let yer mug me to one. I'm not one to bear grudges, I'm too soft-hearted for that.'

Steve snapped his fingers to draw her attention. Knowing what his mam was like for talking, he knew she would talk about everything under the sun except the weddings. They'd be lucky to get the guest list sorted out, never mind all the other details that had to be settled. 'Mam, in case yer've forgotten, we're all sat around the table here to make arrangements for two weddings. And I think yer'll agree they're far more important than your liking for cream slices.'

Nellie's face was a picture of innocence as she spread out her hands. 'Of course they are, son. And I'd be the last one in the world to say any different. So me and Molly will sit as quiet as mice, we won't interrupt yer no more. Just you go ahead and we'll sit and listen.'

'How the hell can I just sit and listen when I'm supposed to be doing a list of guests?' Molly shook her head. 'I need some sort of number by tomorrow, so I can start making enquiries about a hall. It won't matter if the number is not exact, we can always add a couple if necessary, but I need some idea.'

'Calm down, there's a good girl.' Nellie patted her hand. 'If yer keep this up yer'll be worrying yerself into an early grave. And I know yer'd kill yerself if yer died before the wedding, 'cos it stands to sense yer wouldn't want to miss that. Not after yer taking all this time to make the guest list out.'

Molly leaned back in her chair and chewed on the end of the pencil. 'Seeing as yer've got me dead and buried, perhaps you'd like to take the list over in case I conk out before I've got all the names down?'

'No, girl, you carry on while ye're able. Get as much out of life as yer can, that's what I say.' For once Nellie's chins were all in harmonious agreement. 'Start writing like the clappers and yer'll have it done in no time. There's Ruthie's friend Bella and her parents, Maisie and Alec from the corner shop and seven from the Corkhill family.'

Tapping the pencil on her teeth, Molly let her eyes travel around the table at the grinning faces. 'Do any of yer ever get the feeling that yer life is all mapped out for yer? That although yer think ye're in control, some mysterious hand is working yer like a puppet?'

'Sod that mysterious hand malarky, Molly Bennett, and try using yer own,' Nellie said. 'Get writing and put down the names I've just given yer.' She waited until Molly's head was bent over the paper, then caught her son's eye. Her lips doing the most comical contortions, she mouthed, 'How many is that?'

Steve had no idea but made a guess and mouthed back, 'Thirty-four'.

Nellie put a hand to her mouth and coughed in a refined sort of way. 'I think yer'll find that comes to thirty-four.'

Molly grinned. Her mate was absolutely hopeless at adding up. Three numbers were her limit, so there was no way she could have added all these together without using her fingers and toes. No, it was purely a guess, a shot in the dark. 'Is that what you get it to, sunshine?'

'Yes, that's what I get it to.' Nellie raised her brows for her haughty expression. 'Why, what do you get it to?'

'I don't know, I haven't added it up yet. And neither have you! Yer've just plucked that number out of thin air.'

'I have not! I bet yer a tanner that I'm right.' When Molly looked undecided, Nellie pressed her point. 'Go on, clever clogs! Put yer money where yer mouth is.'

'No chance!' Molly threw the pencil down and folded her arms. 'I wouldn't trust yer as far as I could throw yer. If you've got that number right, then someone has helped yer.'

'Yeah, I hold me hand up, girl, I have had help.' The chair creaking was the first indication of the laughter to come. 'Yer know this mysterious hand of yours, what works yer like a puppet? Well, I've got a mystery voice that whispers in me ear. And it was the voice that told me how many guests' names yer've got down. And it told me to have a bet with yer and to put me shirt on it 'cos it was a sure thing.' The creaking became more urgent as Nellie's body shook. 'I told the silly bugger I didn't wear a shirt, so it said to bet my blue fleecy-lined bloomers against your pink ones.'

Everyone around the table was doubled up, and even though Molly was laughing as loud as anyone, the back of her mind was registering the urgent creaking of the chair. She got to her feet and pulled on her mate's arm. 'Come on, sunshine, before the chair falls to pieces. Yer can get back on it when yer've stopped laughing.'

Nellie laid her arms flat on the table and rested her head on them. 'I'm nearly finished, girl, just give me a minute. Yer know what a vivid imagination I've got, well it's working overtime right now and I might as well enjoy meself.' Another loud burst of laughter followed and it was a while before she could get her words out. 'Those bloomers of yours wouldn't go near me, girl, I know that. They'd take one look at me and fall apart at the seams. But I'd like to win them just to see the look on the face of that nosy cow next door when she sees them blowing in the breeze on me washing line.'

It was five minutes before order was restored and the meeting got back on track. 'Right,' Molly said, 'I'll reckon on forty guests in all, 'cos there's bound to be a few more people to invite. Jack's

155

brother went to live in Wales years ago and we haven't seen hide nor hair of him since, but Jack might want to try and get in touch.'

'I haven't got no family, girl,' Nellie interjected, 'only some longlost cousins who I wouldn't know if I fell over them. But George's sister Ethel only lives in Seaforth, and he'll probably think it right and proper to invite her and her husband.'

'I'll definitely cater for forty, then – that should do it.' Molly put the pencil down and stretched her arms over her head. 'Thank goodness that's sorted out. What's next on the agenda?'

Jill put her hand up. 'Me and Doreen have been wondering what happens at a double wedding, mam. I mean, the father usually gives the bride away, but how would me dad manage with two of us? The aisle in the church wouldn't be wide enough for three to walk down, not without a crush, anyway.'

Molly frowned. 'I hadn't thought of that, sunshine. And I know yer dad hasn't or he would have mentioned it. He'll want to give both of yer away, that's only natural. And he'd be the proudest man in Liverpool with a lovely daughter on each arm. But I can see it might cause problems, so we'll have to sit and talk to him tonight and see what he says.'

'I was going to ask Father Kelly,' Doreen said, 'but Phil said it wasn't the priest's job to advise on who does what. So the sooner we get it sorted out the better. Then Phil and Steve can say who they want as their best man.'

Nellie patted her friend's arm. 'There's more to getting married than meets the eye, isn't there, girl? Still, it'll all come out right, you'll see.'

'The hardest thing is trying not to leave anyone out. I feel lousy not asking Rosie to be a bridesmaid, but it's not possible. I mean, yer've got to draw the line somewhere.'

'I've had a word with Rosie about it, Mam, 'cos I felt mean as well,' Jill said. 'But she understands and doesn't mind in the least.' Her pretty face broke into a smile. 'She said, "As long as I'm the bride at me own wedding, then, sure, won't I be the happiest girl in the whole wide world?".'

Three streets away, Rosie and Tommy were sitting side by side. As soon as Bridie and Bob had climbed the stairs to bed, the sweethearts had retired to the comfort of the couch and each other's arms. 'They're all in our house tonight, making plans for the big day.' Tommy kissed the tip of her nose. 'Me mam's going to have her hands full, with two daughters getting married the same day. It'll take some organising, that.'

'Sure, hasn't yer mother got a good head on her shoulders?

There'll be no slip-ups on that day, I'll be bound. And while there's a lot of worry, sure isn't there a lot of happiness as well? She's gaining two sons, and doesn't she love the bones of them?'

'Don't yer wish we were getting married?' Tommy asked. 'I can feel meself becoming jealous.'

'Of course I wish we were getting married, and I'd be telling a lie if I said different. I love yer very much, Tommy Bennett, and I can't wait to become yer wife. But as me mammy would say, patience is a virtue and brings its own reward. Our day will come, me darlin', in a year's time, please God.'

'I'm reckoning on eighteen months,' Tommy said quietly. 'That's how long it will take to save up enough money.'

'Not at all, me darlin'! Would yer not be forgetting that we'll be living here with yer nan and grandad, and won't be needing to buy furniture. Sure, it's more than enough we'll have in twelve months' time.'

Tommy pulled one of her curls and smiled when it sprang back. 'Not for the wedding present I want to give yer.'

'I'll not be wanting a wedding present off yer, Tommy. Sure, aren't you the only present I'll ever need in me life?'

'I was sixteen when yer gave me my first kiss outside this front door. And I was seventeen when I knew yer were the girl I was going to marry. It was then I made meself a promise to give yer this wedding present. And I've never wavered from that promise.'

Rosie's deep blue eyes gazed into his. 'And what is this present yer've kept a secret all these years?'

'That on the day we get married, your mam and dad will be here to see their beautiful daughter wed to a man who adores her.'

The blue eyes filled with tears. She'd been fifteen when she'd left her home in Ireland to find work in Liverpool. Her family couldn't afford to keep her because times were hard and money very short. There were no jobs for young girls in the beautiful countryside of County Wicklow, and a distant cousin of Bridie's had written to ask if the Jacksons would take her in. She'd been lost and afraid at first, not being used to a big city. But she'd soon grown to love her Auntie Bridget and Uncle Bob, and when their grandson, Tommy, fell in love with her, her happiness was complete. But she'd never forgotten her family, and every four weeks she sent them a postal order for five shillings. 'Oh me darlin', there's nothing I'd like better in the whole world. I haven't seen me family for five years and I still miss them. But it's impossible, they couldn't afford to come all the way from Ireland.'

'We'll make it possible, Rosie, I promise yer. We'll put a little bit extra aside each week, in a separate money box, and when the time comes we'll have enough to pay their fares.' Tommy wiped a

157

tear from her cheek with his thumb. 'I want to meet the two people who brought someone as beautiful as you into the world and into my life. And I think . . .'

But his words petered out when his lips were claimed for kisses.

Chapter Twelve

'I can't go for a pint every night, yer know, love,' Jack said as he hung his coat up. 'It's not that I don't enjoy it, mind, but we need to be saving our money.'

'There'll be no need for yer to go again, we sorted most of the things out tonight.' Molly uncurled her legs and slipped them over the end of the couch. Nellie had gone home, Ruthie was in bed and Doreen had gone across to Miss Clegg's with Phil. So with only Jill and Steve in, she had taken the opportunity of putting her feet up for a while. 'We've made a list of guests and so far there's thirty-one. But there's bound to be people we've forgotten, so I'll reckon on catering for forty to be on the safe side.' She slipped her feet into her shoes and pulled a face when a corn on her little toe complained at the discomfort. 'What about your Bill and his wife? D'yer think we should invite them?'

'Molly, we haven't heard a word from him for over twelve years. I wouldn't even know how to contact him.'

'Yer could try writing to the last address yer had for him. But it's up to you, sunshine, you please yourself. It's a long way to come from Wales, and we don't know their circumstances, but it wouldn't hurt to drop him a line. He can always say no if he doesn't want to come, but then again he might be glad to see yer again after all this time. There's only the two of yer left of your family, so it would be nice to keep in touch if only for old times' sake.'

'I'll write the letter for yer, Dad, if yer like,' Jill offered. 'I don't remember him at all, but if he's me uncle then I'd like to meet him.'

'All right, sweetheart, I'll try and root his last letter out.' The more Jack thought about it, the more the idea of seeing his brother again appealed to him. Bill was two years older than him, and they'd always got on well together as kids. In fact, it had been an advantage having an older brother, someone who the street bullies shied away from. 'Yeah, I've got an idea where his last letter might be, I'll see to it as soon as I come in from work tomorrow night.'

'Nellie said George will probably want to invite his sister Ethel and her husband. They only see each other every Preston Guild, so if they come, and your Bill and his wife, it'll be a real nice get-together.'

Jack lit a Woodbine before stretching out in his favourite chair. 'And what other arrangements did yer sort out at this meeting of great minds?'

Steve's dimples deepened when he chuckled. 'Me mam insisted that this wedding is going to be a posh do and there's no riff-raff allowed. We also found she has a great liking for cream slices and that she wants to borrow your wife's pink fleecy bloomers.'

Jack grinned. 'What's this mother of yours been up to now?'

'Don't you tell him, Steve,' Molly said. 'Don't you dare say another word. Every night in bed I tell my feller about yer mam's shenanigans. It's become a ritual we both look forward to. We laugh ourselves silly, then go to sleep with a smile on our faces. Now yer wouldn't want to spoil it for us, would yer, sunshine?'

'I wouldn't dream of it, Mrs B. I shall say no more on the subject. And I'll leave you to open the discussion on how one father can give two daughters away. I don't think Jill will rest in her bed until that's sorted out.'

Jack threw his cigarette stump in the grate. 'Me and George were only talking about that in the pub. Neither of us has ever been to a double wedding and know nothing of the procedure. But I told him there was nothing to worry about because you'd know what everyone had to do, and when.'

'Aye, well yer told him wrong, love, 'cos we haven't got a clue. I think the best thing I can do is call at the church tomorrow and have a word with Father Kelly. It's no good us making arrangements and just hoping for the best 'cos the whole thing could end up a shambles. And I'm not taking any chances on that happening. I want the day to be perfect in every way. One we'll remember all our lives.'

'It will be, Mrs B., so don't be worrying.' Steve pulled Jill closer. 'I'm sure no wedding goes without a hitch, but it doesn't matter 'cos at the end of the day me and Phil will be married to our sweethearts and be the happiest men in the world. And you and Mr B. will have got yerselves two brand new sons-in-law.'

Molly grinned. 'You've always been like a son to me, sunshine. And I've had me eye on yer as a future husband for Jill since yer were toddlers. Ask yer mam to tell yer how we used to sit at that table and discuss what we were going to wear at yer wedding.'

'But yer like Phil as well, don't yer. Mam?' Jill asked. 'He's a lovely bloke and he'll be a good husband to our Doreen.'

'Of course, I'm very fond of Phil! I couldn't wish for a better husband for Doreen or a better son-in-law. But don't forget I've known Steve since the day he was born, and that's a long time.'

'That shouldn't make any difference, love,' Jack said. 'It's not Phil's fault yer haven't known him since the day he was born. He's a decent bloke and yer can't make fish of one and flesh of the other.'

'Don't you dare accuse me of that, Jack Bennett!' Molly was indignant. 'I would never favour one against the other, and you should know that by now. But I can't forget all the memories I have, nor would I want to because they are precious to me. In me mind I can still see Steve picking Jill up when she'd tripped over in the street. She was two, he was three. I can still see him pushing Billy Knox because the lad had pulled Jill's hair and made her cry. And Billy Knox was two years older than him at the time. And the first day Jill started school, I walked one side of her while Steve walked the other, holding her hand.' Molly had become emotional and wiped a tear away. 'Those are memories, Jack, and I treasure them. But I have memories of all me children at different stages in their lives and they are all precious to me. Like the day Tommy's mate Ginger broke next door's window when they were playing footie, and Tommy got the blame for it. I thought Nobby Clarke was going to kill our Tommy that day. And he probably would have done if Nellie hadn't stopped him.'

Jack reached for her hand. 'Come on, love, don't be getting yerself all upset.'

Molly sniffed up. 'It's all right, 'cos the next thing that has always stuck in me mind about our Tommy, was the day Rosie O'Grady arrived from Ireland and me ma and da brought her around to meet everyone. I think they were both about fifteen and our Tommy hated girls. You were all here, so yer know what happened. But I still carry the memory of me son's face when Rosie said he was a fine figure of a man, and asked if he had a girlfriend. His face was as red as beetroot and he told me to shut her up.'

'I remember that, Mam!' Jill giggled. 'It was dead funny, but I couldn't help feeling sorry for Tommy when we all laughed. He couldn't get out of the house quick enough and he always made it his business to go up to Ginger's when he knew she was coming.'

'It's funny how things turn out, isn't it? Rosie knew at first sight that Tommy was the lad for her, but it took a couple of years for it to sink in with him.' Jack's mind was now going back in time. 'She played her cards right, did Rosie. She chased him for twelve months and got nowhere, only the cold shoulder. Then she changed tactics and began to ignore him. That's what did the trick. Oh, and Ginger telling Tommy he fancied Rosie himself

161

and was going to ask her for a date.'

'Yeah, but I don't think yer were told the full story on that,' Molly said. 'Yer see, Ginger plucked up the courage to ask Rosie for a date, but the crafty little minx said she thanked him kindly, but she couldn't go out with him because she already had a boyfriend. And it was when Ginger relayed the news to his mate, that Tommy realised if Rosie was to have a boyfriend he wanted it to be himself.'

Molly looked at the clock. 'Ay, look at the time, we'll never get up in the morning. But isn't it nice to have memories, Jack? Life would be very empty if yer had nothing to look back on. And before we hit the hay, I'll just quickly say that I do have memories of Phil, even though we haven't known him long. I remember the terrible family he was brought up with, through no fault of his own. He walked away from them with dignity and pride, a decent, hard-working lad. I've seen the way he loves and looks after Victoria. He has been her reason for living for the past six years. And I've seen the change he's brought about in our Doreen. I love the bones of her, but she used to worry me because she was the bossy, pushy one. But when she fell head over heels for Phil Bradley, it was the best thing that could have happened to her. She's no longer the loudmouthed girl she was, but is more thoughtful of others and kind and caring. And I believe this has come about through Phil's influence.' She pushed herself up. 'Now, that's me heart stripped bare, except for all the loving memories I have of me darling husband, and those I'll have of Ruthie as she grows older. So confession time is over and it's time for bed. I'll let yer know tomorrow what Father Kelly has to say to put yer mind at rest. But no committee meeting tomorrow, eh? Let me and my feller have a night to ourselves for a change.' She reached for her husband's hand. 'Come on, love, and if I don't fall asleep first, I'll tell yer what Nellie's latest caper was.'

'I won't keep Jill up long, Mrs B,' Steve said. 'Just a quiet five minutes on our own.'

As Molly led her husband from the room, she called over her shoulder, 'Jill, remind me to put Ginger's name on the guest list. We can't leave him out.'

'He's got a girlfriend now, Mam.'

Molly stopped halfway up the stairs. 'The list is on the sideboard, sunshine, so put Ginger down for two.'

Business was brisk in the corner shop and Maisie was kept on the go. As quick as she served a couple of customers, more would come to crowd the tiny shop. They'd run out of bundles of firewood and firelighters, and Alec had gone to pick some up. She hoped he wasn't long because her feet were killing her. What she wouldn't do for a sit-down and a cuppa. She'd noticed a young girl standing at the back of the shop but she was so busy it didn't strike her that the girl didn't move forward to be served. Then when she was down to just two customers, Maisie beckoned to the girl. 'Yer'll never get served standing there, love. Come on over and tell me what yer want. These ladies won't mind waiting because I know you've been here for ages.'

The girl shook her head. 'It's all right, I'm in no hurry. Serve them first.'

Maisie thought there was something strange about the girl. Why would she stand there and let all those customers be served before her? Girls her age would usually push themselves forward. And she wasn't from around these parts unless her family had just moved in. But when yer worked in a corner shop there was little went on in the neighbourhood you didn't hear about. And as far as she knew, there'd been no families moved out or in.

'There yer are, Mrs Ashton, two ounces of corned beef.' Maisie took the coppers from the old lady and threw them in the till drawer. 'See yer tomorrow, love. Ta-ra!'

Maisie waited until the shop door closed then looked across to the only person left in the shop. 'What can I get for yer, love? Yer've waited long enough.'

The girl approached the counter. 'I don't want to buy anything, I just thought yer might be able to help me. I'm looking for a girl who lives around here who goes out with a boy called Lofty?'

Maisie lowered her head to straighten the bags on the counter. It was a move to buy her some time. As soon as the girl mentioned the name Lofty, it rang a bell. Lily McDonough was going out with a bloke called Lofthouse, and the obvious nickname to come from that was Lofty. But it wasn't up to her to tell that to a perfect stranger. 'I couldn't tell yer, love. Yer see, not many young girls come in here, it's usually the mothers. If yer knew the girl's name I might be able to help yer.'

'I don't know her name, just that she lives down one of these streets and goes out with this bloke.'

Thinking there was something fishy about the whole thing, Maisie asked, 'Don't yer know where the bloke lives either?'

'Oh yeah, I know that. He lives in Tetlow Street in Walton.'

'Well, why can't you ask him for his girlfriend's address? Surely that would be the easiest way of finding her?'

'Er, well . . . er, yer see, he's working away from home at the moment or I would ask him. His firm has sent him to Blackpool to do a job there and he won't be home until next week.'

I don't know who you are, Maisie thought, but I know when

163

I'm being told a lie. 'Surely you can wait until next week? It's not a matter of life and death that yer find this girl, is it? I can't help you, and yer'd have a job on yer hands knocking on all the doors and asking for a girl who goes out with a bloke called Lofty. Yer'd get some pretty strange looks, I can tell yer. But that's up to you, it's none of my business what you do.'

The girl, who was of medium height, had a slim figure, short dark straight hair, brown eyes and a healthy complexion. But she had a bold expression and Maisie got the impression that if you got on the wrong side of her she'd lash out with her fists.

Just then, the shop door was pushed open and Alec came through, his two arms full of bundles of firewood. 'Seeing as ye're not busy, will yer give us a hand to carry the stock in, love?'

'Yeah, OK.' Maisie put on a smile for the girl. 'I'll ask around for yer. If I do find the girl ye're seeking, who shall I say is looking for her?'

'Me name's Joan, but she won't know me. Lofty does, though, so tell her to ask him when she sees him.'

Maisie saw her out of the shop before going to help her husband. 'I've just had a very unusual conversation with that young lady. I'll tell yer about it when I've made us a cuppa. But it sounds to me as though, somewhere along the line, there's dirty work afoot.'

Alec took a sip of tea and sighed with contentment. 'Now if only the customers will stay away so we can drink this while it's hot. A good strong cup of tea is better than a pint of beer any day.'

'I'm glad those are yer sentiments, love, because seeing as we only close half an hour before the pubs shut, I'd be left high and dry most nights while you propped the bar up. And that wouldn't make for harmony between us, lover boy.'

'We've been in harmony for nearly thirty years, Maisie, and I ain't about to change me habits now.' Alec put his cup down on top of a wooden crate. 'Now, what's all this about dirty works at the crossroads?'

'It's probably nothing at all, but I've got a feeling that young girl was looking for trouble.' Maisie explained what had been said. 'When she said Lofty, the first person I thought of was Lily McDonough's feller. I've never met him, but Nellie's told me enough about him. To say she wasn't keen would be an under-statement.'

'It does sound a bit queer to me. Are yer going to tell Nellie, or d'yer think it's best to leave things be?'

'If this Lofty feller is Lily's boyfriend, then I know something that Nellie doesn't know, and that's where he lives. But whether

I'll tell her or not remains to be seen. One part of me is saying not to get involved, then another part is telling me I should warn Nellie in case there's trouble coming to her door.'

'I know what I'd do if I were you.' Alec drained his cup, wiped the back of his hand across his mouth and put the cup down before reaching into his pocket for a packet of Capstan cigarettes. 'I'd have a quiet word with Molly first, see what she thinks.'

'I've thought of that, and it would be the best thing because I might be barking up the wrong tree. The trouble is, yer very seldom see Molly without Nellie.'

'Ye're bound to see her over the next few days. I wouldn't let on to Nellie until yer've spoken to Molly, because yer know how quick she flies off the handle. If Molly thinks it's something she should know, then she's the best one to tell her.'

Maisie heard the shop door bell tinkle and got to her feet. 'No rest for the wicked. But it's been an interesting half-hour. Life behind a shop counter may be tiring, and some of the customers so awkward yer feel like strangling them. But there's one thing it never is, and that's dull.' She squared her shoulders, put a smile on her face and walked through to the shop.

When Molly and Nellie walked out of the church into the sunlight, they were both smiling. 'There yer are, girl, all yer little problems sorted out. Five minutes with Father Kelly and all yer fears laid to rest. It was a good idea of yours to come, otherwise yer'd have been worrying yerself sick for nothing.'

'I know – I hardly slept a wink all night. I had visions of the girls' dresses being squashed to blazes, or Jack having to walk behind them, which would have spoilt the whole thing. But that aisle is plenty wide enough for the three of them, and now Father Kelly has explained how the service will go, I'm over the moon.'

'Then let's celebrate and mug ourselves to a nice cream cake to have with the cup of tea you're going to make us after we've done our shopping.'

'Yer can sod off, sunshine, 'cos I've loads to do before I go home. I've got to start making enquiries about a hall, and then find someone to do the catering. But first I want to get to Hanley's before they sell out. I'd rather have their bread than any of the big shops'. It might be a penny or so dearer, but the smell of fresh baking alone is worth that.' Molly's arm was tired trying to steer Nellie in a straight line, so she pulled clear. 'You're a dead weight on me arm, sunshine, so let's see if yer can walk straight without my help.'

'Well, swap over and I'll link you!'

'No, let's swing our arms for a while and we can walk faster.'

Nellie jerked her head and tutted. 'I dunno, the next thing is yer'll be wanting me to race yer to Hanley's.' She spied a familiar figure and nudged Molly. 'There's Vera Patterson up ahead. She's probably going to the cake shop as well.'

Molly quickened her pace. 'Come on, let's catch her up. I've been wondering how she's managing with the kids from number sixteen.'

'If you think I'm going to break into a run, girl, then yer've got another think coming. I know me limits, and trotting along like a horse is outside of them.' The chubby face creased into a smile. 'I'll tell yer what, girl, if I started to run me legs would move but me body would stand still. So yer'd look a bit of a nit running along with just a pair of legs at the side of yer. I reckon yer'd be at Hanley's before me tummy and me bust caught up with yer.'

Molly had a strong desire to give her friend a hug. But yer didn't do things like that in the middle of a main road. 'Ah, God love yer! I wouldn't leave you on yer own, sunshine, not for no one. We'll just take our time and stick to a pace that ye're comfortable with.'

'I know yer've got a lot to do today, girl, so if it would help yer get around a bit faster, I wouldn't mind yer giving me a piggy-back.'

Molly chuckled. 'Oh, aye, ye're not soft, are yer? The next thing, yer'll be asking me to buy yer a whip so yer can gee me along.'

'Yeah, like Tom Mix! I've always fancied meself riding the prairie on me faithful steed, rescuing women what have been kidnapped by the Indians.'

'Blimey, sunshine, I thought I had a good imagination but yours knocks mine into a cocked hat! For the life of me I can't see you sitting astride a horse, riding the prairie in search of women what have been kidnapped by the Indians.'

'Neither can I, girl, but talking about it has passed the time away, hasn't it? Here we are, outside Hanley's and there's Vera at the back of the queue. So yer wouldn't have gained anything by running after her hell for leather.'

Three women had joined the queue by the time the friends arrived, but they all lived locally and knew each other by sight. So they didn't object to Molly talking across them. 'How have yer managed with the kids, Vera?'

'They've been as good as gold, no trouble at all. In fact, me and Bill have enjoyed having them and we'll be sorry to see them go. It's a nice change to have company.'

'When is Mavis due back?'

'Tomorrow, supposed to be. At least, that was the plan when

she went away. But I imagine it depends on how she finds things down there. We'll just have to wait and see. I did tell her not to worry though, because an extra day or two won't matter to me.'

'It's good of yer to have the children, Vera.' Nellie would never change her mind about the woman she'd always called the fly turn, but her children couldn't help what their mother was. That went for her husband as well, the poor bugger. 'There's not many would have taken three kids in, like you did.'

Molly tutted. 'Just listen to hard-hearted Hannah! Yer make out ye're as hard as nails, Nellie McDonough, when I know ye're a real softie. Are yer trying to tell me you wouldn't have taken the three kids in if they didn't have anywhere else to go?'

'No, I'm not saying that, girl.' Nellie shuffled forward as the queue moved. 'What I'm saying is, yer could have counted on me to stand shoulder to shoulder with you when you offered to take them in.'

'Take no notice of her, Vera, she makes out she's a real tough guy. The trouble is, she watches too many gangster films. My heart-throbs are Cary Grant and Robert Taylor, but me mate's hero is Edward G. Robinson. Haven't yer ever noticed that she even walks like him? All she's short of is a shoulder-holster with a gun in.'

Nellie saw the funny side and tapped the woman in front of her on the shoulder. 'See this, Missus?' She pressed a finger into her mountainous bosom. 'Well, this isn't what it seems, yer know. Oh no, I've got a pistol stashed in there in case an Indian comes to try and kidnap me.'

The woman laughed. 'He'd have to bring the whole tribe with him, queen, 'cos it would take more than one brave to carry you off.'

The queue had moved forward again and Vera was now inside the shop. 'I'll let yer know when there's any news, Molly.'

'OK, sunshine, and don't forget – if yer get stuck, give us a knock.'

When they reached the counter, the woman in front of them pointed to Nellie and told Edna Hanley, 'Watch this one, she's got a gun down the front of her dress.'

Edna studied Nellie for a few seconds before the laughter burst. 'No, she hasn't got no gun down there. Two cannonballs, yes, but never a gun.'

'Oh, very funny, I must say!' Nellie put on her hard-done-by expression. 'Ye're only jealous 'cos yer've got no bust. Flat as a ruddy pancake, yer are. And because yer've insulted me, I don't want yer two meat pies, yer can keep them. Stick them where Paddy stuck his flaming nuts.'

'What meat pies are they, Nellie?'

'The two I was going to buy off yer. But I'll hang on to me money instead.'

'I haven't got two meat pies, Nellie.'

'Of course yer have! I've just seen your Emily put two in a bag for that woman.'

Edna was made-up with the lively exchange. It brightened the day for her and was in contrast to the constant moans of women who wanted more than the Hanleys could give. 'Yes, I saw that, Nellie, but I can't take the pies back off the woman, she wouldn't like that.'

'Look, there's another woman getting two!' Nellie's voice was shrill. 'So yer have got pies, yer see. Yer can't pull the wool over my eyes.'

'I'm not trying to, love. But I don't know what all the fuss is about when yer've said yer don't want any pies. She did say that, didn't she, ladies?' Everyone in the shop was in agreement, and Edna also noticed that every face had a smile on it. That very seldom happened in these days of rationing. And all because of one little fat woman who had been blessed with the ability to bring laughter and smiles wherever she went.

Nellie spotted Molly being served by the shopkeeper's daughter, Emily, and a bag with the juice already seeping through, was being handed over. 'Well, I'll be buggered! How come me mate can have pies, but me, who should have been served before her, doesn't get a look in?'

'I can't make yer take two pies when yer've told me yer don't want any. I mean, I can't force anything on me customers.'

Nellie drew herself up to her full four feet ten inches, and gave a sharp shake of her head. 'Yer could coax me. I'm not unreasonable and always open to offers.'

Edna chuckled. 'Two pies and a loaf, is it, Nellie?'

'That's it, girl! And could yer put the pies in two bags so I don't get the juice running up me sleeve?'

Molly had been served and was watching the procedure with more than a little pride. How lucky she was to have Nellie for a mate.

Edna came down the counter and picked up a tin from the rack. 'She's a corker, is Nellie. I wish there were a few more like her.'

'I wish there were a lot more like her! The world would be a much happier place.' Then Molly had a thought. 'Ay, Edna, yer know me two daughters are getting married soon, and I've got to book somewhere for the reception. Can yer recommend anywhere?'

168

'Well, I know they say self-praise is no recommendation, but what's wrong with our room upstairs.? We haven't done much for years because of the war, but before that it was used nearly every week.'

Molly's eyes were wide with interest. 'I didn't even know yer had a room here. I thought the upstairs rooms were yer living quarters.'

'The ones over the shop are, but above the bakery is just one big room. It's not large enough to cater for a hundred guests, but it'll seat fifty in comfort.'

'That would suit us fine.' Molly could feel her tummy stir with excitement. But it seemed too good to be true, there had to be a catch in it. 'Do yer have to come through the shop to get to it?'

Edna shook her head. 'There's a door at the side of the shop that leads up to it. Yer probably haven't noticed 'cos it doesn't get used much, except by courting couples. I haven't got time to take yer up there now, but why don't yer come down about three o'clock and have a look around. If it's not suitable then yer haven't lost anything.'

'Thanks, Edna, I'll do that.'

Nellie sidled up. 'Yer mean we'll do that. You ain't going anywhere without me, girl, 'cos don't forget that as mother of one of the grooms, I have certain rights.'

Molly could see the shopkeeper was itching to get back to the customers who were muttering about being kept waiting. 'Me and my shadow will be back at three, Edna, so we'll see yer then.'

Nellie waddled out of the shop after her friend. 'Ay, it looks as though yer've hopped in lucky there. Ye're a jammy bugger, you are.'

'I'm keeping me fingers crossed that it's suitable, sunshine. It would be a load off me mind if it is. So close to home, too!'

'I might as well have a bite to eat in yours, eh, girl? Seems daft to go home and then have to come out again at three o'clock.'

Molly stopped in her tracks. 'Yer don't miss a trick, do yer? What would yer say if I told yer I wanted to put me feet up on the couch for half-an-hour?'

'I'd think that was a good idea, girl! I know we can't both get on your couch, but I wouldn't mind putting me feet up on your Jack's chair. And I'd be as quiet as a mouse, so if yer wanted to close yer eyes for the half-an-hour, I wouldn't stop yer.'

'D'yer know what me biggest nightmare is, Nellie? That when all me children are married and left home, you'll move into me spare room.'

'What! Yer'd expect me to sleep at the back of the house? No fear! If you want me to come and live with yer, girl, then I'd expect no less than the front bedroom.' Their shoulders shaking with laughter, the two friends linked arms and made their way to the butcher's. If their luck hung out, they might be able to coax Tony into giving them something they could make a pan of stew with for the dinner.

Edna slipped the key out of the lock and flung the door open. 'I keep the place dusted and the windows clean, but it needs a thorough good going-over. So yer won't be seeing it as it will look if yer decide it's what yer want. I'll lead the way upstairs.'

Molly's first impression was of a room flooded with light. It ran from the front of the building to the back, so had windows at both ends. There were trestle tables stacked against one wall and chairs against the other. 'It's nice and bright, Edna, and seems plenty big enough.'

'It would look a lot different on the day, with the trestle tables placed as yer wanted them, with nice white cloths and vases of flowers in the centre of each. Usually they are set out like three sides of a square, with the bride and groom's family seated at the top table, and guests on tables that run down the sides. That way, everybody can see each other and they don't have to keep turning around.'

Nellie, whose eyes were everywhere, pointed to a corner. 'What's under those sheets, girl?'

'Come and I'll show you.' Edna led the way across the room to where Nellie had pointed, and whipped off two sheets to reveal a piano and a gramophone. 'Most people like a bit of music at a wedding.'

'Oh, I think it's just the job.' Molly had a good feeling about this room. With the sunlight streaming through the windows, it looked light and welcoming. 'Don't yer think so, Nellie?'

'I think it's the gear! We'll not do any better than this, girl.'

'No, I don't think we will.' Molly was hugging herself. 'How would I go on about the catering, Edna – any ideas?'

'We could do the catering, Molly, but yer know how tight things are, so we'd need help. It's a summer wedding, so a nice boiled ham salad wouldn't go amiss. The salad itself we could manage, but not the boiled ham. That is something yer'd have to come up with yerself. We could make the tables look really attractive, with plates of small meat pies, sausage rolls and a selection of iced fancy cakes. And of course there'd be wine glasses and serviettes.'

'It sounds so marvellous, I feel like pinching meself to make sure I'm not dreaming. I can't wait to tell the girls.'

'Molly, I think yer should ask the girls, not tell them. Their

170

ideas might be a lot different to yours and mine. Let them see the room and leave it up to them. If they like it, then we can go ahead and sort out the catering. If it's not what they had in mind, then there's nothing lost and yer can look elsewhere. I certainly won't be offended.'

'Would it be all right if they come tonight, the brides and the grooms? Yer see, I'd like to get it settled and off me mind.'

'Yeah, that's fine. But don't come with them, Molly, let them come on their own. Tell them to ring the shop bell and I'll be waiting for them. I'll bring them up here and then leave them to have a good look around without being embarrassed.'

'If they don't like this, then it's just a pity about them,' Nellie mumbled. 'They'd be hard pressed to find anything better.'

'Don't you dare have a go at your Steve as soon as he comes in from work, Nellie, or I'll clock yer one,' Molly warned. 'Like Edna said, they should have some say in where they have their reception. So not a word until they've been and seen for themselves. D'yer think yer can manage to hold yer tongue for that long?'

'That's asking a lot, that is, girl! If I don't exercise me tongue every few minutes, me brain starts to worry.'

'What brain, Nellie? You never told me yer had a brain.'

'There's a lot of things I haven't told yer, Molly Bennett! I mean, after all, we've all got our little secrets.'

Edna was smiling as she covered the piano and gramophone. It would be a luxury to stand and listen to these two, but she felt guilty because she'd left her husband cleaning the bakery and preparing everything for his five o'clock start the next morning. Emily would be helping him in her own way, but she was only a young girl and didn't know the meaning of elbow grease. 'Come on, ladies, your families will be in from work before yer know it. I'll see yer tomorrow and yer can tell me what the brides have decided. Because it will be the brides who have the say, the grooms won't get a look-in.'

'They'll be too busy thinking about the wedding night. They'll get a look-in then, all right.' Nellie had that mischievous twinkle in her eye which Molly recognised only too well. It was time to make their exit while she still knew where to put her face.

'Come on, Tilly Mint, out we go.' Molly led her friend to the top of the stairs. 'You go first, sunshine, so I'll have something soft to land on if I fall.' She stood for a while to make sure Nellie was using the banister, then looked back over her shoulder. 'Thanks, Edna, we'll see yer tomorrow. Ta-ra for now.'

Chapter Thirteen

Molly watched the four young ones as they walked down the street laughing and joking. Then before closing the door she crossed her fingers and said softly under her breath, 'Please, please, come back full of praise.'

'What it is to be young, eh, love?' Jack lifted his eyes from the *Echo*. 'Seeing them takes me back a bit.'

'Yeah, it doesn't seem like more than twenty-five years since we were talking about getting married. Time certainly flies over.'

'Mam, the hem of me gymslip is hanging down.' Ruthie lifted her leg to show the uneven hem. 'If I change into me old skirt, d'yer think yer could stitch it for me tonight, ready for school tomorrow?'

'I haven't got any navy-blue cotton, sunshine, so yer'll have to run up to the corner shop for a reel.'

'Ah, ay, Mam!' Ruthie pulled a face. 'I promised to go over to Bella's for a game of Ludo, and if I don't go now I might as well not bother 'cos yer'll be knocking on her door and telling me it's time for bed.'

'I'll slip up for yer, Mam,' Tommy said. 'I can be there and back in five minutes.'

'No, I'll go meself.' Molly had visions of Maisie telling her son she didn't have navy-blue cotton, only white. And Tommy would take it, not knowing any different. One reel of cotton was the same as any other to him. 'If ye're going round to see Rosie, I'll walk to the corner with yer.'

Ruthie looked relieved. 'I'll change me skirt before I go over to Bella's, Mam.'

'OK, I'll have yer gymslip ready for yer to wear tomorrow. But you be back in the house by nine at the latest. D'yer hear?'

The young girl's eyes rolled to the ceiling. Anyone would think she was a baby, instead of a twelve-year-old going on thirteen. 'I hear yer, Mam, I hear yer.'

Tommy was grinning as he stepped on to the pavement. With a wide sweep of his hand, he bowed from the waist. 'It is my pleasure to escort you, Madam.'

'Go on, yer daft ha'porth,' Molly said, loving it. He was really handsome, was her son. And he had a nice nature to go with it. Being the only boy, she'd probably miss him more than anyone when the time came for him to leave the nest.

Just then their neighbour's door opened and Phoebe joined them on the pavement. 'Ye're looking very nice, Phoebe,' Molly said. 'Have yer got a date?'

'Only with one of the girls I work with.' Phoebe's smile was shy. 'I don't know where we're going yet, probably to the flicks.'

'No boyfriend on the scene, then?' Tommy asked.

'No.' Phoebe blushed. 'I don't go anywhere to meet boys, and anyway I'm too young to be really interested.'

'Yer want to try going to dances,' Tommy said. 'Yer'll meet plenty of lads then, and with your looks they'd be queuing up to dance with yer.'

'Come on!' Molly wanted to get the skirt done and out of the way before the gang came back from the Hanleys'. 'We're going your way, so we'll walk up together.'

But they only got as far as the McDonoughs' house before being joined by Paul. With a smile on his face, his hair slicked back and his dance shoes tucked under his arm, he was all ready for a night out. 'Well, fancy bumping into you lot!'

'I only came out to go to the corner shop for a reel of cotton,' Molly told him. 'But it looks as though I'll have a procession behind me by the time I get there.'

Tommy chuckled at his mother's exaggeration. 'Three people hardly constitute a procession, Mam.'

'Well, yer know what I mean.' Molly eyed Nellie's youngest son. 'And where are you gadding off to, Romeo?'

Paul's grin was full of devilment. 'I haven't made up me mind yet, Mrs B. I don't know whether to honour Blair Hall with me presence, or Barlow's Lane.' He fell into step beside them. 'It's like this, yer see. There's a couple of crackin' girls go to Blair Hall, but Barlow's Lane has got a sprung floor and it's smashing to dance on.'

'My God, if that was all I had to worry about in the world, I'd be laughing sacks.' Molly came to a halt outside the corner shop. 'Anyway, this is where me and our Tommy bid yer farewell. I'm going in the shop and Tommy's going round to me ma's. So you can play the gentleman, Paul, and escort Phoebe up to the tram stop.'

'No, there's no need!' Phoebe stepped back, her face the colour of beetroot. 'I'm in no hurry, I've got plenty of time. You go on, Paul, and I'll walk at me leisure.'

'I wouldn't dream of leaving a young lady to walk on her own.'

Paul changed the dance shoes to his other arm before cupping her elbow. 'We'll walk to the tram stop together.' Before they were out of earshot, Molly heard him say, 'Yer look very nice, Phoebe, where are yer off to?'

The girl's answer was lost to mother and son standing on the corner. But the look on Molly's face wasn't lost on Tommy. 'Mam, forget about it, 'cos they're as different as chalk and cheese.'

Molly blinked rapidly with surprise. 'What are yer on about, sunshine?'

'I can read yer like a book, Mam! Yer had that soppy look on yer face and I know that in yer mind yer were matchmaking.'

'Was I heckerslike! It's coming to something when I can't watch two of me neighbours' children without being accused of marrying them off!' Then Molly grinned. 'It would be nice, though, wouldn't it?'

'I know yer like everything to be neat and tidy, Mam, but yer'd be wasting yer time with Paul and Phoebe. They are definitely not cut out for each other. He's very outgoing and loves a good time, and she's just the opposite, quiet and shy.'

'Stranger things have happened, son.' Molly tilted her face. 'Give us a kiss in case I'm in bed when yer get home.

'I hope yer have good news about the room over Hanley's. Once the hall and catering are booked, yer'll feel easier.'

'Yer said a mouthful there, son.' Molly lifted the latch on the shop door. 'Tell me ma I'll be round to see her and me da tomorrow, and I'll give her all the news then.'

There were no customers in the shop and Alec was alone behind the counter. 'An empty shop, Alec? My God, you and Maisie will never get rich at this rate.'

'We're glad of the breather, Molly. Honest, we've both been on the go all day. That doesn't mean we're rich, though, Mrs Bennett – I'd hate yer to get the wrong idea.' Alec grinned. 'Maisie said there was sparks coming from her feet with running all day. She's in the stockroom with her feet on a sack of spuds. Go through and have a word with her.'

'I haven't got much time, Alec, I only came for a reel of navy-blue cotton. Our Ruthie's gymslip needs sewing for school tomorrow.'

Alec glanced towards the stockroom. 'Maisie's been waiting for yer to come in, she's got something to tell yer.'

'If it's good news, Alec, I'm all for it. If it's bad news, I don't want to know.'

'We don't know about that, Molly, but I think yer should hear what the wife has to say.' He lifted the hinged part of the counter to let her through. 'We found it strange, but you might think we're reading too much into it.'

'Yer've got me curious now.' Molly made her way through to the back room where Maisie was reading the *Echo*. 'My God, just look at the state of you! Ye're a lazy so-and-so, Maisie Porter, moaning 'cos yer've got to work fifteen hours a day! It should be a doddle to a young slip of a girl like you.'

Maisie folded the paper and put it on top of a wooden crate. 'Park yer backside on there, Molly, and take the weight off yer feet.'

'No, I'll stand, sunshine, 'cos I haven't got long. What's the big mystery?'

'There might not be anything in it, but I thought I'd tell you to see if yer think I should mention it to Nellie.' Maisie went on to tell her about the young girl and the conversation they'd had. 'I know Lily's boyfriend is called Len, but with a name like Lofthouse he's bound to get Lofty off his workmates. And like I said, there was something in the attitude of this young girl. She certainly wasn't backward in coming forward, I can tell yer.'

'And she said he lived in Walton?'

'Yeah, in Tetlow Street. And if I was to give an opinion, Molly, I'd say the girl was trouble with a capital T. When I asked her why she didn't ask this Lofty where his girlfriend lived, she stared me out as bold as brass and said she couldn't 'cos he was working away from home this week.'

Molly looked puzzled. 'And she told yer her name was Joan?'

'That's right. According to her, the girl she was looking for wouldn't know who she was, but she could ask Lofty, 'cos he knew her.'

Molly rubbed her fingers in a circle on her forehead, as though to clear her mind. 'I'd say to leave things and see if anything further comes of it, except for one thing. Well, I suppose yer could say two things, really. One is that it would be stretching the imagination a bit too far to say it was just a coincidence she happened to pick on this street out of the dozens of streets around here. And the other is that I can't stand the feller. I wouldn't trust him as far as I could throw him.'

'D'yer think one of us should mention it to Nellie?'

'Will yer let me think about it tonight, Maisie? Yer know what Nellie's like for flying off the handle. It could cause murder between her and Lily, and I wouldn't want that. Especially as it might turn out to be a storm in a teacup.'

'I think ye're right, Molly, and I hope it does turn out to be a storm in a teacup. I had to tell yer, though, to get it off me chest.

I didn't like the girl, I had a bad feeling about her. But I could have misjudged her.'

'I'm glad yer told me, sunshine, so I can keep my eyes and ears open. I feel sorry for Lily, 'cos she must think a lot of Len to put up with his sulks, and knowing none of the family have any time for him. But if there's something in his life she knows nothing about, it would be better for it to come out now before she marries him.' Molly picked up the evening paper and handed it to Maisie. 'Here yer are, sunshine, you keep yer feet up and have a read. I can't hear much noise coming from the shop so Alec can't be busy. I'll get me reel of cotton and go home and sew our Ruthie's gymslip. I'll see yer tomorrow. Ta-ra.'

As soon as Molly put the key in the door and heard the excited chatter, her heart jumped for joy. 'Yer like it, then?'

Her two daughters ran towards her and put their arms around her. 'Mam, it's ideal,' Doreen said, laughter in her voice. 'Much better than we expected.'

Jill couldn't wait to have her say. 'Mrs Hanley was very nice and explained how the room would look on the day. And her husband is going to make a wedding cake for us.'

Molly's legs were weak and she groped for a chair. 'Go 'way! Yer mean yer've ordered a cake, too?'

The girls nodded. 'We're only having one between us, 'cos it would be daft to have two. So he's making a three-tier one.' Doreen was so excited she couldn't keep still. 'He's going to ice it and decorate it, the whole works.'

Jill gently pushed her sister aside so she could get a word in. 'Mr Hanley said it was hard to get hold of dried fruit, Mam, so we're having a sponge one. I don't mind because I don't like fruit cake anyway.'

Molly looked across at the two boys sitting at the table. They looked so happy anyone would think they'd just heard they'd been left a fortune by an unknown rich relative. 'Are you both happy with the arrangements?'

'Never been so happy, Mrs B.,' Phil said. 'Yer couldn't have found anywhere better.'

'Over the moon, Mrs B.' Steve's dimples told of his delight. 'Over the moon.'

Molly turned to Jack, who was overjoyed at the way things had turned out. 'Not a bad day's work, eh, love?'

'Not bad? I think yer've achieved more in one day than yer expected to in a week. Just think! Between yer, yer've booked the hall, sorted the catering out and the wedding cake's been ordered!' Jack was feeling very proud of his wife, and his two lovely

177

daughters. 'They were the most important things, so now yer can slow down and take things in yer stride.'

'There's another thing we've decided tonight, Mam,' Jill said. 'Steve is having Paul as his best man.'

'Oh, that's nice, sunshine. I bet Paul's cock-a-hoop!' Molly raised her brows at Phil. 'Have you decided who you're having, son?'

'The person I would really like, because he's always been so good to me, is Mr Corker. But I don't know whether he'll be home for the wedding.'

'Yer can ask him in a couple of days 'cos he's due home near the end of the week. I saw Ellen in the shop today and she told me.'

Phil's face lit up. Corker was his hero, the person for whom he had so much respect and admiration. 'Oh, that's the gear! Will yer all say a little prayer tonight that he'll definitely be home for the wedding and agrees to be me best man?'

'He'll be home for the wedding, son, yer can be sure of that,' Molly said, nodding her head for emphasis. 'His actual words were, "Nothing on earth could keep me away. Seeing the girls walk down the aisle on Jack's arm is a sight I'll not miss, even if I have to jump ship".'

Steve pushed his chair back and stood up. He patted Phil on the shoulder and said, 'It looks as though ye're going to get yer wish, and I'm glad for yer. Now me and Jill had better go and bring me mam up-to-date or she'll give us the rounds of the kitchen because she had to wait ten minutes after Mrs B. to find out what's going on.'

Molly grinned. 'I bet she's had her nose to the window. And she'll have counted the seconds, never mind the minutes. So go and put her out of her misery and tell her I'll see her in the morning.'

Steve was holding Jill's hand and they were in the hall when Jill remembered something. 'Eh, Dad, did yer think on where yer'd put that last letter from Uncle Bill in Wales?'

'Yeah, I'll root it out in a minute and yer can write to him tomorrow.'

Jill looked pleased. 'I hope he can come – I'd like to meet him.'

'Don't build yer hopes up, sunshine,' Molly said. 'It's a good way from here and would cost them a few bob in fares. They might not be able to afford it.'

'We'll never know if we don't ask, Mam.' Jill allowed herself to be pulled through the front door, shouting over her shoulder, 'I'll drop them a line tomorrow.'

'We'd better make tracks as well.' Phil set his chair neatly under the table. 'It's getting near Aunt Vickie's bedtime.'

Doreen gave her mother a hug as she passed. 'Yer've done well, Mam, and me and Phil are grateful.'

'And proud,' Phil reminded her.

'Oh yeah, we're dead proud of yer.'

'It was pure luck that I mentioned to Mrs Hanley that we were looking for a hall. Or, as me mate said, "Ye're a jammy bugger, you are".'

The two sweethearts were giggling as they walked out, their joined hands swinging between them. 'You're a jammy bugger getting me for a wife, Phil Bradley.'

'Uh uh! It's you that's a the jammy bugger 'cos I picked yer for me wife.'

Molly and Jack grinned at each other. 'This makes up for all those lean years, when we didn't have two ha'pennies to rub together.' Molly was feeling emotional. 'I'd go through them all again just to see the children as happy as they are now.'

'Those years weren't so bad, love,' Jack said. 'We might not have had any money, but we had things all the money in the world can't buy. Things more precious than pounds, shillings and pence. And that's health, happiness, friends and laughter.'

Molly's face creased into a grin. 'Ye're getting very sentimental all of a sudden, aren't yer, sunshine? The next thing, yer'll be writing me romantic poems.'

Jack uncrossed his legs and stood up. He cupped his wife's face and gazed into her eyes, remembering her as she was when she was young and as pretty as a picture. And how lucky their three daughters were to have inherited her good looks. 'The day I stop feeling romantic about you, Molly Bennett, will be the day I give up on life.'

'That won't be for another forty years, I hope, love, 'cos we've got too much to look forward to. I want to be holding your hand while we watch our grandchildren growing up, and then their children.' She puckered her lips. 'Give us a kiss and then get that letter for our Jill. Where did yer put it, by the way?'

'I think it's with some other papers in a box I put in the loft. I'm hoping so, anyway.'

The word loft brought to mind the name Lofty, and the incident with the girl in the corner shop. 'Sit down a minute, Jack, while I tell yer something. I'll make it quick before our Ruthie comes in.' Molly repeated word for word what Maisie had told her. 'I don't know what to think. I mean, if it had come from anyone else I might pooh-pooh the idea. But Maisie isn't a jangler, nor is she stupid. What do you make of it?'

'Without being there and seeing the girl for meself, it's hard to

179

say. But I agree with yer that Maisie isn't one to talk just to hear the sound of her own voice. And after all these years working in the shop, dealing with all types of people, she should be a good judge of character by now. As for telling Nellie though – well, that's something yer'll have to make up yer own mind about. And if I were you, I'd give it some careful thought because yer might just put yer foot in it.'

'Yeah, I'll mull it over for a few days. I've got enough on me mind to be going on with. I'm made up that the hall and reception have been booked, but I haven't a clue what it's all going to cost. I'll find out tomorrow, though, when I see Edna Hanley. I'll ask her to write everything down so we're not caught on the hop when the time comes to pay. The cost of the hall, the catering, wedding cake and flowers for the tables.' Molly pulled a face. 'And when I've got a list of the damages, you and me can sit and worry about where the money's coming from.'

'We'll make it, love, so don't worry. By hook or by crook, we'll make it. But won't the Hanleys want a deposit?'

'I can manage that 'cos I've got enough saved up. When the war in Europe was over, I knew it wouldn't be long before we had two weddings on our hands. So every week since then, I've been putting some money by. Some weeks it was only five bob but others I managed ten bob or even a pound. So I should have enough for the deposit.'

Jack looked surprised. 'Woman, you never cease to amaze me.'

Molly winked and clicked her tongue. 'That's the way to keep a man on his toes. Never tell him everything, always hold something back that yer can amaze and mystify him with. Some women say the way to a man's heart is through his tummy, but that's an old wives' tale. I bet any man would rather see a female performing The Dance of the Seven Veils than sitting down to a good roast dinner.'

Jack leaned against the door jamb, his smile wide. 'I'm one of those men, so where d'yer keep yer seven veils?'

'Ah well, yer see, love, I'm keeping them as a last resort. As soon as I think yer interest is on the wane, I'll bring the veils out. But as that isn't likely to happen right now, I suggest you go and find the letter while I sew our Ruthie's skirt.'

'So, everything in the garden's rosy, eh, girl?' Nellie's swaying hip knocked Molly a few inches nearer the gutter. 'Our Steve never stops smiling and I'm surprised his face didn't stick like that.'

'It's better than having a face on him like a wet week, so don't be moaning.'

'Oh, I'm not moaning, girl, far from it! As I said to him last

180

night, the mother of the girl he's marrying is a jammy bugger, and a bit of good luck might rub off on him.'

By this time Molly was walking along the edge of the kerb and she came to a halt. 'Nellie, ye're pushing me into the road!'

'Oh, for crying out loud, don't start that again! If yer end up under a tram this time, I'm going to tell your Jack straight, he's not to take any grapes into the hossie 'cos I'll only get accused of eating them.'

'Look, sunshine,' Molly said, with infinite patience. 'Let's start all over again. I'll walk on the inside, and you walk on the outside.'

'Suit yerself, girl, it doesn't make no difference to me.'

And indeed it didn't. They'd only gone twenty yards before the sleeve of Molly's coat was brushing against the windowsills of the houses they passed. 'I give up!' She bent her elbow and showed her friend the dirty marks. 'See that!' Then she turned and pointed in turn to the nearest six houses. 'I've just cleaned every one of those windowsills with me coat.'

Nellie put on her angelic expression. 'Well, I'm sure the women will be very grateful to yer, girl. But yer hadn't ought to have done it, 'cos look at the mess yer've made of yer sleeve.'

Molly didn't know whether to laugh at her friend's comical expression, or cry at the mess she'd made of her one and only decent coat. In the end the happy events of the day before made her decide that laughter was on the menu today. 'Listen, sunshine, yer can drop that Little Girl Lost look 'cos it doesn't cut no ice with me. And when we get home, you're the one who's going to sponge me sleeve and get the dirt off.'

'If you say so, girl,' Nellie said meekly. But her thoughts were anything but meek. Inside she was laughing her socks off. 'If it'll make it easier for yer, why don't we just walk without linking arms, eh?'

'The best idea yer've had all day.' Molly put her basket on her left arm. 'We'll get along a lot quicker.'

Nellie took note and put her basket on her right arm. 'Come on, girl, or the day will be over before we do anything.' Now the two baskets were bumping against each other, and with Nellie having the added benefit of her wide hip to use as a ledge for her basket, which added to her pushing power, she had Molly up against the wall in no time. 'If I didn't know yer better, girl, I'd swear yer were drunk.'

Molly dropped her head, pinched the bridge of her nose and counted to ten. Then she looked up and saw Nellie shaking with laughter. For once, the little woman's cheeks, chins, bosom and tummy were in harmony and moving in an upward direction.

181

'Sod it,' Molly said under her breath. 'If yer can't lick 'em, join 'em.' So she let the laughter rip until tears were rolling down her cheeks. 'Oh dear, oh dear, oh dear.' She felt in her pocket for a hankie, found she didn't have one, so wiped her eyes with the back of her hand. 'They reckon if yer laugh too much yer'll cry before the day is out. So I'm warning yer, Nellie McDonough, if anything crops up to spoil my feeling of well-being, I'll hold you responsible.'

'That's all right, girl, me shoulders are wide enough to take it.'

'So are yer ruddy hips! If it wasn't for them we'd have been at Hanley's by now and I'd know how much money I've got to find in the next nine weeks.'

Nellie shook her head sadly. 'You don't appreciate me, do yer, girl? I spend all me life thinking of ways to put a smile on yer face and I get no thanks for it. Me hip will be black and blue by now, and it's sore into the bargain. But I don't mind the pain, not when it's for me best mate. I just wanted yer to feel happy, and strong enough to stand the shock when Edna Hanley hands yer the estimate. If yer don't faint, or start bawling yer eyes out, then my suffering will not be in vain.'

'Nellie, me heart bleeds for yer.' Molly's mind was racing to find something that would match what her friend had said. Then it came, like a flash of lightning, causing her to feel very pleased with herself. 'Never in the field of battle, has anyone had a more true and loyal comrade, ready to lay down their life if necessary.'

'Ah, ay, girl, don't be getting carried away now. A laugh is one thing, but laying down yer life is getting serious. I'd have to have words with my feller before agreeing to that.'

Molly stood aloof now, her nose in the air and her two hands holding the basket in front of her. 'That is the difference between us, you see.' Speaking as posh as she knew how, she looked down on Nellie. 'While I am prepared to laugh at your jokes, you are not prepared to lay down your life for me. Now we know who the true friend is.'

Just at that moment a woman from the top of the street came by, and it was obvious from the sly glance she gave that she'd heard Molly's words. She would have walked on, but Nellie was in one of her mischievous moods and this was a chance too good to miss. 'Hello, there, Milly! In case ye're wondering why we're standing here like two lemons, I'll tell yer. Yer see, my mate has joined an amateur dramatic society, and she asked me to listen to her saying her lines. Just to get a bit of practice in, you understand.'

Milly didn't understand, but she wasn't going to say so. 'Fancy that, now!'

While Molly stood with her mouth gaping, her friend went on, 'She's not half good, too! I'm definitely going to see the play when it's on. Would you like to order some tickets, Milly, for you and your feller?'

'If yer let me know when it is, Nellie, I'll think about it.' Milly knew, like everyone else in the street, that it was wise to take everything Nellie said with a pinch of salt. But it was best not to take any chances, so the poor woman had to think of an excuse. 'Mind you, to be truthful, it's not something me and my feller go in for. So I don't think we'll bother, if yer don't mind.'

'It's your loss, girl!' Nellie called, as the woman made her escape. 'She's better than Bette Davis any day.'

Molly found her tongue. 'Yer've gone too far this time, Nellie McDonough. Yer've made a flaming holy show of me.'

Nellie wasn't the least bit put out. She thought the whole thing hilarious. 'No, girl, I've made a holy show of meself, and I couldn't care less. If Milly was daft enough to believe a word I said, then she wants her ruddy bumps feeling. And if you didn't see the funny side, they yer'd better go back home and see if yer've left yer sense of humour on the table.'

'I haven't left nothing on the table, clever clogs! I distinctly remember picking me sense of humour up and putting it in me pocket. So there!'

'So yer did think it was funny, then?'

'I thought it was bloody hilarious, sunshine, one of yer best stunts.' The two women smiled at each other and Molly jerked her head. 'Come on, let's get cracking. And when we get home, over our cup of tea, I'll practise some more of me lines on yer.'

'Ye're too good to me, girl! Yer'll be spoiling me.'

The laughter around the table had the rafters ringing. 'An amateur dramatic society?' Jack was pressing at the stitch in his side. 'How does she think all these things up?'

'God alone knows,' Molly said. 'Every day is something different, and it's been like that for the twenty-five years I've known her. But the funniest thing today was Milly Crossen's face. Talk about a picture no artist could paint. She couldn't get away quick enough, and she legged it down the street as though the devil was on her heels. In fact, given a choice, I think she'd rather have had the devil on her heels than Nellie. The lesser of two evils.'

'You're lucky, Mam,' Tommy said. 'Yer've got yer own comedy show every day.'

'Yeah,' Doreen grinned. 'I think you should pay Auntie Nellie.'

'Don't tell her that, for heaven's sake! Every morning when I open the door to her, she'll be standing there with her hand out.'

Jill put her knife and fork down on her plate before pushing it aside. 'Mam, yer said yer had some good news for us but wouldn't tell us until we'd eaten our dinner. I've just finished mine and I can't wait any longer.'

'Ruthie and Tommy, come on, hurry up. I know yer would have all been finished ages ago if I hadn't started telling yer about Nellie, but once I start on her there's no stopping me.' Molly saw that all knives and forks had been laid down and began to reach for the plates. 'Let's get these out of the way and we'll have a nice clear table. Stack them up in the kitchen, girls, and I'll wash them later.'

When they were all seated, and five pairs of eager eyes were on her, Molly took a piece of paper from the pocket of her pinny. 'I think the Hanleys are giving us a very good deal. We have to supply the ham for the salad, but they'll supply everything else. That includes all the food, the table decorations and flowers et cetera. It works out a twenty-five bob a head, and that price includes the use of the hall.'

There were murmurs of surprise and approval. 'That is a good deal, love,' Jack said. 'Yer couldn't fall out with that.'

'I couldn't get over it,' Molly said. 'I thought it would be a lot more. Edna said it would have been if we'd been having a hot dinner. But it'll be July, no one would expect a hot dinner.'

'What about the cake, Mam?' Doreen asked. 'Has she given yer a price for that?'

'No, they want to talk to you first about how big yer want it. But Edna said it won't be too dear because of being sponge. She guessed between five or six pounds, depending on the size of each of the three tiers.'

'Will yer be able to manage all that money, Mam?' Jill asked. 'Because me and Doreen would help yer out.'

'I know yer would, sunshine, but this is something me and yer dad want to do. You and Doreen are seeing to the bridesmaids' dresses, Miss Clegg's buying the flowers, the boys are paying for the cars and drink, so there's only the reception left! We'll manage fine, so don't be worrying. If I get stuck, I'll sing out.'

Later, when they had the house to themselves, Molly and Jack were able to discuss finances without having to sound as though everything in the garden was rosy. 'If we'd had a little more time, there wouldn't have been a problem,' Molly said. 'An extra few weeks and I'd have been laughing sacks.'

'How do we stand now?'

'Well, the reception for forty people is fifty pounds. I had twelve pounds saved, which I told yer about, and I gave Edna ten pounds today as a deposit. So that leaves us owing her forty.'

'We should be able to manage that,' Jack said. 'There's nine pay days before the wedding.'

'You need a new suit, shirt and shoes, love! I'm not having you letting the side down. I want my husband walking down that aisle looking like Gentleman Jim, with a beautiful daughter on each arm. And I'll settle for nothing less.'

Jack sighed. 'I'd forgotten about clothes. You'll be needing a decent rig-out, being the mother of the brides.'

'Don't worry about that, sunshine, 'cos I fully intend to look the part. Doreen's making me dress, so that won't cost very much. But I want a real posh hat, a ruddy big one, and that'll cost more than a few bob.' Molly sat forward and smiled into his face. 'Me and Nellie have talked about this wedding for donkey's years. How we were both going to wear hats as big as cartwheels. I think George has talked me mate into something smaller, but my heart is still set on a big hat.'

'Then you shall have one, 'cos yer deserve it. Look, love, I'll not go near a pub for the next nine weeks, and I'll cut down on me ciggies. If I do that, and if the overtime keeps coming in, I'll be able to give yer at least an extra ten bob a week. More if I possibly can.'

'Yer've no need to cut down on yer ciggies, sunshine, a working man is entitled to some pleasure in his life. But any extra cash yer can hand over I'll be grateful for. I'll be cutting corners meself to save a bob here and there. Every little helps, as they say.'

'What about me getting a good second-hand suit? That would cut down the cost.'

'Forget it! The fifty-bob tailors do good suits, no one will be any the wiser.' Molly clasped his hand. 'With your good looks, everyone will have their eyes on you, not on the tailor's name inside yer jacket. Ye're still the best-looking feller down our street.'

Jack's free hand covered hers. 'When yer look at me like that, love, all I can think of is why don't we have an early night in bed?'

'It's only a quarter to ten.'

'So what! Ruthie's in bed and she's the only one we've got to worry about these days. The others can let themselves in.'

Melting brown yes locked with vivid blue ones. 'OK, yer talked me into it.' Molly kept her smile back as she ran her hand down the front of her dress. 'Mind you, I'm not a bit tired so I won't be able to sleep.'

Jack put his arm around her waist. 'Sleep was the last thing I had in mind.'

Chapter Fourteen

'I wonder who that can be?' Molly put the iron back on the gas ring before looking through to the living room. 'I'm not expecting anyone, so it can only be one of the neighbours on the cadge. Be an angel and open the door for us, Jack, save me leaving my ironing.'

'Yer know I'm not one for gassing to neighbours.' There was a rustling of paper as Jack pushed the *Echo* down the side of his chair. 'If I'm not back in ten minutes, come and rescue me.'

Molly grinned as she pressed the iron over the piece of damp cloth covering the crease in Tommy's trousers. 'The size of him and he wants me to rescue him.'

'Someone to see yer, love,' Jack called. Then to warn his wife who the visitor was, he said, 'Sit yerself down, Maisie.'

Molly immediately thought of the girl and the name Lofty. And as she laid the iron down safely, she muttered under her breath, 'I wasn't expecting to hear any more about that, I thought it was all a flash in the pan.'

Maisie was still standing. 'I won't sit down 'cos we'll be closing in half-an-hour and my feller will go mad if he's left with all the clearing up.'

'Sit on the arm of the couch, if yer don't want to make yerself too comfortable,' Molly said. 'Yer'll make me feel guilty if I sit down and you're standing to attention. Besides, yer make the place look untidy.'

'Oh, OK, but only for two minutes. I only called to tell yer that girl was in the street again about an hour ago. I saw her passing the window and Alec went outside to make sure I wasn't mistaken. There might be nothing in it, but I still have this feeling about her. She's after someone and I wouldn't like to be that person when she finds them.'

'Did Alec see where she went?'

'He said she just walked down to the main road, but she was looking closely at the houses as she went.'

'I don't know what to think.' Molly stroked her chin. 'If only we knew someone who lived in Tetlow Street, we could find out if

187

Len and Lofty are the same feller.'

'I don't know what yer'd gain by that, love,' Jack said. 'If his name's Lofthouse he's bound to be called Lofty, especially by his workmates, anyway. But there's nothing wrong in that – it doesn't mean the lad's done anything wrong.'

'I know that, Jack, I don't need yer to tell me. By the same token though, it doesn't mean he's as pure as the driven snow! Apart from Lily, not one in Nellie's family like him. And I believe yer'd be hard pushed to find one in our family who likes him.'

'I only know the lad by sight, I've never spoken to him,' Maisie said, 'so I can't pass judgement. But I thought I'd let yer know about the girl being in the street again, just in case it turns out it is Nellie's daughter she's looking for.'

'It's good of yer to be concerned, Maisie, and I'll have a little think about it.' Molly's mind went to her iron which would be going cold, and she got to her feet. 'I've sorted the wedding reception out, as yer know, so me mind's a bit clearer now.'

'I've done what I thought was right, Molly, so it's up to you what yer do.' Maisie turned towards the door. 'I'll get back or I'll have a moaning husband on me hands.'

'I'll see yer out.' Molly followed her down the hall. 'Have yer heard that Corker's ship's due in tomorrow? He's one person I'm always happy to see.'

'Ye're not the only one,' Maisie laughed. 'Young Gordon was in the shop before and he seemed to grow a couple of inches with pride when he said his dad was coming home.'

Molly's hand was on the door ready to close it. 'They idolise him and it's no wonder. He's a man and a half, is Corker.'

'Yer'll not find anyone to disagree with yer.' Maisie began to walk away. 'I'll see yer tomorrow, Molly. Ta-ra.'

Molly went straight through to the kitchen to put the iron back on the gas ring, then popped her head around the door. 'Yer wouldn't know what to think, sunshine, would yer?'

'I think the whole set-up is a mystery, love. I haven't said anything before because it's really none of our business, but doesn't it strike you as queer that Lily doesn't know where he lives? She was going out with him before he went in the army, so she must have known him over two years. Yer'd think she'd have met his family by now, and know all there is to know about him. It's a funny how-d'yer-do for a courting couple.'

'Yer can say that again! I never say a word to Nellie 'cos I know she's worried sick about Lily – which is only natural seeing as she's her only daughter. If it wasn't for the fact I can't go anywhere without her, I think I'd be paying a visit to Tetlow Street and doing a bit of detective work. I could always ask in one of the local shops if they know the family. I could say they were old neighbours of mine I was trying to get in touch with, and while I knew they lived in Tetlow Street I couldn't remember the number.'

'Don't try it, love, 'cos yer might take on more than yer can chew.' Jack ran his fingers through his mop of dark hair. There were a few grey hairs at the temples now, but they suited him. 'What would yer do if Mrs Lofthouse was standing next to yer in the shop when yer asked? Yer'd have a hard job talking yer way out of that!'

'No I wouldn't,' Molly chuckled. 'I'd either take to me heels and run like the clappers, or come straight out and say her son was courting me best mate's daughter.'

'Ye're going to have me worried to death! Promise me yer won't do anything so stupid, love?'

'Yer've no need to worry because I wouldn't do anything like that unless I had Nellie with me. I'm not brave enough to do it on me own. So I'll promise yer I won't do anything stupid on me own, but I won't promise not to do it with her. Because if the time comes when I think there's something she should know, then I'll tell her. And if she wants any help doing a bit of detective work, I'll be right beside her. Because, Jack Bennett, we both know full well that she'd be the first to come to my aid if necessary. She's a true friend, is Nellie, and has always been there for me. And I'll be there for her.'

'OK, I get the message.' Jack grinned. 'Why didn't yer just tell me to mind my own ruddy business?'

'Now, that wouldn't be a nice way to talk to me husband, would it? Him what I love with all my heart and soul.'

'What about yer body?'

Molly tutted. 'Now ye're getting greedy. And anyway, what about our Tommy's trousers? I started them twenty minutes ago and I haven't done one leg yet!'

Jack dropped his head in his hands in a dramatic pose. 'Now ye're telling me I'm not even as important to yer as one leg of our Tommy's trousers. Oh, woe is me.'

'Ah, yer poor thing! Never mind, dry yer eyes and when I've finished me ironing I'll kiss yer better.' Molly disappeared for a few seconds, and when she reappeared, she was brandishing the iron. 'But there's no early to bed tonight, sunshine, so get *that* idea right out of yer head.'

'What the heck are yer doing here this time of the morning?' Molly's hands went to her hips as she stared down at Nellie. 'Is yer clock fast, or something, 'cos it's only just turned half nine!'

'Listen, girl, the only fast thing in our house is me! And if yer

189

rubbed the sleep out of yer eyes yer'd see that I'm not dressed for visiting. I've only come to borrow a couple of rounds of bread 'cos I've run right out.'

'Yer mean yer've had no breakfast yet?'

Nellie hesitated, wondering whether to tell a fib or not. Then she went all virtuous and decided she stood more chance of getting in God's good books if she was honest. 'I had one round, that's all that was left. And my tummy would be complaining in no time if I had nothing to eat until dinnertime.' She narrowed her eyes as she gazed up at her friend. 'If ye're thinking of refusing me, I think yer should know the pitfalls to that! When my tummy gets hungry it also gets very angry. And it rumbles so loud it sounds like thunder. So we could be standing in a shop, or even walking down the street, and suddenly there'll be this loud clap of thunder and everyone will run for shelter thinking a storm's on the way. And when they found out it was me what was making the noise, yer'd be dead ashamed to be seen with me. Yer know what a delicate disposition yer've got.'

Molly knew when she was beaten and lifted up her hand. 'OK, yer've talking me into it. But yer ain't getting in me house, not this time of the morning, or I'll never get me work done. So stay there and I'll fetch the bread for yer.' When she turned to walk, there was a smile on her face. And when she spoke, it was supposed to sound like sarcasm. But after over twenty-five years of friendship, she should have known better. 'I don't suppose yer'd like me to butter it for yer?'

'Ooh, would yer? I didn't expect that, girl, it's very good of yer.'

'You can just sod off, Nellie McDonough. It's bad enough giving yer a cuppa every morning and wasting time gabbing. I'm not feeding yer as well, so yer can get lost.'

Nellie had a knowing look on her face when she folded her arms and turned her head. 'Did yer hear that, Corker? That's how me so-called friend treats me when no one's around.'

Molly was suspicious. It might just be a leg-pull and her mate would have the laugh on her. On the other hand, though, it could be true because the gentle giant was due home today. So she inched closer to the edge of the step and poked her head out. When she saw him walking towards them just three doors away, she jumped down to the pavement and ran towards him. 'Corker! Oh, it's lovely to see yer. A sight for sore eyes, that's what yer are.'

Corker dropped his seaman's bag and welcomed her with open arms. Lifting her up in the air, he twirled her around. 'And it's lovely to see you, me darlin'. Sure, yer haven't changed a bit, ye're still as pretty as ever.'

'I'm keeping me eye on you two,' Nellie said. 'And if yer kiss on the lips I'm going to snitch to Jack and Ellen.'

'Put me down, Corker, 'cos she would too! She's run out of bread and wants a couple of rounds to keep her going until we go to the shops. You stand and have a natter to her while I cut a couple of slices.'

'That's all right, girl. Ye're bound to be inviting Corker in for a cup of tea, seeing as he's come home to an empty house, with Ellen at work and the children at work or school. So I might as well eat me butties in your house.'

Corker's head fell back and his throaty chuckle filled the air. 'Nothing's changed, has it? The day I left, you two were going at each other hammer and tongue. I wouldn't be surprised if it was still the same argument!'

'Huh!' Nellie's bosom was hitched and she adopted her haughty expression. Well, as haughty as a four foot ten woman can give while gazing up at a six foot five man. 'Yer must think we lead a very dull life, Jimmy Corkhill. Well, for your information, me and me mate change our argument every day, don't we, girl? In fact, sometimes three times a day.'

'But we only ever come to blows once a day, Corker,' Molly said. 'I'd hate yer to think that me and Nellie are always rolling our sleeves up to knock spots off each other.'

'I'd not be thinking that in a million years, Molly, me darlin'. Not about two sweet, gentle, ladylike women as yerselves.'

Nellie touched his arm. 'Before I invite yer into Molly's house for a drink, I've got a bone to pick with yer. And I'm going to stand on the top step to do it so me eyes are on a level with yours. That way yer don't have an advantage over me.' Nellie waddled to the steps, held on to the wall for support, and when she was standing in the hall, she turned to face him. 'How come, Corker, that every time yer come home yer tell Molly how pretty she is, but yer never say a dickie-bird to me?'

Blue eyes twinkled in the weatherbeaten face as the big man stroked his beard. 'I didn't think yer needed telling, Nellie. I thought yer knew how pretty yer are.'

Every part of Nellie's body grew in stature, except her chins. They were on the alert to see which way they were going. 'Now that's very nice of yer, Corker, and I'm beholden to yer. I won't tell Ellen what yer said in case she gets jealous. So yer've no need to worry, I'm not a clat-tale-tit like someone I know who is standing not a million miles away from us right now. And she's got such a miserable gob on her, I'm surprised the cat hasn't packed its bags and made for pastures new.'

Corker's bushy eyebrows shot up. 'Have yer got yerself a cat, Molly?'

191

'Have I hellslike! Take no notice of her! Don't yer think I've got enough to put up with, with her? And has she ever told yer that she got a cat once, and it left home after a week because she was giving it a dog's life!'

The howls of laughter reached the ears of Miss Clegg, and she came to the window to watch. She had no idea what had been said to make the three people on the opposite side of the street double up with laughter, but it was infectious and she laughed with them. And when she returned to her rocking chair she was still smiling and the day seemed brighter.

Molly wiped her tears away with the corner of her pinny. 'A good laugh is better than a kick up the backside any day, isn't it, Corker?'

'I miss you two when I'm away. Oh, we have many a laugh on the ship, but it's not quite the same. Watching and listening to you, is like sitting in the Astoria laughing me head off at Laurel and Hardy.'

Nellie, who had taken over tenancy of Molly's front step, her frame filling the doorway, said, 'Come on in, Corker, and I'll tell yer a few jokes while me mate is making yer a pot of tea and some sandwiches for me.'

'If you don't get down off me step, Nellie McDonough, I'll drag yer down. And as for sandwiches, well, yer can forget it. Yer asked for a few slices of bread and that's what yer'll get. And yer'll take them home to eat. I want to tell Corker how the plans are going for the wedding, and with your mouth going fifteen to the dozen, I wouldn't be able to get a word in edgeways.'

Nellie wasn't going to be put off. 'If you give me enough to eat, me mouth will be full and I won't be able to talk. So there!'

Corker was smiling as he picked up his seaman's bag by the drawstrings. 'I'd give in if I were you, Molly, 'cos ye're flogging a dead horse.'

'I can't afford to keep her, Corker! I haven't got six in me family, I've got seven! And me mate seems to forget everything's on ration. I'm sure she thinks I'm a magician who can pull half-a-pound of butter out of thin air.' But Molly knew she might as well talk to the wall. If Nellie made up her mind she was staying, then nothing would shift her. 'Would yer kindly move aside, Nellie, and let me in me own house?'

'If yer didn't talk so much, girl, we'd be sitting down at your table enjoying a nice cup of tea by now. And I'd have a plate of dry bread in front of me. Not that the thought of dry bread appeals to me, but yer won't hear me complain. I'll grin and bear it.'

'Mrs Woman, yer've got until I count to ten to move yerself.'

192

Nellie turned and walked down Molly's hall, calling over her shoulder, 'Come in, Corker, and make yerself at home. Yer can put yer feet up on the mantelpiece if yer like.'

'What would yer do with her?' Molly asked, mounting the steps.

'Enjoy her, Molly.'

'Oh, I do, Corker, I really do. But it doesn't do to tell her or she'll be getting big-headed.'

'Yer seem to have everything in hand, Molly,' Corker said, after being filled in with all the news. 'I think yer've done really well. Mind you, I've always said yer were a good manager.'

Nellie had been very quiet while Molly was talking, but now she'd eaten all the jam butties she decided her friend had been in the limelight long enough. 'I was standing next to her when she did all this, yer know, Corker – she didn't do it all herself.'

'Oh, I get it now! Some of your excellent management capabilities transferred themselves to Molly, did they?' The big man's smile was hidden behind his enormous beard and moustache. 'Well, that explains everything.'

Nellie was looking at him as though he'd either gone mad or was speaking in a foreign language. 'Did you understand all that, girl?'

Molly nodded. 'Of course I did! I don't agree with what Corker said, but I certainly had no trouble understanding it.'

Nellie put a little finger in each of her ears and wiggled them about. 'Either me hearing is going for a burton or me ears want cleaning out. Now, go ahead, Corker, and repeat what yer've just said. Only do it slower this time.'

Corker could feel Molly kicking him under the table and knew that, like himself, she was having trouble keeping her face deadpan. Speaking very slowly and pronouncing each word clearly, he said, 'I said I thought yer had a hand in it somewhere, Nellie.'

Keeping her face as straight as his, Nellie stared him out as her brain worked overtime. Then her eyes lit up when she thought of a good reply. Swinging her legs back and forth under the dining chair, and with an air of nonchalance, she said, 'It would have been extremely selfish of me *not* to offer my renowned negotiating skills to a friend in need, Corker. And knowing how caring I am, I'm sure you would have expected nothing less of me. Am I right?'

They were never to find out what Corker thought of her negotiating skills because they were doubled up with laughter. It wasn't so much what Nellie had said, but the way she said it. And the look of pleasure on her face at getting all those big words out, was a joy to behold.

When Molly had calmed down, she put an arm across her friend's shoulders. 'Nellie, yer are one cracker. Yer deserve a medal for remembering all those long words and for putting them in the right place.'

'Can I go to top of the class, Miss?'

'Yer certainly can, sunshine! In fact, I think yer should have the honour of being milk monitor for the week.'

'Higher praise than that yer can't get, Nellie.' Corker leaned sideways to reach into his pocket for a packet of Capstan Full Strength cigarettes. After lighting up, he drew deeply a couple of times, blowing the smoke in the direction of the door and away from the faces of the two women. 'If we can be serious for a while now, let's get back to the most important event in both your lives. If there's any help yer need, Molly, then all yer have to do is sing out. With regards to the ham, yer can leave that to me. I've already had a word with the ship's cook and he's promised me a ten-pound tin, like the one we had a few years ago. I don't remember what that do was for, unless it was when me and Ellen got married. Anyway, it'll cater for forty people easily. Cut properly it would work out at a quarter of ham per person.'

Molly jumped from her chair and rounded the table. With her arms around his neck, she smothered him with kisses. 'Corker, ye're a smasher. Yer always turn up trumps.'

Nellie was looking on with a smile so wide her chubby cheeks reached her eyes. 'Didn't I say yer were a jammy bugger, girl? Honest to God, if yer fell down the lavvy yer'd come up with a gold chain.' The table began to wobble when her tummy shook with laughter. 'Mind you, yer'd still ruddywell moan because it wasn't clean!'

When Molly returned to her chair, she was looking fit to burst with pleasure. 'Corker, I don't know how to thank yer. That's one big worry off me mind.' She turned to her mate and wagged a finger. 'If you were any sort of a friend, Nellie McDonough, yer'd offer to wash the gold chain for me.'

'I will on one condition. That yer let me wear it for the wedding.'

'It's a deal, sunshine!'

'Good!' Nellie waited expectantly for a few seconds, then jerked her head. 'Well, go on, what are yer waiting for?'

'Go where?'

'Go and fall down the ruddy lavvy! I dunno, girl, sometimes ye're that ruddy slow yer need a kick up the backside.'

'I don't need to worry about that, do I, 'cos yer can't kick that high.' Molly reached over and took a chubby cheek between her thumb and forefinger. Pinching gently, she asked, 'Can yer behave

194

yerself for a while so me and Corker can have an intelligent conversation? I haven't even asked him how he is, or if he called into the shop to see Ellen?'

'Yes, I called in to see her,' Corker said, a smile on his face as he recalled the warmth of his wife's welcome. 'She looks well and tells me all the children are fine.'

'They are lovely kids, Corker, and really well behaved. And they're all excited about yer coming home.'

Using both hands, Corker ran his fingers over the bushy moustache, twisting the ends until they curled upwards. 'I'm a very lucky man, Molly, to have such a fine wife and children. As me ma is always telling me, I might have left it late in life, but I ended up with the best.'

'We call in and see Lizzie a couple of times a week, Corker,' Nellie told him. 'We always give her a knock when we're going to see Molly's folks.'

'Yes, I'm grateful for that, Nellie. And Ellen said Jill and Steve go and keep her company as well. It's good of them to do that, 'cos it means when they're married and move in with her, they'll be used to each other. It makes me easier in me mind to know there's someone calling in every day to see she's all right.'

'Corker, yer mother has more visitors than I do!' Molly said. 'Never a day goes by that Ellen or one of the four children don't pay her a visit. I often wonder how she manages for tea because the kettle is never off the boil!'

The big man just smiled. He wasn't going to say that he made sure his mother never went short of anything. Instead, he asked, 'Jack and the children all right, Molly?'

'Yeah, everyone's in good health. There's lots of excitement about the weddings, as yer'd expect. And it'll be worse in the weeks to come with Doreen making dresses for the five brides-maids. And she's making my outfit, and Nellie's. So she'll have her hands full.'

'And your family, Nellie? How's George, the boys and Lily?'

'George is the same old George, he never alters. Steve is walking around in a dream, with a permanent smile on his face. Paul is as mad as ever, thinking the only reason he was put on this earth was to have fun. As soon as he's had his meal every night, he's off gadding here, there and everywhere. And our Lily is fine.'

'Paul hasn't got a girlfriend, then?'

'It'll be a good one that catches our Paul! He says that with all the lovely girls in Liverpool, why should he just pick one? He's the love 'em and leave 'em type, I'm afraid.'

'Lily's courting though, isn't she?'

'That's a sore subject, Corker. I wish to God she wasn't

195

courting! I'd rather have her an old maid than married to that miserable bugger.'

'Still no love lost between the two of yer, then?'

'Never will be, I can't stand the feller. And I'm not the only one, none of the family can. They're civil to him in the few minutes he deigns to honour us with his presence, but they only do that for Lily's sake.'

'It's a great pity that, for everyone. Yer can only pray that things work out, one way or another.'

As Molly listened, an idea sprang to mind. Who better to confide in than the man she would trust with her life? Deciding quickly, she made a show of looking at the clock and feigning surprise that it was nearly half ten. 'In the name of God, will yer look at the time! If we don't put a move on there'll be nothing left in the shops by the time we get to them. I'll leave the housework until I get back, it won't come to no harm. So you nip home and get yer coat, Nellie, and I'll be ready for when yer get back. Corker can have another cup of tea while he's waiting to be thrown out.'

'No, I'll go out with Nellie and let you go about yer business, me darlin'.' Corker made to get to his feet. 'I'll see yer tonight anyway, 'cos I'll be calling in to see Jack and the kids. And I'm home for ten days so yer'll soon be sick of the sight of me.'

'I'd never get sick of the sight of you, Corker.' Molly was willing him to read the message in her eyes. 'There's still tea left in the pot and I'd hate it to go to waste. So I'll pour yer a cup out while Nellie goes for her coat. All I've got to do is run a comb through me hair, it's not as though anyone's going to look me up and down.'

Molly followed her neighbour to the front door to make sure it was firmly closed after her so she couldn't walk in on them unannounced. Then she hurried back to the living room. 'Nellie will only be about five minutes, so I'll have to hurry. I want to ask yer advice about something Maisie told me, and which I'm in two minds whether to mention to me mate or not. I'd like to hear your opinion.'

Corker listened intently to Molly's hurried version of events, and when she'd finished he stroked his beard thoughtfully. 'It should be easy enough to find out if Len and Lofty are the same person, and I might be able to help yer solve the mystery. There's quite a few pubs near Tetlow Street, and while I won't say I'm well-known around there, I've been in a couple of them with some of the lads off the ship. In fact, one of me best mates, Ken Roberts, lives in the next street. He's on leave, too, like meself. So it wouldn't hurt if I paid Ken a visit. But it'll have to wait until

196

Monday now, 'cos the kids will be off school over the weekend.'

When a loud bang came on the window, rattling the glass in the frame, Corker was startled. 'In the name of God, what's that?'

'That's me mate, announcing herself. I'm fed-up telling her about it, but I might as well talk to the wall. I'll let her in, but not a word, Corker, I don't want her worrying if there's no reason to.'

Nellie waddled in and stood in the middle of the room. With her basket over her arm and her fingers laced across her tummy, she eyed Molly up and down. 'Oh, aye! Yer hair's a mess and yer skirt is around yer hips. If I was a bad-minded woman, I'd say there's been a bit of hanky-panky going on here. I can understand yer being desperate after being away at sea, Corker, and being obliging, I'd have invited yer into my house for a cuppa if yer'd given me the eye-eye.'

Corker chuckled as he got to his feet and stretched to his full height. 'It's a good job ye're not bad-minded, Nellie, 'cos think what yer could have come up with if yer were!'

'Oh, I could have come up with a lot more, but I've got to watch what I say in front of me mate. I'm under instructions that there's to be no dirty talk, no swearwords and I'm not to mention the bedroom under any circumstances. I'm not even allowed to tell her when I'm changing me ruddy sheets!' The chubby cheeks creased. 'After I leave her, step into me own house and shut the door, I talk filthy to me four walls. I come out with every bad word I can think of, and I don't half feel better after it.'

'May God forgive you, Nellie McDonough.' Molly slipped her arms into her coat. 'You'll never get to heaven, you won't.'

'Listen to me, girl! I'm relying on you to get me to heaven. If I'm good enough to go to the shops with yer, then I'm good enough to go to heaven with yer. And I promise I'll have a clean pair of bloomers on, and I won't have no tidemark.'

'I'm sure Saint Peter will take note of that, sunshine. But before we make our way up the stairway to heaven, d'yer think we can make our way to the shops?' Molly pushed her friend towards the door. 'Come on, Corker, before she thinks of some other gem to keep us talking.'

Nellie turned her head, and gave a very good impression of Schnozzle Durante. 'I've got a million of 'em, kiddo.'

'They'll keep, sunshine!'

Corker donned his seaman's peaked cap and swung his bag over his shoulder. 'I'll see yer tonight, Molly.'

'We'll have a full house, I'm afraid. The bridesmaids are coming to choose the pattern for their dresses and to have their measurements taken. But the more the merrier, eh, Corker? You can come with yer two daughters.'

'I'm not having no favouritism,' Nellie said. 'If he can come with his daughters, I'm coming with our Lily.'

'Not on your life, sunshine! By the time we get back from the shops I'll have had enough of you for one day.'

The two women turned to the left, facing the main road, while Corker turned to the right. As he put the key in the lock of the house next door, he could still hear Nellie complaining: 'That's not right, that! If I'm yer mate during the day, I should be yer mate at night, too!'

'Yer can talk till ye're blue in the face, sunshine, but it won't make no difference. You and me are clocking off at two o'clock.'

Chapter Fifteen

There was a mad scramble after dinner that night to clear the table away and get the dishes washed. Ruthie, excited about being measured for her bridesmaid's dress, didn't need any coaxing to help her mother tidy the living room while her two sisters did the washing up. And they'd just finished, with seconds to spare, when Corker arrived with his two stepdaughters. He had a hand on each of their shoulders and looked as proud as Punch. 'I know we're early, but they've had me and Ellen moth-eaten. They're so excited they hardly touched their dinner.'

Jill rushed to hug each of the girls. 'Well, they've waited long enough for it, heaven knows. I was only sixteen, and Steve seventeen, when we asked them to be bridesmaids. That's five years ago.'

Phoebe's smile was shy and gentle. 'It was worth waiting for.'

'I'll say!' Dorothy, at fifteen, was more outgoing than her older sister. 'I mean, if yer'd got married before, it would be over by now. As it is, we've got it to look forward to.'

'That's a very sensible way of looking at it,' Corker said. 'Now sit yerselves down until Doreen's ready for yer. I'm going to drag Jack down to the pub for a pint.'

Having in mind the need to save every penny, Jack's eyes went to Molly. He was about to make an excuse, but Molly got in before him. What was a few coppers spent in the pub when the ham Corker had promised them would have cost pounds? It would be churlish and stingy to refuse to go for a pint with the man. 'Go on, Jack, it'll get yer from under our feet. We can't have men sitting around while the girls have their measurements taken, it would be too embarrassing.'

'I'm getting thrown out early, too!' Tommy said. 'They're not even giving me time to let me dinner settle.'

'Hark at him! Any other night he can't wait to get round to see Rosie.' Molly gave her son a loving smile while pushing him gently towards the door. 'Give me ma and da a kiss and say I'll see them tomorrow.'

'Hang on, son, we'll come out with yer.' Jack moved quickly to

199

get his jacket from the hallstand. 'We'd be better going out under our own steam than being thrown out.' He winked at Molly. 'How long d'yer want us out for, love?'

'Give us two hours, at least. The measurements won't take long, but choosing a pattern will. We could hop in lucky and have all five agreeing they like the same dress, but I think the chances of that are pretty remote. So if yer hear raised voices when yer pass the window, turn around again and go back to the pub.'

'There'll be no arguments,' Doreen said with confidence. 'The two patterns I've got for them to choose from are both smashing and they'll be spoilt for choice.'

'I'm glad men don't have the same fuss,' Jack said, following Tommy down the hall with Corker walking behind. 'I wouldn't like to be one of these toffs what has to wear top hat and tails, I'd feel a right nit.'

When the men had gone, Dorothy asked, 'Have you and Jill got a favourite between the two patterns, Doreen? 'Cos if yer have, then that's the one me and Phoebe would like. Isn't that right, our kid?'

'I think the brides should choose, anyway,' Phoebe said, in her softly spoken voice. 'After all, it is their big day.'

'Well, I'm going to wait and see which one I like the best.' Ruthie, who was perched on the arm of the couch, firmly believed that being a bridesmaid was a pretty important job. After all, it was no good the brides looking like fairies if the bridesmaids looked like frumps. That would spoil the whole effect. 'I don't know why yer won't let me see the patterns, our Doreen, ye're dead mean. I could be looking at them while I'm sitting here.'

'Maureen and Lily will be here any minute, so yer can hang on. Then we'll sit around the table and yer'll all see them at the same time.' Doreen threw her kid sister a warning glance before answering Dorothy's question. 'Me and Jill both like the same one, but we'll wait and see what the majority think.'

Just then there was a knock on the door and Ruthie flew off her perch. Usually she pulled a face if asked to open the door, but not tonight. 'I'll go.' She was back within seconds. 'It's Maureen and Lily, they came together.'

'Where's your manners, young lady?' Molly asked sternly. 'Yer don't leave visitors at the door to let themselves in.'

'It's all right, Mrs B.' Maureen Shepherd's white teeth flashed in a wide smile. She had been Doreen's friend since the day they'd met at Johnson's Dye Works where they'd gone for an interview after leaving school. They'd been best mates ever since and Molly treated her like one of the family. She was a vivacious girl, with short black bobbed hair, a rosy complexion and an attractive, slim figure. 'I wasn't left to close the door, it was Lily.'

Lily McDonough slipped out of her coat and draped it over the back of the couch. 'At least she didn't bang the door in me face.'

'There's no excuse for bad manners,' Molly said, pulling the chairs out from the table. 'Sit yerselves down. Come on, Phoebe and Dorothy, yer've got as much say in this as anyone else. And don't be afraid to speak up.'

They were a chair short, so rather than go upstairs for the one in the bedroom, Jill and Doreen decided to share, even though it meant only half their bottoms were seated. 'I've got two patterns,' Doreen said. 'And I'm hoping the five of yer will agree on the same one to save me a lot of work.' She handed the packets, with pictures of the made-up dresses on the front, to Lily, who was nearest. 'See which one yer like, then pass them around. Don't say anything until everyone has seen them.'

Molly, sitting on the couch with her feet under her, watched and listened with interest. Both dresses were nice, but she knew which one she'd pick if she had her way.

Finally the patterns were back in Doreen's hands. She looked at Lily 'Well?'

'They're both lovely, but I'd go for the one with the heart-shaped neck.'

Maureen didn't wait to be asked. 'Yeah, me too!'

When Phoebe felt Doreen's questioning eyes on her, she blushed as she said, 'I think it's really beautiful.'

Dorothy couldn't keep still she was so excited. 'Really, really, beautiful.'

Molly was over the moon and felt like clapping. Until she saw her youngest daughter's stubborn expression. Oh dear, she thought, if that little madam is the odd one out, so help me, I'll clock her one.

But Doreen had her sister weighed up. 'What's wrong with your face?'

'I think I like the other one better.'

'That's all right, kiddo! I'll make the sweetheart neck for these four, and I'll make the other one for you.' Doreen knew she would never be required to do this, or she wouldn't have been so generous. 'No problem.'

This wasn't going Ruthie's way; she'd expected to be coaxed. 'I only said I *think* I like the other one better, I didn't say definitely.'

'Well, make up yer mind because we haven't got all night.' Doreen expected capitulation within two minutes or her patience would run out. 'It's no skin off my nose which one yer have. But it'll be too late to change yer mind after tonight because I'll be measuring up for the material, and the dress you like wouldn't need as much because it's not as full.'

'I'll have the sweetheart-neck one.' Ruthie's surrender came through knowing Doreen wouldn't put up with any messing from her. Jill would, 'cos she was more patient, but Doreen was a different kettle of fish. Anyway, in her mind the young girl had visions of the other four with sticky-out skirts, and hers being dead straight. 'I don't want to put you to no bother.'

'That's very thoughtful of yer,' Doreen said with a smile on her face as she reached down to pick up her handbag from the floor. There was never any doubt that Ruthie was going to have the same style as the others, but there was no point in rubbing it in. 'I nipped into town in me dinner-hour and went to Blackler's. Since we all decided on blue, that's the colour I looked for. I liked two of the materials I saw, one satin and one a type of silky crêpe. The assistant was smashing and cut me a piece off each of the bales.' She pulled two strips of material from her bag and laid them in the centre of the table. 'Different shades of blue and different material. Which one is it to be?'

Molly, from her ringside seat, watched the pleasure on each of the faces as the strips of material were fingered. And there was happiness and laughter in the raised voices as opinions were exchanged. When they'd been asked to be bridesmaids it had seemed too far off to start getting excited about. But tonight it was different. Seeing on paper how beautiful the dresses were going to be, and the lovely blue of both pieces of material, they were overjoyed in hearts and minds.

'I hope they pick the crêpe,' Jill whispered in her sister's ear. 'I think it's lovely.'

'Yeah, me too!' Doreen grinned as she whispered back. 'If they don't we'll have to try a little gentle persuasion. And if that don't work, kid, we'll get out the rolling pin.'

Lily tapped her on the arm and passed the strips of material back. 'Maureen and meself like the crêpe the best. I don't know about the others.'

Out of the corner of her eye, Doreen caught the mutinous expression on Ruthie's face. Oh Lord, the little minx was going to be awkward again. She would have to try and nip it in the bud right away or they would be here till all hours. 'That would be the best choice, girls, 'cos the crêpe will fall into folds beautifully. What about you, Phoebe, and Dorothy?'

Phoebe nodded. 'That's the one I like.'

Dorothy, who wanted to be the same as the grown-up girls, agreed. 'Me too, I think it's beautiful.'

In an effort to remove the look of mutiny from Ruthie's face,

Doreen played her trump card. 'I'm glad about that. I think satin is more for children, don't you?'

Molly chuckled. My God, she's getting as crafty as Nellie McDonough! I just hope it does the trick or the little article is going to cause ructions.

Ruthie was still feeling mutinous, but now it was for a different reason. She wasn't a child, she was nearly thirteen! And their Doreen needn't think she was going to be treated like one. 'Am I the invisible woman, or something? Aren't yer going to ask me what I think?'

'I certainly am, dear. What do you think?'

'The same as the others, of course! I am not a child, even though some of yer try to treat me as one.'

'Thank goodness that's settled,' Jill said. 'Now Doreen's got what she wants, except for yer measurements, it's my pleasant task to discuss what sort of headdress yer'd like. I'll tell yer what I've got in mind, and see whether it appeals to yer.' Her pretty face radiated the happiness she felt in talking about her marriage to her childhood sweetheart. 'I thought if yer wore hair-bands, and they were decorated with the same blue and white flowers as yer posy they would look really attractive. But perhaps some of yer might have other ideas.'

There was not one voice objected. Not even Ruthie's. A smile like the rising sun came to her face and it was still there when she climbed the stairs to bed. She didn't even complain when Doreen was telling her off for not keeping still while she was trying to take her measurements. All the girl could think about was bragging to her best friend, Bella, who was bound to be dead jealous.

Doreen had written all the measurements down in a notebook. 'Maureen, you and Lily are exactly the same in height, waist, hips and bust. The dresses are going to be identical, yer won't know which is which.'

'That'll make it easier for you, won't it? And while me and Lily will be putting them on in here, we won't be taking them off here because Lily will be going home in hers.'

Phoebe, who was blissfully happy but too shy to show it, asked, 'Will we all be getting dressed here, Jill?'

'It'll be a tight squeeze, but we'll have to. We wouldn't want the neighbours to see yer until the wedding cars come. We'll manage somehow, using the two bedrooms.'

Molly groaned when she heard a rap on the knocker. 'This can't be yer dad and Corker back already, surely? The two hours are not up yet.'

Doreen made for the hall. 'I'll go.'

Molly had an ear cocked, and when she heard a man's laughter her face lit up. 'It's Archie!' She tutted when Tommy's army friend walked into the room. 'What lousy timing, Archie! Yer've just missed the girls getting measured for their bridesmaids' dresses.'

Looking as happy as ever, Archie snapped his fingers. 'Just my luck, Mrs B.! That's the story of my life.' His eyes travelled the room and when he spoke it was with a posh accent. 'I say, what a bevy of beauties! Jolly hockey sticks, what!'

'Keep yer eyes off them,' Molly laughed. 'They're being kept under wraps until the big day. And, oh boy, will yer get an eyeful then!'

'I shall await the day with great eagerness.' Archie spotted Phoebe who was sitting as far back on the couch as she could get. 'Are yer going to dance with me at this wedding, Phoebe?'

The girl seemed to shrink with embarrassment. 'I can't dance.'

'Yes, yer can, our Phoebe!' Dorothy piped up. 'Yer've been practising with me when no one's looking.'

Her blushing sister gave her a dig in the ribs. 'That's not proper dancing, we were only acting the goat.'

'Then yer'll have to act the goat more often,' Archie said. 'Because I intend to dance with every pretty girl at the wedding.' He looked across to where Jill and Doreen were standing next to each other. They were alike as two peas, with their long blonde hair, vivid blue eyes, peaches and cream complexion and stunning figures. Girls that would turn any man's head. 'And that includes the brides.'

'Oh, yer'll have to ask my new husband about that,' Doreen said. 'I don't think he'd like me dancing with another man a few hours after we become man and wife.'

'Yer wouldn't want to dance with me anyway, Archie,' Jill told him with a smile. 'I've got two left feet.'

'Oh dear, knocked back by two of them already! Never mind, that still leaves four. And I know you can dance, Maureen, so yer've no excuse. Nor have you, Lily, 'cos I've heard ye're pretty nifty on yer feet.'

'I don't know who told yer that, but if yer don't mind having yer feet trodden on, then I'm game.' Lily thought, why not? She might be able to talk Len into coming to the wedding, but she'd never get him on the dance floor. And she didn't want to look a spoilsport by refusing a pleasant bloke like Archie. 'Take a bit of advice and ask me up for a slow waltz.'

'Me and our Phoebe will keep practising, Archie.' Dorothy could feel her sister pinching her arm but she ignored it. After all, they'd never been to a wedding before, never mind being

204

bridesmaids. And they were going to look lovely in pretty dresses and flowers in their hair. She wanted to show off, not sit down on the sidelines like a wallflower. 'And when the time comes we should be good enough to dance with yer.'

'I'm sure yer will. And if not, I'll lift yer off yer feet and twirl yer around the room.' Archie grinned at the wide-eyed, open-mouthed expression on the young girl's face. 'You see if I don't!' He turned his head and winked at Molly who was pleased Ellen's girls were being included. 'I suppose Tommy's round at your mother's, Mrs B.?'

'Yeah, he's round there most nights. Him and Rosie usually have a few hands of cards with me ma and da. Why don't yer slip round there? They'd be glad to see yer.'

'I think I will. I might even have a game of cards with them. I won't stay long though, 'cos it's such a lovely night I'm going to walk home instead of getting the tram. The exercise will do me good, I'm getting lazy since I came out of the army.' He saw Lily lift her coat from the back of the couch and immediately hastened to help her into it. 'Since we're leaving together I'll escort you home.'

'That's very gallant of you, sir! But are you sure you won't tire yerself out before your long walk home? After all, I live all of three doors away.'

'Yer should be flattered, Lily.' Molly was thinking it was a long time since she'd seen Nellie's daughter so relaxed. 'He's a handsome lad, is Archie.'

Lily gave a slight curtsey. 'I am suitably honoured.' She was giggling when she turned to Molly. 'I'm not very high up on etiquette, so what do I do now? Do I offer him my hand or does he cup my elbow?'

Jill and Doreen were looking on with amusement, as was Maureen. But the two young girls from next door were listening with wonder and taking in every word so they could repeat it to their mother when they got home. They weren't as shy as they were a few years ago, before their real father died and their mam married the man they adored and now called Dad. But the violence and abuse they'd endured as youngsters had left them with a low opinion of themselves and the inability to mix in company. The scars might have faded, but bad memories still came back now and again to hurt them and their younger brothers.

'Don't worry about etiquette, Lily, I'm quite good at improvising.' Archie bowed and made a wide sweep with his hand. 'I'm sure I can come up with something in the twenty yards I'll have at my disposal.'

205

'Ooh, er, that sounds very interesting,' Doreen said. 'I won't make a show of yer by coming to the door to watch, but I'll be looking through the window.'

'Me too!' Maureen was leaning on the table, her face cupped in her hands. 'I could do with a few hints.'

'Mrs B. I'm relying on you to keep them in their place. I'm not at me best when I know I'm being spied on.'

Molly knew from what Tommy told her, that his old army mate had no trouble attracting the girls. And why would he, a nice handsome lad like that? But apparently he hadn't yet met one he wanted to spend the rest of his life with. 'Have no fear, Archie, I shall guard that window with me life.'

'Ay, come on, soft nit,' Lily said. 'I could have been home by now.'

'Ah, but you wouldn't have had the pleasure of my company.' Archie's smile covered everyone. 'I'll bid you goodnight, ladies, until we meet again.' He dropped to his haunches in front of Phoebe and Dorothy. 'And don't forget, you two, that practice makes perfect. I'll be brokenhearted if I don't get to dance with you at the wedding.'

'Oh, we will practise, Archie.' Dorothy's face was so serious, as though she spoke straight from the heart. As indeed she did. Tonight she'd been treated like an adult and revelled in it. 'Me dad's home now, and him and me mam used to go dancing, so I'll ask them to teach us.'

Lily got fed-up waiting. 'I'm going without yer,' she warned, waving her hand in a general goodbye. 'I thought it was only women who talked so much.'

'Farewell, ladies.' Archie made a hasty retreat, leaving laughter in his wake.

'He's funny, isn't he?' Dorothy said. 'He didn't half make me laugh.'

'He's everything, sunshine, and I really love the bones of him. He's funny, pleasant, polite, honest and handsome. Whoever gets him will be getting a good 'un.'

'In that case I think I'll swap him for Sammy.'

Molly smiled at Maureen's words, but behind the smile was a trace of sadness. The one person at the wedding whose heart wouldn't be celebrating the marriage of her long-time friend, would be the girl who had fallen for Phil Bradley the night she and Doreen first met him at Barlow's Lane dance hall. But Phil had fallen for Doreen at first sight and had eyes for no one else. And such was the loyalty of the girl, she had never, by word or deed, allowed her feelings to affect her friendship with Doreen. No one guessed her secret, except Molly, who hadn't failed to see

206

the way the girl's eyes followed Phil's every movement, or the way her face lit up at the sight of him. And only Molly knew she still carried a torch for him. When it was Maureen's turn to get married, she wouldn't be marrying the man of her dreams.

'I don't know why yer'd want to swap Sammy,' Doreen said. 'I think he's a smashing feller.'

'So do I,' Molly agreed. 'And he thinks the sun shines out of yer backside. Yer'd go a long way to find anyone better.'

'Yeah, I know that.' Maureen stifled a sigh. 'I was only kidding.'

'Ye're going to be late meeting yer boyfriend tonight,' Archie said as they stood outside the McDonoughs' house. 'It'll be time to come home before yer get there.'

'I'm not seeing him tonight,' Lily said. 'He's working late.'

'In that case, why don't yer walk round to the Jacksons' with me? I know it's not far, but the fresh air would do yer more good than being stuck in the house.'

'I couldn't do that. If I walked in there with you they'd wonder what was going on!'

'And what is going on?'

'Nothing.'

'Precisely. So what's the problem?' Archie lowered his head to meet her eyes. 'It's coming to something when two ordinary people can't walk along the street together without worrying what people think. Unless yer boyfriend objects to yer talking to another man?'

'Len is me boyfriend, but he doesn't tell me what I can or cannot do. I don't take orders from him.'

'Then walk with me to the Jacksons' and keep me company. We can have a game of cards, a good laugh, and yer can leave whenever yer want.'

Lily was sorely tempted. Her dad would be in the pub with his mates, Paul would be out enjoying himself and Steve would be going to Jill's any minute. That would leave her in the house with her mother, and these days the atmosphere between them wasn't exactly warm. 'OK, I'll walk round with yer for half-an-hour. It'll pass the time away, and as yer say, it is a lovely night.'

They started walking with a respectable distance between them, and Lily feeling very self-conscious. But Archie was so easygoing, and so funny, by the time they were outside the Jacksons' house she was at ease with herself.

It was a surprised-looking Tommy who opened the door. 'Well, I'll be blowed! Come in, and welcome to yer.' He was made up to see his friend, but curious as to why Lily was with him. As he closed the door after them, he called, 'Make yerselves respectable, we've got visitors.'

Bridie, Bob and Rosie were sat at the table with a fan of playing cards in their hands and open-mouthed expressions on their faces. They didn't get many visitors, especially at this time of night. But once they'd got over the initial shock their welcome was warm and sincere.

'Come in, me darlin's,' Bridie said, laying her cards face down on the table before pushing her chair back. 'It's happy we are to see yer.'

Rosie jumped to her feet. 'Give me yer coat, Lily, or yer'll not feel the benefit of it when yer leave.'

Lily shook her head. 'I'll not be staying long, I got talked into taking some fresh air by me laddo here.' She jerked her head at Archie. 'He must think I need some colour in me cheeks.'

'Yer'll not be going without a cup of tea, me darlin', so let Rosie take yer coat.' Bridie's tone said she wouldn't take no for an answer.

Bob chuckled as he laid his cards down. 'Yer may as well do as ye're told, lass, because my dear wife thinks it's an insult if anyone leaves this house without tasting her hospitality.'

While Rosie was relieving Lily of her coat, Tommy was slapping Archie on the back. 'It's good to see yer, mate! If I'd known yer were coming down I'd have waited in for yer.'

'I'm glad yer didn't, 'cos I had six beautiful young ladies all to meself. No, make that seven because yer mam was there. If I'd arrived half-an-hour earlier it would have been better still because they'd been getting measured for their bridesmaids' dresses.'

'I know! Me and me dad practically got thrown out.' Tommy's curiosity finally got the better of him and he raised his brows at Lily. 'Not seeing yer boyfriend tonight, then?'

'No, he's working overtime. Anyway, I knew I'd be a long time in your house so I wouldn't have made arrangements to see him even if he hadn't been working.'

Bridie was fussing over Archie, who was a great favourite with all of Tommy's family. He wasn't to know it, but they'd all been told about his exploits when they were overseas in the army. He'd received a commendation for bravery after saving the lives of some of his comrades who had strayed into an area which had been heavily mined by the German soldiers before they retreated. It was something Archie never mentioned, but something that Tommy would never forget because he was one of the soldiers saved. People thought that because the war was over, there was no danger, but the enemy had left deathtraps everywhere for unsuspecting soldiers who hadn't had much training and were nothing more than raw recruits. And frightened ones into the bargain. If it hadn't been for Archie keeping a cool head and leading them through the minefield, a lot of them wouldn't be alive today.

'Sit yerselves down at the table and I'll have the tea made in no time, so I will.'

'No you won't, Auntie Bridget,' Rosie said with a determined nod of her head. 'Sure, it's meself that'll make the tea. And isn't it the luck of the visitors that yer baked those lovely scones today?'

Bob began to collect in the cards. 'We won't be needing these now. If yer feel like it after we've had a drink, we can deal a new hand.'

Lily smiled but didn't answer. She wouldn't be staying to play cards because it would set tongues wagging. If her mam found out she'd walked here with Archie she'd never hear the end of it. She'd get her leg pulled soft. And if Len found out there'd be holy murder.

Half-an-hour later Lily was so busy laughing she forgot her good intentions. Archie had to be the funniest, most entertaining person she'd ever met. He was a marvellous observer of human nature, and when he was talking about his workmates, or the girls he met at dances, he got their voices, facial expressions and body language just right. He had tears of laughter running down Bridie's and Bob's faces, Tommy was in convulsions and Rosie's infectious giggle filled the room. And Lily herself was in a pleat.

Archie was into his stride about one of the blokes at work. 'He's a lazy so-and-so. It takes him about five minutes to hammer a nail in. In fact, more often than not the nail gets fed-up waiting and drives itself into the wood. And he has more time off than anyone else. D'yer know, he's taken six days off in the last few years to go to his grandmother's funeral! And I think it's five times his grandad's been buried! Now my boss had got a very dry sense of humour. He comes out with the funniest things without a flicker of a smile on his face. The last time this Fred Berry went into the office to ask for a day off to go to his grandmother's funeral, the boss looked up at him and said, "This is the seventh time yer've dug the old dear up. Is it because yer want to make sure she's dead? Or is it because yer want a bleedin' day off? Now the next time yer come in here asking for a day off to go to a funeral, permission will only be granted if it's yer own".'

'God rest the poor woman's soul.' Bridie lifted the corner of her pinny to wipe her eyes. 'That man, Fred, sure he has no respect for the dear departed and will never be allowed inside the Pearly Gates.'

'Respect is not the only thing he's lacking in, Mrs Jackson.' Archie was grinning all over his face. 'He's as thick as two short planks and thinks everyone else is the same. His own mother is eighty years of age, so by my reckoning the grandmother he keeps burying must be about a hundred and ten.'

'Bet she feels every day of it,' Tommy said. 'Being popped up and down so often, it's enough to put years on her.'

'How does he keep his job?' Bob wanted to know. 'He wouldn't have got away with it where I used to work.'

'The boss said he was keeping him on just to see how many lies he could come up with. He doesn't get paid while he's off, so it doesn't cost the firm anything. I'll tell yer just a few of the excuses he's given for not turning into work. His wife has fallen down the stairs twice and couldn't move 'cos she'd hurt her back. Now, a lot of people who fell from the top of the stairs to the bottom would probably break their necks, but not Fred's wife! She is very accommodating and her injuries only require him to take one day off. Then there was the time she was running down the yard to the lavvy in the middle of the night and she stepped on the sweeping brush. The handle flew up and knocked her out. She was unconscious when Fred went down to see what was keeping her. And she stayed unconscious until dinner-time, when it was no use him turning into work then, was it? His own mishaps are too numerous to mention, but a small example is the day he was walking down the street on his way to work when he tripped on a shoelace that he hadn't tied properly. He ended up face down on the ground and cut his nose open. Now nobody would expect him to turn up for work after that, would they? He showed up the next day like a wounded soldier with a plaster on his nose, and all morning he moaned about being in agony. Everyone was fed-up listening to him, so one of the lads, as a dare, pulled the plaster off. And there wasn't even a scratch to be seen.'

'Sounds like a queer bloke to me,' Bob said, scratching his head. 'How can he afford to take so many days off?'

'The day Fred Berry stops taking days off, Mr Jackson, will be the day my job becomes very dull. He doesn't think it's funny, mind, 'cos he's got no sense of humour. I don't think I've seen him laugh in all the time I've known him. But he keeps all his workmates amused, I can tell yer. We even have bets on who can guess what his next excuse is going to be! But he's got us licked 'cos we've never even been close. I mean, how many of yer would guess that a bloke could turn up for work one morning and tell the boss he was sorry for being absent the day before, but he'd fallen into the River Mersey!'

There were hoots and shrieks of laughter. 'Archie, is this the truth ye're telling us?' Rosie's deep blue Irish eyes were bright and shining. 'Or is it yerself that's making it up for our benefit?'

'Rosie, my love, nobody could invent a character like Fred Berry. And nobody but him could come up with these outlandish excuses and expect to be believed! He's a miserable so-and-so at the best of times, but yer should see the look of self-pity on his face when he's spinning these tales to the boss. He told him he'd been walking to work along the Dock Road the day before, and it was such a lovely morning he'd stopped to look into the river. But just as he bent down a sudden gust of wind came and blew his cap off. Without thinking, he leaned forward to try and catch it, and that's when he fell in the water. But luck was with him as a docker saw his plight and threw him a lifebelt. But of course his clothes were sopping wet so he was forced to make his way home.'

'Do they take women on in your place?' Lily asked. 'He sounds like a bundle of fun, that bloke.'

'The only women are the two in the canteen. If they did take them on in the factory I would personally chuck Fred Berry in the Mersey, Lily, and make sure there was no docker around with a lifebelt. Then, after he'd been buried on top of his grandmother so she couldn't be dug up again, I'd ask the boss to give you his job.'

'Ooh, I'd not be having anything to do with that, Lily, indeed I wouldn't.' Rosie's thick dark curly hair swung about her shoulders. 'Me mammy used to say it was unlucky to step into a dead mans shoes.'

Tommy couldn't resist and pulled her close. 'I can't wait to meet yer mammy. I wonder if she'll have a saying for me?'

'Oh, she will that, Tommy Bennett. Sure, as I told yer the first time I saw yer, me mammy will say it's a foine figure of a man yer are. And I'll bet she says that ye're beef to the heel like a Mullingar heifer.'

Bridie and Bob reached for each other's hand as they watched the two young sweethearts with happiness and pride. Archie looked on hoping that one day he'd meet someone and share the same sort of love. And Lily looked on with longing in her heart. If only Len could be as demonstrative and loving as Tommy.

Thinking of her boyfriend brought Lily down to earth. 'I'm going to be making tracks or me mam will wonder what's happened to me.'

'I'll walk yer back, Lily,' Archie offered.

'No, I don't want to break up the party, you stay and enjoy yerself.'

'Are yer sure?'

'Yes, I'm sure! I want to thank all of you for a very pleasant evening. And Mrs Jackson, the scones were lovely, yer'll have to give me the recipe sometime.' Her coat on and her handbag clutched between her two hands, she looked at the man who'd entertained them for the last two hours. 'Before I go, though, Archie, I want to hear the end of the story. Had this man really fallen in the river?'

'Had he hellslike! Me boss even went to where he said he'd fallen in and asked a couple of dockers that were there. They said if it had happened they would definitely have known. They had a damn good laugh about it and said someone was pulling his leg.'

'What did yer boss have to say?'

'What he said was not fit for the ears of ladies.'

Lily grinned. 'Come on, Rosie, throw me out.'

Chapter Sixteen

Corker washed the breakfast dishes after Ellen and the children had gone out, then tidied the living room and gave a quick dust around. His wife wouldn't go to work without making the beds because she said that was a woman's job and he didn't do it properly anyway. So with nothing else to do, and all day to do it in, he left the house to go on the errand he'd promised Molly.

It was a lovely spring morning and Corker decided to walk to Walton. He cut a fine figure with his bushy beard and moustache, and his peaked cap set at a jaunty angle. That, combined with his height and a body built like a battleship, caused many heads to turn. But he was oblivious to this as he stopped every so often to window shop. When he was passing a confectioners, he promised himself to call in on his way back and buy a couple of cakes to take to his mother's. She had a sweet tooth and would enjoy a cream cake with a cup of tea. He'd make it his business to be home by lunch-time and they'd spend the rest of the afternoon together. The time spent in each other's company was precious to both of them.

Corker stopped at the corner of a street and looked up at the name sign. This was Tetlow Street where the mysterious Lofty lived. It would be interesting to know if he and Len Lofthouse were one and the same person. And if he was, why had the girl who was called Joan come in the corner shop looking for Lily? Hopefully his mate could throw some light on the subject.

Walking up the next street, Corker checked the numbers until he came to fifty-seven. This was where Robbo lived, and with a bit of luck he wouldn't have gone out yet. The door was opened by a woman in her forties, with a rounded figure and steel-grey hair. Her hand flew to her mouth. 'In the name of God, it's Corker!'

'Hello, Alice. Long time no see, eh?'

'Come in, come in.' Alice grabbed his arm as though she thought he might run off. 'It's nice to see yer.' She pulled him along the hall of the six-roomed house and didn't let go until they were in the living room. 'What brings yer to this neck of the woods?'

213

'I wanted to have a word with Ken if he's in.'

'The lazy bugger's still in bed! When he's on leave I can never get him up before twelve. And then it's the hunger that shifts him, not my bawling.'

'Still in bed! On a lovely morning like this? He should be ashamed of himself.' Corker jerked his head towards the ceiling. 'D'yer mind if I give him a shout?' When Alice nodded, he walked to the bottom of the stairs and yelled, 'Robbo, yer lazy blighter, get down these stairs before I come up and drag yer down.'

There was silence for a while, then Corker heard feet slithering along the lino on the landing. He looked up to see his mate standing at the top of the stairs wearing a vest and long johns, and rubbing his eyes as though he didn't believe what he was seeing. 'Corker, what the hell are yer doing here at this time of the morning?'

'Robbo, the streets were aired off hours ago. And before I get a kink in me neck looking up at yer, will yer get dressed and come down?' Corker's guffaw echoed in the rather gloomy hall. 'I'll tell yer what, mate, ye're not a pretty sight to see. I just wish the crew were here to see yer now, yer'd never live it down. And I'm glad I've had me breakfast because I wouldn't be wanting it now, that's for sure.'

Ken Roberts grinned. With an arm across his waist holding the long johns up, he scratched his head. 'You don't look any better when yer first get up. In fact, yer look twice as bad 'cos ye're twice the size of me.'

'Put some clothes on and get down these stairs before I run off with yer wife.'

A loud whisper came floating down. 'Is that a threat or a promise, Corker?'

Alice came into the hall brandishing a fist. 'I heard that, yer lazy swine! If I could get meself another feller I'd be off like a shot. And I wouldn't care if he had a face like the back of a bus, as long as he had a few bob in his pockets.' She tugged on Corker's arm. 'He'll stand there talking all day if yer let him. Come and sit down, the kettle's nearly boiled.'

'How's the family?' Corker asked as he sat across the table from Alice. 'Keeping well, I hope?'

'Yer know our Janet's got a baby, don't yer? They called it Gary, after the flamin' film star, would yer believe. Still, everyone to their own taste. Six months old he is now, and as bright as a brass button. Janet wheels him around every afternoon, and as soon as he sees me his arms and legs start kicking until I lift him up. I get told off for spoiling him, but what the hell! If can't spoil me own grandson, who can I spoil?'

'And Shirley?'

'She's still at home but courting strong. She works at Vernon's and is saving up like mad for her bottom drawer.' Alice rested her chin in her hand when her husband came into the room. 'I didn't hear yer coming down the stairs.'

'I'm in me stockin' feet, aren't I? I've looked everywhere and I can't find me ruddy shoes!' Ken grinned and slapped Corker on the back as a way of welcome. 'We went out on the razzle last night and I don't even remember going to bed.'

'Hang on a minute, let's get this story straight,' Alice said. '*I* went out for a drink, *you* went out on the razzle. For every drink I had, you had three.'

'That explains why me head's spinning, but it doesn't explain why I can't find me shoes.'

'If you want to go out and get yerself plastered, Ken Roberts, then that's your lookout. Don't come crying to me 'cos yer can't find yer ruddy shoes.'

'But I need them to go down the yard! I can't go in me socks.' Ken was rubbing the back of his neck and grimacing. 'Me flamin' neck's sore, as well. I feel as though I've slept on a sack of coal.'

At that moment, Corker just happened to glance at Alice as she lifted the cup to her lips, and caught a smile playing around the corners of her mouth. She's having him on, he thought. I bet she knows where his shoes are. 'It's a wonder you didn't see what he did with his shoes, Alice. Haven't yer any idea?'

The smile was still hovering as she said, 'He could try looking under his pillow.'

'Why the hell would I do that? No matter how drunk I was, I wouldn't be daft enough to put me shoes under me pillow. I must have left them down here somewhere.'

'No, yer didn't.' Alice was very definite about that. 'I've cleaned this place from top to bottom while you were lazing in bed.'

'Try under yer pillow, Robbo,' Corker suggested. 'Yer never know.'

'Oh, for crying out loud!' Alice's cup was returned to its saucer. 'I'll go and get yer flamin' shoes for yer! And yes, they are under yer pillow.' She pulled a face at Corker. 'I put them there hoping they'd stop him from falling into a deep sleep and snoring his head off. Yer've no idea what it's like sleeping with him when he's had a few. He sleeps on his back with his mouth wide open and it's like listening to a symphony orchestra. One what hits all the wrong notes and plays loud enough to split yer eardrums.'

Corker's head went back and he roared with laughter. 'Yer don't have to tell me about Robbo's snoring, or any of the other lads. We've all suffered from it. But I've never heard it compared

215

to a symphony orchestra before.' Once again his head went back and his laughter filled the room. ' "One what hits all the wrong notes and plays loud enough to split yer eardrums." I'll have to remember that to tell the rest of the crew. I think it's bloody brilliant.'

Alice scraped her chair back and with her hands flat on the table she pushed herself to her feet. 'I was being polite, Corker. Yer should hear some of the things I call him when he's in full flow and I'm tossing and turning, and can't get to sleep even though I'm dead tired.' She gave her husband a withering look before making for the stairs to retrieve his shoes.

'I've never realised it before, but your wife is quite a wit.'

'Yeah, I know.' Ken stood with his hands on the back of a chair. It was no good sitting down because his need to go to the lavvy was now becoming desperate. He hoped Corker said nothing to make him laugh. 'And she's also a bloody good liar! She forgot on purpose to tell yer she can lick me when it comes to snoring. That's why I always have a few drinks so I can get to sleep before her. Otherwise I lie there thinking the blitz has started all over again. Air-raid sirens, ack-ack guns and bombs dropping, she goes through the whole lot. But if I tell her that she goes all huffy, like women do, and says she doesn't snore at all and won't speak to me for days.'

'But yer wouldn't swap her for a big clock?'

'Indeed I wouldn't, Corker! I know when I'm well off.'

'Here yer are, misery guts.' Alice thrust the shoes at him. 'And don't sit down there on yer throne for too long, or this pot of tea will be stiff.'

When Ken had completed his ablutions and sat at the table next to his wife, Corker said, 'Now yer look more like me shipmate! Standing at the top of those stairs I didn't recognise yer as Robbo, the bloke I share watches with.'

'You're the only one who calls him that, yer know,' Alice said, hoping to impress Corker with the delicate way she held her cup. 'He gets Ken off everyone else.'

'Not on the ship he doesn't. The only one he gets his full title off is the skipper.'

'I don't dare what anyone calls me.' Ken offered his packet of Woodbines. 'Here yer are, have a fag and tell us what brought yer here.'

'I'll have one of me own if yer don't mind.' Corker brought out his Capstan Full Strength. 'I never feel I've had a smoke after one of them.' He waited until both cigarettes were lit, then said, 'I was asked if I know a family called Lofthouse, who live in Tetlow Street. Now I've never heard of them, but I thought with you living so near, you might have. So, with the sun cracking the flags, I decided to take a walk down and ask yer.'

'Yeah, they live at the back of us, don't they, love?' Ken began to show interest. 'Their entry door is about four doors down from ours. Why?'

'Nothing really, just a bit of information. What sort of a family are they?'

'Ada and Jim Lofthouse are the salt of the earth,' Alice said. 'Always got a smile for yer and never fail to stop and ask how the family is.'

'Have they got any children?'

Ken put a hand on his wife's arm to tell her to leave him to do the talking. After all, he was the one Corker called to see. 'They've got two lads. The eldest, Alan, is about twenty-three and Len is roughly two years younger.'

'Nice lads, are they?'

'Alan is, he's a really good bloke. Takes after his dad, always friendly.'

'And his younger brother?' Corker asked. 'Is he the same?'

'Don't his parents wish he was! He's caused them nothing but trouble from the time he started school. And what a miserable, surly bugger he is! Yer never get a word out of him, never mind a smile. And he's a right bad 'un.' Ken took a last drag on his cigarette before flicking it into the grate. 'There's a rumour—'

Alice put a hand over her husband's mouth and cut off his words. 'Don't say anything else, love, not one word! Keep it to yerself or we could end up in trouble.' With her hand still keeping Ken quiet, she looked at Corker for understanding. And what she said next kept him amused all day. 'I had to shut him up, or he'd have said something he shouldn't. The rumour he nearly told yer is rife in the neighbourhood. The lad is supposed to have got a girl in the family way before he went in the army, but now he's saying the baby isn't his. But true or false, my feller has no right to repeat it.'

Corker studied her face to see if she had deliberately let the cat out of the bag but her expression was one of innocence. Not knowing what to say, he looked at Ken and they both burst out laughing. 'I don't know quite how to answer that.'

'Don't bother, Corker,' Alice said, chuckling away merrily. 'I don't think men are any good with gossip, they don't make the best of it. My feller isn't anyway, he always gets the wrong end of the stick. So I thought I'd do it for him.'

'What sort of information were yer after, Corker?' Ken asked. 'Is it old friends of the family who want to get in touch?'

'No, nothing like that.' Corker dropped his head for a few

seconds to give himself time to think. When he looked up, it was on Alice he fastened his eyes. 'Can I trust yer to keep a secret, Alice? It's important.'

'Of course yer can! I've been acting daft with yer, but I'm not always like that. What I told yer about the lad at the back, that's no secret, everyone in the neighbourhood knows. The girl that had the baby to him, she's practically shouting it from the rooftops. She said he promised to marry her, but now he runs a mile if he sees her. Her whole family are gunning for him.'

'Her name wouldn't happen to be Joan, would it?'

'How did yer know that?'

'Come on, Corker, out with it,' Ken said. 'Yer didn't walk all this way out of idle curiosity, did yer?'

'No, I didn't. This Len feller is courting the daughter of a very good friend of mine. None of the family like him, but the girl is infatuated and won't hear a wrong word against him. This Joan turned up at the corner shop last week, asking if anyone knew a girl who was going out with a bloke called Lofty. It was through her we found out he lived in Tetlow Street. We connected the nickname and here I am! There's only one other person beside meself who knows about this. The girl he's courting doesn't know and neither do her family. And I'm going to have to consider very carefully whether I tell them or keep me mouth shut.'

'If it was a daughter of mine going out with him, I'd want to be told,' Ken said. 'Because believe me, Corker, the lad is a bad lot. Ask anyone in the streets round about and they'll tell yer the same thing. He was always pinching children's toys when he was young, then it went on to bikes and footballs. I used to feel sorry for his parents 'cos they're nice, decent folk, and they had years of neighbours knocking on their door with complaints. Mind you, that was before he left school and started work.'

'Oh, he doesn't pinch bikes or footballs any more, I'll grant yer that.' Alice's voice had more than a hint of sarcasm. 'He gets a girl in the family way, instead! His mam walks down the street with her head bent in shame, and his dad's put years on, poor bugger. If I were you, Corker, I'd find some way of letting the girl know. Better she finds out now before it's too late. If she married him, she'd be letting herself in for a life of heartache.'

Corker sighed. 'I'll have to think of something. But are yer sure that the baby is his?'

'I don't think there's any doubt. The girl, Joan, is a bit of a hard knock, but I don't think she'd lie about a thing like that. She was writing to him when he was called up, but when she wrote and told him she was expecting, then his letters stopped. And she wouldn't be the first girl he's messed around with 'cos I've seen him down this entry with different ones. He was only sixteen the first time I caught him with his hand up a girl's dress. I chased the pair of them, calling them all the names I could think of. And threatening to tell both their parents. I never did, though, 'cos I didn't want to cause no trouble and I thought that after me catching them in the act they wouldn't do it again.'

'It gets worse by the minute,' Corker said. 'He sounds a right bad lot. The girl he's going out with has two brothers and they'd kill him if they knew. But I'm going to have to be careful because I don't want to embarrass her or dent her pride. If I can put her wise without her family finding out, I will do. She's too nice to be made a fool of, and I'll have to make sure that doesn't happen.'

Corker looked sad as he stroked his beard. 'God knows how I'm going to do it though. I mean, I couldn't tell her, it would be far better coming from a woman. But if I told her mother it would only make matters worse because she's been telling her daughter the lad was no good from the day she clapped eyes on him. And there's nothing so humiliating as somebody saying "I told yer so".' He was very careful not to mention Lily's name in case it ever rebounded on him. 'The best thing I can do is talk it over with the woman whose concern brought me here today. She's me best bet.'

'Will yer keep us informed, Corker?' Alice could think of hearing no better news than that Len had got his comeuppance. The hard-faced rotter had got away with far too much. 'I'd like to know if the girl's got the sense to chuck him.'

'I'll let yer know if I can, but things are not going to happen that quick. No one is going to blurt it out, it's got to be done sensitively so as not to hurt her. And I'm hoping the matter will be in the hands of a very capable lady later today who will decide if, when and how. So it could be I won't know anything meself by Sunday, when me and Robbo are due back on the ship. But I promise yer'll be brought up-to-date as soon as possible. After all, you've been a fountain of information. When I came here I was thinking I'd be lucky if yer just knew the Lofthouse family. I never expected to get the whole low-down on them.'

'I'm glad me and Ken were able to help, but I would be grateful if yer could let me know the outcome, some time.' Alice felt the teapot standing on a chrome stand in the middle of the table. 'This has gone cold, I'll make us a fresh one.'

'Not for me, thanks, Alice, I'll be on me way. When I'm on leave, I spend a few hours every day with me ma. And I'd lay odds that right now the kettle is whistling on the hob and she's back and forth to the window to see if there's any sign of me.' Corker stood up and pulled on his peaked cap. 'It's been nice seeing yer again, Alice, and I'm grateful for all yer help. It's not a very pleasant story I'm taking back with me, but it's definitely one a certain person should be aware of.' He grinned down at his shipmate. 'I'll see yer on board, Robbo, and while I promise not to tell the lads about this apparition appearing at the top of the stairs, I won't be able to resist the shoes under the pillow lark. I think that's one of the funniest things I've ever heard.'

Alice preened. 'I could tell funnier tales than that if yer weren't in such a hurry. Yer want to come up some time with yer wife and we can go for a drink.' She pushed her chair in. 'I'll see yer to the door.'

Ken jumped to his feet. 'We'll both see yer to the door. It's not that I don't trust yer, Alice, but it wouldn't be the first time yer'd concocted tales about me so yer could get a laugh.'

So it was that Corker was waved off by man and wife, their arms around each other's waists. They could be fighting like cat and dog one minute, then laughing their socks off the next. They were lucky enough to have what every marriage needed – a sense of fun.

Corker was so deep in thought as he walked home that nothing he passed registered in his mind – not the people or the rattling of trams or the noisy motors of buses coming and going to the city centre. He didn't even see the confectioner's shop where he intended buying cakes for his mother. He kept going over all he'd heard and the more he went over it, the more sad and disgusted he was. Sad for the distress this was going to cause Lily, and disgust for the bloke who'd been stringing her along. She had to be told, there were no two ways about it. It would be a poor friend who had this knowledge and kept it from her.

Lizzie Corkhill was standing on her front step looking down the street for sight of her son. Her face registered surprise when she heard her name called and turned her head to see him coming from the opposite direction. Her heart filled with love, as it always did when she saw the man whom everyone called the gentle giant. He was that, of course, but to her he was the best son any mother could have. 'Where've yer been? I've been looking out for yer.'

'I had to take a message to one of me shipmates.,' Corker put his massive hands around her waist and lifted her back into the hall. There he held her frail body close and planted a kiss on her lips. 'I suppose yer've had the kettle on the boil for an hour.'

'More than that, I expected yer ages ago.'

'I did intend getting the tram or the bus, but it's such a lovely

220

day I decided to use shanks's pony and it took me longer than I thought it would.' As they walked into the living room, he said, 'I've got confession to make, Ma. I was going to treat us both to a cream cake, but I clean forgot about it on the way home until I was well past the shop.'

Her head as far back as her neck would allow, she gazed up at him. 'Well, it's a good job I made some fairy cakes this morning, isn't it? I must have remembered me son's got a head like a sieve.'

'Only when it comes to things that aren't really important. Like I'll never forget I have the best mother in the world and I love the bones of her.'

'Away with yer! Anyway, now ye're here, I've got a job for yer. As yer can see, I've got no net curtains on me back window. That's because the hook the wire goes on has come out of the wood. So while I'm seeing to the tea, would yer mind screwing it back in again for me? I feel naked without the nets up, 'cos the people at the back can see in from their bedroom window.'

Corker chuckled. 'And what would they see if they were nosy enough to peep? Yer haven't got a secret fancy man, have yer?'

Lizzie huffed. 'I don't comb me hair in the morning until I've had a good wash, nor do I put me teeth in.'

Corker's chuckle became a loud guffaw. 'Ma, they'd need a ruddy good telescope to see yer hair was out of place and yer didn't have yer teeth in! Anyway, when did this hook have the cheek to come out of the wood?'

When Lizzie grinned the lines on her face became deeper. 'An hour ago.'

'What am I going to do with yer, Ma? Fancy leading me on to believe the folk at the back had a free peepshow! Especially the feller with the telescope.'

'What feller with the telescope?'

'The bloke who went out and bought one the minute yer curtains fell down! He might have been of the opinion that a young bit of stuff lived here and he'd be quids in.'

Lizzie clicked her tongue on the roof of her mouth. 'Big and all as yer are, ye're not too big to have yer ears boxed.'

'Shall I get the chair for yer to stand on, Ma?'

'Yer'll get that hook in, that's what yer'll do. And give me less cheek, that's another thing yer'll do. Otherwise there'll be no fairy cakes for you!'

'Then let's get about our business, eh? I'll get the screwdriver while you see to the tea.'

Facing each other across the table a short time later, Lizzie asked, 'Is Ellen all right?'

221

'Yeah, she's fine. I wish she wouldn't go to work, though. There's no need for it now, with two of the girls working. There was no need for it before, because I can keep the family, but she can be stubborn when she wants. But having said that, I really think it does her good to be meeting people all day. She's a completely different woman to the one she was years ago.'

'I hope I'm not speaking out of turn,' Lizzie said, 'but she's saving up to buy herself a nice rig-out for the wedding. With the two girls being bridesmaids, she said she wants them to be as proud of her as she will be of them. And I for one don't blame her because I remember the years she had to walk around like a tramp. So I hope she splashes out and buys herself whatever takes her eye, and to hell with the ruddy cost.'

Corker smiled. His mother had really taken his new family to her heart. Being part of that family had filled her life with interest and love. 'I hope you too are going to be dressed up to the nines on that day?'

'I'll surprise the lot of yer, son! I'll probably even surprise meself! Molly and Nellie are taking me into town one day to help me choose a rig-out and they've warned me they won't let me buy anything old-fashioned. So don't be surprised if yer see yer old ma looking like a twenty-year-old.'

'It should be some wedding! I thought I might have to skip a trip, 'cos there's no way I'd miss seeing some of me very favourite people married. But as luck would have it, I think we're due to dock about four days before.' Corker had his fingers laced and was circling his thumbs around and around. 'I was so pleased, and proud, when Phil asked me to be his best man. I wouldn't disappoint him for the world.'

'Yer'll need a new suit, son, 'cos being a best man is important.'

'I'll get one on me next trip. They're cheaper abroad and they're made to measure. Yer choose yer material and get measured up one day, then go back for it the next. Yer can't beat that, can yer?'

'It's just as well, 'cos yer'd never get one off the peg to fit yer.' Lizzie's frail, veined hand covered his. 'Get a nice grey one, son, to please yer old ma.'

'Grey it shall be, Ma, if that pleases yer. And what shall I wear with it? A white shirt and a deep maroon tie?'

'That sounds just the ticket, son. How did yer guess what I was going to say?'

'Because I can read yer like a book. And because we have the same taste. Yer see, I'd already decided on grey, white and maroon. So that makes two satisfied customers, eh?'

'Like mother like son, eh?'

'And I know no one who I'd rather take after than you, Ma.'

222

When Corker got home from his mother's he began to prepare the evening meal for when Ellen and the two girls got in from work. And he had his eye on the clock for the boys coming in from school expecting a cup of tea and a jam buttie to see them over until their hot meal was ready. But his mind wasn't really on what he was doing, it was too full of what he'd heard about Lily McDonough's boyfriend. He needed to get Molly on her own to pass the information on to her, but how he was going to do that he didn't know. She was very seldom on her own and it was important that nobody else heard what he had to say.

'I'm in, Dad!' Peter, at twelve the baby of the family, poked his head around the kitchen door. 'When I've had me cup of tea, can I go out to play? I've promised to have a game of ollies with Harry.'

'Then change into your old kecks before yer go out. Yer mam will have yer life if yer kneel in the gutter in those.' Corker put the pan of potatoes on the stove and turned the tap on to rinse his hands. 'You get changed while I pour yer tea out. And I want yer to do me a favour and take a note to Mrs Bennett. I'll write it out while ye're upstairs.'

Peter's socks were around his ankles and he bent to pull them up. 'Why can't I just tell her the message, Dad?'

'Because it's private. And I want yer to make sure she gets it. Don't pass it on to Ruthie in yer hurry to be with yer mate, either. I want it put into Mrs Bennett's hands and nobody else's. Understand, son?'

'Yeah, OK, Dad!' Peter took the stairs two at a time, whistling happily, a twelve-year-old boy without a care in the world. Except that he was determined to beat Harry at ollies tonight. He'd lost one to his mate last night and intended to win it back.

While he was out of the room, Corker sat at the table putting a note together for Molly. In it he said he had something important to tell her but it had to be in strict privacy. And he asked her to let him know how that could be arranged. He was folding the slip of paper when Peter came bounding down the stairs. 'Pass me an envelope out of that drawer, will yer, please, son.'

'Yer've no need to put it in an envelope, Dad, it's only going next door! I promise not to read it and I won't put me dirty hands all over it.'

'Peter, do as I tell yer.'

The boy grinned and shrugged his shoulders as he pulled open a drawer in the sideboard. Grown-ups didn't half have some daft ideas sometimes. What a waste of a good envelope!

'What's this?' Molly ran her hands down her pinny before reaching for the envelope. 'Yer dad hasn't written me a love letter, has he?' She was running a finger under the flap as she smiled down at Peter. 'I should be that lucky, eh?'

The lad could see his mate beckoning impatiently and was eager to get away. He had to win back the ollie he lost last night because it was his bobby dazzler with lots of different colours running through it. 'I'll see yer, Mrs Bennett!' With that he took to his heels and ran, his socks falling back around his ankles as he did so.

Molly couldn't wait to read the letter so she opened it standing on the step. It would be one of Corker's jokes and she was smiling in anticipation as she started to read. But the smile faded as she read the contents. Corker hadn't actually said he had bad news, but she had a foreboding that there was trouble.

Slipping the envelope in the pocket of her pinny, she stepped down on to the pavement and hurried the few yards to the house next door. She didn't waste time in case Nellie was looking through her curtains as she often did, nor did she waste words in case there were ears listening. 'The girls are both going out tonight. Jill and Steve are going to the flicks and Doreen will be over the road at Miss Clegg's until about eleven. So can yer nip down about ten? Ruthie should be in bed by then.'

'Suits me, Molly.'

She searched his eyes for a clue, but they weren't giving anything away. But the thought of waiting until ten o'clock didn't appeal, 'cos she'd be a nervous wreck by that time. So she asked, 'Is it to do with a certain feller?'

Corker turned his head and cocked an ear. He'd heard the latch on the kitchen door being dropped and knew it was fourteen-year-old Gordon letting himself in from school. 'Yeah, ye're right, Molly. But I'll see yer later, OK? I can hear our Gordon, and he'll be wanting a drink and a jam buttie.'

With that Molly had to be satisfied. 'See yer later, then.'

There was mounting horror on Molly's face as she listened to what Corker had to say. He started at the very beginning and didn't leave anything out. And as he talked, Jack kept shaking his head and clicking his tongue in disgust. He was very straitlaced, was Molly's husband, and having a baby out of wedlock was against everything he believed in. And he had no time for thieves or liars.

When Corker had finished, Molly fell back in her chair. 'Oh, my God!' Her tummy was churning over. 'What a rotten swine he is! Lily doesn't say much about him, but I do know she told Nellie the reason he was quiet and didn't like mixing in company was because he'd had an unhappy home life.'

'No truth in that at all,' Corker told her. 'My mate and his wife said Len's parents are two of the nicest people yer could meet. He's led them a dog's life since he was old enough to go to school. My mate isn't one for gossip, and I'd take every word Robbo said as gospel. And his wife, Alice, she wouldn't make anything like that up.'

Molly took a deep breath and then blew it out slowly. 'Where do we go from here? Nellie and George will go mad, not to mention the boys.'

'I don't think it would be a good idea to tell them,' Corker said. 'It's going to be bad enough for Lily to find out her boyfriend is a rotter, but it would be ten times worse if she knew everyone was aware she'd been taken for a fool. If she could be taken aside and told quietly it would be better for all concerned.'

'That's not going to be a very pleasant task for anyone,' Jack said. 'I know I wouldn't like to be the one to do it. Lily could hold it against the person for the rest of her life, even if that person was only doing it for her sake.'

'I know of only one person who could do it in such a way that Lily would harbour no ill-feelings. Someone who is caring, and would know the right words to use to soften the blow.' Corker raised his bushy eyebrows. 'And that person is you, Molly.'

'I couldn't do it!' Molly was horrified at the thought. 'Lily would hate me if I told her all you've told us. She'd never look me in the face again.'

'What's the alternative?' Corker asked. 'Who else is there? Not one of her family, because the first thing they'd do would be to march en masse up to Tetlow Street to knock hell out of the bloke! And that would mean the whole world knowing Lily's business. I don't think that's what she'd want, do you?'

Molly sighed and cupped her chin in her hand. 'I don't think I could do it, Corker. I know I sound as though I've every confidence in meself, but I'm really a coward at heart.'

'She's yer best mate's daughter, Molly, so do it for Nellie's sake.'

Molly gripped the arms of the fireside chair and closed her eyes. She couldn't do it! She couldn't stand in front of Lily and tell her something that would break her heart. Then in her mind's eye a picture of Nellie appeared. And her chubby face was creased in a smile while her eyes were glistening with mischief. If the roles were reversed and it was one of Molly's girls in trouble, there'd be no hesitation on Nellie's part. She'd be right there to help her mate out.

'OK, I'll do it, Corker – but it'll have to be in me own way and the time and place will have to be just right. And that's going to be the biggest problem, for I only see Lily on her own once every blue moon.' Molly didn't relish the thought and she was shaking inside. But as Corker said, what was the alternative? They couldn't leave the girl in the dark, it wouldn't be right. 'I'll put me thinking cap on and see what I can come up with. But I'm going to tell her a lie and say I'm the only one who knows. That way, if she sends him packing, which she's bound to do, she'll be able to look people in the face and say they'd had a blazing row and she'd finished with him.'

'It's only a white lie, Molly, and all in a good cause. Apart from yerself, there's only me and Jack knows. Robbo and his wife haven't a clue about Lily 'cos I never mentioned her name or anything about her.'

'It'll knock her for six, love, of course it will,' Jack said. 'But she'll get over it and find herself a decent lad. And given time, she'll thank yer.'

Corker rubbed his hands together, glad he'd got all that off his chest and the matter was in the capable hands of Molly. 'Now, seeing as I've made yer both miserable, I'll have to do something to cheer yer up. Yer see, me visit to me mate's wasn't all doom and gloom. His wife Alice is an absolute scream and she had me in stitches.'

Molly thought nothing would bring a smile to her face, not tonight anyway. But hearing about the apparition at the top of the stairs, and Robbo's state of undress, brought forth a low chuckle. And Corker was so good at describing the expressions on Alice's face when her husband was hopping from one foot to another because he wanted to go down to the lavvy but couldn't find his shoes, the chuckle became a laugh. By the time he'd told them about the shoes being under the pillow, and Robbo's snoring being likened to a symphony orchestra that was out of tune and played loud enough to split yer eardrums, both Molly and Jack were laughing heartily.

'This Alice seems a good sport,' Molly said. 'Yer'll have to bring her and Robbo down one night and we'll have a good laugh.'

'He's as funny as her! When she'd gone up to get his shoes, he told me she snores worse than him! He said it was like being in an air raid, with sirens going, ack-ack guns blazing and bombs dropping. But if he tells her she gets a cob on and won't speak to him for days.'

'Yer've cheered me up, Corker,' Molly said, wiping her eyes. 'Life doesn't seem as miserable as it did ten minutes ago.'

'I'm glad about that, Molly, 'cos I wouldn't like to think I'd left yer with a load of worry on yer mind. But if yer feel all right, I'll love yer and leave yer. Ellen will think I've left home and will have the bolts on the door. I'll see yer both tomorrow. Goodnight and God bless.'

Chapter Seventeen

'How about going into town today, girl, and looking at the wedding hats?' There was eagerness in Nellie's eyes as she grinned at her friend. This wedding couldn't come quick enough for her, but she wouldn't dare say that to Molly, who was wishing she had a few extra weeks. 'Just to look, yer know, not buy.'

'There's not a snowball's chance in hell of me buying, sunshine! A hat is not on top of me list of priorities.' Molly sighed inwardly. If her mate knew what she knew, the smile would soon leave her face. But, please God, she would never have to know. 'Not that it isn't important, 'cos it is! As soon as I've got the reception in hand, like having the money to pay for it, then it's you and me down to Lewis's to buy two of their poshest hats.'

'We could still go and have a look, girl, that wouldn't cost nothing. We could try some on to see what style suits us, and we'd get an idea on price.'

Molly didn't have the heart to disappoint her. In fact, she felt like gathering her in her arms and giving her a big hug. 'OK, but I'm not spending any money. Every penny counts at the moment. I remember me mam saying once that if yer look after the pennies, the pounds will look after themselves. Well, I've been working on that and looking after me pennies, but I can't see the pounds looking after themselves.'

'I'll mug yer on the tram there and back, girl, so it won't cost yer nothing. I just want to see what these middling hats look like and if one would enhance me natural beauty.'

Molly chucked her under the chin. 'With your natural beauty, sunshine, it wouldn't matter if yer wore a beret.'

Nellie huffed. 'I'm not wearing no ruddy beret! How soft I'd look with everyone else got up like a dog's dinner! No, ta very much, I intend outshining the lot of them. If I've got to have a small hat, it'll have such a bloody big ostrich feather in that yer won't be able to miss me.'

'That is something I've got to see.' Molly grinned and waved to a chair. 'Sit yerself down while I go upstairs and put a pair of stockings on. I'm not going into town bare-legged.'

'There's no need for that! Now if yer'd said bare-arsed, then I'd agree. But who the hell is going to look at yer legs?'

'Yer never know yer luck in a big city, sunshine.' Molly made for the door. 'I'll only be two ticks.' It was with a heavy heart she climbed the stairs. The knowledge she carried with her was becoming more of a burden every day. It was Thursday now, and she'd never even set eyes on Lily, let alone got her on her own. And it was hard trying to keep a smile on her face when she was with Nellie. Something had to happen soon or she would make herself ill.

'There's a bus coming,' Molly said. 'D'yer want to get that or wait for a tram?'

'We'll wait for a tram. The steps on the bus are high, and me legs are too short. By the time I get one foot on the platform me knee's under me chin and the driver gets a good look at me bare flesh, me garters and me bloomers. And I have to pay for the privilege! It should be him what pays me for the peepshow!'

Molly pulled Nellie aside to make way for a man and woman who wanted to board the bus. They were both smiling, and when the man was on the platform he turned and winked at Nellie. 'I'm in the wrong job. I should have gone in to be a bus driver. It seems to be more fun than driving trains.'

When Nellie stood to attention her bosom and chins also stood to attention. 'Well, I never! The flamin' cheek of him!' She watched the bus draw away and when she turned to Molly the expression on her face had turned to one of mischief. 'Eh, wait until I tell George I nearly got a click. Not that he'll believe me, like, but just wait until I tell him.'

'The man was with his wife, sunshine, and he was only being friendly.'

'D'yer know, girl, you are as big a spoilsport as my feller! If it makes me happy to think the man was admiring me voluptuous body and trying to get off with me, it's no skin off your nose, is it?'

'No, it isn't. You stick to yer dreams, sunshine.' A tram shuddered to a stop in front of them and Molly stood aside to let her friend get on first. 'D'yer think yer can negotiate the steps without making a holy show of me?'

Nellie had one foot on the step and was gripping the upright bar with both hands. But try as she might to pull herself aboard she couldn't make it. She could see the driver grinning, and turned her head. 'Give us a hand up, girl.'

Molly put her two hands on her friend's backside and pushed until she was red in the face. Then taking a deep breath, she gave

230

one final, successful push. 'Thank God for that!' While Nellie straightened her skirt she glared at the driver. 'Have yer got nothing better to look at? Yer want to keep yer eye on the road or yer'll be running someone over. Then yer'd be laughing on the other side of yer face.'

'I'd have a job to run someone over, wouldn't I, Missus? The ruddy tram's not moving!'

'Well, how come there's a dog under yer front wheel?'

'Pull the other one, Missus, it's got bells on.'

'It's a pity the dog didn't have a bell on or yer might have heard it and pulled up in time.' Nellie was biting on the inside of her cheek to keep a straight face. She'd have the last laugh on this smart Alec if it killed her. 'OK, please yerself if yer don't want to believe me.'

The passengers heard what Nellie had said and had their noses pressed against the window to see if they could see the dog. It was their actions that caused the driver to curse as he left his seat and jumped down on to the pavement. He cursed even more when he found the road clear and looked up to see Nellie standing on the platform with her arms folded and a smile of triumph on her face. 'Have yer ever been had, Mister?'

The man was not amused. 'I've a good mind to throw yer off.'

'Oh, I wouldn't advise it, lad! I'm handy with me fists and pack quite a wallop. One belt from me and you'd be at the Pier Head before the tram.'

The passengers thought it was hilarious, all except Molly, that is, and there were shouts of encouragement. 'Where's yer bleedin' sense of humour, mate?' one man called. And another one answered him with, 'He hasn't got no sense of humour, the miserable bugger.'

But the one who enjoyed it most was the conductor. He'd just come down from collecting fares on the top deck when Nellie took off on the driver, and he was pleased as Punch. All the lads at the depot had this bloke noted for his bad temper and there was always a groan when they found they were paired with him. It was about time someone took him down a peg or two. He treated all passengers as though he was doing them a favour. And he was really nasty with elderly people who couldn't board the tram as quickly as he would like them to. He was not a nice man to know or work with, and the conductor felt like raising his hat to the little fat lady who had just made a fool of him.

Nellie swayed down the aisle to where Molly was sitting with her face turned towards the window. 'Are yer pretending ye're not with me, girl? Would yer like me to sit on the back seat, all on me lonesome?'

'Sit down, Nellie, before I strangle yer.' Molly wasn't as annoyed as she sounded; she had really enjoyed hearing her friend wipe that smirk off the driver's face. But if she were to admit that, then Nellie would think it a licence to come up with even more outrageous acts and heaven knows where it would all end. 'It's coming to something when we can't even get the tram into Liverpool without yer causing a scene. Now sit down and behave yerself.'

Nellie sat down quickly. At least half of her sat down quickly, the other half was suspended in mid-air. She really needed one of the long seats to herself, but nothing would part her from her mate, even though she had to hang on like grim death to the bar of the seat in front when the tram shuddered to a halt at the next stop.

There were several people getting off the tram so the conductor used the bustle to get to the little fat woman without being seen by the driver. Dinging his ticket machine he made his way down the aisle, shouting, 'Any more fares, please?'

'Here yer are, lad.' Nellie opened her hand to reveal the exact coppers to cover the fare. 'Two to Lime Street.'

'Put yer money away, Missus, this ride is on me for pulling a fast one on Misery Guts.' He bent down so not even finely tuned ears could hear. 'If an inspector gets on, say yer just got on the stop before.' He patted her on the back. 'Nice work, love.'

If Nellie's smile had been any wider, it would have split her face. She looked as though she'd won a thousand pounds on Vernon's. 'How about that, then, girl? I get a very handsome compliment and save fourpence into the bargain! Yer see, I do have me uses.'

'Don't look so smug, Nellie, it doesn't become yer.'

'Smug? What does smug mean, girl?'

'It means showing off. Like thinking ye're the whole cheese when ye're only the maggot.'

'Ay, that's good, that is, girl! I'll have to remember that if my feller starts throwing his weight around.' Her feet dangling a few inches from the floor, she swung her legs back and forth under the seat in front. 'I've got an idea, girl, and it's a good 'un.'

'Don't even think about it, sunshine!' Molly's shaking head was saying she'd had enough of her friend's ideas to be going on with. 'One caper a day is about all me heart can stand.'

Now Nellie wasn't as daft as she made out. She knew curiosity would get the better of Molly and before they reached the next stop she'd be asking, in a roundabout way, what the idea was. And she was proved right.

'I suppose yer were thinking of making it a cat under the wheel next time, were yer?' Molly tried to sound as though she didn't

232

care one way or the other. 'I don't know what's going on in yer head half the time.'

'I wasn't thinking of no cat, girl. No, I'll stick with the dog. After all, why change a winning hand?' There was a sly look on Nellie's face. 'I know it's no use asking you to lie down across the tramlines 'cos ye're not so obliging.'

'Before yer have me in hospital again, with you sitting on the side of me bed eating the grapes what Jack brought in, can I ask yer to move yerself 'cos we get off at the next stop.'

They were in the entrance to Lewis's when Molly took hold of her friend's arm. 'Now let's be serious for once, sunshine. A lot of posh people buy their hats from here because they have such a large selection to choose from. So can we show a little decorum, please?'

'I'll show anything yer like, girl, as long as it isn't that birth-mark I've got on the left cheek of me backside.'

Molly gave up. How could you fall out with someone who had an answer for everything? 'Come on, I'm only wasting me breath. But if yer turn around and I'm gone, don't say I didn't warn yer.'

There were no customers in the millinery department on the first floor, so the two friends were able to browse in peace. That is, until an assistant came over to ask if she could help. 'I'm looking for a middling hat to wear at a wedding,' Nellie said, showing her best haughty expression.

The assistant looked confused. 'A middling hat? I'm afraid I've never heard of the make or style, Madam.'

'Oh, dear!' Nellie's expression became haughtier. She glanced at Molly who was standing near, not knowing whether to laugh or cry. 'Shall we try elsewhere, my dear?'

That did it. Molly decided laughter was the only answer. 'My friend has a warped sense of humour, sunshine. It was me that told her she needed a middling hat, meaning one that wasn't too small or too big.'

'It was my feller what started all this,' Nellie informed the assistant who was beginning to think these two were going to brighten her day. 'He said if I wear a big hat he won't sit next to me in the church 'cos no one will be able to see it's me. And Tilly Mint here, who's supposed to be me best friend, she said I might end up wearing a beret! Well, they can both sod off because I'm going to wear a hat everyone can see me in. One with a ruddy big feather sticking up at the side, like Robin Hood wears.'

'Has Madam seen anything she fancies?'

'Yeah, I have!' Nellie knew a sympathetic voice when she heard one. 'But me mate said I hadn't got to touch any of them.' The round body began to shake with laughter. 'She didn't say it as nice as that, though. What she said was, "Keep yer flamin' hands off".'

Molly was worried that the assistant might think she'd make a sale, and thought they should be honest with her. 'Nellie, I think yer should tell the lady that we're only looking. We won't be buying our hats for a few weeks.'

The assistant, a woman in her forties with sharp features and her hair marcel waved, looked around for sight of her supervisor. She'd get a ticking off for encouraging people to try hats on when she knew full well there wasn't going to be a sale. 'It wouldn't hurt to try one on so you'll know which style suits you. Which hat was it that took your fancy?'

Nellie grew six inches, upward and outward. 'The velvet one over there, with the big ostrich feather in.'

'We have that in two colours, Madam, a soft shade of green and the one on the stand which, as you can see, is a deep lilac. I'll get it down for you.'

Nellie had never had a posh hat before, and she held it in her hand as if it was a precious gem. It was a close-fitting, hard-crowned hat with a short rolled brim. And the ostrich feather curled from one side of the crown to the other. The price tag told her it was three guineas which was a lot of money for a hat, but Nellie had fallen in love with it and was determined she'd be wearing it for her son's wedding.

'Allow me, Madam.' The hat was taken from her hand and placed on her head at an angle the assistant thought suited her. Then she led her to a mirror. 'I think it suits you very well.'

Nellie couldn't believe it was her own reflection in the mirror. 'Ay, girl, it does look good on me, doesn't it?'

'It looks lovely, sunshine,' Molly said. 'Yer'll not get anything that suits yer better.'

That was all her friend needed to hear. But what if she came back in a couple of weeks and this particular hat had been sold? It didn't bear thinking about. 'If I give yer a ten-shilling deposit, could yer put it away for me until Saturday, when I come with the rest of the money?'

'Of course, Madam. If you'll come to the counter with me I'll take some particulars and give you a receipt for the ten shillings.'

'Hang on a minute.' Nellie caught Molly gazing at a light beige, wide-brimmed hat she's said was just what she had in mind. 'Can me friend try that hat on? The one not quite as big as a cartwheel?'

'Of course.' The assistant hurried away, not caring now if the supervisor did come. She'd made one sale and there was every prospect of a second.

Molly was all hot and bothered. 'Yer shouldn't have said that, Nellie, 'cos I won't have the money to pay for it on Saturday! I've got plenty on me mind as it is, trying to save enough for the reception.'

'Yer don't need to buy it, girl, no one is twisting yer arm. But I know ye're dying to try it on, so why not when yer've got the chance?'

Molly should have stuck to her guns because the move was fatal. The hat was a real glamorous mother-of-the-bride hat, and once on her head she felt she never wanted to take it off. Looking at her reflection in the mirror, she told herself she wanted her daughters to be proud of her, and they would certainly be proud of her in this.

'Give her ten bob deposit, girl,' Nellie said. 'Go mad for once in yer life. Throw caution to the wind, break eggs with a big stick and go stark staring bonkers.'

'Nellie, I won't have the money to pay for it on Saturday, no matter how many eggs I break with a big stick, or how bonkers I go! It's four guineas – twenty-one shillings more than yours.'

'Well, you've got two getting married to my one, so it's only right yer have a better hat. And yer'll have the money on Saturday 'cos I'll lend it to yer.'

'I'm not going to borrow when I know I won't be able to pay yer back.'

'Holy suffering ducks! Ye're a stubborn bugger, Molly Bennett.' Nellie handed the amused assistant a pound note. 'Take no notice of what she says, just take a ten-bob deposit off the two hats. If push comes to shove I'll wear both the flamin' hats meself at the wedding.'

And the assistant didn't think for one moment that she wouldn't.

They sat on the back seat of the tram going home because all the other double seats were occupied. Nellie's smile had never left her face, while Molly's head was spinning. 'I don't know why I let yer get away with it! If I borrow the money off yer, Jack will go mad. He hates borrowing, and God knows when I'll be able to pay yer back.'

'But yer really fell for that hat, didn't yer, girl?'

Molly's features softened. 'It's the hat I've always dreamed of, sunshine. I fell in love with it straight away.'

'Well, to hell with everything else! If I know your Jack, he'd be

235

the last one to moan about yer getting something yer'd set yer heart on.'

'I'm not going to tell him – or anyone else. No one is going to see that hat before the wedding, I want it to be a surprise. Mind you, the biggest surprise will be if I'm ever able to pay yer the money back.'

'It won't matter if yer can't pay me until after it's all over, girl, 'cos with four working in the house I'm not exactly skint. And I don't have the worries you have. But it's yer own blinking fault for having so many daughters.' Nellie's eyes squinted sideways. 'If ye're not going to tell anyone about the hat, where are yer going to hide it? If yer've got a good speck yer can put mine with it 'cos I'd like to surprise my lot.'

'There's only Corker's mother we can ask. I did think about Miss Clegg, but our Doreen's never away from there and while I don't think she goes rooting, I'd rather not take a chance.'

'We'll ask Lizzie tomorrow then, girl, and take the hats straight there on Saturday.'

Corker's name brought Molly's mind to the horrible task ahead of her. The sooner she got it over with, the sooner she wouldn't be nervous and on edge all the time. 'I see plenty of your Steve, but I haven't seen Paul for about a week. Is he still out enjoying himself every night?'

'He's never in! Him and Archie have palled up and they go to dances all over the place. Last night it was New Brighton Tower, tonight it could be the Grafton or Blair Hall. The pair of them are dance mad.' Nellie was quiet for a while as she stared out of the tram window. 'If I tell yer something, girl, yer won't think I'm going barmy, will yer? And cross yer heart yer won't repeat it to a soul?'

'Have I ever done anything yer've asked me not to do?'

'No, yer haven't, but I had to make sure. Yer see, if it got to Archie's ears, he might stop coming to our house and that's the last thing I want.'

'Will yer spit it out, sunshine, and don't keep me in suspense!'

'I don't think Paul is the only reason Archie comes to our house. I reckon he's got a soft spot for our Lily.' Nellie held up her chubby hand. 'Don't tell me it's wishful thinking on my part because I thought it was that meself the first time I caught him looking at her with a soppy look on his face. But it's not wishful thinking, girl, I'm sure of that. He gets to our house long before Paul's ready, and I'm convinced he does it deliberately to see our Lily before she goes out.'

'But he knows she's courting, doesn't he?' Molly's heart had briefly flared with hope, until she asked herself what good was it going to do if Archie *did* have a soft spot for Lily, if she didn't return his feelings? Still, please God, sometime in the near future Archie might be in there with a chance. 'She is still going out with Len, I suppose?'

'Yes, worse luck! Every flippin' night like clockwork! Archie comes at half seven and Lily leaves the house at a quarter to eight on the dot. She never says where she's going or where she's been. And our Lily was never like that until the queer feller came on the scene. She used to tell me everything and we'd have many a laugh together. She's changed, and I blame him for it. I hope one day he rots in hell.'

'Don't give up hope, sunshine, I think she'll come to her senses one of these days.' Molly had made a decision, and also a vow to stick by it. No matter how sick, or how afraid she felt, she wasn't going to put it off any longer. Nothing would prevent her from seeing Lily tonight, even if it meant standing on the street corner until midnight. The sooner the whole sorry mess was out in the open, the better for all concerned.

'Here's our stop coming up, sunshine, so I'll make me way to the front to let the driver know we're getting off. You take yer time, there's no need to rush.'

'What are yer doing here, Auntie Molly?' Lily grinned at seeing one of her favourite people. 'Are yer standing on the corner hoping to get a click?'

'I wish I was, sunshine, I really wish I was.' Molly's mouth was dry with nerves and she told herself to get it over with quickly before her nerves deserted her altogether. 'I've been waiting for you 'cos I've got something to tell yer.'

'Why didn't yer come to the house to tell me?' Lily asked, still wearing a beaming smile. 'Or is it all cloak and dagger stuff?'

'I have to talk to yer, Lily, and I don't think yer'd appreciate hearing what I've got to say in front of yer family. So shall we walk down the entry to the main road, save being seen? Yer know what yer mam's like for standing at her front door.'

As they walked down the cobbled entry their two minds were having very different thoughts. Lily was thinking it was either a joke, or Mrs Bennett wanted to tell her something about the wedding, while Molly was worrying how her mate's daughter was going to take it.

Just before they reached the exit to the main road, Molly put a hand on the girl's arm. 'Can we stop here, Lily? I don't think we'll be disturbed.' Molly couldn't control her shaking hands, so she folded her arms and tucked them under her armpits. 'Before I start, I want yer to know I'm the only one who knows what I'm going to tell yer. It's the worst thing I've ever had to do in me life, sunshine, and I hope yer don't hate me for it. But because ye're like one of me own family, I'd hate meself if I didn't tell yer.' She closed her eyes and let out a sigh of sadness and weariness. 'It's about Len.'

As Molly talked, she saw the girl's face draining of colour and decided it wasn't necessary to tell the full story, a shortened version should be sufficient. So she explained that it was by a strange coincidence she met someone who knew Len. They told her his parents were nice, decent people and he came from a good home. Then, before she lost her nerve, she went straight on to tell of the girl Joan, and the baby she said had been fathered by Len.

Lily went as white as a sheet and fell back against the wall. Her lips were moving but no words would come, and her eyes were beseeching Molly to tell her all this wasn't true.

Molly felt terrible. Fancy standing in an entry with a girl she'd known since the day she was born, and telling her these awful things about the boy she was courting. 'I'm sorry I'm the one having to tell you all this, but no one else knows and I couldn't stand by and do nothing.'

Lily ran her tongue over her lips, and when she spoke her words were barely audible. 'Is this all true, Auntie Molly? There's been no mistake?'

'I wish to God it wasn't true, sunshine, but I'd be lying if I said it wasn't. D'yer really think I'd do something like that to you? I've been out of me mind for a week now, wondering what to do for the best.'

'And me mam doesn't know?'

'No, sunshine, I haven't told anyone.'

'I don't believe what yer said about the baby, Auntie Molly, because it can't possibly be Len's. He only came out of the army a few weeks ago.'

'He was going out with her before he was called up. And they were writing to each other while he was away, until she wrote and said she was expecting a baby. Then his letters stopped, and when he came home he said the baby wasn't his. But the girl is adamant he's the father and is chasing him. There's trouble brewing, sunshine, and I wanted to put you on yer guard. It's your life, and yer have to decide for yerself what to do. But if yer take my advice, yer'd be well out of it.'

'The person yer were talking to, how do they know all this?'

'They're neighbours of the Lofthouses in Tetlow Street. The only reason it was mentioned is because a young unmarried girl having a baby is bound to cause gossip. But they know nothing about you. I just listened and said nowt.'

Lily moved away from the wall and squared her shoulders. The colour was slowly returning to her cheeks and when she spoke her voice was stronger. 'I'm on me way to meet him now, so I'll see what he has to say for himself.'

'Are yer sure yer feel up to facing him?'

'I'm sure, Auntie Molly. I want to ask him to his face, and if he's telling me lies I'll soon know. If what yer said is all true, he's certainly taken me for a sucker with his hard luck tales about coming from a bad home, and how he was saving up for us to get married. But I'll give him the benefit of the doubt until I've spoken to him. It wouldn't be fair not to hear his side.' Lily touched Molly's arm. 'Don't look so worried, it's not the end of the world. And yer were right to tell me. I'm not going to say I don't care whether it's true or not because that would be a lie. I've known him for two years, and I'd be devastated if we split up. I'd probably cry me eyes out for weeks, but I don't think many people of my age die of a broken heart, do they?'

'No, they don't, sunshine.' Molly cupped her face and gazed into troubled eyes. 'If yer need anyone to talk to, yer know where I am.'

'Don't tell me family, will yer?'

'That's one thing yer don't have to worry about. Now be on yer way, and the best of luck.'

There were tears in Molly's eyes as she watched Lily turn into the main road and disappear from sight. Once again she asked herself had she done the right thing, because the poor girl must be feeling in a right state. With her head down, she walked back down the entry. Of course I've done the right thing, she told herself, there was no question about it. What would have happened if that girl, Joan, found out where Lily lived and confronted her on the McDonoughs' doorstep? There would have been ructions then, with the whole family getting involved while the neighbours learned enough gossip to keep them going for weeks. Lily would never have been able to hold her head up in the street again. It wouldn't have embarrassed Nellie because she didn't embarrass easily. But she would be very angry for her daughter and create merry hell.

Molly passed the corner shop but kept her eyes averted. She didn't want to be asked any questions and had no intention of ever talking about it to anyone. Except Jack and Corker, they would have to be told. A sigh came from deep within her. She didn't like telling lies and she'd told Lily quite a few about where she got her information from. But she'd done it with the best of intentions. At least when the girl met her husband or Corker, she could look them

239

in the face without feeling ashamed or humiliated.

Jack put his paper down when he heard the key in the lock and his eyes were on the door when Molly came in. 'I expected yer before this, love. I was beginning to get worried.'

Molly glanced towards the kitchen. 'Where's Ruthie?'

'She went over to Bella's for a game of snakes and ladders. I told her to be in for nine o'clock. And the other three are out, too, so we've got the house to ourselves. Tell me how yer got on?'

Molly slipped out of her coat and threw it on the couch before sinking into a fireside chair. 'Jack, I wouldn't go through that again for all the money in the world. When I was looking into Lily's face and telling her her boyfriend was a two-timing rotter, I felt like the wicked witch. And I didn't tell her everything, not about him stealing and all the other things. I felt bad enough telling her about the baby.'

'Did she ask yer how yer found out?'

'She didn't ask too many questions about that, thank God! I told her it was by pure coincidence I got talking to this person who lived in Tetlow Street and she happened to mention the name Lofthouse. The woman didn't know who I was from Adam, but she was a gossip and there's nothing a gossip likes more than a young unmarried girl having a baby. That was the gist of it, Jack, and I just pray she doesn't ask for more details because I've told enough lies as it is. I keep telling Nellie she won't get to heaven, but the way I'm going I won't have much chance, either!'

'What d'yer think she'll do?'

'I don't know. She was going to keep her date with him and ask if it's true about the baby. I think he'll deny it, so it's a case of whether she believes him.' Molly kicked her shoes off and sighed with relief as she wiggled her toes. The shoes were on their last legs but they'd have to do until she bought new ones for the wedding. 'Lily isn't as boisterous as Steve and Paul, but she's all there and I don't think she'll be taken in by him. I just hope anger comes before the tears because anger can rid yer of a lot of pent-up emotions. But the ball's in her court now, there's nothing else we can do.'

'Yer look all in, love, and I'm not surprised. I couldn't have done what you did.' Jack left his chair to give her a hug. 'I'll make yer a nice cup of tea, then I'll fetch a bowl of warm water and yer can soak yer tired feet.'

'Is that me consolation prize, sunshine?'

'Is it hell! *I'm* yer consolation prize.'

'Oh no, you're the star prize that I won over twenty-five years ago. And if we live another twenty-five years, yer'll still be me star prize.'

Molly lifted a finger when she heard a knock. 'This must be Ruthie, she's dead on time. Not a word about what we've been talking about because yer know she can't keep anything to herself.'

'I'm not soft, love!'

'I know that, sunshine! Haven't I just said that in the lottery of love I won the star prize?'

Chapter Eighteen

Even though she knew she was very late, Lily didn't walk as quickly as she would have done any other night. She wanted to collect her thoughts and calm her rapid heartbeats before facing Len. Nothing would be gained by allowing her temper to take over and starting a row before she'd heard what he had to say. A tiny voice in her head was telling her that her Auntie Molly wouldn't have said such things if there wasn't a grain of truth in them. But she didn't want to believe them, so she ignored the tiny voice. She was hoping with all her being that when she confronted him with the story, Len would laugh and say it was a load of rubbish, and that whoever was spreading this rumour had got him mixed up with another bloke.

Len saw her approaching and came out of the shadow of the wall to meet her. 'What the hell time d'yer call this? I was nearly giving up and going home! We'll have missed half of the big picture by now.'

'I don't want to go to the pictures,' Lily said, keeping her voice even. She wanted to stay cool so she could question him in a conversational sort of way. But she was hurting so much inside she wanted to blurt it out so he could deny it and chase away the hurt. It would take just a few reassuring words from him to ease the pain. But caution overruled her heart. What if Auntie Molly was right? She would rather know the truth than carry on in ignorance. 'There's something I want to ask yer, so let's go for a drink.'

'I don't want to go for a drink – yer know I hate the pubs around here.' There'd been no smile of welcome on Len's face; he looked like a spoilt child who hadn't got his own way. 'Let's go to the flicks like we said.'

The first warning bell sounded. Why would he never go in any of the pubs around here? They were no different to pubs in any other part of the city. Was it too near his home and he was afraid of being seen? 'I've told yer I don't want to go to the pictures! I want to talk to yer, and a picture-house is no place for that.'

'What the hell have yer got to talk about that is so important? Why can't it wait?'

'Because I say so! I'm always giving in to yer, doing what you want, but tonight is different. We'll do what I want for a change.'

'Then let's take a tram or bus to the Prince Albert, by Walton Hospital. I don't fancy going in one around here.'

But even though her heart was pounding, Lily stood her ground. She pointed across the road. 'See that pub on the corner? Well, that's where we're going, Len, whether yer like it or not.'

His lips curled. 'Considering yer've kept me waiting for three-quarters of an hour, it's a bit much to start throwing yer weight around, don't yer think?'

'If yer want to look at it that way, I suppose it is. But I'd say it's because I'm fed-up being told where we're going without having a say in the matter. Most boys ask their girlfriends where they want to go. And they usually get a kiss, when all I get is a snarl and sarcasm.' Lily walked to the edge of the pavement. 'If yer'd rather go to the pictures, then you go. But me, I'm going over there for a port and lemon.'

Len didn't believe for one second that she'd really go off and leave him in the lurch. And girls didn't go into pubs on their own anyway – it just wasn't done! But when he saw her look both ways before stepping off the kerb, he knew she was in earnest and this was one time he wasn't going to get his own way. She had never defied him like this before and although he wasn't very happy about it, he quickly followed and caught up with her halfway across the road. 'I don't know what you've got to be in a temper about, it's me what's been hanging around waiting for yer.'

'Who said I was in a temper?'

They'd reached the pavement by now, and Len put his arm around her waist. 'Come on, what's upsetting yer?' His voice was soft and coaxing. 'Tell me all about it and I'll give yer a kiss and make it better.'

But this time his smooth wheedling didn't work. Until she knew the truth, Lily didn't want him near her and she moved away from his arm. 'Let's go, shall we?'

There weren't many in the pub, just a few workmen standing by the bar and a few sitting at the small round tables. Thursday night was hard-up night, and many married men with families couldn't afford the money for beer.

Lily pointed to an out-of-the-way table. 'I'll sit there, you get the drinks.' She hadn't failed to notice his eyes scanning the room as soon as they were through the door. And she recalled the number of times he'd done that. Even when they were walking in the street he always seemed to be on the lookout. She hadn't thought anything of it until now, but then she'd had no reason to.

Lily sat tapping her fingers on the table as she watched Len waiting for the barman to fill his pint glass. Her whole inside was turning over as she asked herself how she was going to put the questions she needed answers to. For a fleeting moment she even thought of not asking him at all in case the whole thing was a misunderstanding. But she quickly dismissed that idea. If she didn't get it off her chest she wouldn't be able to sleep tonight.

'Here yer are, love.' Len put her glass of port and lemon on the table before pulling out a stool and sitting opposite her. 'Yer'll feel better after that.'

'I hope so.' Lily wasn't a drinker, she only ever had one to be sociable. And then she'd take ages to drink it, just taking tiny sips at a time. But she needed something to bolster her courage tonight and she drank half the glass in one go. Then, after running her tongue over her lips, she took the plunge. 'Len, do you know a girl called Joan?'

He looked startled and dropped his eyes – but not before Lily had seen a look in them that could only be described as fear. 'Er, no, I don't think so.'

'Oh, I think yer do! Yer went out with her before yer went in the army.'

Len's face went as white as chalk. Lily was on to something, but how much did she know? He'd have to take a chance that she wasn't in possession of all the facts. 'Yeah, I know who yer mean now. I went out with her before I met you. Why, what made yer ask that?'

Lily was beginning to shake, so she finished off the remainder of the port and lemon before answering. 'Because I believe she had a baby to yer.'

'Yer what!' Len was flustered but it didn't stop him from brazening it out. 'I'm going to the police about that one! She's been spreading these rumours about me just because I chucked her when I met you. She's had a baby all right, but it certainly isn't mine! And I'm going to have to put a stop to her blaming me. The father of the baby could be anyone, 'cos she's a fly turn and generous with her favours.'

'How would yer know that unless she's been generous with you?'

'Because the whole neighbourhood knows!' Len had been telling lies since he was old enough to talk, and it was second nature to him. 'She's a slut and I wouldn't touch her with a bargepole.'

Lily looked at him and sighed. Either he was a bloody good liar or there was a grain of truth in that he said. 'She also says yer were writing to each other after yer were called up. I suppose that's a lie, as well?'

'She wrote to me! Me mam was daft enough to give her me address without asking me first. But I never wrote to her and her letters stopped after a while.' Len's eyes became slits. 'Who's been telling yer all this, anyway? They want to get their facts right before they go shouting their mouth off. If anyone said it to me face I'd belt them one.'

'I heard it by sheer chance.' Lily felt so confused she didn't know what to think. She thought he would have looked guilty if it was true, but instead he'd given what could be a genuine reason for the girl to want to get her own back on him for packing him in. And he seemed angry that these rumours were flying around. That is, of course, if they *were* rumours. She just didn't know what to think. What she did know was, she wanted to be out of that pub and in the fresh air.

'Look, it was such a shock to me, I've got a splitting headache thinking about it. So I'd like to go home.' She reached down for her handbag which was standing between her feet. 'You stay and have another drink.'

'I'm not staying here on me own, I'm coming with yer.' Len emptied his glass in two gulps. 'Besides, yer can't just walk out on me like that! Yer make it sound as though yer believe all this rubbish about me being a father.'

'To be honest with yer, I don't know what to believe. But me headache's so bad I can't think properly right now.' Lily got to her feet. 'I need to get out in the fresh air.' Without waiting to see if he was following, she made her way out of the pub. There was a slight breeze blowing and she stood on the pavement to breathe in the welcoming air. This had to be one of the worst days of her life.

Len came up behind her and took her arm. 'I'll walk yer home if yer don't feel well. And I'm not leaving yer until yer say it's me yer believe, and not this cock-and-bull story someone's been telling yer. Whoever it was did it to split us up, and I'm not having that.' He led her across the road and his voice was so convincing it would have fooled anyone. 'Last night we were talking of saving up to get married, and now this! I'll kill that Joan when I get me hands on her, the evil cow.'

It was on the tip of Lily's tongue to say she'd also heard his parents were nice people and he came from a good home. But she bit the words back because she knew he'd say whoever told her that was a liar. And she'd have no way of knowing whether it was the truth or not. In fact, she had no way of knowing if anything he'd said tonight was the truth. She was all mixed up in her head, and she felt let down, sad and heartbroken. Perhaps when she was able to think clearly she might feel differently. Might even believe it was the girl, Joan, who was the mischief-maker and he wasn't the one telling lies. But she didn't want to talk about it any more tonight because nothing would be gained by it, they'd only be going around in circles. 'Look, I really don't feel well and would like to walk the rest of the way home on me own. An early night in bed would do me the world of good, and it wouldn't do you any harm.'

'Ye're not going to believe the words of a liar, are yer?' Len shook his head in anger and frustration. 'I thought yer were supposed to be in love with me? Yer were last night, before someone filled yer head with a load of rubbish.'

'Len, I don't think yer understand what a shock it was for me to be told a girl had had a baby to yer. I nearly fainted with the shock! So stop thinking about yerself for once and put yerself in my position. I need time to sort meself out, time to clear me head. And I'm not going to go over it all again tonight, I'm too sick at heart and weary. I just want to go home and crawl into bed.'

But Len wouldn't leave it there. 'I'm going round to see that Joan's mam and dad and have it out with them. She's not going to get away with this.'

'Stop it, Len! I don't want to hear any more! I'm going home now and I suggest you do the same.'

'Will I see yer tomorrow night, then? Same time, same place?'

'No, let's skip tomorrow night. I'll meet yer on Saturday as usual.'

'Give us me goodnight kiss, then.'

Lily backed away from him. 'I'm not in the mood, Len, so leave it until Saturday.' With that she turned from him, and her feet seemed to take on a life of their own as they covered the ground quickly in their eagerness to put a distance between them. And although Len watched until she was out of sight, he couldn't see the tears rolling unchecked down her cheeks.

Lily knew her eyes and cheeks would be red, a tell-tale sign of crying. So she stood for a while and let the light breeze fan her face. There'd be questions asked at home anyway, because she usually didn't get home until eleven. And although she wasn't sure of the time now, she reckoned it couldn't be later than half nine to a quarter to ten. She'd plead a headache and go straight up to bed.

Nellie and George were listening to the wireless when they heard the front door being opened and closed. 'Who the heck can that be?' Nellie moved quickly for her size and opened the door leading to the hall. 'You're early, girl, is something the matter?'

'No, I've got a headache, that's all.' Lily forced a smile. 'I thought if I went to bed it might go away.' She intended going straight upstairs but her mother had different ideas.

'Come and sit down, love, and I'll mix yer a Beecham's powder. They're good for getting rid of headaches as well as colds.'

'It's not like you to have a headache,' George said, turning to the shelf at the side of him to lower the wireless. 'And yer can't be sickening for a cold, not in this nice weather.'

'No, it's not that, Dad,' Lily said, putting on a brave face. 'It'll probably go away when I lay me head on the pillow.'

Nellie came bustling in, a steaming cup in her hand. She stood over Lily and fussed like a mother hen, telling her to drink the mixture while it was still hot and she'd soon feel better. And George looked on thinking how quickly his wife could drop her mantle of the joker who was always happy and hadn't a care in the world. When it came to her children she'd take on the world to protect them. If she could she would take Lily's headache and suffer the pain herself. And she'd always been like that with her children. Nursing them with love and tenderness through the chicken-pox, measles, and mumps. And she'd shown infinite patience, sitting up all night with them until the fever had gone and their temperature was back to normal.

'Where did yer get to tonight, then?' Nellie asked. 'The pictures?'

Lily was glad she had the cup in her hand, it was something to focus on instead of looking into her mother's eyes. 'No, I could feel the headache coming on, so we just went for a drink. And after one port and lemon, all I wanted was me bed.' The drink was piping hot but Lily kept sipping, willing the cup to empty. All she wanted was to escape to the privacy of her bedroom. 'I'll take this upstairs with me, Mam, and finish it when I'm in bed.'

Nellie went to take the cup from her. 'I'll carry it up for yer, sweetheart.'

'There's no need, Mam, I'll take it up meself. It's only a flippin' headache I've got.'

'If that's what yer want. But if yer need anything, give us a shout.' Nellie followed her into the hall and watched her climb the stairs. 'If yer don't feel well in the middle of the night, just give us a knock.'

Lily turned on the landing to look down at her mother. 'I'm hoping to sleep all night, Mam, but if it makes yer feel better, I promise to give a knock if I need yer. Goodnight and God bless.'

Nellie walked back into the living room and closed the door behind her. 'Just a headache, me foot! I think her and the queer feller have had a row. She's been crying over something.'

'Nellie!' George warned. 'Don't be making something out of nothing. What if they have had a row? God knows, we had plenty when we were courting. I remember yer walking off the dance floor at the Rialto one time, just because I'd said something yer didn't like! Yer left me swinging in the middle of the dance floor, and I felt a right nit! Then there was the time yer walked out of the Stella in the middle of the big picture because I'd tried to kiss yer!'

'Me heart bleeds for yer, George.' Nellie's face was one big grin. 'Yer've had twenty-five years of hell being married to me, haven't yer? Yer deserve a medal, and I'd be the first one to say it.' She dropped her head to try and rid herself of the grin, but her thoughts were so funny it only grew wider. 'D'yer know what I'm going to do for yer, so the whole world will know what a lousy wife yer had? I'm going to put an epitaph on the headstone of yer grave, and it'll say, "Here lies the body of George McDonough. A decent man until he married a shrew who drove him to drink and his grave". How about that, George? Don't yer think that's very thoughtful of me?'

'Nellie, I'm overwhelmed by yer thoughtfulness.' George placed his two open palms on his tummy as it shook with laughter. 'But ye're overlooking one thing. What happens if you are the first one to go?'

'Oh, yer've gone and spoilt it now! I had it all figured out! I was going to leave word with the kids that when I die, I wanted to be buried in the same grave so I could go on tormenting yer. And my epitaph would read "Here lies the body of Helen Theresa McDonough, the shrew what drove George to drink and his grave".'

'This is a very pleasant conversation,' George said. 'Anyone listening would think we can't wait to get rid of each other.'

'Yeah, we shouldn't be talking about death, it's tempting fate. And anyway, I've made me plans for the future. I'm going nowhere without me mate, Molly. Yer see, I've got a feeling I'd have a hard job getting into heaven without someone to give me a good reference. And as she's such a goody-goody, she's a dead cert for a place on the front row. And that's with wings and a harp. So, when she goes, I go.'

'Thanks very much! And what about me?'

'It's all in hand, light of my life! I'll take yer along with me and Molly, and once she gets me in, I'll put a word in for you. I'll tell them I made yer life on earth a hell, and yer deserved a medal but didn't get one. And in me very poshest voice, and borrowing some of Molly's big words, I'll ask them to give your case their careful consideration.'

249

'It's you that'll have to be careful about that, Nellie,' George said, pursing his lips and shaking his head slowly from side to side. 'Yer see, yer'd be leaving yerself wide open. You tell them that it was you who ruined me life, they'll say ye're not fit for heaven. And they'll boot yer down to the place below, where they've always got a fire going.'

'Ah, well, yer've stumped me now, I hadn't thought of that. So it's back to the drawing board, Nellie McDonough, if yer ever want to get to heaven.'

'There is another way yer can get there, love, but yer've probably never even given it a thought, either.'

'Oh, aye? And what's that?'

'Yer could take a leaf out of Molly's book and start behaving yerself.'

'And yer say I've never given that a thought! Well, that's where ye're wrong, George McDonough because I thought of that twenty years ago.' Nellie rolled her eyes to the ceiling. 'I tried it for about four weeks, but life was that bloody boring, I decided to be me own sweet self and take me chances.'

Lying in her bed overhead, Lily could hear the roars of laughter. And it added to her confusion. She'd hovered from believing Len, to thinking he was a liar. She wanted to believe him with all her heart. But her head didn't agree with her heart. And hearing her parents laughing together, and enjoying each other's company as they'd done for as long as she could remember, a voice in her head asked if she really believed it possible that she and Len could ever enjoy the same closeness and love as her mother and father?

Lily sighed and pulled the sheets over her ears. I'll never get to sleep if I keep going over it again and again. Take your mind off it, she told herself, and think of something nice. And the one nice event she was really looking forward to was seeing her brother marry the girl he'd loved for so long and who was like a sister to her. Then she thought of the design she'd seen of the bridesmaids' dresses and imagined them made up in that blue material. And she saw herself wearing one, with a band of flowers in her hair and a posy in her hands. The girl she could see in her mind's eye looked happy and was smiling. And when Lily finally dropped off to sleep, that was the vision she took with her to dreamland.

Molly opened the door to Corker the next morning. 'My God, ye're early, aren't yer? Yer might at least give a girl time to make herself, er, presentable. I was going to say pretty but thought better of it. It would take more than half-an-hour to make me pretty.'

250

'Molly, me darlin', ye're a fine-looking woman. Always have been, always will be.' Corker glanced sideways before lowering his voice. 'Nellie's not here yet, is she?'

'No, but she's due any minute. Come in and I'll put yer in the picture.'

'I won't sit down, Molly, I'd rather not be here when she comes. Yer know what Nellie's like for asking questions and I can't think of an excuse for being here, not off the top of me head, anyway. And this is the only time I knew I'd get yer on yer own. It's Saturday tomorrow and the kids will be home, then I'm away first thing on Sunday morning.'

'I'll make it quick, then, Corker, and yer can slip out the back.' Molly pushed a lock of hair out of her eyes. 'I saw Lily last night and told her. Only about the baby and Len's parents, I thought that was enough to throw at the girl in one go. She looked as though she was in shock for a while, and I got worried. But she seemed all right when she left me, and she's not turning against me, which was me biggest fear. She was going to meet him and said she'd ask him to his face. God love the girl, she said it was only fair to hear his side of the story. And that's all I know, Corker, I'm afraid. Whether she gives him his marching orders, or stays with him, only time will tell. But whatever happens, I think you and I did the right thing. Nothing will convince me otherwise.'

Molly cocked an ear when she heard a door bang nearby. 'This will be Nellie, Corker, so yer'd better make yerself scarce.' She opened the kitchen door for him. 'If I hear anything before yer go away, I'll try and let yer know. If not I'll tell Ellen and she can write to yer.'

Corker was down the yard and by the entry door when he said, 'Ellen knows nothing about it. I thought the fewer people who knew, the better. I'll give yer an address to write to when I see yer tomorrow. We're away for six or seven weeks, so the letter would catch up with me at one of the ports.'

Molly jerked her head backwards. 'Me mate's knocking the door down, I'd better let her in. Ta-ra, sunshine.' She closed the door and hurried through to let her friend in. 'Good God, Nellie, can't I go to the lavvy in peace?'

'How the hell was I supposed to know yer were on the lavvy! I'm not a ruddy mindreader!' Nellie stepped into the hall, squeezed past her friend and waddled into the living room. She was grinning from ear to ear when she faced Molly. 'Eh, girl, d'yer know those fellers we've seen on the pictures what go around with a stick and say they can tell where there's water by this stick shaking?'

251

'That's only in countries where they don't get much rain, sunshine. Yer won't find any of them here. They're called water-diviners.'

'Well, if I'd been one of them, and I had one of them sticks what tell yer where there's water, I'd have known yer were on the lavvy, wouldn't I? The stick would have led me to yer.'

'Thank heaven for small mercies! I'm sure I'd have been delighted if you'd opened the door when I was sitting in state. It would have made my day!'

'Yer haven't got nothing I haven't got, girl!'

'No, but I'd like to keep mine to meself, if yer don't mind.' Molly opened a drawer in the sideboard and searched through an untidy mess of papers, hairbrushes, pencils and other odds and sods that had just been pushed in any old how. 'I can't find me ruddy comb.'

'I can't help yer there, girl, 'cos I don't carry one around with me. Just run yer fingers through it, no one will know the difference.'

'I will! I'm not going out looking like something the cat dragged in. I'll have to use a brush, but I much prefer a comb.' Molly had quite a few white hairs in her head now, but with being blonde they weren't noticeable unless you looked closely. Which she did now as she stood in front of the mirror with the brush in her hand. 'I don't suppose I can complain because me mam's hair was snow-white by the time she was my age.'

'Oh, stop yer worrying. What's a few white hairs between friends?'

'That's just it – I got these white hairs *because* of a friend! You're the one who put these in me head. Ye're more worry to me than me whole family put together.'

'Ah, ay, now, girl, yer can't blame me for it! Me, what's yer best friend and goes out of me way to make yer happy. I could just as easy say it's your fault I'm so fat.'

Molly grinned at her friend through the mirror. 'I don't know whose fault it is that ye're fat, sunshine, but they made a good job of it 'cos ye're nice and cuddly.'

'That's kind of yer to say so, girl. And I think yer suit the white hairs, they make yer look very distan . . . distun . . . what's the ruddy word I'm looking for?'

'Distinguished, sunshine!'

'I knew what it was, but I just couldn't get it out.' Nellie turned her head so their eyes weren't meeting. 'It's funny how yer know all these big words but still let yerself down on fiddling little things.'

'What d'yer mean, fiddling little things?'

'Well, yer know before, when yer said yer weren't going out like something the cat had dragged in? That was wrong, yer see, wasn't it? For it to make any sense, yer would have had to go out first, before the cat could drag yer in. And for the life of me I can't see yer being daft enough to let a flippin' cat do that to yer!'

Molly spun around, the brush handle in one hand, the bristles in the other. 'Only you could think up something like that, Nellie McDonough! It was a real tongue-twister, that was.' She grinned and threw the brush on the table so she could put her arms around the little fat woman she adored. 'Shall I tell yer what yer are, sunshine? Ye're a little treasure.'

'Blimey, it's taken all these years for the penny to drop! I've told yer over and over again that I'm a treasure, but yer wouldn't believe me. It's taken a ruddy cat to make yer see what's been staring yer in the face for years.'

'All right, sunshine, don't let yerself be carried away. One compliment a day is all ye're going to get.' Molly picked up the brush, plucked the hairs from it and threw them in the grate. 'I've only got to put me stockings on, then I'm ready. Yer don't mind if I put them on in front of yer, do yer? After all, as yer said, I haven't got nothing you haven't got.' She lifted her arm as though fending off a blow, before adding, 'Only you've got more of it.'

'I'll let yer off with that for now. But I'll get me own back by making a show of yer in the butcher's.' Nellie watched her friend pulling a stocking on and wished she could reach her feet like that. It was a performance for her to put stockings on, her tummy got in the way. 'George said I was making something out of nothing, but I'll tell yer anyway 'cos I'm hoping to God I'm right. I think our Lily had a row with the queer feller last night. She was home by half nine and I'll swear she'd been crying.'

Molly kept her head down as she reached for the other stocking. Her heart was beating like mad and her mouth had gone dry. 'Yer might be imagining it, sunshine, because that's what yer'd like to happen. Didn't she say anything?'

'Yeah, she said she had a headache and couldn't get to bed quick enough. But I've never known our Lily have a headache before.'

'Well, yer'll soon know if she goes out with him tonight. If she does, then she was telling the truth about having a headache.'

'I lay in bed last night, girl, and felt like saying a prayer that she'd finish with him. Then I thought I better hadn't 'cos God would think that was wicked.'

'I'm not saying anything, sunshine, 'cos all the talking in the world won't make any difference. It's Lily's life, and although I understand how you feel, no one can tell her how to live that life.'

As Molly got to her feet, she was hoping her best friend would never discover the part she'd played in her daughter's life. 'Let's get cracking, Nellie. I haven't seen Vera Patterson all week, and I'd like to know how that Mavis's husband is. We'll give her a knock on our way to the shops.'

'Come in a minute, don't be standing on the step.' Vera Patterson held the door wide. 'I've been keeping an eye out for yer.'

Nellie couldn't resist. 'Which one?'

Vera looked blank. 'Which one what?'

'Which eye have yer been keeping out?'

Molly gave her friend a dig, but she couldn't help laughing inside. The trouble was, not everyone shared Nellie's humour. 'Take no notice of her, Vera, she has a funny half-hour about this time every day.'

'I could do with her staying and keeping me company, then. I don't know what to do with meself all day since the kids went back next door. I know they were at school most of the day, but cooking and washing for them gave me something to do. And me and Bill don't half miss them at night, it's like a graveyard without their chatter.'

'How did Mavis find her husband?' Molly asked.

'She got the shock of her life. He's only half the man he was, she said, but the doctors told her that with time, rest and the right food, he'd put back the weight he lost. It's his mental condition they're more concerned about. He's in a world of his own most of the time, and Mavis said he jumps at the slightest sound and looks terrified if anyone comes near the bed. He wouldn't let her touch him at first, he would back away as though she was a stranger.'

Molly sighed. 'Poor man, it just doesn't seem right! All because some jumped-up swine called Hitler wanted to rule the world, thousands of men have been killed and wounded. If he wasn't already dead I'd offer to hang him meself.'

'Mavis said there were a lot more men in the ward like Frank. Some worse, some not so bad. It's had an effect on her, I can tell yer. Going in that hospital was worse than any horror picture she's ever seen.'

'Any sign of him being moved nearer home?'

Vera nodded. 'This week, she hopes. But it won't be to Walton or the Southern, it'll be to a special hospital in a place called Mossley Hill. At least she'll be able to see him every day, and the kids might be allowed in. Mavis thinks that seeing the kids will be the best medicine he could get. It was the only time he showed that he was even listening to her, when she told him how the kids were doing at school. She's asked me if I'll go with her the first time she visits the hospital, just for a bit of moral support, like.'

Nellie felt she'd been left out of it long enough. 'Me and Molly will always go with her, won't we, girl?' She was thinking about all the bad things she'd had to say about Mavis Sheild over the years, and this had taught her a lesson. You should never say bad things about anyone because the day might come when you'd regret it. 'You could go with her one day, Vera, and we'd go the next. Just until she got used to going on her own, that is.'

'That's kind of yer. I'll tell Mavis and she'll be pleased. She hasn't got many friends, I'm afraid, because of the life she led. But I'm sure everyone will rally round when they know all the circumstances, and how ill Frank is.'

Molly knew most of the neighbours would rally round, but it was the two with poisoned tongues she was afraid of. 'Has Fanny Kemp and that mate of hers, Theresa Brown, had any more to say?'

Vera sighed. 'Every time they see Mavis they call names after her. They're always standing on their doorsteps gossiping, and they've only got to see her opening the door and they're at it. So she hardly ever goes out now because she's afraid of bumping into them. I get all her main shopping, and the kids run to the corner shop for the little things.'

'She can't be stuck in the house all the time just because of those two!' Molly was disgusted. 'It's a free country and she has as much right to walk the streets as they have. And what's getting my goat is they'll be laughing their socks off because they know she's frightened of them. It's just what they want! Her best bet would be to stand up to them, Vera, and lift her two fingers to them.'

'She's got no fight in her, Molly! She knows she's done wrong and is paying the penalty for it. And although I feel like giving them a mouthful when I hear the things they shout over to her, I'm no match for those two.'

Nellie squared her shoulders and thrust her bosom forward. 'You might not be, Vera, but me and Molly are. If I hear one word out of them about Mavis, I'll belt them so hard they won't know what day it is.'

Molly couldn't help smiling. 'Ay, sunshine, don't be expecting me to roll me sleeves up and have a go, 'cos I'm no fighter. I'd run like hell if they came at me. But I'd be in your corner, ready with a sponge and towel for when Fanny clocked yer one. She's got muscles on her like a man, has Fanny, and I'd not like to tangle with her.'

Nellie looked really put out. 'Thank yer for the vote of confidence, girl, it's nice to know yer've got faith in me.' Her shaking head had her chins flying. 'I've a good mind to go and knock on her door this minute just to prove me point. Before she had time to ask what I want, I bet any money I could floor her with one belt.'

'If she was standing on the top step, sunshine, and you were on the pavement, that would make her two foot taller than you. So the only place yer could belt her would be in her tummy. Now that wouldn't floor her, but it might knock the wind out of her for long enough for you to make good yer escape.'

Nellie looked at Vera with a sweet smile on her face. 'Doesn't my friend have a lovely way of putting things? Me, I would have said, "Ye're bloody pathetic, you are. Yer couldn't punch a hole in a ruddy paper bag". That's the difference between us, yer see. She can be real hoity-toity, while I sound as common as muck.'

'Ay, ye're as good and as clever as anyone,' Molly said. 'Yer pretend to be as thick as two short planks, but I know different.'

Nellie was well pleased. 'Did yer hear that, Vera? I knew she'd stick up for me 'cos she's me best mate. But I still say I could knock the stuffing out of Fanny Kemp.'

Molly jerked her thumb towards the door. 'Let's get to the shops before they close. If yer want us, Vera, give us a knock.'

Vera stood on the step and waved them off. And she grinned when she heard Nellie say, 'I won't go looking for a fight, girl, 'cos I know yer don't think it's ladylike. But if Fanny stands in me path, I won't walk around her, I'll walk through her.'

Chapter Nineteen

Lily glanced nervously at the large round clock on the factory wall, and sighed when it told her it was a quarter to twelve. All morning she'd been chopping and changing her mind, but she couldn't afford to waste any more time because the dinner buzzer would be going soon and then it would be too late. She moved closer to the girl she was working next to on the bench. 'I feel lousy, Ginny, me tummy's upset and me head is whirling. D'yer think Miss Birch would mind if I asked her if I could go home?'

'Of course not. It's you that'll have yer pay docked, not her.' Ginny was a pleasant woman in her late thirties. Her husband had been killed in the war, and with two children to keep she had to work to survive. Life was no bed of roses for her, but she never complained and was always smiling. 'I thought there was something wrong with yer 'cos yer face is as white as a sheet. Go now, before the break, otherwise yer'll miss her and she wouldn't be happy if yer took the afternoon off without asking permission.'

'I better had, I couldn't face standing here much longer.' Lily gazed around the workshop and saw the supervisor near the office door. 'I'll come back for me things, Ginny, before the buzzer goes.'

Miss Birch was a stern-looking woman and strict with the women under her. But she was also fair, and willing to listen. 'I noticed you didn't look well, Lily, and if you had mentioned it earlier I'd have sent you to the nurse for something to settle your stomach. However, it's too near dinner-time now, the nurse will probably have left for the canteen. So perhaps it would be better if you went home and took yourself off to bed. I'm sure your mother will get something from the chemist to cure whatever ails you.'

'Thanks, Miss Birch, I'll do that. I should be all right for work tomorrow, seeing as it's only half a day.'

'Off you go then, before the mad rush for the canteen starts.'

Lily took off her overall and folded it before placing it under the bench and reaching for her handbag. 'I'll see yer in the morning, Ginny, please God.'

'All right, queen, and I hope yer feel better soon.'

As Lily took down her coat from a hook in the cloakroom, she asked herself if the lies had been worth it. She probably wouldn't have the nerve to do what she'd spent the morning planning, and which had brought on the headache. Still, she'd carried out the first part of her plan, and when she was out in the fresh air, she might just find the courage to complete the rest.

Lily was shaking like a leaf as she walked up Tetlow Street. She hadn't a clue what number she was looking for, and so far there'd been no one around to ask. Then one of the doors opened and Lily took her courage in her hand and stood at the bottom of the path, outside a small wooden gate. 'I wonder if yer can help me, please? I'm looking for a family called Lofthouse.'

'Number forty-six, pet, and yer should catch Ada in 'cos I've just seen her coming back from the shops.'

Lily thanked the woman, and although her heart was pounding and she felt like turning around and running miles away, she forced her feet to carry on walking up the street. The houses she passed were three-bedroomed terraced houses, with a small garden in front and a path running down to gates that were either wrought iron or wood. They were all well-kept and it seemed a nice area to live in. And handy for shopping. Walton Road was lined both sides with shops selling everything you could wish for, a pub on every corner and a Mary Ellen at the top of every side street selling fruit and vegetables from small carts or barrows.

But all of these things were far from Lily's mind as she came to a stop outside number forty-six. Her teeth were chattering and her tummy was knotted with fear. But it was important to do what she'd come for because it was the only way to find out the real truth. So mustering all of her willpower, she pressed down the latch on the gate and pushed it open. She couldn't feel her legs as she walked up the path, and although she only knocked lightly on the door, it sounded to her ears like a clap of thunder.

'Yes, love, can I help yer?'

The woman looking down at her was the opposite to what Lily was expecting. For so long she'd been hearing from Len about how hard his mother was, but the woman she was seeing now had a kindly, pleasant face. 'Mrs Lofthouse?'

'That's me, love. What can I do for yer?'

'My name is Lily McDonough, Mrs Lofthouse, and I've been courting your son Len for nearly two years.'

The woman looked startled. 'He never mentioned to me that he's courting! Are yer sure yer've got the name right, love?'

'I'm positive. I see him nearly every night! At least, I did before he went in the army, and since he came home. I wouldn't tell lies about a thing like that, I'd have no reason to.'

'No, of course yer wouldn't, and I didn't mean to imply yer were a liar.' Ada Lofthouse was asking herself if her wayward son was bringing yet more trouble to her door. 'Did yer want to leave a message for him, or something?'

Lily shook her head. 'No, I wanted to talk to you. Could yer spare me ten minutes, please? I promise I won't keep yer any longer.'

Ada could see fear in the girl's eyes and her heart sank. What the hell had her younger son been up to now? Hadn't he caused her and her husband Jim enough heartache? But chasing the girl away wouldn't solve anything, and besides, she seemed a decent lass. 'Come in, love, I've just put the kettle on so yer timed it nicely.'

The hallway was three times the length of the one at home, and sported a very ornate coat-stand with spaces at the side for sticks or umbrellas. Although it was on the dark side, Lily could see everywhere was spotlessly clean and highly polished.

'Sit yerself down, love, while I see to the kettle. I'll have a cup of tea on the table in two minutes, then yer can tell me what yer came for.'

After Ada had placed the two cups of tea on the table, she moved an aspidistra plant out of the way before sitting down facing Lily. 'I was going to ask if yer were hungry and would like me to make yer a sandwich, but ye're all tensed up so yer'd probably prefer to get what yer've got to say off yer chest.'

'Yer might not want to tell me what I want to know, Mrs Lofthouse, but I think I have a right to know. I've heard some things about Len which are not very nice, and although he denied them when I put them to him, I can't bring meself to believe him. Yer see, he hates coming to my home, and when I've asked why he didn't bring me here, he always made excuses. I've been courting him for so long, yet you've never even heard of me! I've thought that was strange for a long time, but because I really loved him, I believed everything he told me. But I've been knocked for six by the things I've been told and I don't trust him to tell me the truth. That's why I'm here, to try and get to the truth.'

'What have yer heard, love?'

'I won't tell yer everything, Mrs Lofthouse, 'cos there's no point in hurting someone who has never done me no harm. So I'll stick to the one thing I would never forgive him for if it's true. I've been told a girl called Joan has had a baby to him.'

'What did Len say when yer faced him with that?'

'He said the baby wasn't his and that the girl was blaming him

259

to get her own back because he chucked her for me. According to him, she's no good and the baby could be anyone's. He blames her for spreading rumours about him and said if she doesn't stop he'll go to the police. He can be so convincing I almost believed him! But there's been so many times I've had my suspicions that he was lying, I had to find out for meself this time. And now I've seen you, I know he is a liar. I'm sorry to have to say that, Mrs Lofthouse, 'cos he's your son. But I can't ruin my life by marrying someone who is a liar and a cheat.'

'So yer've gone as far as talking about marriage, have yer?'

'Yes, of course we have! We've been courting for two years and he told me he was saving up to get married.' Lily was nearly in tears. 'I mean, that's what sweethearts do, isn't it, Mrs Lofthouse? They get married!'

Ada's sigh came from her heart. 'Lily, if you married my son it would be the worst thing yer could ever do. Yer'd be letting yerself in for a life of misery, not ever able to believe a word that comes out of his mouth. I should know because I've had twenty years of it. He's broken my heart so many times, it will never heal. It grieves me to say it, but he's deceitful and doesn't know what the truth is.'

Lily could hear the catch in the older woman's voice and her heart went out to her. 'I'm sorry, my coming here has upset yer and I didn't mean for that to happen. It's just that I didn't know what else to do!'

'You were right to come, love, and I'm glad yer did. At least I can stop him from ruining another girl's life. Joan has had a baby to him, she got pregnant before he was called up. He says it's not his, but the whole neighbourhood knows it is because the baby is the spitting image of him. And although Joan is a forward, outgoing girl, she is certainly no trollop. She's a good mother to the boy, who is about eighteen months old. And if she and her family have their way, Len will do the right thing and marry her. Me and me husband Jim agree. We both think it would be the makings of him, 'cos Joan wouldn't stand any of his nonsense, she'd knock it out of him. And we'd both be over the moon to have a grandson.'

Lily's sadness was turning to anger. Len had not only made a fool of her, he'd broken his mother's heart, allowed Joan to bear the shame of being an unmarried mother, and worst of all he'd denied his own son. Thank God she came here today to hear the truth. And thank God Mrs Lofthouse was a decent woman who wasn't blind to the faults in her son. 'I appreciate yer being so honest with me, it can't have been easy for yer. It hasn't been easy for me either, 'cos I cared deeply for Len. But I'm only young, I

260

can pick meself up and start all over again.'

'I hope yer do, love. Yer'd be better off without my son. And if yer take my advice, if he tries to talk yer round, tell him to get lost and in future give him a wide berth.'

'Would yer do me one more favour?' Lily asked. 'I'm supposed to be meeting him tomorrow night, but that's out of the question now. So would yer tell him for me? He'll know his lies have been found out when yer tell him I've been here, but he's cheeky enough to come to our house to try and get round me. I don't want him to do that, I don't want to set eyes on him again. And if he's wise, he'll stay away. My two brothers wouldn't take kindly to him bothering me.'

'I'll tell him that, love, and I'm sorry he's hurt yer. But as yer say, ye're only young and can start again. Just think of it as a lucky escape.'

'I suppose most people will say I've had a lucky escape, Mrs Lofthouse, but it'll take me a while to see it that way. After all, two years is a long time to love someone and I can't just snap me fingers and forget all about it. But he's let me down, lied and cheated, and I feel I've been made a fool of. If I think of it that way, then I'll get over it a lot quicker.' Lily pushed her chair back and stood up. 'I won't take up any more of yer time, yer've probably got work to do. But I thank yer for being so honest with me. Len doesn't realise how lucky he is to have you for a mother, but I hope one day he will. And I hope for the sake of everyone concerned, particularly the baby, that he does right by Joan and marries her. Perhaps she can make a proper man of him. Then you'll not only gain a grandson, but you'll have a son yer can be proud of. A bit late in the day, but better late than never.'

When Ada opened the front door to let Lily out, she said, 'I'm glad yer came, love, and I'm sorry my son has caused yer pain. But bear this in mind. If you'd married him yer'd have regretted it every day of yer life. Yer see, Joan could tame him 'cos she's tough, but you never would because ye're too nice a person and he'd have walked all over yer.'

'He has done for the past two years, Mrs Lofthouse, and like a fool I let him. But it's over now and I just hope things turn out the way you'd like them to.' Lily closed the gate behind her and lifted a hand in farewell. 'Ta-ra, and thank you.'

Lily walked slowly along Walton Road, stopping to look in shop windows to pass the time away. If she went home so early there'd be questions asked and she didn't feel up to telling the truth, or lies. The family would have to know soon that she'd finished with Len, but she wanted to be calm when she told them. She wouldn't tell them the reason, of course, because they'd go mad. She was passing a small café, but as it seemed to be quite busy, she walked on by. It was after she'd gone a little way, she asked herself what did it matter if the café was busy? She wouldn't know anyone because it was miles away from home, she was hungry, and it would pass an hour away. Besides, *she* had no reason to avoid people. She hadn't done anything to be ashamed of and should be walking with her head held high!

So Lily retraced her steps and pushed open the door of the café. She was taken aback for a few seconds by the noisy chatter, but while her ears were getting accustomed to the din, her nose was welcoming the smell of bacon and chips. She saw all of the tables were occupied and was about to turn heel and walk out, when a woman behind the counter pointed to a table near the window where two men in working overalls were deep in conversation. 'They'll be leaving in a minute, queen, so hang on.' She came from behind the counter with a plate of egg and chips in her hand, and when she'd served them to a customer, she beckoned Lily to follow her. 'Come on, queen, and I'll get yer sorted.'

'Oh, don't chase them on account of me, I'd feel terrible!'

'I'm not going to chase them! They're two of me regulars and if I tried they'd tell me in no uncertain terms where I could put meself.' The woman tapped one of the men on the shoulder. 'Ned, will yer make room for this girl, please, she's red with embarrassment. I've told her yer would be going soon, so yer won't mind her listening to yer conversation until then, will yer?'

By this time Lily's face was crimson. 'No, please, it doesn't matter!'

Ned grinned up at her. 'It's no trouble, girl. We'll just have to watch our language, that's all.' His grinning face was turned to the woman who worked behind the counter. 'I was just telling Bill about the bird I met last night, Nora, she was a real cracker.'

'Oh, had a good dream, did yer, Ned? That's the only way you'd pull a cracker these days.' Sticking her hands into her overall pockets, Nora tutted. 'I don't know, the older men get the worse they get. Why can't yer just grow old gracefully like we women do?'

'I'm trying, Nora, but I can't help it if I've got a roving eye.'

'Well, just keep yer roving eye to yerself and pull a chair out for the girl. And you and Bill mind yer manners.' She waited until Lily was seated. 'What can I get for yer, queen?'

Feeling decidedly uncomfortable, and wishing the men would hurry up and leave, Lily said, 'I'd like egg and chips, please, and a cup of tea.'

'I've got a feeling I've just served the last egg, but I'll ask my

262

feller what else we've got. How about a slice of Spam with yer chips?'

'That will do fine, thank you.'

Nora had turned to walk away when Bill said, 'Ay, Nora, why can't you lay an egg for the girl? Ye're good at everything else.'

'Listen to me, smarty pants.' The woman wagged a stiffened finger. 'One more crack like that and I'll bring my feller out to yer.'

'Take no notice of him, Nora, he should know by now that yer finish laying at twelve o'clock,' Bill said with a huge grin on his face. 'But do us a favour on yer way back to the kitchen, will yer? Walk gracefully, like yer say all women do when they're growing old.'

'That's enough lip out of you, Ned Shearing, and if yer haven't made yerself scarce by the time I bring the girl's dinner, I'll throw yer out meself.' Nora saw the smile on Lily's face and with a mock seriousness, warned her, 'If he tries to act his dream out on you, queen, then either clock him one or shout for reinforcements.'

'I'll do both!' Lily was surprised at her own daring. The lively exchange meant she hadn't thought of Len or her troubles for ten minutes. 'Then I'll run like the clappers.'

'Yer'd be knocked over in the scramble, love,' Bill said as he watched Nora walk back behind the counter. 'Me and me mate wouldn't wait around, I can tell yer. I've seen men twice the size of us being thrown out by Nora, because they complained or misbehaved.'

'Fair dos, though, Bill, they've deserved it.' Ned put his cigarette out in the ashtray and leaned back in his chair. 'Some of them complain over nothing. One guy even had the cheek to call her over, moaning because she'd left an eye in a potato and it had landed in one of his chips. All the miserable bugger had to do was cut it out, but no, he had to complain. And he wasn't quiet or gentlemanly about it either, he was shouting at the top of his voice so everyone in the café could hear. And he used some words that should never be said in front of a lady. If he'd been a regular, he would have known better, but it was his first time in the café.'

Lily's eyes were wide with interest. 'And what happened?'

Both men roared with laughter. 'Let's just say, girl,' Ned said, 'that the potato wasn't the only one to have a black eye.'

Lily's mouth was now as wide as her eyes. 'Go 'way! Yer mean the woman gave him a black eye?'

'A belter! And she escorted him out of the door with instructions never to show his face in here again. She didn't have to, because some of the regulars were ready to take him on for using bad language to a woman, but Nora waved us aside and said she

263

could manage. And, by God, she managed better than any of us could have done.' Ned picked up his cigarettes and matches from the table and slipped them in his pocket. Then giving Bill the eye, he said, 'It's time we were back at work, mate, while we still have a job to go to.'

The men bade Lily a cheery goodbye, and she was left alone at the table. But it wasn't long before Nora was putting a plate down in front of her with a slice of bacon on top of golden chips. 'That looks very appetising, thank you. I didn't realise I was so hungry until yer put that plate down in front of me.'

'Yer hopped in lucky, queen, that's the last slice of bacon. I think my feller had put it away for his breakfast tomorrow, but what he's never had he'll never miss.'

'I'm sorry for yer husband, but I'm not going to tell yer to take it back. Bacon is a luxury these days.'

'You muck in, queen, and enjoy it. I'll bring yer tea in a minute.' Nora walked away thinking the girl looked a damn sight better than she did when she came in. She'd looked like a frightened rabbit, ready to turn and flee.

The bacon and chips were tasty, and Lily was enjoying them. But it wasn't long before her mind went back to the reason for her being here. She had her family to face and lie to, then there was the thought of the lonely nights ahead. She'd stayed true to Len since she'd met him and had lost touch with a lot of the girlfriends she used to go out with. They'd all be courting or married by now, their lives running smoothly. While she, at twenty-one years of age, was going to have to pick up the pieces and start all over again.

Lily took her purse from her bag and approached the counter. 'That was very nice, thank you. How much do I owe yer?'

'One and six, queen. And any time ye're passing, drop in for a cup of tea or a bite to eat.'

'Yes, I'll be sure to do that.' Lily handed over a two-shilling piece and waited for her change. 'I'll try to do it on a day your husband has put a slice of bacon away for himself.'

Nora laughed as she handed over a silver sixpence. 'You take care, queen, and look after yerself. Ta-ra for now.'

'Ta-ra, and thank you.'

'Where are you gallivanting off to tonight?' Steve asked his brother as the family sat around the table having their evening meal. 'Jazzing as usual, I suppose?'

'Yeah, me and Archie are going to the Grafton.' There was mischief in Paul's eyes. 'Mind you, I'll swap with yer if yer like. I'll take Jill out and you can go with Archie.'

'That and cut me throat are the last two things I'm likely to do.'
Steve's dimples appeared. 'That's not being disrespectful to
Archie, because I think he's a smashing bloke.'

'You find yer own girl,' Nellie told her youngest son. 'God
knows, there's enough of them in Liverpool. The trouble is, ye're
too hard to please. If yer tell me exactly what yer want in a girl,
I'll flamin' well knit yer one! Yer can have her fat or thin, blonde,
dark-haired or a ruddy redhead! I won't give her a mouth, so yer
won't get fed-up with her nattering, she'll have long legs and feet
that can trip the light fantastic like a fairy.'

'Mam, what a brainwave! If yer knitted her tall enough, I could
practise me tango with her in the bedroom. Try a few new
fandangled steps out, like. Then amaze everyone at the dance with
me skill on the floor.'

'Me and Jill are going to the flicks,' Steve said. 'We haven't had
a night out for ages with trying to save up. But a few bob's not
going to skint us.'

'I suppose you're going out too, love?' Nellie's eyes squinted
sideways to where her daughter was sitting. 'Off to the pictures,
are yer?'

This is it, thought Lily. It's no good putting it off, they've got to
know sometime and the sooner I get it out of me system the
better. Trying to keep her voice casual, she said, 'I'm not going
out, so you and me dad are stuck with me. Yer see, me and Len
had a row and I've finished with him.'

There was silence as the family digested the news. It was the
best thing Nellie could hear, but she was sensitive enough not to
say so. 'Oh, yer've had a lovers' tiff, that's all.'

'No, Mam, it's over between us. We've been rowing a lot lately,
and I reached the end of me tether last night and packed him in.'

'He'll be knocking on the door any minute,' George said. 'I
don't think yer'll get rid of him that easy. He'll be round, mark
my words.'

'I don't think so, Dad. I certainly don't want him to. But if he
did, I'd like whoever opens the door to tell him straight I don't
want to see him.'

'It must have been some row yer had,' Nellie said. 'Whatever
brought it on?'

'It wasn't just last night, Mam, it's been building up for a while.
I'm not thrilled about it, not after two years, so don't expect me to
go around with a smile on me face. But I will get over it in time.'

'There's no need for yer to stay in and mope tonight,' Paul said,
hoping to cheer his sister up. 'Come out with me and Archie.'

'I will not! And don't yer dare tell him in front of me, either, or
I'll never speak to yer again. It's my business and nobody else's. I

don't want people asking me questions and looking at me as though they feel sorry for me.'

Paul pulled a face at his mother across the table, as though to say he was only trying to help. 'OK, Sis, keep yer hair on. I just thought yer might enjoy a night out.'

Lily was already sorry she'd bitten his head off. She shouldn't take it out on her family because Len had let her down so badly. 'Take no notice of me, I'm feeling down in the dumps. I'm not fit company for anyone, and I'd only spoil yer night out.'

'That's all right, kid, I understand.' Paul didn't understand, of course, because he'd never been in love. 'Perhaps some other night, eh?'

'Yeah, some other night.'

Nellie was dying to know what Len had done that was so drastic her daughter had turned against him. She prayed Lily wouldn't have second thoughts, but they'd have to wait and see. In the meantime though, she decided silence was the best policy. And to act normally, that was important. So she began to gather in the empty plates. 'You can give us a hand with the washing up, Lily, seeing as ye're not going out. We'd better do it now before the boys want to get washed at the sink.'

As Paul was pulling the front door closed behind him and Archie, Phoebe Corkhill was coming out of her house. She turned to the left to walk up the street, the boys turned right and the three came face to face. 'Hi, Phoebe, it's not often we bump into you,' Paul said. 'Where are yer off to?'

'I'm going to meet one of the girls from work. We go out together once or twice a week.'

Archie was eyeing the paper bag under her arm. 'I'm not going to ask if ye're going to the flicks, 'cos if I'm not mistaken, there's dancing shoes in that bag.'

Phoebe blushed. 'Ye're not mistaken, but we're not going to a dance.'

Paul chuckled. 'Well, ye're not taking them to be soled and heeled, not at this time of night. So where are yer going?'

'Ye're very nosy, Paul McDonough! I don't ask yer where you're going.'

Not in the least put out, Paul said, 'Yer don't need to ask, it's no big secret so I'll tell yer. Me and Archie are off to the Grafton.'

'Where I'm going is no big secret, either,' Phoebe was stung into saying. They must think her very childish and immature. 'If yer must know, I'm going to a dancing class with one of me mates. Now, are yer satisfied?'

'Connie Millington's?' Archie asked. 'I bet it is.'

Phoebe looked surprised. 'Yer know it?'

'That's where I started off. I couldn't put one foot in front of the other until I went there. I was as stiff as a board, with no rhythm in me head or me body. But three months after starting with Connie, I could flap me wings like a butterfly. If she can't teach yer, nobody can.'

This news lifted Phoebe's spirits and she didn't feel so self-conscious when she said, 'I've only been a couple of times, but already I'm getting the hang of it.'

'I know why ye're learning,' Archie said, pulling her leg. 'It's so yer can dance with me at the wedding.'

'Well, if yer ask me, at least I won't make a fool of meself.'

'Me and Archie can teach yer to dance, yer don't need to go to no dancing school, does she, Archie?'

'I know you, Paul McDonough! If I tripped up, yer'd laugh yer blinkin' head off.'

'Cross my heart, I wouldn't even titter,' Paul told her. 'Come with us to the Grafton and we'll mug yer to a tea in the interval.'

'No chance!' Phoebe was quite definite. 'I wouldn't let me friend down for one thing, it would be mean. And I'll not be going to the Grafton before I feel ready for there. So you go and enjoy yerselves while I go and learn how to waltz without looking down at me feet.' She walked around the side of them. 'I'll be seeing yer, ta-ra.'

'She's a pretty little thing.' Archie said as they continued down the street. 'Give her a bit more time to gain confidence, some stylish clothes and make-up, and she'll be a stunner.'

'I must be losing me touch.' Paul sounded surprised. 'She's the second girl to knock me back in the space of one hour.'

'Why, who was the other one?'

'Our Lily. She's packed that Len in, thank goodness, and I thought I was doing her a favour asking her to come with us. But she wasn't having any.'

Archie pulled him to a halt. 'Your Lily's packed that bloke in?'

'That's what I said. What have we stopped for?'

'Because yer've just given me the best news I could hear. I've liked your Lily since the first time I saw her, but I didn't think I had a chance with her courting. Me luck might change now.'

'Our Lily?' Paul looked stunned. 'Nah, yer don't fancy her, do yer?'

Archie's face couldn't have been happier. He'd taken a shine to Paul's sister at the Welcome Home party, and each time he saw her his feelings of tenderness grew. He didn't take to the bloke she was with; didn't think he was good enough for her, and was hoping for a miracle. But he didn't expect it like a bolt out of the blue. 'I thought she was out with him tonight when I didn't see her.'

'No, she was upstairs in her bedroom 'cos she wasn't in the mood for talking to anyone. She'll come round, me mam said, but it might take a few weeks.' Paul was thinking of all the dancing time they were missing and pulled his friend along. 'If that's what love does to yer, then I don't think I'll bother.'

'When love hits yer, yer don't have much choice.' Archie lengthened his stride to keep up with Paul. 'Anyway, to answer yer question, yes, I do fancy your Lily. And as a mate, I'm expecting yer to help me get in her good books. Without being obvious, like, 'cos that would put her off. If yer could coax her to come dancing with us one night, that would be a start.' He glanced sideways. 'I am serious, Paul, so don't be making a joke out of it. I don't want yer telling her that I fancy her, 'cos that would be goodbye to any chance I might have.'

'I might act daft, mate, but I'm not daft.' Paul was beginning to realise that Archie was indeed serious. And what a hundred per cent improvement he was on that Len bloke. Always a smile and a joke, ever courteous and gentlemanly with women, and very handsome into the bargain. 'I'm on your side and will do what I can. But as yer say, I mustn't overdo it.'

'I'll more likely than not see her tomorrow night when I call for yer. She can't keep running up to her bedroom every time there's a knock.'

Paul wasn't so sure of that. His sister had looked dead miserable tonight, and definitely not a good advert for love. In fact, it was enough to put anyone off for life. But Archie had set him thinking. With Lily being his sister, and seeing her all the time, he'd never given a thought to the way other men would see her. He did now, though, as he conjured up a picture of her in his mind. She was dressed to go out, with her face made-up, her hair brushed till it shone, and white teeth flashing when she smiled. Yes, she was an attractive girl all right who would catch any man's eye. For looks, she could knock spots off most of the girls he danced with at the Grafton. Funny, he'd never seen her in that light before. But then, being her kid brother, that was probably natural.

'I'm going into town tomorrow afternoon, love,' Nellie told her husband. 'It's something me and Molly have bought for the wedding, but we didn't have enough money on us so we put a deposit down and said we'd pick them up tomorrow. I can't tell yer what it is because it's a secret. But mine's a lovely colour and I know yer'll like it.'

'Yer've got a cock-eyed way of putting things, love,' George said. 'If yer not going to tell me what it is, why bother to mention it at all?'

'Because I'm that excited I had to tell someone.'

'But yer haven't told me anything! Except that ye're going into town. And that's not heart-stopping news, is it? Anyway, I'll see whatever it is when yer bring it home.'

'Ah, but yer won't, yer see, that's why I told yer. Me and Molly have found somewhere to hide them so they won't be seen until the big day.'

George shook his head. 'I wonder if Jack if being told the same useless information that I'm hearing? I'll ask him when I see him, to see if he made any sense of it.'

'Oh, yer mustn't do that' I said it was a secret and I only told yer in confidence. I'm sorry I did now 'cos yer can't keep anything to yerself.'

'Nellie, will yer remind me what the secret was that yer told me?'

'George McDonough, yer can be a stupid nit, sometimes.' Nellie tutted, but inside she was really enjoying herself. 'How could I have told yer anything when it's a secret?'

'I give up, Nellie, before yer start asking me to guess what it is.'

'I won't, yer know, 'cos I haven't got time for guessing games. I'm going down to me mate's to ask what time we're going tomorrow. And while I'm gone, yer can make a pot of tea and take a cup up to our Lily.'

Nellie couldn't wait to get down to Molly's. Leaving aside her joy and relief when her two sons came back safe from the war, the most welcome words she'd heard since Winston Churchill came on the wireless and told the nation the war was over, were those that came out of Lily's mouth, saying she'd finished with her boyfriend. And she couldn't share her relief with George because men didn't think like women. If he so much as guessed she and Molly had already made arrangements for tomorrow and she was only using that as an excuse to have a conflab with her mate about Lily's love life, he'd go mad and tell her she should grow up and learn to mind her own business. But her daughter's happiness was her business, and always would be. And there wasn't a mother in the land worth her salt, who didn't share that sentiment. 'Knock on her door softly, like, in case she's asleep. I don't think she will be, though, and she might be glad of a drink.'

Nellie hummed as her short, chubby legs covered the short distance to the Bennett house. And when Molly opened the door it was to see her grinning from ear to ear. 'Hi-yer, girl, I've got some news for yer.'

'From the look on yer clock, I'd say yer've come up on the pools!'

'How the hell can I have come up on the pools when there's no football until tomorrow?' Nellie used both hands to press her tummy in while she squeezed past Molly. 'Honest, girl, there's times I'd swear yer were tuppence short of a shilling.' She waltzed into the living room and gave Jack a beaming smile. 'I've only come to see what you two are up to. I know the two girls are out and Ruthie will be in bed, and I thought I might find yer in a compat . . . Oh, yer know what I mean.'

Molly raised her brows. 'I think yer trying to say yer hoped to find me and my feller in a compromising situation. Am I right?'

'Are yer ever wrong, girl? Are yer ever ruddywell wrong?'

'Nellie McDonough, if yer've come down here this time of night just to say that, well all I can say is, it's a pity yer've nothing else to do.'

Jack chuckled. 'I should be so lucky, Nellie! My wife is not so adventurous.'

'A stick-in-the-mud, isn't she? I have the same trouble with my George. There's a time and place for everything, he says, with a face as long as a fiddle. And apparently our couch isn't the place and there's never a right time.'

'Nellie, how come your mind is only ever on one subject?'

'Oh, it isn't, girl! Not tonight, anyway. I was only winding yer up, 'cos I like to see yer get all hagitated.'

'There's no "h" in agitated, sunshine.'

'I know that, I just threw it in for good measure 'cos I'm feeling generous. And if yer ask me nicely, I'll tell yer why I'm feeling generous.'

Molly sighed. 'If I don't ask yer, yer'll be here all night. So go on, why are yer in a generous mood tonight?'

When Nellie parked her backside on one of the wooden chairs, the chair disappeared from view and she appeared to be suspended in mid-air. With her arms folded across her tummy, she smiled from Jack to Molly. 'Our Lily has given the queer feller his marching orders.'

'Go 'way!' Molly said, while her heart sank. She felt really guilty about causing Nellie's daughter any heartache, and once again asked herself if she'd done the right thing. 'What brought this about?'

'They had a blazing row last night, which she said was only one of many. She wouldn't tell us what the row was over, but it was the final straw for her and she told him she didn't want to see him again. I didn't ask any questions because she is upset.'

'It's sad for her, Nellie,' Molly said. 'After all, she courted him for two years.'

'Sad be buggered! It's the best thing that could have happened! I've said all along he was no good. There's something wrong when a person can't look yer straight in the eye. She's well rid of him and I'm over the bloody moon. She'll have a chance to meet someone decent now.'

'Yes, ye're right, sunshine, she'll have a chance to meet someone decent.' Molly wondered what her friend's reaction would be if she knew the truth about Len Lofthouse? She'd probably seek him out and strangle him. 'Seeing as yer've made yerself comfortable and look set to stay for an hour, I'll put the kettle on for a cuppa. But keep yer hands off my feller while I'm in the kitchen, 'cos this is neither the time nor the place.'

Chapter Twenty

'There's a letter for yer, Jill,' Molly said when her daughter came in from work on Saturday dinner-time. 'And it's from Wales.'

Jill's face lit up. 'Ooh, it'll be from Uncle Bill.' She stared down at the envelope her mother handed over. 'I wonder if he's coming?'

'There's only one way to find out, sunshine, and that's to open it.'

Jill ran her finger under the flap and tore open the envelope. 'Me hands are shaking and me tummy's all of a do-dah.' She took out the letter and unfolded it. Her eyes scanned the first few lines and she let out a shriek of delight. 'They're coming, Mam! Uncle Bill and Auntie Annie are coming! Isn't that great!' She read further. 'He said not to worry about transport because they've got a car. And he says him and his wife were delighted to be invited and they're looking forward to seeing us all again.'

Molly was smiling. 'Yer dad will be pleased.' She held out her hand. 'Let's read what Bill's got to say.'

Doreen and Ruthie left their seats to peer over their mother's shoulder. 'I don't remember them,' Ruthie said. 'I must have been very little when they went to live in Wales.'

'Yes, yer were, sunshine. Uncle Bill is yer dad's older brother, and he's a smashing man. It'll be nice to see him and Annie again. They must have come up in the world seeing as they've got a car.'

'Me dad and Tommy are late, aren't they?' Doreen glanced at the clock. 'They're usually home by now.'

'Yer dad was hoping to get an hour's overtime in, and Tommy must be working with him. It's a few extra bob and we need all the money we can get.' Molly was thinking of the four-guinea hat, and what she was having to borrow off Nellie to pay for it. 'I'll put our dinners out and put theirs in the oven with a plate over.'

When they were seated at the table with their dinners in front of them, Doreen said, 'Me and Jill are meeting Maureen in town at half-two.' She speared a chip and bit off the end. 'We'll get all the material for the bridesmaids' dresses in one go, in case they sell out. And we'll get two reels of white tacking cotton and two as near to the colour of the material as possible. Then I can make a start on them.'

'That'll be a load off yer mind, won't it?' Molly never mentioned that she too was going into town because she knew they'd ask what she was going for. The likelihood of them bumping into each other was pretty remote, but if they did, she could make some sort of excuse. 'It's a lot of material, for five dresses.'

'I won't be carrying it all, don't worry. Our Jill can carry half, seeing as it's her wedding as well.'

'I'll carry it all!' Jill said. 'It's the least I can do, seeing as you're making the dresses. I don't mind being yer skivvy until after the wedding.'

'Whose dress are yer making first?' Molly asked, thinking the house would be a mess for the next eight weeks, while all the sewing was going on. There'd be patterns, pins, bits of material and cotton all over the table, sideboard and floor. She remembered what it was like when Ellen married Corker and Doreen had made her dress, and Nellie's and Ruthie's. It had been bad enough then, it would be ten times worse this time.

'Seeing as Lily and Maureen are the same measurements, I'll cut theirs out first. I can use Lily as the model, save Maureen coming up all the time.' Doreen didn't fail to notice that her kid sister had stopped chewing and was awaiting her answer with bated breath. 'Then I'll do Ruthie's, before the two girls next door.'

That's not bad, at least I'm not being left until the last, Ruthie thought before asking, 'How long will it take yer to make each dress?'

'I'm going to have to work flat out to get everyone sorted out in time. That means every night and Saturday and Sunday.' Doreen put on a pleasing expression when she looked at her mother. 'Do yer mind yer house being turned upside down, Mam? Miss Clegg said I could work over there 'cos there's more room, but I don't think it would be fair, not at her age, to have the place like a tip and the sewing machine going.'

'No, ye're right, it would be too much for Victoria. Anyway, seeing as it's my two daughters getting married, I'm not likely to mind, am I? That's not to say I won't ever lose my temper, but yer'll have to put up with it.'

'I'll start cutting the two dresses out tonight, then I can tack them together tomorrow and ask Lily if she'll try one of them on. If I keep at it, I'm hoping to have both dresses finished in a week.'

'I wish I could help,' Jill said. 'But I wouldn't know where to start.'

'Oh, yer won't be idle, kid,' Doreen told her. 'You can clear the mess up as I make it. And yer'd better tell Steve he won't be seeing much of yer. I've already told Phil, and he said he won't mind as long as he still gets his goodnight kiss.'

'We'll all have to muck in and do our share.' Molly was thinking Steve wouldn't be happy if he had to go a night without seeing Jill, so she thought of a compromise. 'But I don't want to go to bed every night knowing I'm coming down the next morning to a pigsty. So how about saying all work finishes at ten, the place tidied up, then yer've got an hour to be with yer boyfriends.'

The mention of boyfriends brought a certain person to Ruthie's mind. 'Mam, did yer know Gordon leaves school in a couple of weeks? He should have left at the last holiday, but because the term had started before his birthday, they made him stay on.'

'Yes, I know, sunshine.'

'And did yer know Uncle George is trying to get him a job where he works, as an apprentice?'

'Yes, I know that too, sunshine.'

Ruthie looked disgusted. Was there anything her mother didn't know?

Molly saw the look and chastised herself. Why couldn't she have pretended she didn't know about Gordon? It wouldn't have hurt her to listen to what her daughter had to say. So she hastened to make amends. 'I'm going out with Aunt Nellie, so if I give yer a penny for some sweets, sunshine, will yer go and play with Bella until I get back?'

That cheered the girl up. She'd buy a pennyworth of humbugs, 'cos they were Gordon's favourites. 'Yeah, OK, Mam!'

'I'll wash up, you two get yerselves ready so yer won't keep Maureen waiting. And leave the letter from yer uncle. I'll prop it up on the table so yer dad will see it when he comes in. It'll cheer him up if he's been working hard.'

'Here it is, Mam.' As Jill passed the letter over, she felt a gentle kick on her shin. She didn't need to look at Doreen because she knew what the signal was for. 'By the way, what colour are you wearing for the wedding, Mam?'

Taken unawares, Molly floundered for a few seconds. 'Well, I've got me eye on a smashing hat, and it's in a very light biscuit colour. So I thought I'd buy a material in a darker beige. The two colours should go well together.'

'So yer've seen a hat yer like?' Doreen asked. 'Where did yer see it?'

'I'm not saying no more. Except that as the mother of two brides, I intend to look the part, and make the most of the occasion. It'll be the best day of your lives, and the best for me

275

and yer dad.' There was fondness in Molly's eyes as they rested on her youngest daughter. 'And of course there'll be two more very special days in our lives. When Tommy gets married next year, and some years later when my baby is old enough to find herself a sweetheart.'

Ruthie was well pleased as she pushed her chair back. Flinging her arms around her mother's neck, she said, 'When I do get married it'll be to someone who likes this street, 'cos I'm not moving away from yer.'

Doreen gave a hearty laugh. 'The way things are going, the McDonoughs and Bennetts will own this flippin' street.'

'I'm going over to Bella's, Mam, I'll see yer later.' When Ruthie turned at the door there was mischief in her eyes. 'I'm going to brag about me auntie and uncle coming to the wedding in their posh car.' With that she scarpered before being told it wasn't nice to brag.

'The little tinker,' Molly said. 'It would be the price of her if the car turns out to be an old clapped-out banger.'

'If it's got four wheels, Mam, and it goes, I wouldn't mind having it,' Jill said. 'I rather fancy seeing Steve behind the wheel of a car.'

'Blimey! Yer'd be the talk of the wash-house!' Molly got to her feet and waved a hand. 'Get yerselves off while I wash up. Nellie will be here before I can turn around.'

'Can I have the use of the table after tea, Mam, so I can cut the pattern out and pin the pieces to the material? The sooner I make a start the better.'

'Yeah, OK. Me and yer dad might make ourselves scarce so yer can get on with it. We could walk round to me ma's and have a game of cards with them. And we'd take Ruthie to get her out from under yer feet.'

'That sounds like a very good idea,' Doreen said. 'Not you and me dad, of course, but I'd get on much quicker without Ruthie chattering down me ear fifteen to the dozen. I can't remember talking as much as she does when I was her age.'

'What? Yer were ten times worse than Ruthie will ever be! Even when yer were told to shut up, yer defied me and kept on talking. And yer were a damn sight more argumentative than she is. And louder! The whole street could hear yer when you took off. Once yer got something in yer head, no one could talk yer out of it. A stubborn little article, yer were.'

Doreen chuckled. 'I haven't changed much, have I?'

'Enough, sunshine, enough! In fact, from the day yer met Phil Bradley yer've changed a lot. Ye're more kind, gentle, caring and understanding. And,' Molly grinned, 'yer don't fly off the handle if things don't go your way.'

'He's been good for me, Mam, and I love the bones of him.'

'I know yer do, sunshine, and yer'll never know how happy I am that both of my lovely daughters are marrying fine, upstanding men who will take good care of them. And now, if yer don't mind, will yer put a move on before the afternoon is over?'

'My God, yer don't half look smart, sunshine!'

Nellie drew herself up to her full four foot ten inches. 'Slept in ruddy curlers, didn't I? They gave me hell through the night, and a few times I was going to take them out. But I persevered, girl, 'cos I didn't want to go to pick up me three-guinea hat with a turban on me head, dirty nails and me stockings all wrinkled. I wasn't going to have no hoity-toity snobs looking down their noses at me.'

'Well, yer look a treat.' Molly picked up her coat from the arm of the couch where she'd draped it in readiness. 'I thought Jack and Tommy would have been home by now. I've lowered the gas in the oven and I'm hoping their dinners don't dry up.' When she was fastening the buttons on her coat, she asked, 'How is Lily?'

'If looks are anything to go by, she's feeling bloody awful. She went into work, even though I told her she should take the morning off. She's going to be at a loose end, having no friends to go out with. I do feel sorry for her, but I hope to God she sticks it out. If she gets back with that swine, I'll go mad, because I know in me heart she wouldn't find happiness with him.'

'Is she in the house now?'

'Yeah, she was reading a magazine when I came out. At least she was pretending to. She's got the house to herself because Liverpool are playing at home and George and Steve have gone to the match. Paul went out right after he'd had his dinner, heaven knows where to, so Lily is on her lonesome.'

'My two girls have gone to town to buy the material for the bridesmaids' dresses. Doreen is cutting one out tonight, and she said when she's got it tacked she'll ask Lily to try it on for size. D'yer think I should tell her to leave it, 'cos Lily's not feeling well?'

'No, don't do that, girl. She'll sit and mope for ever if she's let! The best thing we can all do is treat her as we normally would. Let Doreen ask her to try the dress on – at least it will take her mind off things for a while.'

'Does she know that yer've told me about her falling-out with Len?'

Nellie started to shake her head before she remembered the curls she'd suffered all night for; she didn't want them to fall out.

'I haven't said nothing, girl. I thought it best to keep me mouth shut and say nowt.'

Molly had a thought. 'How about if I give a knock and tell her about the dress? I can't see her saying she won't try it on, that wouldn't be like Lily. And she might mention about her and Len, so I can pass it on and she won't have the embarrassment of having to tell everyone herself. D'yer think that's a good idea, or not?'

'It'll be a good idea if she opens the door to yer. But I've got a feeling she won't, in case it's the queer feller himself.'

Molly needed to see Lily for her own sake. To make sure she wasn't responsible for the girl doing something she didn't really want to do. Perhaps she would have stood by the bloke, even knowing what he was, if she thought nobody else knew. It was possible she'd packed him in to save face, and that wouldn't be right. 'I'll give a knock and see. But you stay outside, Nellie, because she won't say anything if you're there.'

'OK, girl, but don't be all day, will yer? I'll look a right nit standing outside me own house. The neighbours will think George has thrown me out.'

'Well, stand on my step if it makes yer feel better.'

There was no answer to Molly's first knock, so she lifted the letter box and called through. 'It's Molly Bennett, sunshine!'

The door was opened just enough for Lily's ashen face to be seen. 'Me mam's not in, Auntie Molly.'

'I know that, she's standing on my front step calling me for everything for keeping her waiting. But I wanted a word with yer, so can I come in?'

Lily hesitated briefly, then stepped aside. 'Come in.'

'I won't come right in, sunshine, or yer mam will be spitting feathers. Let's just stand in the hall.' Molly leaned back and felt pity for the girl who looked as though the bottom had dropped out of her world. 'Our Doreen's getting the material for the dresses today, and she's hoping to have one cut out tonight. She mentioned she was going to ask you to try it on when it's tacked, but when I told yer mam, she said yer weren't feeling too well.'

'I feel ruddy awful, Auntie Molly, and that's putting it mildly. Yer see, I finished with Len and it's really upset me.'

'I'll be quick about this, sunshine, or yer mam will be coming for me. It's something I've got to get off me chest. If you really love Len, then take no notice of what I told yer about him. You follow your own heart, Lily; don't be put off by what others say.'

'This is between you and me, Auntie Molly, and I'm trusting yer to let it go no further. As far as anyone else is concerned, I packed Len up because we were always rowing. That's what I

278

want them to think. But the truth is, I wasn't put off by what you told me, I found out for meself. I went to his house and saw his mother. She was a lovely woman, not the hard person he'd told me she was. That was the first lie I found him out in. Then she told me about the girl, Joan, and the baby she has that is the spitting image of Len. There was a lot more said, Auntie Molly, and perhaps I'll tell yer when we've more time. But don't you go on thinking this is all your fault, because it isn't. The blame lies with the man I thought I was in love with for two years. But I've found out that man doesn't exist, and while I'll miss him for a while, I hate him for stringing me along with his lies.'

To say that Molly was surprised would be an understatement. 'That took some spunk, sunshine, and I take me hat off to yer. It was a very brave thing to do. And if yer keep thinking along those lines, yer'll get him out of yer system in no time. He'll just be a distant memory.' Molly put her hand on the door latch. 'I'll have to go, but we'll have a good talk sometime. Now, can I tell Doreen yer'll act as her model when she's got the dress ready for trying on?'

Lily managed a weak smile. 'Of course yer can. Tell her to give me a shout when she wants me.' As Molly began to open the door, Lily put out her hand. 'Will yer tell the girls and everyone I've finished with Len, please, Auntie Molly, to save me having to do it?'

Molly gave her a quick hug and a kiss. 'Of course I will, sunshine. And take my word for it, it'll be a nine days' wonder.'

Nellie snorted when Molly walked towards her. 'I've taken root here! I've been expecting the neighbours to come out and water me.'

'Shut me front door, sunshine, and stop yer moaning.' Molly waited until her friend had closed the door and they began to walk down the street. But she shook her head when Nellie tried to link arms. 'Not today, sunshine, I ain't cleaning any windowsills with me coat.'

'What did our Lily have to say?'

'She told me she'd finished with Len, but she didn't say why and I didn't ask. And she said of course she'll help Doreen with the fitting.'

'That's all she said?'

'Well, I've made it brief for you, but that was about the size of it, yeah.'

Nellie held an open hand out and began to tick off her fingers. 'I've finished with Len. That's four words. Of course I'll help Doreen with the fitting. That's another eight words. So it took yer half an hour to listen to her saying twelve words. There must be something very wrong with your ears, girl, 'cos ye're obviously hearing everything in slow motion. Unless our Lily has suddenly developed a stutter.'

Molly chuckled. 'Yer hate to miss anything, don't yer, Nellie McDonough? And yer don't half exaggerate. I was no longer than five or six minutes. I didn't even go in yer living room – me and Lily stood in the hall. I've a good mind not to tell yer what I think now, seeing as ye're so blinking bad-tempered.'

'Bad-tempered! Me – bad-tempered? Never on your life, Molly Bennett, and well you know it. I'm noted for me sweet and even temper. Mind you, I think I could get really mad if someone upset me enough. Like, for instance, one of me so-called friends refusing to tell me what she thinks about me loving daughter's situation.'

'Yer so-called friend is of the opinion that yer daughter has no intention of ever making it up with Len Lofthouse. And the same so-called friend believes that if the girl is not asked too many questions, nor treated as though some great sadness has befallen her, then she'll get over it in her own sweet time.'

'Yer really don't think she'll get back with him, then?'

'Nellie, don't take what I say as gospel. I'm only giving yer my opinion for what it's worth. Don't you come after me with the rolling pin if I'm wrong.'

But Nellie trusted her friend's instinct. And with her heart lighter, her hair in curls and the seams of her lisle stockings straight, she felt well satisfied with her lot in life. 'I can't wait to see me hat again, can you, girl?'

'Oh, let me give yer some money off mine.' Molly fished in her bag for the well-worn purse. 'I've paid ten bob deposit, so that means there's three pound fourteen shillings to pay on it. If I give you fourteen shillings now, that'll mean I owe yer three pound.'

'Listen, girl, yer've no need to pay anything until after the wedding. You hang on to yer money to pay all the other bills yer'll have coming in.'

'No, I'll pay yer the fourteen shillings and I'll know where I'm working.' Molly took a ten-shilling note and two two-bob pieces from her purse and handed them over. 'That's three pound I owe yer, and I'll pay it back as soon as I can. Out of debt, out of danger, as me ma always says.'

'OK, girl, have it yer own way. But if yer find yerself skint, yer know where to knock. There's many a time in the past when I've been glad to borrow off you.'

'And vice versa, sunshine, don't forget. It's always been share and share alike.'

Nellie smiled and winked. 'Aye, we've been good mates, girl, no doubt.'

★　★　★

Molly had not long gone when there was a knock on the McDonoughs' door. Thinking her auntie had forgotten to tell her something, Lily had no qualms about opening the door. But she gasped in dismay when she saw Len standing there. 'What do you want? I asked yer mother to tell yer I didn't want to see yer again.'

'I don't know what me mam told yer, but it must have been a load of lies. I'd warned yer what me parents were like, so I'm surprised yer took any notice of her.' Len knew Lily was alone; he'd been watching the house from an entry a bit higher up the road and had seen all the family going out. 'Can I come in and talk to yer?'

Lily moved to stand in the middle of the doorway, with her arms folded. 'No, yer can't come in. I don't want to hear anything yer've got to say because I know it'll be lies. And I don't know how yer've got the nerve to face me, anyway!'

'Why shouldn't I face yer? I've done nothing wrong. Just give me five minutes to tell yer my side of the story.'

'Ye're not getting in this house, Len Lofthouse, so yer'd best be on yer way. I know the truth about yer now, and just looking at yer makes me sick. Yer get a young girl into trouble, then deny ye're the father of her child and leave her to face the shame. If yer were a man, yer'd face up to yer responsibilities and marry her. But ye're not a man, just a poor excuse for one. And I'm only glad I found out in time what ye're really like. And when I look at yer now I wonder what the hell I ever saw in yer. I must have been blind and stupid.' Lily watched the effect her words were having and for a second was afraid of him. His face was red with temper and his eyes were blazing because things weren't going the way he'd planned. 'Do yerself a favour and get away from this front door.'

Len was so used to her believing everything he said, he was convinced he could talk her around if he got the chance to hold her in his arms and sweet talk her. He'd always got away with it before. So he moved fast: so fast he almost succeeded in getting past Lily. But she anticipated his action, and with her two hands flat on his chest, she pushed with every bit of strength she possessed. 'If yer don't go, I'll scream at the top of me voice.'

He now realised that this time she wasn't going to be talked round, and his temper flared. Like a child who'd had his pet toy taken from him, he wanted to smash his fist in her face. 'You won't scream, Lily, 'cos yer'd be too frightened of what the neighbours would say.'

'Go away!' Lily, close to tears, stepped back and tried to close the door. But she wasn't quick enough and his foot shot out to keep it open. 'Please go, Len, I don't want any trouble.'

The fear on her face pleased him, and filled him with a sense of power. 'Ye're a stupid bitch, d'yer know that? A stupid cow and as cold as a bleedin' iceberg.' There followed a string of obscenities that had Lily reeling and clinging to the door for support. 'You and me have got some unfinished business to sort out. I'll leave when I'm good and ready, bitch, and not a second before.'

Len was so incensed his vision was blurred, and he didn't see the figure come up behind him. Before he knew what was happening, he was lifted off his feet and held in a vice-like grip around his waist. His arms and legs thrashing, he tried to turn his head to see who was behind him, but he was being held so tightly his movement was restricted.

'I heard Miss McDonough asking yer to leave, son,' Corker said. 'And I think yer should do just that. Not when ye're good and ready, but right now. And unless Miss McDonough tells me otherwise, I'm here to make sure you do.'

'I want him to go away, Uncle Corker. I don't want him here now, or ever again.'

'Yer heard what the lady said, so I suggest yer start walking unless yer want me to carry yer.' Corker set Len down on the pavement. 'I want yer to walk up this street with a warning ringing in yer ears. If I ever see yer walking down it again, I'll give yer the hiding of yer life. And if I hear yer've tried to contact Miss McDonough, or give her any grief, I'll come looking for yer. And I promise if I do that, yer'll regret the day yer were born. Now have I made myself clear?'

Len was shaking like a leaf, his arrogance and bravado gone. Bullying women was one thing, he thought that was all they were fit for. But tackling a man, especially one built like Corker, was an entirely different proposition. Pulling his jacket back into shape, he began to slink away. But the big man stepped in front of him. 'I asked if I've made myself clear?'

'Yes!' The word came out through teeth Len couldn't stop from chattering. 'I heard yer.'

Lily moved back into the shadow of the hall, praying no one had witnessed the incident. She'd die of humiliation if her family found out. 'Will yer come in, Uncle Corker?'

'Just for a minute, me darlin'.' Corker seemed to fill the living room with his huge frame. He patted his pocket. 'I'd been down to the shop to get some meat off Ellen for our tea, and I couldn't help hearing your young man. I didn't know whether to interfere or not, but he seemed to be in a right temper. And when I heard yer asking him to leave, and he wasn't inclined to do so, I thought

I'd come to the rescue of a damsel in distress. I hope I did the right thing?'

'He's not me young man any more, Uncle Corker, I've finished with him. But he came down to try and talk me round, like he always does. I've fallen for it time and time again, but not any more.'

Corker feigned ignorance of the whole situation. 'Well, it's not for me to pass judgement, me darlin', but from what I've just seen and heard, I'd say ye're well rid of him. I can't abide a man who doesn't treat a lady with respect. And if he doesn't treat yer with respect now, he certainly wouldn't if yer married him. D'yer remember Ellen's late husband, Nobby Clarke? I know I shouldn't speak ill of the dead, but he was a rotter. A violent drunkard who used to beat her and the children. Well, from the little I heard coming from Len, I'd say he was another Nobby Clarke in the making.'

Lily sighed. 'I know. I've been a fool. No man will ever treat me like that again, Uncle Corker, I can promise yer that.'

'Oh, don't let him put yer off men, me darlin', because there's more good ones than bad ones. You shouldn't need me to tell yer that, living in a house with three of the best. They don't come any better than yer dad and yer two brothers.'

'I know that, they're smashers.' Lily's heart had stopped pounding and the trace of a smile played around her lips. 'I'd marry me dad, but me mam won't part with him.'

Corker chuckled. 'Yer mam acts daft, but she's far from it. She knows when she's on to a good thing. They're well matched, yer mam and dad.'

Lily had to rid herself of the niggling worry in her head. 'Uncle Corker, were there any neighbours in the street when Len was acting up?'

'No, there were a few kids playing at the top of the street, that's all. None of the neighbours were out.'

'I don't want the family to know he's been, yer see. None of them liked him, which shows they're better judges of character than I am. Especially me mam. She couldn't stand the sight of him and was always telling me he was no good. I wish I'd listened to her.'

'Sometimes when Cupid fires his arrow, he hits the wrong target. He won't make the same mistake with yer again, though. Next time he takes aim, he'll make sure it goes straight through the heart of Mr Right.'

'It'll be a long time before I trust another man.' Lily's head was still hearing the dreadful words that had been hurled at her by a man she'd thought loved her as she loved him. Oh, how wrong she'd been, and how gullible. 'I'll not be made a fool of again.'

'I don't think yer've been a fool, me darlin'. I think yer've been very sensible in finishing with someone you found yer didn't like any more. Put it down to a bad experience, a mistake, and get on with yer life.' Corker chucked her under the chin. 'Ye're a lovely looking girl, Lily, and there'll be no shortage of boys wanting to date yer. And one of those boys might turn out to be Mr Right. Yer'll know him when yer meet him, 'cos yer'll go to bed at night with a smile on yer face and dream of him.'

'Uncle Corker, ye're an old romantic.'

His deep guffaw filled the room. 'I'll also be a dead romantic if I don't get home and put this meat on. Ellen will have me guts for garters.' He tilted his head and looked into her face. 'Are yer feeling all right now, me darlin'?'

'Yes. Thanks to you, I feel a lot better. Heaven knows what would have happened if you hadn't come along. I thought he was going to hit me.'

'When yer let me out of the front door, Lily, I want yer to let Len, and everything he stood for, out of your head for good. Will yer do that for me?'

'Yes, and thank you for everything. Yer've been an angel.'

Corker made his way down the hall. 'It's a good imagination yer have. I don't think they make angels in my size, they'd take up too much room in heaven.'

Molly and Nellie sat on the long back seat of the tram, their precious hats in Lewis's bags on their knees. 'A posh hat in a posh bag, eh, girl? If it wasn't a secret, I'd walk up our street with me arm out so everyone could see we'd shopped at Lewis's.'

'Nellie, if you let on to anyone about these hats, so help me I'll clock yer one. We're going up the entry to Mrs Corkhill's so no one will see us, and what a waste of time that's going to be if you start shouting yer mouth off.' Molly clicked her tongue on the roof of her mouth. 'I don't know, yer can't keep anything to yerself.'

'Of course I can!' Nellie quivered with indignation. 'I can keep a secret just as well as you can, so there!'

Molly too was quivering, but it was with suppressed laughter. 'I remember years ago, not long after we'd moved into the street and we barely knew each other. I distinctly remember saying to meself, "Stay clear of that woman, Molly, 'cos she can't keep anything to herself".'

Nellie looked at her in amazement. 'Yer can remember saying that to yerself twenty-five years ago! My God, girl, yer should be on the stage with that Leslie feller ... the one they call the

Memory Man. Yer've missed yer chance in life, yer could have been famous! Mind you, ye're too ruddy slow to catch cold.'

'It might have been twenty-five years ago, sunshine, but I can still remember. I can even hear meself saying it!'

'And what, pray, Mrs Woman, did I do twenty-five years ago that made yer think I couldn't keep anything to meself?'

Molly had to turn her head to look out of the window, otherwise she'd have burst out laughing. 'It was the day yer found out yer were pregnant with your Steve. Yer told everyone in our street, and all the streets around. The whole neighbourhood knew before yer husband.'

'Ooh, aye, yeah! I remember that, too, girl. My feller was coming home from work and couldn't understand why people were shaking his hand, slapping him on the back and congratulating him. He thought we must have come up on the pools until I reminded him we didn't do them.' The bag containing her hat began to slip off Nellie's lap and she made a grab for it. Holding it as though it was a baby, she went on, 'Ye're not the only one with a good memory, girl. I can see George standing one side of the table and me the other. He said, "Well, if we haven't won the pools, what have we won?" I said we hadn't won nothing, but I did have a present for him, of a kind. He said, "It must be some present if everyone in the street knows about it. Come on, let's have the good news." And d'yer know what, girl? When I told him he was going to be a father, he just scratched his head and said, "And that's what all the fuss is about?".'

Molly was smiling as her friend spoke. She'd heard this tale hundreds of times over the years, but it never failed to touch her emotions.

'I couldn't believe it, girl, 'cos I thought he'd be over the moon! I was just thinking of picking up the poker to flatten him, when I saw he was smiling with his eyes. The next minute I was in his arms and being whirled around the room.' There was no regret in her voice, just pleasure at conjuring up a happy moment from the past. 'Mind you, I was a slim young thing in those days. If George wanted to twirl me round now, he'd need a block and tackle.'

'Your George still sees yer as that slim young thing, sunshine, yer can see it in his eyes every time he looks at yer. Besides, what can yer expect after having three children in three years? Just look at the state of me and think back. My hair used to be as bright blonde as the girls' is now, and my figure the same as theirs. But if yer think about it, the same applies to all the neighbours down our street. Everyone loses their figure as they grow older and start a family; it stands to sense yer can't stay young and beautiful all yer life.'

'You speak for yerself, girl! I might not be young, but my feller still thinks I'm beautiful.'

Molly gave her a dig. 'Come on, this next stop is ours. Give me that hat to carry so yer don't squash it.'

'I'd cut me throat if I squashed that hat, girl, I'm telling yer. Three guineas for a ruddy titfer, my feller will think I've lost the run of me senses.' Nellie passed the bag over before struggling to her feet. 'At least, that's what he'd think if he knew. I'm going to tell him I got it from TJ's for thirty bob.'

'I'm telling Jack the truth,' Molly said, swaying down the aisle of the tram behind her friend. 'I always get paid back if I tell lies, and it serves me right. So I'm not taking a chance of anything going wrong on the day of the wedding.'

Nellie waited until she was safely on the platform, gripping the bars with both hands, before nodding. 'Ye're right, girl, as usual. If George asks, I'll tell him the truth. If he doesn't ask, then what the eye don't see, the heart don't grieve over.'

'Ye're a crafty article, Nellie McDonough.' Molly pressed her feet firmly on the floor as the tram came to a shuddering halt. 'You get off first, then I can pass yer one of the bags.'

Nellie looked at the driver and saw a chance to brag. 'You be careful with my bag, girl, 'cos it's not every day I buy a three-guinea hat.'

Molly couldn't help but chuckle. Her mate never missed a trick. If she could keep the hats a secret for the next nine weeks, it would be a flaming miracle.

While Molly and Nellie were walking up the back entry, hoping no one came out of their back door until they were safely in Mrs Corkhill's, Lily was sitting quietly staring into an empty grate. The weather was so nice her mam hadn't bothered lighting a fire. Although she wasn't cold, the girl thought it would be nice to stare into dancing flames. She was a lot calmer now, and her heart was filled more with anger than sorrow.

Lily knew the precise moment she realised that Len Lofthouse wasn't worth a moment's thought. It was when Uncle Corker's hearty guffaw had rung out. He had brightened the quiet house, bringing a normality to it. And it had also brought her to her senses. It wasn't the end of the world, and she'd do as he said and put the past two years out of her mind. In fact, she was glad that Len *had* come down – it had given her a chance to see what he was really like. Mind you, it could have turned out nasty if Uncle Corker hadn't put in an appearance. Funny how he always seemed to be around when help was needed. She used to call him

Sinbad when she was younger, like all the other kids in the neighbourhood, because he reminded them of the man in their storybooks. And although she was no longer a kid, she still thought of him as that larger-than-life fictional character who was there when people needed him.

Chapter Twenty-One

When Nellie got home her husband and son were back from the match and looking very pleased with themselves. 'Yer're no need to tell me, Liverpool won!'

'What else did yer expect?' George asked, his tone so superior anyone would think it was he who scored the winning goal. 'They're on top form, it was a cracking match.'

'Both teams were good, Dad,' Steve said. 'They certainly gave us our money's worth. Liverpool were lucky to score that last goal five minutes before the whistle, otherwise it would have been a draw.'

Nellie came back from hanging her coat in the hall. 'Don't say that, son, or yer'll put yer dad off his meal. Him and his ruddy football team! I hope Liverpool are not playing at home on your wedding day, otherwise I'll be sitting in the church pew on me own.'

George chuckled. 'No fear of that, love, 'cos there'll be no football. The season finishes next week.' He eyed his wife. 'Anyway, where've you been until now? I was beginning to think yer'd run off with the coalman.'

'I've been shopping with me mate, if yer must know. Blimey, just 'cos I'm not here when yer get in, yer think I've done a bunk with Tucker! I'd have done that years ago if he'd have had me, but he knocked me back. He was nice about it, mind, so I wasn't upset. In fact, he paid me a compliment and said I was too much of a woman for him.' Nellie turned to smile at her daughter. 'I see yer've made them a cup of tea, love, that was thoughtful of yer. How about pouring one out for me, I'm gasping?'

Lily jumped up. 'It won't be very hot now, so I'll make a fresh brew.'

'Put a light under the pan of potatoes for us while ye're at it, love, and I'll rest me poor feet for ten minutes. Me corn's giving me gyp.'

'Where's yer shopping?' George asked.

'What shopping is that, love?'

'Yer said yer'd been shopping, but yer came in empty-handed!'

'I said I'd been shopping with me mate. It was Molly what did some shopping, I didn't buy nothing.'

'What are we having for tea, then,' cos I'm starving!'

'It's the fresh air what's done that, love. That and shouting yer ruddy head off every time Liverpool looked like scoring. Yer come home puffed with glory and decide ye're starving! Then, horror of horrors, yer find yer dutiful wife isn't here to put a plate down in front of yer the minute yer come through the door. And why isn't she? Because she's run off with the ruddy coalman, that's why!'

Steve had a smile on his face as he listened. He was lucky with his parents and he loved them dearly. He'd miss these exchanges when he left, especially his mam's fantastic sense of humour. But he'd still be living in the street and would see them every day.

'When yer've calmed down, love, will yer tell us what we're having for tea?' George asked. 'Then I can picture it in me mind until I see it with me eyes.'

'Mashed potato, one and a half sausages each, and beans out of a tin. If yer've any complaints let's hear them now, while me hand is in reaching distance of the poker.'

George decided to quit before his wife got too far ahead of him. 'No complaints, love.'

'Right – well, I've got one for you!' Nellie's chins got ready to sway when she nodded her head. 'The Bennetts got a letter from Jack's brother in Wales today, and him and his wife are coming all that way to the wedding. But you, yer lazy so-and-so, haven't been to ask your Ethel yet, and she only lives in ruddy Seaforth!'

George looked suitably chastised. 'I'll go tomorrow afternoon, love, I promise. Yer could come with me if it's a nice day, the outing would do yer good.'

Nellie glanced towards the kitchen where she could hear Lily pottering about. She wasn't going to leave her daughter in the house on her own again to sit and mope. Not that she looked as though she was moping, but you never could tell what was going on in her head. 'Sod off, George McDonough, I don't call going to Seaforth a day out. Now if yer'd said yer'd take me to Southport . . . that's what I'd call a day out.'

George looked down at his clasped hands so she couldn't see the glint in his eyes. 'I took yer to Southport once, woman, so don't be trying to make out I never take yer anywhere.'

'Holy suffering ducks! Did yer hear that, Steve? Ay, Lily, come in and listen to this.'

Lily came through carrying a pot of tea in one hand and a chrome teapot stand in the other. She had heard all the conversation and knew there was laughter on the way. After putting the stand and teapot on the table she perched herself on the arm of the couch. 'What is it, Mam?'

'I want yer both to know how good yer dad thinks he's been to me. Like taking me on days out and such. So go on, George, tell them about the day yer took me to Stockport.'

'What's there to tell? We went on the train, and I remember buying yer an ice-cream cone on the promenade. I ate mine, but you insisted on licking yours to make it last longer. The trouble was, it was a hot day and the ice cream melted and ran down the front of yer dress. Yer tried to wipe it off with my hankie, but yer only succeeded in making it worse. And yer made me walk in front of yer so no one could see the mess yer'd made.'

'How's that for a memory, eh?' Nellie too remembered that day and she felt like hugging him to bits. And she would when she'd got her point across. 'If yer can remember that so clearly, yer must remember when it was.'

Oh, George remembered it all right, as if it was yesterday. But he knew his wife wanted the last word, so he said, 'Ah, come on, love, I've forgotten.'

'It must have been when I was in the army,' Steve said. 'It's the first I've heard of it.'

'Well, yer wouldn't have heard of it, son, because it was twenty-three ruddy years ago and you were only a twinkle in yer dad's eye! That's how long it is since my beloved husband took me on a day out.'

George chuckled. 'After the mess yer made of yerself I didn't fancy taking another chance. The only suit I possessed in those days was me wedding outfit and I couldn't afford to get ice cream or candy floss all over that. It had to last me years, did that suit.'

'George, yer've just said yer only possessed one suit in those days. Well, how many suits have yer got in the wardrobe now?'

'Yer know damn well I've only got the one.'

Nellie know how this was going to end and was looking forward to it. 'George, in all yer life, have yer ever owned more than one suit?'

'No! How could I afford more than one when I was spending all me money taking you to Southport and buying yer ice cream?'

The laughter was so loud, no one heard the door opening, so Nellie was surprised to see Paul framed in the doorway. 'In the name of God, look who's here! The return of the Prodigal Son!'

Paul grinned. 'It's nice for some people to be able to sit around laughing and joking. Me now, I've been hard at work, dancing the feet off meself.'

Nellie gasped. 'Yer've never been to a dance this afternoon, have yer?'

'I certainly have.' Paul held one arm up and curved the other around the waist of an imaginary girl. 'Reece's tea dance, very enjoyable.' He used the small space available in the living room to show off his prowess. 'I just wish all these Yanks would go home, though. Our blokes don't stand a chance with them. They've got far more money than us, and seem to be able to get plenty of chocolate, pure silk stockings and lipsticks. They can't dance, most of them just move around the floor with lovesick girls gazing up at them. Even those that are as ugly as sin can get a click.' He dropped his arms and his cheeky grin appeared. 'What I say is, now the war's over, let's send them back home.'

'Pure silk stockings and lipstick?' Lily feigned interest. 'Now I wouldn't mind acting lovesick for a pair of pure silk stockings. I've never even seen a pair, but one of the girls in work went out with an American when they were stationed in Aintree, and he used to get pure silk stockings for her. She said they're so fine she was afraid of putting them on in case she laddered them.'

Nellie knew Lily was pulling her brother's leg and would never in a million years play up to a man for a pair of stockings. But there had to be a laugh here somewhere. 'Ooh, I wouldn't half love a pair for the wedding. How d'yer fancy taking yer mam and yer sister to this tea dance next Saturday, son? We'd dress up so yer wouldn't be ashamed of us, and once yer got us inside, yer could pretend yer didn't know us and go about yer own sweet business.'

'And have you two cramp me style? Not ruddy likely!'

'Not just the two of us, son! I was thinking of asking Molly, Miss Clegg and Corker's mother. Between the five of us we should at least come up with two pair of these flaming pure silk stockings.'

'I hate to break this up,' George said, 'but didn't Lily put a light under the potatoes about half-an-hour ago?'

'Oh, good grief, I forget all about them!' Lily made a bee-line for the kitchen. 'They're well done, Mam, they're all falling to pieces.'

'Drain them off, love, and I'll come and see to the sausages. One of the men can open the tin of beans because the ruddy tin-opener is hopeless. I usually end up on the floor struggling with the ruddy thing. I'm sure it's got a mind of its own.' Nellie turned at the kitchen door to ask, 'Did Archie go to the dance with yer?'

'No, I didn't know I was going meself until this lad in work mentioned it and I thought I'd give it a try. But I don't think I'll bother again 'cos I can't really afford Saturday afternoon and Saturday night out. Me money wouldn't run to it.'

'If that's a hint, lad, then ye're not on. When I was your age I used to get sixpence a week pocket money and daren't ask for a sub through the week.' Still talking, Nellie went into the pantry under the stairs for the sausages. 'I bet there's not many lads can afford to go dancing every single night of the week like you do.'

Paul knew he was well off. His mam was more than generous with all her children. But it didn't pay to let her know that. 'Archie can afford it.'

'Well, he would, wouldn't he? He's served his time and is on a man's wage.' Nellie appeared holding the link of eight sausages which she began to twirl like a skipping rope. 'In another ten months, yer'll be in the money yerself and can please yerself what yer do. But while ye're waiting, get out here and open this tin.'

Steve winked at his dad before calling after her. 'Ay, Mam, who's going to be the lucky one today?'

The voice came back, 'What d'yer mean, son?'

'Well, yer've got eight sausages and yer only need seven and a half if we're getting one and a half each. So who gets the extra half?'

'My God, yer don't miss much, do yer? If yer must know, it's going to the man of the house. And in case yer don't know who that is, it's yer dad. It's my way of saying thank you for the ice cream he bought me twenty-three years ago. He must think I've no manners, just taking it off him and nodding.'

'I admit I was waiting for a word of appreciation,' George said dryly. 'It's a good job I didn't hold me breath while I was waiting.'

'Well, yer patience is being rewarded, light of my life.' To the sound of fat sizzling in the frying pan, she added, 'I'd rather have half a sausage than a thank you, any day.'

'Will yer put a move on, Mam?' Paul emptied the tin of beans into a small pan. 'Ye're late with the tea tonight – Archie will be here before I'm ready.'

'Tough luck, son, 'cos he'll just have to wait, won't he?'

But Nellie was sorry she hadn't put a move on when Archie arrived just as they were finishing their tea. 'Yer'll have to take us as yer find us, lad, dirty plates and all. And it's yer own fault, anyway, for coming so early.'

'I know, and I do apologise.' Archie sat on the couch, crossed his legs and made himself at home. 'Me mam's got a sister living not far from here, and she goes to see her a couple of times a week because me Auntie Elsie is not in the best of health. It's only one tram stop before here, so I came with her tonight for company and walked the difference.'

'Oh, yer should have brought yer mam in for a cup of tea!' Nellie grinned as she cast an eye over the dirty plates. 'Perhaps tonight wouldn't have made a good impression, eh? She'd think we live in a hovel. But next time she's down this way, bring her in, I'd like to meet her.'

'Yeah, I'll do that. Perhaps next Saturday, before she goes to me auntie's. Yer see, me mam does a bit of work for her, seeing as she's not well. Just a spot of washing and ironing, you know, to help out.'

Nellie, forever the inquisitive, asked, 'What's wrong with yer auntie?'

'She's got a bad chest and sometimes she can hardly breathe. Me mam said she's been like that since she was a child. She's married but got no children. Her husband's a nice enough bloke and he's good to her in his own way. But he's useless around the house, wouldn't know what to do with a duster if yer gave him one.'

'Most men are the same, Archie, so he's not on his own.' Nellie's chins wobbled, agreeing with her opinion. 'They're all pretty useless.'

George and his two sons voiced their disapproval. 'Ah, ay, Mam, that's not fair,' Steve said. 'Who washed the dishes for yer when yer hand was sore?'

'And who gets the coal in for yer when the weather's bad?' Paul asked. 'And makes sure yer've got enough in to last for the day?'

George scratched his head. 'I know I do something, but I can't for the life of me think what it is, now.' Then his face lit up. 'I dusted the picture rail for yer a few times, 'cos even standing on a chair yer can't reach. And I once put the washing out on the line for yer. There's not many men would do that.'

Nellie's look of surprise was very exaggerated. 'Oh, my God, I don't believe it! The day yer put the washing out, George McDonough, I was in labour with our Paul. Did yer expect me to tell the baby to hang on for a while till I put the washing out?'

George had a pained expression on his face. 'Well, he wasn't born till half-an-hour afterwards, so yer would have had time.'

Archie noticed that Lily's laughter was as loud as anyone's, and he thought she looked well. She certainly didn't seem to be fretting over her boyfriend. He wondered whether Paul had asked her to come to the dance with them, but couldn't catch his mate's eye to give him a hint.

'I'll clear the table and wash up, Mam.' Lily began to collect the plates. 'You and your corn sit and relax.'

'If ye're not going anywhere, our kid, why don't yer come to the dance with me and Archie?' Paul had caught his friend watching Lily closely. 'We wouldn't leave yer on yer own and I bet yer'd enjoy yerself.'

'Yeah, why don't yer, love?' Nellie tried not to sound too eager. 'Yer used to like dancing.'

'I can't, not tonight.' It was a lame excuse, but the only one Lily could think of on the spur of the moment. 'Doreen's starting on the bridesmaids' dresses and has asked me to try one on when she's tacked it up.'

That won't be tonight, Nellie thought. But she wisely kept her thoughts to herself. It was no good pushing the girl too soon, otherwise she'd dig her heels in. Give her a bit more time and things might be different.

So Archie had to be content with Paul's company. But there was hope in his heart.

'I want everything cleared away and this place nice and tidy when we get back,' Molly said. 'Yer've got till ten-thirty, no later.'

'Don't worry,' Doreen told her, 'I've told Phil I'll be over there by half-ten. I want to spend some time with him. Yer know what they say about all work and no play?'

'Steve's calling for me at that time, too,' Jill said. 'We're going for a walk, seeing as the weather's so nice.'

'Arm-in-arm looking up at the stars, eh, sunshine? There's nothing more romantic.'

'I'm lucky, Mam, I don't need to look up at the sky to see stars. I see them every time Steve kisses me.'

'Yuk!' Ruthie pulled a face. 'You and our Doreen are proper sloppy beggars.'

'I was a sloppy beggar once,' Molly told her. 'And in a few years you'll be a sloppy beggar too! Now go and give yer dad a shout, tell him we're waiting.'

Ruthie reached the bottom of the stairs to see her father halfway down. He wasn't to know the smile on her face had been brought about by the thought of walking under the stars with Gordon and finding it wasn't sloppy after all.

'We'll give Corker a knock and say ta-ra,' Molly said, closing the door behind her. 'He'll be away first thing in the morning so we won't get another chance.'

When Ellen opened the door to them she smiled and stood back. 'Come on in.'

Molly shook her head. 'We're on our way round to me ma's and I don't want to be too late 'cos they go to bed early. We just wanted to say ta-ra to Corker.'

'Is someone taking my name in vain?' The big man towered behind his wife. And when he put his arms around her, the embrace was so gentle and loving, Molly couldn't help thinking what a remarkable man he was. He was built like an ox, had the strength of a lion, and yet was as gentle as a kitten. 'Are yer not coming in?'

'I promised me ma we'd go round, Corker, so we haven't time tonight. We just called to wish yer well and say the next time we see yer the wedding will only be days off.'

'Yer'll have yer hands full then, Molly, me darlin'. Two daughters getting married is double the trouble. But what a wonderful day it'll be for everyone.'

'It's started to get hectic now, Corker,' Jack said. 'What with the sewing machine out, patterns all over the place and what looks like enough material to make curtains for the Empire Theatre! But why worry about what the house looks like, eh? When it's all over, my one will have it ship-shape in no time at all.'

'I'll be home at least four days before the wedding, Molly, so I can help yer with any last-minute running round.' Corker, as always, had a thought for youngsters. 'I bet ye're looking forward to being a bridesmaid, eh, Ruthie? It's all we can get out of Phoebe and Dorothy, they talk of nothing else. It's a pretty picture yer'll make, like princesses out of a fairy tale.'

Molly put her arm on her daughter's shoulder. 'Watch it, Corker, she's big-headed enough for her age as it is.' She gave Ruthie's shoulder a gentle squeeze to let her know that what she'd said was only in fun. 'Have yer said farewell to the McDonoughs yet? Nellie will lay a duck egg if yer go off without a word.'

'I called this afternoon but they were all out, apart from Lily. I wouldn't dream of leaving without seeing them, so I'll give them a knock later. By the way, Lily told me she'd given a certain person his marching orders . . . have yer heard?'

Molly nodded. 'Good riddance to bad rubbish, that's what I say.'

Ruthie's eyes were wide with interest. 'What's Lily done, Mam?'

'Nothing that concerns you, sunshine, so don't be asking.' Molly turned her daughter to face up the street. 'We'll have to go or me ma will start worrying. Take care, Corker, and we'll see yer soon. Ta-ra Ellen.'

After waving goodbye, Ruthie walked between her mother and father. And as she'd done since she first learned to walk, she reached out for their hands. Jack looked across at Molly and they both smiled. Each sharing the thought that she was their baby and very soon would be the only one of their children at home.

'The material's lovely, Ma, wait till yer see it. Doreen said it was blue, but it's got a lilac tinge to it and it looks good, if yer know what I mean. Not a baby blue.'

'Yeah, it looks great, Nan.' Ruthie had squeezed herself into the side of Bob's chair and her arm was across his shoulders. 'Yer won't know me when I'm all dolled up, Grandad, yer'll get the shock of yer life.'

'If yer think we won't know yer, me darlin', then yer'll have to carry a sign with yer name on, so yer will,' Bridie said, her smile as gentle and loving as her voice. 'Sure, we'd never forgive ourselves if we missed our granddaughter on her big day!'

'Far chance of that, Ma,' Jack said. 'Ruthie will make sure that no one, from here to Woolworth's in Church Street, misses her. She's already got her friend, Bella, green with envy, and probably half the girls in her class.'

'Well now, wouldn't I be the same, Auntie Molly?' Rosie asked from her perch on Tommy's lap. 'Sure, it's a great honour, so it is.'

'Not as great an honour as getting married, love,' Tommy said. 'And yer've got that to look forward to. And best of all, think of the fine figure of a man that yer'll be standing next to at the altar. Thousands of girls would give their right hand to be in your place.'

Rosie's deep blue Irish eyes shone. 'Me mammy used to say that self-praise is no recommendation, Tommy Bennett. And, sure, I can't let yer get away with that, indeed I can't. Yer see, I've a mind to think that when you and me are standing at the altar, there'll be many a one telling themselves that it's a lucky feller yer are 'cos it's yerself who'll be getting the best of the bargain.'

Molly never looked at Rosie without thinking how God must have crafted her beauty with special care. Her face was perfect, as was her nature. 'Ye're my son, Tommy, and I love the bones of yer, but ye're going to have to do better than that if yer ever want to out-talk Rosie. What her mammy didn't have a saying for, she makes up one of her own.'

'Mam,' Tommy said, tongue in cheek, 'is there a man breathing that can out-talk a woman? I don't believe me dad ever managed it.'

Bob chuckled as he gazed at the woman he adored. 'Yer have a point there, Tommy, 'cos I've never managed it with my dear wife. Mind you, I've never really tried, because the sound of her voice is like music to my ears.'

'Watch it, Da, or our Ruthie will be saying ye're a sloppy beggar.'

'I will not!' Ruthie was quiet emphatic. 'It sounds sloppy when it comes from our Doreen and Jill, but dead romantic from me Nan and Granda.' She looked across at Bridie. 'D'yer know what our Jill said, Nan? That she doesn't need to look up at the stars in the sky because she sees stars every time Steve kisses her. Now don't you think that's sloppy? I mean, you and Granda don't say things like that.'

'Oh, when we were young we said all those things, me darlin'. But when yer've been married as long as we have, sure, words aren't necessary. We speak with our eyes, and the touching of hands. And the way we care for each other.'

The tear shining in the corner of the girl's eye told how she'd been touched. 'Wasn't that dead romantic, Mam? Like sitting in the pictures and watching William Powell looking into Myrna Loy's eyes. He doesn't need to say he loves her, she knows, and we can all see it.'

'And you said our Doreen was sloppy! You come a close second, sunshine!' Molly's mind took her back to when she was a child. 'And I'll tell yer something that'll give yer food for thought. When me ma was younger, she would have knocked spots off Myrna Loy for looks. She was a real beauty. And me da was so handsome he would have put William Powell in the shade.'

It took several seconds for Ruthie to digest this bit of information. Then she said, with due solemnity, 'I think me Nan's still beautiful, and me Granda's very handsome.'

'It's a big head yer'll be giving me, child,' Bridie said. 'It's a good job I haven't bought me hat for the wedding yet, so it is, or I'd have to be taking it back for a bigger size.'

'What colour are yer thinking of, Ma?' Molly asked, wishing she could tell them about the beauty now lying on top of Lizzie Corkhill's wardrobe. 'Or haven't yer decided yet?'

'Oh, I know what I want, Molly, me darlin'. The lady in the shop has put it away for me and I'm paying it off weekly. But that's as much as I'm saying because I want it to be a secret.'

'I've seen the one I want.' Molly crossed her fingers and told herself if it was a lie, it was only a white one. 'And I'm not saying, either!'

Rosie's rich, infectious laugh filled the room. 'Sure, we're all very good at keeping secrets, and that's a fact. But I wonder how long we can keep it up?'

Tommy turned her on his knee so he could look into the deep blue eyes that could send his legs to jelly and his heartbeats racing. 'What have you been up to, Rosie O'Grady? Come on, out with it. Yer shouldn't keep secrets from yer ever-loving intended.'

'Like me Auntie Molly, I'll tell yer so much, Tommy Bennett, but yer'll not get any more out of me, so don't be coaxing me with the promises of kisses and hugs.'

Tommy chuckled as he pulled her close. 'I don't need to promise yer kisses and hugs, yer get them anyway. And in abundance. But I'll not coax yer, so just tell us as much as yer want to without letting the cat out of the bag.'

'I've seen the dress I want for me soon to be sisters-in-laws' wedding. I've tried it on and the lady in the shop said it fitted me like a glove, the colour suited me and it was altogether perfect. And didn't the dear soul put it away for me, on the understanding I left a small deposit and paid the full amount off in a month? Wasn't I so happy me boss had to tell me to stop singing while I was serving customers because it wasn't the done thing?'

Her happiness rubbed off on everyone, especially Molly. 'Which shop did yer see it in, sunshine?'

'In a shop on Walton Vale, Auntie Molly. I always go for a walk in me dinner-hour, and when I saw the darling dress on a model in the window, sure I felt like jumping for joy. But don't ask me what it's like 'cos I won't tell yer.'

'That's no way to speak to yer future mother-in-law,' Tommy said with mock severity. 'At least tell her what colour it is.'

'She'll do no such thing!' Bridie wagged a finger at him. 'It's a nosy poke yer are, Tommy Bennett, and a devious one. We women are going to stick together on this. No one will see Rosie's dress, yer mam's hat, or mine, until the big day. And yer'll all stand in open-mouthed amazement when yer see how glamorous we look.'

'Ooh, ay, Ma, did Tommy tell yer Jack's brother and his wife are coming? All the way from Wales, and in their own car!'

'Is that a fact, now. Well, I never!'

'It seems me brother's come up in the world, Ma,' Jack said, with more than a little pride. It was nice to have a family member to talk about. Both his parents had died young and there was only him and Bill left. 'It'll be nice to see him again after all these years.'

'Yes, it will, and on such a happy occasion.' A slow smile spread across Bridie's face. 'We might not have a car to brag about, Jack, me darlin', but I'll bet there won't be a hat to beat mine and Molly's.'

'Don't forget Nellie, for heaven's sake, or she'll have yer life,' Molly cautioned. 'She's dead set on being belle of the ball in her millinery creation.'

'Oh, has she got her hat already?'

'No, Ma, I didn't mean that.' Molly hid her hands under the table-top while she crossed fingers on both of them. This wedding isn't half making a liar out of me, she thought. Then told herself it was all in a good cause. 'I just meant it's her intention to be noticed.'

'No matter what Nellie wore she'd be noticed,' Bob said with a smile. 'It would be very difficult for her to go unnoticed. It'll be a big day in her life, and a sad one. I bet she has the guests laughing the whole day with her antics, but there'll be a tear in her heart at losing her eldest son.'

'Da, she'll be crying her eyes out with me! She's already told me she's taking one of George's big hankies with her. But being Nellie, she has to go one better. And while she was telling me her intentions, I was doubled up with laughter. I'll tell yer in her words, 'cos it wouldn't be funny coming from me. And yer know she sometimes puts this Little Girl Lost look on – well, that's how she looked, and here's what she said. "I'll put George's hankie in the pocket of me bloomers, girl, and just get it out if I'm crying buckets. I'm going to mug meself to a little white, laced-trimmed one for show, just in case anyone's watching. I mean, like, it's no good me wearing a film-star hat, and blowing me nose on a ruddy big navvy's hankie, now is it? One thing would be laughing at the other".'

Everyone thought this was hilarious and there were hoots of laughter. It was made even more funny by Molly's impression of Nellie. She had her friend's voice, facial expressions and body movements off pat, and if you closed your eyes you would think it was the little woman herself speaking.

'She's a darlin' woman, so she is,' Bridie said, wiping her eyes. 'God was very generous when He gave her the gift of making people happy, and that's the truth.'

'That's not all.' In her mind's eye, Molly could see her best friend sitting across the table from her on the day this conversation took place. 'I asked her how she intended getting the hankie out of the pocket of her bloomers in a crowded church. And yer know how her face creases up when she winks? Well, she did that and tapped the side of her head. "I've got it all figured out, girl, so don't be worrying 'cos I won't make a show of yer. I'll pick a time when the priest tells us to kneel down to pray, and I'll pretend I've dropped something. Everyone will have their heads bowed and their eyes closed. That's if they're good Catholics, like. If they haven't I'll have something to say to them later, the flaming heathens. Anyway, I'll whip me hand up me skirt and get the hankie out. Isn't that good? Just like a magician who says, Now yer see it, now yer don't, when he turns a hankie into a rabbit. Mind you, I wouldn't fancy having a rabbit in the pocket of me bloomers, girl, 'cos yer know how quick they breed!".'

Jack was holding his tummy, Bob was beating his clenched fists on the arms of his chair, Bridie was doubled up, Tommy and Rosie were clinging together helpless, and Ruthie was laughing and clapping her hands. 'I love me Auntie Nellie. She's the bestest auntie in the whole world.'

'Oh dear, oh dear, oh dear!' Jack took a deep breath and stretched his arms high. 'This wedding could turn into a comedy if Nellie's let loose. I hope the priest's got a sense of humour, 'cos he'll need one.'

'Don't worry, she'll be as good as gold in the church, I've made sure of that. I told her if she's wearing a posh hat she'll have to act like a lady. But I can't guarantee her behaving once we get to the reception.'

'Leave her be, Auntie Molly,' Rosie said. 'As me mammy would say, laughter is the best medicine in the world.'

Tommy nodded. 'Auntie Nellie will make the party go with a swing, Mam. Yer wouldn't have to worry if people were enjoying themselves 'cos she'd make sure they do.'

'I agree, love,' Jack said. 'She's on her own, is Nellie McDonough.'

Molly could see Bridie and Bob both nodding their heads. They had a great fondness for the little woman with a big heart and the capacity for making the darkest day brighter.

'She's everything yer say, and more,' Molly said. 'She's my best mate.'

Chapter Twenty-Two

'I want to get the tea over early tonight, and the place tidied up,' Nellie said, hands on hips. 'Archie's bringing his mam to meet us and I don't want her thinking we live in a pigsty.'

'Don't worry, Mam,' Paul said with a cheeky grin. 'I'll tell her we only live in a pigsty when we're not expecting visitors.'

'We'll have less lip out of you, son, and more action. Get yerself out to the kitchen and make use of the sink before I start on the tea. You'll be one less I've got to worry about then.'

'I'll stay to meet her, Mam, to be polite, but the dress is finished now and Doreen wants me to try it on.' Lily had been to the Bennetts' every night and was grateful she'd had something to keep her mind occupied. 'If it fits, she's going to start on Maureen's tonight.'

'She's a whizz on that sewing machine, all right. Starting work in Johnson's Dye Works when she was fourteen has stood her in good stead. She's got a trade at her fingertips that'll last all her life.' Nellie grinned. 'Tell her I said I'm waiting for her to tell me how much material I need for my dress.'

'I can't tell her that, Mam, she's got an awful lot on her plate!'

'It's only a gentle hint, girl, that's all. In fact, if you had any nous about yer, yer could find out by asking in a roundabout way. Just say, casual like, that yer were thinking of buying the material for me as a surprise, but yer didn't know how much to get.'

'I'm not telling a lie, Mam, not for a little thing like that. Yer'll just have to wait yer turn like everyone else.' Lily bent her head to look into her mother's eyes. 'Crafty boots, that's what yer are, Mam. Telling me to drop a gentle hint, and you just dropped one so loud they probably heard it next door.'

There was a pained expression on Nellie's face. 'I didn't drop no hint, girl! Fancy you thinking that about yer own mother. I don't know what the world's coming to; children have no respect for their elders these days.'

'Surely ye're not that skint yer can't buy yer own material?' George asked. 'I would have thought yer were well off with us all working, but if ye're stuck, I can let yer have a few bob.'

'Of course I'm not stuck, yer daft ha'porth! I'm rolling in the ruddy stuff! D'yer know when I sometimes stay behind when yer go to bed? Well, that's so I can get me long stocking out and sit and count me ill-gotten gains. And when I've counted all me tanners, bobs, ten-bob and pound notes, I rub me hands together and cackle like a witch stirring that flaming big black boiler thing they have.'

'A cauldron, Mam,' Steve said, his dimples deepening.

'Call what, son?'

'It's a cauldron a witch stirs while she's cackling.'

'Oh, they don't sell none of them around here, son, so I'll just have to pretend.'

'Excuse me!' George looked from one to the other. 'But can someone tell me how we managed to get from Archie's mother coming, to a witch cackling over her long stocking?'

'Oh, aye! I got carried away and nearly forgot. It's all your fault, George McDonough! Once you start gabbing there's no stopping yer.' Nellie nipped each of his cheeks between finger and thumb. 'Now you sit there and be quiet while I rally the troops. Paul, yer've got five minutes to get yerself washed and clean yer teeth. Then Steve can have the kitchen for five minutes. Lily, you run a duster over the furniture for us, there's a good girl.'

Lily looked at the sideboard. 'But yer've dusted here once today, it doesn't need doing again. There's not a speck of dust anywhere.'

'Just a quick going-over, girl, to make sure. Archie's mother might be one of these fussy women who have their houses like a little palace.'

'Give us a duster, then.' Lily held out her hand. 'If I dust that sideboard again, though, it'll get such a surprise it'll think it must be its birthday.'

'Nah, it's too old for anything to surprise it. Don't forget, it's heard all the shenanigans out of you lot for over twenty years. It takes everything in its stride now, even getting dusted twice in one day. Just go over it nice and gentle, it'll enjoy that.'

Lily jumped to her feet when the knock came. 'This'll be Archie and his mam. I'll open the door, but don't forget I can't stay long.'

'Give Paul a shout while ye're at it. What the hell takes him so long to get ready I'll never know.' Nellie gave a quick glance in the mirror and patted her hair. Not that it made any difference because her hair was so fine it never stayed in place. She turned when Archie came into the room. 'Hi-ya, son.'

He moved to one side and led his mother forward. 'This is Mrs McDonough, Mam.'

'Pleased to meet yer.' Nellie held out her hand. 'Archie's told us a lot about yer.'

Ida Higgins was shaking the proffered hand when their eyes met. 'Bleedin' hell – if it isn't Nellie Blackburn! Well, I never!'

Nellie's eyes narrowed. 'Do I know yer?'

'Ida Smethwick, yer daft ha'porth! Yer used to sit next to me in school!'

'Oh, my God, I don't believe it. And *you're* Archie's mother?'

'His one and only, queen.'

'Well, I'll be blowed! I wouldn't have known yer, Ida, yer've not half changed.'

Ida grinned. She was a well-built woman, with raven black hair like her son's, although hers was peppered with grey. And she had deep brown laughing eyes, something else her son had inherited. 'I'm not going to say you haven't changed, queen, because yer were as skinny as a whippet when we were at school.'

George, who'd been waiting to be introduced, decided the two women would go on all night if he didn't interrupt. 'I'm her longsuffering husband, George. How d'yer do?' Then he went on to introduce his children. 'Steve's the eldest, then Lily, and then Paul.'

'I feel as though I know all about yer, 'cos our Archie talks about yer a lot. And I know about Molly and her family, and her ma and da.' Ida's laughing eyes covered everyone. 'Then there's Corker, Ellen and their family, and of course Rosie. I can't tell yer how happy I am to meet yer. Especially little Nellie Blackburn, the girl who got me into more trouble in school than heaven knows what. But we were best friends, weren't we, queen?'

Nellie was shaking her head in disbelief. She couldn't take it in that Archie's mother was the girl she was friends with all through their school years. And to think they'd met up again over thirty years later! 'We lived in the same street, sat next to each other in class and went everywhere together. Our mothers would give us a bottle of water, a ha'penny for lemonade powder, some jam butties and send us off to the park to play.'

George thought it was time to interrupt again. 'Nellie, aren't yer going to take Ida's coat and ask her to sit down?'

When they were all seated, Steve asked, 'Was my mam talkative when she was younger, or was she quiet?'

'She was very quiet. The best-behaved girl in class,' Ida said seriously, then burst out laughing at the expressions on their faces. 'If yer believe that, yer'll believe anything. She was always up to mischief, and she always involved me. My knuckles were permanently black and blue with being rapped by the teacher's ruler. And poor Miss Holland, the English teacher – well, I think she

305

dreaded taking our class. She could be in the middle of reading something out to us, say a poem, and Nellie would stick her hand up and call out, "Could yer say that again, Miss Holland, please, 'cos I didn't hear it all".'

'She hasn't changed much, Mrs Higgins, she's still as mad as a hatter,' Lily said, with an eye to the clock. 'But she's a good mam, and there's never a dull moment with her. Even if yer wanted to be miserable, she wouldn't let yer.' She got to her feet. 'I'm sorry I've got to go, but I'm sure we'll see yer again.'

'Off out, are yer, Lily?' Archie asked.

'Only to the Bennetts'. I'm acting as a model for Doreen. She's finished one of the bridesmaids' dresses and tonight is the big night.'

Ida smiled at her. Archie had told her about all the family, but she'd noticed a change in the tone of his voice when he mentioned this girl's name. 'I'm sure we'll meet again, queen. If I don't see yer before, I'll see yer at the church because I'll be coming to see the wedding.'

Paul was enjoying listening to the reunion of his mother and an old friend, but time was getting on. So when Lily had left, he said, 'Shall we go, Archie?'

'I'll give it a miss tonight, I think. I'll walk me mam down to me auntie's and then call on Tommy. I haven't seen much of him for the last couple of weeks. But you go, Paul. Yer don't need me with yer, the way the girls hang around yer.'

Ida was just about to tell her son to go to the dance, she'd be all right getting to her sister's, when it flashed through her mind that Lily had gone to the Bennetts'. So Archie's excuse about wanting to see Tommy could really be an excuse to see Lily. 'I can't stay long meself 'cos our Elsie will be expecting me. D'yer remember our Elsie, Nellie? You must do, she was always crying to come out with us.'

'Yeah, I remember her now.' Pictures of the past were fighting for a place in Nellie's mind. Seeing her old schoolfriend brought back many memories of things long forgotten. 'She was sickly then, wasn't she? I can remember her missing school a lot.'

'She suffers something chronic with her chest. Me heart bleeds for her sometimes when I see her gasping for breath. So I do a few odd jobs for her 'cos she can't manage anything strenuous. Tonight I've promised to do her ironing.'

Paul was getting fidgety by this time. He didn't want to appear rude, but he was wasting good dancing time. 'Is it all right if I go, Mam?'

'Yeah, go on, I wouldn't like yer to miss the fandango.'

'I'll see yer again, Mrs Higgins.' Paul shook hands then turned to Archie. 'I'll see yer tomorrow, then, mate?'

'Right! Unless that blonde finally talks yer into a date.'

'No chance! Have yer seen the legs on her?' With that, Paul was gone.

Nellie shook her head. 'Any girl that wants to trap him will have to be up early in the morning. He thinks he's God's gift to women.'

'Ye're lucky having three children, Nellie, I've only got our Archie. Mind you, I couldn't be better looked after if I had ten, he's a cracking son.'

'What about yer husband?'

'He died when Archie was a toddler. He was a few years older than me and fought in the first war. I didn't know him then, like, I met him after the war. He was working but it was light work, 'cos he'd been gassed in the trenches and it had affected his lungs. He was a good husband, Nellie, and it broke me up when he died. It's a good job I had the baby or I'd have gone out of me mind.'

'Mam, shall I put the kettle on?' Steve knew his mother was eager for news from such an old friend, but he didn't want Mrs Higgins to leave without having been offered a cup of tea. 'I'll see to it, you stay where yer are.'

'Ooh, not for me, thanks.' Ida held up a hand. 'Our Elsie will have one ready for me and if I drink too much I'll spend more time down the bleedin' yard than on the ironing. But next time I come I'll make sure I'm not in such a hurry. Me and yer mam have got a lot of time to make up, haven't we, queen?'

'We sure have, kid! I can't tell yer how glad I am to see yer after all these years. It's only just sinking in! When yer've gone I'll think of all sorts to ask yer, like if yer ever see any of the other girls that were in our class?'

'It'll have to wait, queen, 'cos I've got a couple of hours' ironing in front of me. But I'll make arrangements through our Archie to come some time when it's convenient.' When Ida pushed herself to her feet it was to Nellie's husband she bestowed a smile. 'Yer must be bored stiff listening to the two of us, George. I'll try and make it an afternoon, next time, when ye're at work so we don't give yer earache.'

'Not at all!' George said, and meant it. 'I'm made up for Nellie that she's met an old friend after nearly thirty years. Ye're welcome to come here anytime yer like.'

'Mrs Higgins, before yer go.' Steve could see Archie's mother had the same sort of humour as his mam, and he couldn't resist. 'Will yer give the sideboard the once-over, please? Yer see, it's been dusted half-a-dozen times in your honour, and it would be really upset if yer didn't even notice it.'

307

Ida's hearty laugh sounded so much like her son's, it was as if only one person was laughing. 'A chip off the old block, Steve! Yer take after yer mother all right, that's just the sort of thing she used to come out with. And she'd act daft when she was saying it. But she was far from daft, believe me! While Miss Holland was writing on the blackboard, your mam would be making all sorts of faces behind her back. All the girls would be in stitches, but it was never yer mam what got the cane. Oh no, she'd have her head bent over her book when the teacher turned round, and some other poor bugger would get blamed. And I have to say that more often than not, that poor bugger was me! I wasn't quick enough in bending me head, yer see.'

When Nellie threw her head back and laughed, her chins and tummy moved to laugh with her. 'Yeah, we used to have some fun, didn't we? Remember the day I put a spider in the drawer of the teacher's desk and she screamed the place down? That was one day I did get the cane because I couldn't stop laughing. I mean, fancy a grown woman being frightened of a fiddling teeny weeny spider.'

'Nellie, it was the biggest bleedin' spider I've ever seen in all me life! If I'd lifted the lid of me desk and found that there, I'd have fainted, never mind screamed.' Ida moved towards the door. 'I don't feel like ironing now, but needs must when the devil drives. The day might come when I need help meself, 'cos none of us know what life has in store for us.'

'It's just as well, girl, otherwise we might be inclined to put our head in the gas oven.' Nellie suddenly grinned. 'Nah, not the gas oven! That would cost me a ruddy penny to kill meself!'

'Pleasant conversation, I must say.' George didn't like talking about death, he thought it was unlucky. 'Nothing is sacred with Nellie.'

'She's not as tough as she makes out,' Ida told him. 'I found that out the day of the spider. She didn't like getting the cane in front of the class one little bit. But she was determined not to cry, so she bit on the inside of her lip until it was bleeding.'

Nellie thought she wasn't coming out well in these tales from the past. So she said, 'When yer come next time we'll talk about the tricks *you* used to get up to. Like the time yer gave cheek to the cocky-watchman and he chased yer down the street and told yer mam.'

'Yeah, I got a good hiding for that and you stood and laughed yer socks off while me mam was belting hell out of me.' Ida saw the clock and jerked her head at Archie. 'Come on, son, or I'll still be ironing at midnight.'

'I'll see yer out.' Nellie walked ahead to open the door. 'Keep in touch, won't yer, Ida? Don't leave it another thirty years.'

'We should live that long, Nellie!'

'I intend to, girl! And don't you dare go and die on me until ye've told me all yer've been up to since I last saw yer.'

Ida waved before taking Archie's arm. 'I'll try not to, queen. I'll make it me number one priority. Ta-ra for now.'

It was Molly who answered Archie's knock. 'Come in, sunshine. Lily's been telling us about yer mam and Nellie being old schoolfriends. That was a turn-up for the books, eh?'

Archie walked ahead into the living room and his heart smiled when he saw Lily was still there. 'I don't know who was the more surprised – me mam, Mrs McDonough or me! I mean, yer wouldn't expect that in a million years, would yer?'

'I bet Nellie was made up?' Jack said. 'It's a wonder she hasn't been down to tell Molly all about it.'

'Well, she knew Lily was trying on her dress, so she probably didn't like.'

'Nellie wouldn't let a little thing like that stop her, sunshine! It would have been a good excuse to nose.'

Archie glanced from Lily to Jill and Doreen. All three were looking very pleased with themselves. 'Who do I ask how it went?'

'As expected!' Doreen was so delighted and excited she could barely conceal it. 'Lily looks a dream in the dress, it fits perfect.'

'But you're not allowed to see it,' Jill told him. 'Only close family until the big day.'

'Doreen got her words mixed up,' Lily said, pulling a face. 'It's the dress that's a dream, not me. But she really has made a good job of it, it's absolutely gorgeous.'

'I'm starting on the next one now, and it should be easier knowing the measurements are right. It'll be cut out tonight, ready for tacking together tomorrow.'

'I'll leave yer to get on with it, then. I suppose it's a daft question to ask if Tommy's in?'

'He's round at me ma's, sunshine, as yer might know.' Molly raised her brows. 'I thought yer were going out with Paul?'

'I didn't feel like dancing tonight. Every night on the trot is a bit too much. Anyway, I haven't seen Tommy for a couple of weeks, so I'll walk round to yer ma's and have a game of cards or a natter with them.'

'Are yer not staying for a cup of tea?' Molly asked. 'It'll only take a couple of minutes for the kettle to boil.'

'No, I'll only be in the way. Doreen's keen to get on with her work.'

'I'll get out of the way, too,' Lily said. 'Yer don't want me under yer feet.'

'I'm sorry to be so unsociable, but if I don't keep at it I'll never get finished on time,' Doreen said. 'It's only for a few weeks, not for ever.'

'Ye're not being unsociable, only realistic,' Lily told her. 'So come on Archie, let's make ourselves scarce.'

Archie breathed in deeply before taking the plunge. 'If ye're not going anywhere, Lily, why don't yer come with me to see Mr and Mrs Jackson? We had a good laugh last time, if yer remember. That's if ye're at a loose end, like.'

When Molly saw the refusal in Lily's eyes, she thought of Nellie's belief that Archie had a crush on the girl. Her mate might have got it wrong, but then again she might have got it right. So she decided there was no harm in trying to fan a flame between the couple. He was a nice lad, Lily was a nice girl, what more could anybody want?

'That's a good idea!' Molly broke in. 'I'd come with yer if I could, 'cos I could do with a good laugh. But Ruthie's over at her mate's and if I'm not here when she gets in, she'll give Jill and Doreen a dog's life.'

'Ooh, yer not leaving us to put her to bed, Mam.' Doreen sounded very definite. 'She doesn't take a blind bit of notice of us.'

'She certainly doesn't! Apart from carrying her, there's no way we could get her to go up those stairs.' Jill felt a pang of guilt, talking like this about her kid sister. There was no doubt Ruthie would be in the way and slow Doreen down, but she wouldn't do it deliberately, it would be just out of childish curiosity. 'Yer can't really expect her to like being bossed around by us, Mam. After all, she's not far off thirteen.'

'I'll see to Ruthie,' Jack said. 'You go round to yer ma's with Lily and Archie, love. It'll do yer good to have a break.'

Oh dear, I wasn't expecting that, Molly thought. I'm sure Archie would love having me chaperone them – I don't think! He needs me like he needs a hole in the head. 'I'll tell yer what, you two go on and I'll come round when Ruthie comes in.'

There was a look of astonishment on Lily's face. She had every intention of saying no to Archie, but she hadn't been given the chance. And things had gone too far now to back out. She had no reasonable excuse and they'd think she was a miserable beggar if she pleaded a feeble excuse like a headache. Anyway, what the hell! She was only going to sit in and listen to the wireless with her mam and dad, and that wasn't a very exciting prospect for a girl her age. 'Yer'll have to take me as I am,

Archie, 'cos I'm not dressed for going out.'

'Yer look all right to me. Lily.'

'I'll see yer out.' Molly watched them walk up the street, a good yard between them. But she hadn't missed the look of joy on Archie's face, nor was she imagining the spring in his step. Nellie had been right, he did have a crush on Lily. She must remember to tell her mate tomorrow, and see if between them they could work towards bringing the matter to a mutual and satisfactory conclusion.

'Surprise, surprise!' Tommy jumped to his feet when Archie walked in. He was, as ever, pleased to see his old army mate, and never failed to show it with a firm handshake. 'I thought yer were going out with Paul?'

'Certain events changed me mind, mate.'

Tommy cocked an ear. 'Who's Rosie talking to?'

Archie's face gave nothing away. If there was any leg-pulling, it would spoil his chances. 'Lily walked round with me.'

'Well, now, isn't that nice?' Bridie, like everybody else, knew of Lily's falling-out with her boyfriend. And while she didn't know any of the circumstances, she thought the girl had done the right thing. 'Come in, me darlin', it's lovely to see yer, so it is.'

'What have you two been whispering about?' Tommy asked, while his brain was trying to work out why something had cropped up to stop Archie from going dancing, but it hadn't stopped him from being here with Lily.

'Now it wouldn't be of any interest to yer, Tommy Bennett,' Rosie said. 'But because ye're me intended, I'll tell yer. Doreen has finished one of the dresses and Lily said it is the most beautiful creation she's ever seen. Fit for a film star, indeed!'

'I didn't say that, Rosie.'

'Not in so many words, yer didn't, and that's the truth. But God gave me an imagination and I'm making use of it now.'

Bob chuckled. 'I wonder why God gave women the power of imagination, and not us men? Sounds like favouritism to me.'

'Now, sweetheart, don't be blaming the good Lord,' Bridie said. 'He gave yer imagination, same as us. Sure, how was He to know that men weren't going to be very good at using it?'

'That's put us in our place, Mr Jackson.' Archie grinned as he sat on the chair Bridie had pulled out for him. 'We'll have to think of something we can do that women can't.'

With Bridie and Bob settled in their fireside chairs, and Rosie and Tommy on one side of the table holding hands, Lily had no option but to sit next to Archie. 'I can think of lots of things men can do that we can't. Like being a coalman, for instance. Or riding a horse in the Grand National.'

'I can go one better than that, so I can, Lily.' Rosie's face beamed. 'We wouldn't be brave enough to be a soldier and fight for our country. Like Archie did, and me very dearly beloved intended.'

Tommy stuck his chest out. 'I feel better already! At least we're good for something.'

'We're not as nosy as women, that's a plus,' Archie said. 'For instance, Tommy, you don't seem to be interested in the event that made me change me mind about going dancing with Paul. It was the biggest surprise I've ever had in me life and I'm dying to tell someone.'

'Go on mate, we're all ears.'

'Let me tell them?' Lily pleaded. 'Just up to the time where I had to leave?'

'No!' Archie leaned towards her until their faces were nearly touching, and the closeness sent shivers down his spine. 'Yer can join in, but let me tell them the first part, please.'

'Now I am interested,' Tommy said. 'Come on, let's be having it.'

'Well, yer knew I was bringing me mam to see Mrs McDonough, didn't yer? Me mam doesn't get out much, and when Mrs Mac said she'd like to meet her, she was over the moon. Anyway, I was introducing them, and they were shaking hands, when me mam said—' Archie broke off and turned to Lily. 'Are yer any good at impersonating people?'

Lily grinned. 'I'll have a go.' She stuck out her hand and Archie took it. 'Pretend you're my mam, and I'll be hours. You go first.'

With the best will in the world, Archie couldn't impersonate Nellie, so he just said, 'Pleased to meet yer. Archie's told us a lot about yer.'

Lily was shaking his hand when she narrowed her eyes. 'Bleed-in' hell! If it isn't Nellie Blackburn! Well, I never!'

Archie tried the narrowed eyes bit, but didn't even attempt the voice. 'Do I know yer?'

'Ida Smethwick, yer daft ha'porth! I used to sit next to yer in school.'

'Oh, my God, I don't believe it! And you're Archie's mother?'

'His one and only, queen!' Lily pulled her hand free. 'That's my part done, you can just tell them the rest.'

'Ay, that was a surprise, wasn't it?' Tommy said. 'And did they know each other well?'

'Best friends all through their schooldays. They lost touch when me mam's family moved to another district. And until today they hadn't seen each other for thirty years.'

'That's a lovely story, so it is,' Bridie said. 'Friends meeting after all those years. I bet yer mother was pleased, Lily?'

'She was, until Mrs Higgins started giving us the lowdown on her. Apparently she was a little devil in school, always up to mischief. I didn't hear it all because I had to go down to the Bennetts', but I'm glad I was there to see them meeting for the first time. And I had to laugh when me mam said she wouldn't have known Mrs Higgins 'cos she hadn't half changed, and was told, "I'm not going to say you haven't changed, queen, because yer were as skinny as a whippet when we were at school".'

'Sounds as though Nellie has met her match,' Bob said. 'I never thought I'd live to see the day.'

Archie grinned. 'My mam and Lily's are very much alike in temperament. Both have a marvellous sense of humour and have an answer for everything. It was good to listen to them and imagine what they were like as kids. Mrs Mac sat while me mam told of all the tricks she used to get up to, giving the teachers a dog's life, and she laughed as loud as the rest of us. Then she got her own back by reminding me mam that she'd been no angel. They were so funny, it was better than going to any dance or the pictures.'

'I'd love to have been there.' Tommy said. 'Are they seeing each other again?'

'Oh yes, definitely.' Archie was thoughtful for a while, then he said, 'I'd like to tell yer how they parted, but I couldn't do it justice on me own. So would yer mind, Mrs Jackson, if I took Lily into yer kitchen and we rehearsed?'

Lily looked shocked. 'I'm not going into no kitchen with yer!'

Tommy whispered into Rosie's ear and they began to chant, 'We want Lily, we want Lily.'

When Bridie and Bob joined in, Lily had no choice. 'But if yer make a fool of me, Archie Higgins, I'll never speak to yer again.'

There was a lot of laughing and giggling in the kitchen before the couple made their entrance. His face straight, Archie said, 'I am taking the part of Mrs Higgins, and my partner is Mrs Mac.'

Lily crossed the room and folded her arms. She couldn't believe she was doing this, it was so unlike her to be the centre of attention. But, funnily enough, she was beginning to enjoy it. Pretending to hitch up a mountainous bosom, she said, 'Keep in touch, won't yer, Ida? Don't leave it another thirty years.'

In a high-pitched voice, Archie answered, 'We should live that long, Nellie!'

'I intend to, girl! And don't you dare go and die on me until yer've told me all yer've been up to since I last saw yer.'

'I'll try not to, queen. I'll make it me number one priority. Ta-ra for now.'

Lily didn't hear the laughter because she was laughing so heartily herself. She could picture her mother saying those words, her arms folded and her face dead-pan. Oh, she was so lucky to have such a wonderful woman for a mother.

'That was brilliant!' Tommy couldn't get over Lily. She'd always been the quiet one of the McDonough family. Mind you, that feller she was going out with wasn't exactly a bundle of joy.

'Isn't that the truth?' Rosie said. 'Sure, haven't I got the feeling, Archie, that yer mam is going to enrich all our lives?'

Bridie spoke her mind. 'I think you make a good double act. Have yer no more for us?'

'Plenty more, Mrs Jackson,' Archie laughed. 'But I don't think I'll get Lily to come in the kitchen again with me. Not tonight, anyway.'

'In that case I'll put the kettle on. We'll pretend it's the interval and the show will start again in fifteen minutes.'

'I won't be in the cast next time, Mrs Jackson,' Lily said. 'Someone else can make a fool of themselves.'

'Ah, child, making people laugh doesn't make yer a fool!' Bridie said. 'Would yer say yer mam was a fool? Of course yer wouldn't! She has a wonderful gift which she uses well.'

When Rosie nodded in agreement, her thick curls bounced up and down on her shoulders. 'My mammy used to say, if yer can put a smile on someone's face, then sure, yer day hasn't been altogether wasted.'

'I'm not like me mam, I'm afraid.' Lily grinned. 'My two brothers are, but somehow I got missed out.'

'I don't agree with yer,' Archie said. 'I think ye're very much like yer mother. Except perhaps a little more shy and afraid to let yerself go. And I mean that as a compliment, before yer clock me one.'

'No amount of flattery will get me back in that kitchen with yer, Archie Higgins, so yer may as well save yer breath.'

'How about a new act after the interval, then?' Bob asked. 'Archie can bring us up-to-date with the bloke who has a vivid imagination when it comes to excuses for staying off work.'

Archie laughed. 'Oh, yer mean Fred Berry! Let's see now. Last week he came up with a smasher, and me boss has started writing them down. He says one day, when he retires, he's going to write a book about this bloke. No one will believe it's true, but he reckons it'll be so funny it'll be a bestseller.'

Bridie had put the kettle on and now came to stand by the kitchen door. 'And what was this smashing excuse, Archie?'

314

'He reckons he was halfway to work, and so deep in thought he didn't look where he was going. And didn't he slip on some dog dirt and go flying? According to him, he sat right in it and it was all over his trousers. He told the boss he couldn't come in to work because the smell was something awful. And I have to say that I've watered it down for the sake of the ladies. He had another name for dog dirt which was very ungentlemanly.'

Tommy chuckled. 'I don't know how he gets away with it. If I tried, I'd be out on me ear.'

'I think the boss is keeping him on until he's got enough excuses to fill a book. But the best of it is, the next day he was wearing the trousers that he'd said were covered in dog dirt! And he used the same trousers for this week's excuse! This time he said a dog went for him and tore a big rip down one of the legs. And he actually had the trousers on when he was telling the boss! When he was asked where the rip was, he pointed to the back of one of the legs and said yer couldn't see it because his wife had invisibly mended it!'

And the fun and laughter lasted until it was time for Lily and Archie to bid their friends goodnight.

They were nearing the side of the corner shop on their way home, when Lily's footsteps faltered. 'Oh, my God, there's Len!'

'Would yer rather I walked on and left yer to talk to him?' Archie asked.

'No – don't leave me! I don't want to talk to him ever again! Why doesn't he just leave me alone!'

Len moved away from the wall and stood in front of them. 'Can I talk to yer, Lily?'

Archie cupped Lily's elbow. 'She doesn't want to talk to you.'

'I'm not asking you, I'm asking her. Who the hell are you, anyway? She's my girlfriend.'

'Not any more she's not. She's my girlfriend now and I want yer to move out of the way before I make yer.'

'Oh, aye?' Len said, his manner cocky. 'You and whose army?'

'Don't get involved, Archie,' Lily said, her voice shaking. 'He's not worth fighting over.'

'No, he's not, but you are.' Archie took a step forward. 'Now, are yer going to move?'

Len was blazing. He couldn't believe any girl would pack him in, it was a blow to his ego. His anger made him reckless. 'You won't get anywhere with her, mate, she's as cold as a wet fish.'

'You go on, Lily, and wait for me outside yer front door.' Archie swept Len aside to let her pass. 'I won't be a minute.'

Lily didn't see the blow, but she heard it. And when she turned,

315

Len was on the ground rubbing his chin and groaning, while Archie stood over him. 'I'll repeat what I said. Lily is my girlfriend now and she doesn't want to speak to yer or set eyes on yer again. If I ever hear yer've been bothering her, I'll put yer in hospital.'

'I am so sorry,' Lily said tearfully when Archie caught her up. 'I shouldn't have asked yer to stay with me, I should have faced him on me own.'

'Nonsense, I quite enjoyed it. I'm just sorry that where he fell hadn't been used by a dog as a toilet!'

Lily managed a tearful smile. 'I certainly know how to pick 'em, don't I? I should have seen through him ages ago.'

'Better late than never. And don't worry, we'll keep what happened to ourselves. I hope yer didn't mind me telling him yer were me girlfriend, I thought it was one way of keeping the blighter away.'

'Yer've been very kind.' Lily sighed. 'I'd really enjoyed meself tonight, and he had to come and spoil it. I hope to God I've seen the last of him.' And she really meant it. She'd stopped loving him the day she went to see his mother, but deep down there was still a spark and she couldn't help thinking of him and missing him. Not now though. Not after the incident with Uncle Corker, and now Archie. Twice he'd been the cause of her being humiliated and her feelings for him were of intense dislike, fringing on hatred.

'I hope this won't send yer back into yer shell, Lily. I mean, yer won't hide yerself upstairs when yer know I'm coming? I would like us to be friends.'

'Of course we're friends, Archie. And I promise I won't hide from yer. But I'd better go in now because I can see me mam watching us through the curtains. And she's a nosy beggar – she'll want to know what we're talking about.'

'Tell her about Fred Berry, the dog dirt and the invisible mending. That should give her a laugh. And thanks for coming with me tonight, Lily, I enjoyed her company.'

'Same here! Goodnight, Archie.'

Chapter Twenty-Three

'That's the last pound I owe yer off the hat.' Molly handed the crinkled note over to her friend. 'One load off me mind.'

'I've told yer I'm not waiting for it, girl,' Nellie waved her hand away. 'It'll do any time after the wedding.'

'Take it, then I'm straight with yer.' Molly threw the note across the table. 'Yer were very kind to lend it to me, and I'm grateful, but I don't want anything on me mind after the wedding. No worries, no hustle and bustle, and no debts. I'm going to put me feet up for a whole week and rest.'

'OK, if ye're sure.' Nellie put the pound note in the pocket of her pinny. 'Only three more weeks to go, girl, they'll fly over.'

'Yeah, I keep saying I'll be glad when it's over, but that's daft really when the best has yet to come. I can't wait to see me two girls in their wedding dresses, and Steve and Phil dolled up in their suits. It'll be a proud day for me and Jack.'

'Ay, aren't yer forgetting something, Missus? My beloved son is one of the grooms, so haven't I got the right to be proud, too?'

'Of course yer have, sunshine! We'll both be proud together because it's something we've always talked about and longed for, our two families being joined together in holy matrimony. It won't make us blood relations, but as good as.'

Nellie thought about this for a while. Then she said, 'If we were Red Indians we could become blood relations.'

'How d'yer make that out?'

The chair started to shake first, then the table rocked to herald a loud belly laugh from Nellie. 'If yer get me yer bread-knife, I'll show yer. We cut our arms here, then hold them together so the two bloods mix. Easy peasy, girl!'

'Sod off, Nellie, yer might be me best mate but I ain't cutting me arm for yer. Anyway, I think sometimes friends are better than family or relations. Yer can't pick yer family, but yer can pick yer friends.'

'Ye're right there. Phil's a good example of that, isn't he? Remember his family? A gang of rotters if ever there was one. Liars, thieves every one, except Phil.'

317

'They weren't his family, though, sunshine, not proper family. Oh, the mother was his, but Tom Bradley wasn't his dad.' Molly looked thoughtful as she pinched on her bottom lip. 'I've often wondered whether Phil would ever try and contact the family of his real dad. At least his mam had the decency to tell Phil his name and where he was living before he got killed. For all he knows, he might have aunts and uncles that would be glad to hear from him. In fact, he might have grandparents still alive – it's possible.'

'How about McDonough and Bennett going into business again? I wouldn't mind a bit of detective work.' Nellie rubbed her chubby hands together. 'It would give us something to do after the excitement dies down in a few weeks.'

'We'll talk about that some other time, sunshine, when I haven't got so much on me mind. But things have worked out better than I expected, money wise, with Jack working all the hours God sends. When we go down to the shops I'm calling by the cake shop to give Edna Hanley five pounds off the bill. That only leaves me owing her another five, which I'll pay next week. And that's the reception paid for, thank goodness.'

'Yer've done well, girl, I'll say that for yer. And yer've no more white hair in yer head than yer had before.'

'I wouldn't have managed without the two girls, they've been brilliant. Jill's taking me to buy me shoes on Saturday, and she's paying for them. And, as yer know, Doreen bought the material for me dress as a surprise.'

'I think your Doreen's done wonders. Five bridesmaids' dresses, and one for Miss Clegg, all in a matter of weeks.' Nellie's eyes narrowed, as they always did when she was about to drop a hint. 'She's only got yours and mine to make now, then that's the lot.'

'It's taken it out of her, though, she looks tired and drawn. Phil's been telling her for weeks to pack her job in, and I'm glad to say she's giving her notice in today. We can't have her looking haggard on her wedding day.'

'Don't bite me flaming head off if I ask yer something, will yer?'

'How do I know until yer ask me? Go on, try me.'

'Will Doreen be starting on our dresses this week? I know it sounds selfish 'cos she's been working flat out, but I can't wait to see meself all dolled up. I bet that feather on me hat has grown six inches since I last saw it.'

A smile played around Molly's mouth. 'I knew yer'd be asking me that, so I've told Doreen to make yours first. She wants yer to come down tonight to be measured in case yer've put any weight

318

on since the last one she made yer. So does that make yer feel any happier, sunshine?'

Nellie's shining eyes told of her delight, but she didn't want to appear greedy. 'That doesn't seem fair, girl, now does it? You should come before me.'

'I know I should, but I've got a bit more patience than you. I'd rather wait than have to listen to you nattering down me ear every day asking how much longer.'

'I wouldn't do that, girl, not much anyway. I might just make a casual enquiry, and it wouldn't be every day, it would be every half-hour.'

'Get down here for seven o'clock, sunshine, and let's hear no more about it.'

'I'll be as good as gold, you just wait and see. I won't even open me mouth.' Nellie clamped her lips together, but it only lasted seconds. 'Except to ask how many yer've got on yer list of guests now?'

'I think at the last count it was thirty-eight or nine, I'm not quite sure. But we're not far out with catering for forty.'

'Yer've got George's brother and his wife down, haven't yer? And Ida, yer said I could ask her, remember?'

'Nellie, I've got everything under control, sunshine, except you! I don't know what's going to happen when your Lily gets married and you've got to arrange everything.'

'Ye're not thinking of moving house, are yer, girl?'

'Of course not, why?'

'Well, I'll have you to help me. I mean, after this yer'll have had plenty of experience and it'll be a doddle for yer.'

'Ye're a cheeky article, Nellie McDonough! Honest to God, yer face would get yer the parish! Anyway, talking of your Lily and her wedding, how's she getting on with Archie?'

'She's very cool with him, worse luck. I don't mean she's not friendly, 'cos she is nice to him, but it's in a sisterly sort of way. I thought when she went to the dance with him and Paul the week before last, things were looking up. But no, there's nothing doing as far as she's concerned. She'll probably end up an old maid, living on her own with a cat for company.'

Molly tutted. 'Give the girl a chance, Nellie, for heaven's sake! She's had a bad experience and it's bound to have put her off. It's early days yet, and if Archie's keen enough he'll hang around until he thinks she won't turn him down if he asks for a date.'

'He's a good lad, isn't he, girl? Just the sort that would fit in with the family. If it wasn't for upsetting George, I'd marry the lad meself.'

'All joking aside, sunshine, he's one of the best. And so is his

319

mother. I really took a liking to Ida, she's a woman after me own heart. But what we think doesn't count, does it? Lily's the one he's got to win over, not us.' Molly reached for Nellie's empty cup. 'You go and get yerself ready for the shops. I've only got these to wash and me hair to comb, so don't take all day over it.'

'I've been washed, girl, and I'll comb me hair again if it makes yer feel any better. But it won't look no different than it looks now.'

'Vamoose, sunshine, and be back here in ten minutes. OK?'

Vera Patterson was standing at her front door when the ladies walked down the street. 'I'm just getting a bit of fresh air. I've got the dolly tub filled and the sweat was pouring off me. The weather's too nice to be doing ruddy washing.'

'That's what I thought,' Molly said. 'So I'm going to leave me clothes in steep overnight and put them through the mangle first thing in the morning before it gets too hot. They'll be dry in an hour if we have another day like today.'

Nellie put on her downcast look. 'Yer didn't tell me that, girl.'

'There's lots of things I don't tell yer, sunshine! Like what I had for breakfast, how thick I'd cut me slices of bread, or what I gave the family for their carry-out. Me life is full of useless information that I don't pass on to yer.'

Vera was getting used to Nellie's habits by now, and when she saw the eyes narrow and the lips purse, she knew there was some thought being given to a suitable reply.

'What did yer give them for their carry-out, girl?'

'I cut the rounds of bread, spread margarine on as thin as I could, then a layer of fresh air that had a small ray of sunshine in it, and I topped the lot off with conny-onny. Does that satisfy yer?'

Nellie wasn't going to be outdone. 'That's funny, girl, 'cos I gave mine the same! Great minds think alike, eh?' Pleased with herself, she went further. 'What are yer going to tell them tonight when they ask what was in their butties?'

'I'll tell them it was a secret recipe, passed down the family. And if they behave themselves they'll get it again tomorrow.'

Nellie tried a few times to click her finger and thumb, but couldn't manage it. Pity, she thought, 'cos it would have looked good. Still, a click of the tongue on the roof of her mouth would be just the same. So for good measure, she clicked her tongue twice before saying, 'I think yer can read me mind, Molly Bennett, 'cos that's exactly the same as I'm going to tell my lot.'

'Oh, yer mam passed the recipe on to you, did she? She must

have been as hard-up as my mam, then. Skint from Monday to Friday.'

'Are you saying my mam was poverty-stricken? Well, she wasn't, yer know. We had bread and jam every day for our breakfast, so there!'

'I'll believe yer, sunshine. In fact, if it'll shut yer up, I'm willing to believe yer if yer say yer mam was a lady-in-waiting to the Queen!'

Nellie grinned. Oh, she had an answer for that! 'No, that would be telling a lie, girl. The truth is, she was only a chambermaid. But if she hadn't married me dad, she had prospects of becoming a lady-in-waiting.'

Vera was really enjoying herself. She didn't care if the washing never got done. This was far better than pegging clothes on the line.

Molly knew it was her own fault, but she couldn't help egging her mate on. 'Oh, so yer mam lived in London, did she?'

'No, girl, she used to get the twenty-two tram there every morning.'

Molly lifted both hands in surrender. 'OK, I give in.' Then she grinned inwardly. 'Yer see, yer instantaneous responses are too quick for me.'

Nellie nodded her head as though satisfied with the compliment. Not for the world would she let Vera know she hadn't a clue what that long word meant. But she'd get it out of her mate later, in a roundabout way, like.

'How's the bloke next door, Vera?' Molly asked. 'Any improvement?'

'Yeah, Mavis said he's coming on fine. She takes the kids up to see him on a Sunday, and because they wouldn't let them in the hospital, the first few weeks they could only wave to him through the window. But last week Frank was allowed to go outside to them, and Mavis said he was over the moon. The doctor said if his improvement continues he could be coming home in a few weeks. It'll be a long time before he's able to work, but Mavis said she doesn't care, she just wants him home.'

'Oh, that's good news,' Molly said. 'Tell her we were asking about him.'

'Will do!' Vera didn't feel like going back to that condensation-filled kitchen and tried to keep them a while longer. 'Not long off now, eh, Molly?'

'No, sunshine, only three weeks. I lie in bed every night thinking nice thoughts, until I remember they won't be coming back to their own home after the wedding. Then I have to cry quietly so as not to wake Jack. You know, silent tears running down me cheeks.'

Nellie listened with mounting admiration. Her mate didn't half have a nice way of putting words together. It made you feel quite emotional. 'How can tears be silent, girl?'

'When yer don't cry out loud, that's when. Tears usually come with crying, but I can hardly wake Jack up every night because I'm feeling sorry for meself. So I put a hand over me mouth and let the teardrops fall softly.' Molly grinned at the rapt expression on her friend's face. 'I should have been a poet, shouldn't I, sunshine?'

'Yer sound like Janet Gaynor in one of those weepy pictures. If yer keep it up, yer'll have me bawling me eyes out, even though I left the house as happy as Larry, without a single care in the world.'

'Heaven forbid I should make yer feel sad!' Molly took her arm. 'Let's go. We'll see yer, Vera, but don't be sweating cobs trying to get yer washing done. Leave it until tonight, when it won't be such hard going.'

'I think I'll do what yer say.' Vera stepped down on to the pavement and lowered herself to sit on the step. 'My feller would go mad if he could see me doing this, but I'm too hot to worry. So I'm going to sit here for ten minutes, watch the world go by and sod the washing.'

Nellie grinned as she turned away. 'Ye're a girl after me own heart, Vera. Sod 'em all, that's what I say.'

Molly handed five one-pound notes over the counter with a big smile on her face. 'Last one next week, Edna, then I'm square with yer.'

'It would have done after the wedding, yer know, Molly,' Edna Hanley said, before giving a broad wink. 'It's bad policy to pay for anything in advance. Yer should wait and see what ye're getting for yer money.'

'I had to get it off me mind, Edna, 'cos after the wedding I'll be two wages short. Anyway, I trust yer, I know yer won't let me down.' Molly put a hand on Nellie's shoulder. 'If yer did, my mate here would come down and take it out of yer face, wouldn't yer, sunshine?'

Nellie of course had an answer for that. 'She hasn't got fifty pounds' worth of face, girl!'

'Trust you to say that. And here's me hoping we're not too late for pies and bread. If we go out of here empty-handed, sunshine, it's your face that'll be getting rearranged.'

Edna chuckled. 'I don't get upset easily, Molly, thank God. When yer've served behind a counter for as long as I have, yer need a skin as thick as a ruddy rhinoceros. Most of our customers

322

are nice people that we've known for years, but now and again yer get one that loves to throw their weight around and can be downright rude. Then yer have to have the patience of a saint, keep a smile glued on yer face and get them out of the shop as fast as yer can before yer clock them one.'

'That wouldn't do for me, girl,' Nellie said, with the full agreement of her chins. 'If anyone upset me, I'd be round that counter like a ruddy shot, and before they knew what had hit them, they'd be sitting on their arse outside.'

'That's why I'm this side of the counter, and you're there,' Edna said, as her mind pictured the little woman throwing one of their rudest customers, a Mrs Anderson, out on her backside. Oh, what a lovely thought. 'Anyway, I've saved yer the usual loaf and two pies each, and the same for Miss Clegg.'

'Thanks, Edna, ye're an angel. What is she, Nellie?'

'Well, the disguise is perfect, girl, but if you say she's an angel, I'll take your word for it. But just out of curiosity, won't her wings be getting crushed under that overall?'

Molly rolled her eyes. 'Listen, sunshine, yer made a two-minute conversation with Vera Patterson into a ten-minute one, but I'm not letting yer do the same here. So get yer money out and pay the woman.'

Edna was putting the pies into bags when she said, 'I've heard that Frank Sheild is coming on well. They say he could be home in a couple of weeks.'

'Yeah, Vera was just telling us. That's a blessing, isn't it?'

'I wouldn't know about that.' Edna placed the bags on the counter. 'If Fanny Kemp and Theresa Brown get near him, he might be sorry he didn't stay in hospital. It was them what told me he was coming home, and anyone else who was prepared to listen. They were boasting about telling him all about what his wife was up to while he was away. They were really gloating at the thought. I could see some of the customers were disgusted, and one even had the guts to speak up and ask the two evil-minded beggars if they didn't think the man had suffered enough. But they weren't interested in what he'd gone through, they're just out to cause trouble. They've got big mouths and they throw their weight around, so most folk stay clear of them. And, may God forgive me, I just stood and listened. I can't afford to get involved in a slanging match, not with a shop full of customers. But someone should frighten them off before the poor man comes home.'

'Me and Nellie talked about this weeks ago, when Vera first told us what the two women intended to do.' Molly didn't say she'd told Jack as well, she'd rather keep his name out of it. 'We'll get our heads together and see what we can come up with, eh, sunshine?'

'I told yer what I'd do, girl, I'd flatten that Fanny Kemp! Theresa Brown is nothing to worry about, she's got a big mouth, that's all. Hides behind Fanny's skirt and pretends she's as tough, but on her own she'd do it in her kecks if anyone lifted a finger to her.'

'Yer have a very delicate way of putting things, sunshine, I must say. But if we do anything at all, it'll be with our mouths and not our fists.'

'Yer didn't say anything about using our feet, girl, so I take it yer'd have no objection to me kicking her from here to Pier Head, eh?'

'There's no fear of that, sunshine, not if I'm with yer. Anyway, I think I told yer before, yer couldn't kick high enough to reach her backside so forget it. And give Edna yer money so we can get the rest of our shopping in.'

Outside the shop Nellie asked, 'Where are we going now, girl?'

'The butcher's, to see if we can cadge some brawn or corned beef to help out with the pies. And I'm making chips, so it'll be an easy meal for tonight.'

Tony Reynolds was leaning into the window, filling a tray of diced stewing meat when he saw them coming. 'Here's yer neighbours, Ellen. Put those tins of corned beef under the counter so they can't see them. Pretend we've nothing for them today.'

'Tony, yer wouldn't keep that up for two minutes,' Ellen told him. 'Ye're a sucker where Molly and Nellie are concerned.'

'I know. They have that effect on me.' He was all smiles when the two friends entered the shop. 'Good morning, ladies! I hope ye're both well on this beautiful sunny day?'

'We're hoping you can make it even sunnier for us, Tony,' Molly said. 'Perhaps a few slices of corned beef? That would be really nice. But if yer can't manage that, brawn will do, though I don't like the stuff much. Still, beggars can't be choosers, sunshine, so we'll throw ourselves on your mercy.'

'I'll tell yer what, I'll let yer throw yerselves on Ellen's mercy today. Let's see what she can come up with for yer.'

'Now that's what I call very decent of yer, Tony, lad.' Nellie was beaming. 'Why don't you go next door for a packet of fags and leave Ellen to serve us?'

It was that sort of remark that made the two women his favourite customers. 'Oh, aye!' He grinned. 'And I'd come back to find half me stock gone! I might look like a cabbage, Nellie, but I'm not that green. Besides, I want to see the look on yer faces when Ellen serves yer. Seeing as ye're her neighbour, I've got to make sure she doesn't give yer over the odds.'

'Miserable bugger, isn't he, girl?' It was supposed to be a whisper, but Nellie couldn't do anything quietly. 'I bet he saw us coming.'

'Oh, I saw yer coming all right! I told Ellen to put everything out of sight except the scales and me chopping board.'

'Take no notice of him, he's having yer on.' Ellen wiped her hands down the front of her apron. 'What would you like, ladies?'

'Cary Grant on a plate,' Molly grinned. 'But if he's not available, I'll settle for James Stewart or Randolph Scott.'

'I'm sorry, but I can't help yer there, Molly. We had Tyrone Power left until ten minutes ago, then he got snaffled up.' Ellen bent down to the shelf under the counter, and when she straightened up she was brandishing a tin of corned beef in each hand. 'Will these do instead?'

'Oh, you lovely woman!' Molly was highly delighted. 'There'll be enough over to make corned-beef hash for tomorrow. Isn't that the gear, Nellie?'

'It certainly is, girl, it's the bloody gear! If yer'd like to come out from behind the counter, Tony, I'll give yer a big kiss.'

Tony lifted his hands in mock horror and stepped back a pace. He backed into the large round hooks suspended from a bar which ran across the width of the window, and his straw hat was sent flying. 'Stay where yer are, Nellie, for God's sake! I wouldn't be responsible for me actions if yer kissed me, knowing how hot-blooded yer are.' He picked his hat up from the floor and was wiping the sawdust off, when he spied two familiar figures crossing the road from the other side. 'Oh, that's all I need! Here comes Fearsome Fanny and Terrible Theresa. Put those tins out of sight, Molly, before they see them, or there'll be blue murder.'

Molly threw the tins in Nellie's basket and covered them with a loaf just as Fanny Kemp swayed through the door, with Theresa Brown behind her. She walked like a bruiser, did Fanny, with her shoulder movements exaggerated and telling everyone they'd better not mess with her, she was the queen bee.

Molly looked her up and down and asked herself why she should be frightened of this woman. Anyone would think she owned the place, the way she walked around, but all she was, was a woman who bullied everyone into being afraid of her. And she was as coarse and common as muck. I'm not bowing down to the likes of her, Molly told herself. Someone has to stand up to her and put a spoke in her wheel. 'Me and Nellie heard someone talking about you before, Fanny, and it wasn't very complimentary.'

Nellie quickly recovered from her surprise and moved to stand close to her friend. 'No, it wasn't nice at all, what they said about yer.'

'Oh, aye, who was this? I'll break their bleedin' neck for them!'

'Actually, it wasn't only one person, it was a group. We didn't hear every word that was said, mind yer, but I told them they must have got it wrong, 'cos no one would do the terrible thing that they said you were going to do.'

Fanny moved closer and pressed her pugnosed face close to Molly's. Her very manner was threatening and Molly felt a flicker of fear. 'What was said, and who said it? Come on, out with it.'

Nellie wasn't going to stand for that. Pushing in between the two women, she put her hands on Fanny's chest and shoved her back. 'Don't you talk like that to my mate unless yer fancy nursing a broken jaw.'

'Huh! Did yer hear that? And look at the flamin' size of her!' Fanny sneered down at Nellie. 'Is yer mate going to lift yer up?'

When Tony saw Nellie curl her fist and bend her arm back, he was around the counter in the blink of an eyelid. 'All right, ladies, break it up. I don't know what it's all about, but I'll have no fighting in my shop.'

'That's all Fanny Kemp knows, Tony,' Molly said. 'Yer couldn't have a normal conversation with her, she wouldn't know where to start. She can use her mouth and her fists, but seems to be lacking a brain. There would have been none of this if she'd just listened to what I've got to say. But no, unless the words are coming out of her own mouth, she doesn't want to know.'

'Fanny, just back off, will yer?' Tony said. 'And if yer've got anything to ask Molly, then try and be rational about it. And I'll stand here until yer've finished. Any fighting and yer'll not be asked to leave the shop, but escorted off the premises.'

That wasn't a bit to Fanny's liking and she thought about it for a while. But it was a case of giving in or being booted out. 'What is it yer heard people saying about me?'

'Oh, not just you, yer mate was included too. They say that when Frank Sheild comes home from hospital, ye're going to tell him about the men his wife's been going with. I didn't believe them, though, 'cos surely yer wouldn't do that? Not to a man who's been in a prisoner-of-war camp for nearly four years?'

'Who wouldn't? Just you stick around and see whether I would or not. He's got a right to know what the bitch has been up to, and I'll make sure he does.'

'And what gives you the right to interfere between man and wife?' Molly asked quietly. 'It would do you good to keep yer nose out of their business. Ye're a troublemaker, Fanny, and yer

326

sidekick, Theresa Brown. It's a pity neither of yer haven't got better things to do.'

Before Tony knew what was happening, Fanny had closed in on Molly and was jabbing a stiffened finger in her chest. 'If yer know what's good for yer, yer'll keep yer trap shut, right? Me and Theresa are going to tell Frank as soon as we see him, and it's got nowt to do with you, so put that in yer bleedin' pipe and smoke it.'

This was too much for Nellie. She wasn't going to stand by and see her mate being poked by anyone. Mustering all her strength, she turned on Fanny. Using one hip and an arm, she sent the woman tottering backwards towards the window, her arms seeking something to hold on to for support. And for the first time, Theresa entered the fray. But she only had time to curl her fist ready to jab at Nellie before Tony decided things had gone far enough.

'Right, that's it!' The butcher's tone of voice was such that the four women were stopped in their tracks. He was of a mind to throw the two troublemakers out, but first there was something he wanted to know. 'Ye're supposed to be grown-up women, so will yer please act yer age.'

'Serve me and Theresa first, and let's get out of here,' Fanny said. 'Before I marmalise the pair of them.'

Behind the counter, Ellen was standing with her eyes and mouth wide open. In the five years she'd worked in the shop she'd never seen anything like it. It was a good job Tony was here, she wouldn't have known what to do. If it came to tangling with Fanny Kemp, or legging it hell for leather down the road, she'd have chosen the latter option. Molly was very brave for facing up to the neighbourhood bully.

'Before I serve anyone, I'd like yer to tell me, Fanny, what it is ye're so determined to tell Frank Sheild? I don't think me ears heard yer right.'

Fanny squared her shoulders as a boxer would, and her chin jutted out. 'Me and Theresa are going to tell him what no one else has got the guts to. That brazen wife of his has had about fifteen men over the war years, and each one used to sleep the night. And that's not counting the Yank, the one she had a baby to. Frank's going to get his eyes opened all right, and not before time, I say.'

Tony's voice and face were expressionless. 'I don't think that's a good idea, Fanny. The man spent four years in one of the worst prison camps, and saw many of his friends die of starvation or cruelty. The Germans broke his body, his mind and spirit, and now you want to finish the job and break his heart. I think that's such a wicked thing to do, I wouldn't want you in my shop again.

So yer'd better find yerself another butcher, you and Theresa, for I'll never serve yer again.'

'Huh! See if I care!' Fanny was full of bravado. 'There's plenty more butchers' shops will be glad of our custom.'

'I don't think it's only a new butcher yer'll be looking for. Mike from the greengrocer's, his son got wounded in the army and he's never been the same since. I don't think Mike will want yer in his shop when he finds out. And when Andy from the newsagent's hears, yer might find that yer husband has to go elsewhere for his fags and paper. Yer see, Andy lost one of his sons in the war and it's left him a broken man.' Tony walked to the door and gestured for the two women to leave. 'Good afternoon, ladies. Please don't call again.'

There wasn't a sound in the shop as the women left. And when they were out on the pavement, Theresa could be heard saying, 'Ooh, what are we going to do now, Fanny?'

'Oh, shut yer bleedin' face, for God's sake! Yer never opened yer mouth in there, just stood like a bloody statue. Useless, that's what yer are.'

Molly took a deep breath and blew out slowly. 'Tony, I am so sorry. I should have waited until we were outside to tackle them, not start a fight in your shop.'

'I'm glad yer did, Molly, otherwise I wouldn't have known what they were up to. They're bad buggers, the pair of them.'

'But yer've lost two customers because of me, that's not fair!'

'It's meat we're short of, Molly, not customers. Besides, me and Ellen couldn't stand the sight of them.' He looked over to where his assistant stood, her face as white as a sheet. 'Too much excitement, was it?'

'I really thought there was going to be a fight.' Ellen rubbed her hands together for warmth. It was a lovely day, and she hadn't felt cold until the row started and her blood turned to ice. 'Ay, Tony, it's a good job yer went to the abattoir early. If I'd been here on me own, yer would have come back to yer shop wrecked.'

'No, it wouldn't have come to that, girl.' Nellie hadn't turned a hair. In fact, she'd enjoyed it. 'Did yer see the way my mate stood up to Fanny? I was dead proud of her.'

Tony chuckled. 'It'll be something to talk about over dinner tonight. My wife loves a bit of gossip with her liver and onions.' He raised his brows at Ellen. 'Will you see to Molly and Nellie? I want to nip along to the paper shop to have a word with Andy, and then to Mike in the greengrocer's. By the time word gets around to all the shopkeepers, those two villains are going to have to travel far afield to do their shopping. Unless, of course, they have a change of heart.'

328

'Thanks, Tony, ye're a real pal,' Molly said. 'I won't forget yer for this.'

Nellie nodded. 'Yeah, thanks from me too. For everything – including the corned beef!'

Tony turned at the door as a thought entered his head. 'Keep away from those two, they can be dangerous.'

'Don't worry about that,' Molly told him. 'That's the first conversation I've had with them in years, and it'll be the last. I'm not a sucker for punishment.'

'Honest, yer had to be there to believe it.' Nellie's eyes, mouth and hands were all in motion as she related the events in the butcher's shop. 'Never in a million years did I think I'd see Molly standing there, as large as yer like, telling Fanny Kemp what she thought about her. And so calm, as well! When Fanny was poking her in the chest she didn't even bat an eye. That's when I moved in and sent the queer one flying. I wasn't going to have no jumped-up bully doing that to my mate.'

'I should say I'm ashamed of yer for fighting in a shop,' George said. 'But in this instance I think you and Molly did right. And I take me hat off to Tony for sorting the pair of them out.'

'It would be the price of them if none of the shops will serve them,' Steve said, before chuckling. 'I bet Mr Kemp will play merry hell if the newsagent refuses to sell him his fags and paper.'

Lily was only half-listening to the conversation. Her eyes were on Paul, willing him to suggest she go to the dance with him and Archie. She'd been cutting her nose to spite her face for the last week, feeling sorry for herself. Now, after she'd refused so often, her brother probably wouldn't ask her any more. Her mam had given her up as a bad job, too, so she couldn't expect any help from that quarter. Oh, what a fool she'd been, sitting in every night instead of going out and enjoying herself. She'd wasted two years of her life, wasn't that enough?

Nellie hadn't given up on her daughter, she'd just been taking Molly's advice to let the girl move at her own pace. But seeing Lily wasn't even moving at a snail's pace, Nellie decided a little push was in order. So as she was putting her coat on to go to the Bennetts' to have her measurements taken, she asked casually, 'Are yer staying in again tonight, love?'

'It looks like it!'

George lifted his eyes from the evening *Echo*. 'Why don't yer go dancing with the lads?'

'It's manners to wait until ye're asked, Dad.'

'Ye gods! It's no wonder they say all women are contrary.' Paul

329

shook his head in disbelief. 'I've asked yer every blinking night and yer say yer'd rather stay in.'

'I can't help being a woman and contrary, can I? If yer ask me tonight, I'll say yes I'd like to go to the dance with you and Archie.'

'Then go and get ready, girl, 'cos Archie will be here any minute. And wear yer best dress and bags of make-up.' Nellie was well pleased with herself as she closed the front door behind her. That was a turn-up for the books, eh? Wait until she told Molly! All in all, it had been quite an eventful day.

Archie felt like a little boy who'd been given a treat when Paul said Lily was upstairs getting ready to go with them. His flagging hopes suddenly rose again and he felt like singing. And when Lily came down looking so pretty in a pale blue floral dress, with her hair shining and her smiling face wearing just the right amount of make-up, he couldn't help but tell her, 'Yer look very nice, Lily.'

'Thank you, kind sir! And might I say you look very dashing, as always?'

There was contentment in George's smile. He'd been worried about his daughter, but tonight she looked happy, as though she'd put the past behind her. 'Enjoy yerself, love.'

'I will, Dad.' She bent to kiss his cheek. 'If I don't, yer can blame me two escorts.'

Paul was first out of the door, and when he jumped from the top step he landed right in front of Phoebe. 'Yer daft nit!' she said. 'Yer nearly knocked me flying.'

'Nearly, but not quite.' He saw the bag under her arm and grinned. 'Off to Connie Millington's, are yer? Surely ye're good enough to go to a proper dance by now? Our Lily's coming with us tonight, why don't yer come along?'

'No, I'm meeting me friend.' There was a secret behind Phoebe's smile. She *was* good enough to go to a proper dance, but in another couple of weeks she'd be better still. And although the lad grinning down at her didn't know it, she'd made a promise to herself that when the time came for Paul to ask her to dance, she'd be able to match him step for step. And then she wouldn't feel so shy.

'Connie's a good teacher, isn't she?' Archie's smile was directed at Phoebe, but the reason for it was standing by his side. 'She taught me everything I know.'

'I could do with going there for a few lessons,' Lily said. 'I can't keep up with these two, with their fancy footwork. I lack confidence, yer see.'

Oh, Phoebe knew only too well what it was like to lack confidence. She wasn't as shy now as she used to be, not since

330

she'd been going to Millington's. But she needed to feel a lot more sure of herself if she was to compete for a certain young man. 'I'll have to go, I don't like to keep me friend waiting. Enjoy yerselves! Ta-ra!'

'I think I'll go with her one night,' Lily said, as they walked on. 'I could do with a few lessons.'

'I'll teach yer, then it won't cost yer anything,' Archie said. 'We'll start tonight with me favourite dance, the slow fox-trot.'

Chapter Twenty-Four

On Monday morning, when Nellie made her daily call to Molly's for their morning cup of tea, she found her friend in a state of excited agitation. 'What is it, girl?'

'Yer'll never guess! Not in a month of Sundays will yer guess! Honest, sunshine, I couldn't believe me eyes or me ears.'

Nellie pulled a chair from the table and plonked herself down. 'If yer don't tell me quick, girl, either you or me is going to have a heart attack. And if I have a heart attack, twelve days before the wedding, when I haven't even had me posh hat on once, well, I'll have something to say about it, I'm telling yer! And what about me dress and jacket that Doreen made, and what makes me look like a film star, eh, tell me that?'

'Nellie, yer'll be bringing a heart attack on yerself if yer don't watch out. Now just sit nice and calm, so me chair can relax, while I tell yer about me visitor.'

'Yer mean yer've had a visitor, this early in the morning? And yer didn't even think to give us a knock?'

'Will yer shut up and listen, sunshine, before I clock yer one?' Molly leaned her elbows on the table and laced her fingers under her chin. 'When the knock came, I naturally thought it was you. So yer can imagine the shock I got when I opened the door and saw Fanny Kemp standing there! I didn't know whether to scream, faint, or close the door in her face.'

'Fanny Kemp!' It was over a week since the incident in the butcher's and they hadn't seen hide nor hair of Fanny or Theresa. 'What did she want? Did she come to cause trouble?'

Molly shook her head. 'Not a bit of it, she was as meek as a kitten. I was expecting a slanging match outside me front door, and had visions of all the neighbours coming out, but she never even raised her voice. She asked if she could have a word with me, and when I said it depended on what she had to say because I had no intention of getting into an argument, she told me, very quietly, that she hadn't come to cause trouble.' Molly anchored a lock of hair behind her ear and shook her head as though she still couldn't believe what had happened. 'She didn't tell me in so

333

many words, like, but reading between the lines I think her husband created merry hell when the feller in the paper shop refused to serve him his paper and fags. And when he was told why the man had taken the decision to bar him from the shop, he went even more mad! Now I don't know her husband, only to pass the time of day, but I'd say he's laid the law down with her. So the brave Fanny is now trying to mend fences and put things right. She wanted to know if I would kindly have a word with Tony, to see if he will take her and Theresa back as customers.'

The creaking of the chair came before Nellie's laugh. 'Oh, how the mighty have fallen. Well, that's made my day, girl, that has. And what did yer say to her? Did yer tell her to go take a running jump?'

'It's hard to do that when someone is standing there all docile and polite. And, now this might be my bad mind, Nellie, so I don't want yer repeating it to anyone, but I'd swear she's had a belter of a black eye 'cos there's still traces of it.'

'That's why we haven't seen her or Theresa around for the past week. I wondered where they'd got to, and now I know.' Nellie pondered as she pressed at the dimples in her elbow, making deep dents in the flesh. 'I don't hold with a man hitting a woman though. I'd have given her a go-along meself, but that's woman against woman. A man is a different kettle of fish.'

'Perhaps she drove him to it,' Molly said. 'Yer know what she's like when she starts, she's no control over her tongue. Anyway, whatever he did, and for whatever reason, it's brought her to her senses. She won't be spilling the beans to Frank Sheild, that's for sure.'

'Did she tell yer that, girl?'

'She said she probably wouldn't have said anything to him anyway, but we both know that's a load of cobblers. She's only saying that to save her face and because her husband put his foot down. Anyway, Mavis doesn't have to worry any more, thanks to Tony and the other shopkeepers, so that's a blessing. But yer can bet yer sweet life that in a few weeks, when this has died down, Fanny and Theresa will be picking on some other poor bugger.'

'Why didn't Theresa come with her?' Nellie lifted a hand before Molly could answer. 'I know, she didn't have the guts. Without Fanny to stand behind, Theresa Brown wouldn't say boo to a goose. Frightened of her own shadow, she is.'

'Well, it's water under the bridge now – a problem solved, thank goodness.'

'Yer still haven't told me what yer said to her! About having a word with Tony, I mean.'

'I told her I thought she should have the decency to ask Tony herself, because he wouldn't think much of her for getting some-one else to do her dirty work for her. And I got my twopenny-worth in by saying she'd asked for it, because what she and Theresa were planning to do was wicked.'

'Good for you, girl! And what did she have to say to that?'

'That's when she told me they probably wouldn't have said anything to Frank, anyway. But I'd take that with a pinch of salt. She mightn't have the nerve to face Tony, but we'll find out later when we go shopping. Right now I'm gasping for a cuppa, me mouth feels like sawdust. It's been an exciting start to the day.'

Nellie heard the kettle being filled as she mulled over what she'd heard. Molly had been right, she'd never have guessed in a million years that Fanny Kemp would come knocking on the door, cap in hand. Still, it took all sorts to make a world and there was nowt so queer as folk.

'Ay, girl, where's your Doreen?' Nellie called through to the kitchen. 'Wasn't she supposed to be finishing work on Saturday?'

'She did, sunshine. She had an extra half-an-hour lie in, then after breakfast she went over to Miss Clegg's. Phil carried the sewing machine over last night, and Doreen's going to make my dress over there. It's to keep Victoria company, really, and Doreen will be quite happy sewing and nattering away, 'cos she loves the bones of the old lady.'

'I'll tell yer what, girl, she made a ruddy good job of my dress and jacket. I couldn't have got better if I'd gone to the poshest shop in Liverpool and paid a fortune. I tried it on for Lizzie Corkhill before taking it up to her spare bedroom, and she couldn't believe Doreen had made it. And it goes a treat with me hat.'

Molly came through carrying a tray set with teapot, cups, sugar basin, milk jug and a plate with some arrowroot biscuits on. 'I want no wisecracks, sunshine, 'cos I've gone all lah-de-dah. One crack and the tray goes back and yer get a cup stuck in yer hand.'

Nellie was quick to grab a couple of biscuits. 'I'm holding on to these, girl, just in case. I don't have any intention of making a wisecrack, but me tongue is a bit like Fanny Kemp's, it has a mind of its own.'

'Yer've got no manners, Nellie McDonough. I'd be ashamed to take yer anywhere.'

'That's a fine way to talk to yer future sister-in-law, I must say.'

'Where d'yer get that from! Yer don't half get some cockeyed ideas, Nellie, honest yer do! You and me won't be sisters-in-law, yer daft nit.'

Nellie was munching happily away on an arrowroot biscuit, and when she spoke, crumbs flew out of her mouth. 'What will we be, then?'

'Just the same as we are now! The difference will be, I'll be Steve's mother-in-law and you'll be Jill's mother-in-law.' Molly rolled her eyes to the ceiling. 'God help the girl, I wonder if she knows what she's letting herself in for?'

'She should do, seeing as I've known her since the day she was born. Anyway, our Steve has told her what to expect so she can be prepared. He's warned her that I throw things around the house when I get in one of me tempers, that me bad language has been known to turn the air blue, and I've got some really filthy habits.'

Molly smiled as she reached across the table to take hold of one of Nellie's chubby hands. 'And did he tell her she'd have a mate for life, like I have? You and me are better than sisters-in-law, sunshine, we're best mates.'

'Slow down, will yer, girl, I can't walk as fast as you.' Nellie was puffing and blowing. 'What's the big rush, anyway?'

'I'm dying to know if Fanny's been to see Tony.'

'Two minutes isn't going to make any difference. Don't forget, I'm carrying more weight around than you are.'

'I'm sorry, sunshine, I keep forgetting. Let's stop for a while until yer get yer breath back. As yer say, two minutes isn't going to make any difference.'

Nellie's chubby face creased. 'It would if yer had a noose around yer neck, girl! I mean, yer wouldn't want to hang around for two minutes then, would yer?'

'If yer've enough breath to talk, Nellie McDonough, then yer've enough breath to walk slowly. So come on, tuck yer arm in and we'll take it nice and easy.'

They'd only gone a few yards at a snail's pace, when Nellie said, 'I don't know, anyone would think yer were eighty, ye're that ruddy slow. If I had a whip I'd be cracking it on yer backside to make yer gee up. In fact, I'm going to walk on and yer can catch me up when yer decide to put a move on.'

'You cheeky bugger!'

Nellie tutted, put on a sad expression and shook her head. 'One minute I'm yer best mate, the next I'm a cheeky bugger. It's no wonder I've got one of those inferoty things.'

'I know what yer mean, sunshine, an inferiority complex.'

'Oh, have you got one too, girl? Well, I never knew that! It just goes to show that yer learn something new every day.'

Tony and Ellen heard their laughter before the two women came into view. 'They're two good mates, yer neighbours, aren't they?' Tony said. 'I imagine they'd stick together through thick and thin.'

Ellen nodded. 'I don't need to tell yer how good they've been to me, 'cos yer know. The day they talked yer into giving me this job, I didn't even have a penny to put in the gas meter. Me and the kids would have been out on the streets but for Molly and Nellie. I owe them more than anyone will know.'

'Good morning, Tony – morning, Ellen!' Molly's face was alive with eagerness. 'Well, has Fearsome Fanny been in to see yer?'

'She has indeed.' Tony put a finger under the rim of his straw hat and pushed it back off his forehead. 'And from here she went to the other shops. I've been down to see Andy and Mike, and they say the same as me. Yer wouldn't have believed it was the same person. Gone was the tough, loud-mouthed fishwife, and in her place stood a lamb. As nice as pie she was, and very apologetic.'

Nellie and her chins nodded knowingly. 'Her husband's had a go at her.'

'I believe he has, Nellie, I believe he has. She said she would have been in sooner but she hasn't been well. Now, if yer add that to what Andy said about Mr Kemp blowing his top when he refused to serve him, it seems to point to that. Apparently he left the shop blazing with anger and threatening to knock the stuffing out of his wife.'

'I hope she's back in favour with everyone, even though I haven't got much time for the woman,' Molly said. 'If her husband's given her a go-along, and she's had to pocket her pride and apologise to everyone . . . well, I think that's punishment enough.'

'I agree, Molly, and that's why I told her she and Theresa are welcome back and all is forgiven. I don't believe in holding a grudge.'

'So all Mavis has got to worry about now is her own children.' Nellie had her doubts about them. 'They're only young, it'll be a miracle if they don't let anything slip.'

'There's nothing we can do about that, Nellie, it's out of our hands.' Tony leaned over the counter and gave a broad wink. 'But I have got something to put a smile on yer face.'

Within seconds Nellie became an actress. With her hands over where she thought her heart was, a lovesick look in her eyes and a catch in her voice, she purred, 'Oh Tony, I've waited fifteen years to hear yer say that, my darling. I've known all along how yer felt about me and I've been grieved that yer were too shy to bring your love out into the open.' She fell back against the counter and put the back of a hand on her forehead. 'I feel weak with

337

happiness, heart of my heart. But did yer really have to declare your love in the middle of a bleedin' butcher's shop?'

Molly stopped laughing long enough to say, 'Watch yer language, sunshine.'

To which Nellie replied, 'You watch me language, girl, I'm too busy.' Her eyes on Tony, she asked, 'How big is yer stockroom, lover boy?'

'Too small for what you have in mind, Nellie! Small, cold and blood everywhere.'

'Oh, woe is me, I've been denied again. Am I never to know the joy of your heart beating against mine, Tony, or feel the passion in your kisses as you hold me in your arms?'

'Nellie, ye're getting carried away.' The butcher was glad there were no customers in the shop listening to this. It wouldn't be so bad if they knew Nellie, they'd hang around and have a good laugh. But there were others who wouldn't see the funny side. 'When I said I had something to put a smile on yer face, I was talking about shin beef!'

'Shin beef!' Nellie stood to attention. 'Yer mean yer've got some shin beef in?'

Tony nodded. 'I thought that would please yer.'

'Well, I mean no disrespect to yer Tony, but I'd rather have a pound of shin beef any day than the other thing yer were offering me.'

While Ellen turned away to hide her blushes, Molly tutted. 'Nellie, ye're going too far!'

'Too far? Yer heard what the man said, his stockroom is too small, too cold and there's blood everywhere. We'd have to be ruddy contortionists to go too far in there. But I'm not feeling rejected, girl, not when there's a pound of shin beef in the offing.'

'Half a pound of shin beef, Nellie,' Tony corrected her. 'And I'll have to have yer ration books for it. But because yer've been let down in love, I'll throw a quarter pound of stewing steak in to cheer yer up. That goes for you as well, Molly.'

'Thanks, Tony.' Molly opened her bag to get out the ration books. 'Ye're a pal.'

'Well, I'll be buggered.' Nellie's indignant act was one of her best. And right now she was excelling herself. 'Here am I, the injured party what's been cast aside in love, and me mate benefits from it. It's a swindle, that's what it is.'

Molly tapped her on the shoulder. 'Count yerself lucky, sunshine, and shut up before Tony changes his mind. And let's see the colour of yer ration book.'

The two friends were walking back from the shops when Molly

asked, 'How's your Lily's love-life? On the move or standing still?'

'Like a ruddy waltz, girl – one step forward then one to the side. I don't know whether she'd go dancing with Archie if Paul didn't go along. And if I ask any questions, all I get is, "Archie's a good friend, Mam, and lots of fun to be with". So I'm best doing what George says, and leaving them to get on with it. Archie is smitten with her, it's written all over him, but she's playing things close to her chest. I've tried sounding Paul out, but he's too busy having fun himself to think about anyone else. He did say Lily enjoys herself when they go out, and she's up for every dance, but that's about it.'

'So there's no romance on the cards?'

'No, girl, I don't think there's any romance on the cards. Not yet, anyway.'

Archie was of the same mind when he called at the McDonoughs' that night. He didn't seem to be getting anywhere with Lily. They danced nearly every dance together now because Paul had decided that dancing with his own sister wasn't exactly up his street. And they shared the same sense of fun, although her humour wasn't as sharp as his. She was always friendly with him and linked his arm on the nights he took her home when Paul had met someone who took his fancy. But even when they were linking arms, she still kept him at a distance. So much so, he wouldn't have dared ask for a goodnight kiss.

While he was waiting for someone to answer his knock, Archie made up his mind that tonight he would ask Lily if she'd come to the pictures with him one night. Nothing ventured, nothing gained. But when she opened the door to him, still in her working dress and her face wearing no make-up, his heart sank.

'Come in, Archie.' Lily stood aside to let him pass. 'I'm afraid ye're on yer own tonight, our Paul's got a date.'

He smiled a greeting at Nellie and George before saying, 'There's no reason why we can't go. We don't need Paul to hold our hands.'

'I've told her that, the silly article,' Nellie huffed, 'but she said yer mightn't want to take her without Paul, and she wasn't going to get ready and put yer in the position where yer had to take her whether yer liked it or not.'

'That's daft, that, because we don't see much of Paul when we get to the dance.' Archie told himself it was now or never. 'Go and get ready, Lily, I'm not going on me own.'

'But it'll take me ages to get ready – I haven't even been washed yet!'

George came in on Archie's side. 'A cat's lick and a promise, love, that's all yer need. If yer put a move on yer could be ready in twenty minutes.'

'If you won't go with him, I will,' Nellie grinned. 'Do they still do the Black Bottom, Archie? I used to shine at that.'

Archie feigned horror and appealed to Lily. 'Go and get ready, quick!'

She giggled. 'I can just see it! You and me mam doing the Black Bottom.'

'And I could teach him the shimmy-shimmy-shake!' Nellie said, for good measure. 'That's something else I was good at.'

George winked at his daughter. 'Go and get ready, love, before your mam frightens the life out of the lad.'

'I don't frighten easily, Mr McDonough,' Archie said as Lily left the room to dash up the stairs. 'But I've got to admit the Black Bottom and the shimmy-shimmy-shake do send a shiver of apprehension down me spine.'

'The wife has the same effect on me.' With George you never knew whether he was speaking seriously or whether what he was saying was in fun because he had the ability to keep his face straight. 'I feel a shiver running down me spine every time she opens her mouth.'

'That's passion, light of my life.' Nellie preened. 'I know he doesn't look it, Archie, but my husband is a very passionate man.'

'See what I mean, lad?' George spread out his hands. 'That's what gives me a shiver. I never know what she's going to come out with next!'

'At least yer marriage will never go stale, Mr McDonough, not like some do.'

Once again Nellie preened. 'D'yer know what, Archie, the minute I clapped eyes on yer I knew yer were a man after me own heart.'

Lily was ready within fifteen minutes, much to Archie's surprise. 'That didn't take yer long!'

'I put me skates on.' Lily wasn't going to let on that she already had the dress and shoes ready, hoping things would turn out as they had. 'I don't spend half-an-hour plastering me face with make-up, like some girls do.'

'Yer don't need to,' Archie told her. 'I think some girls use a trowel to put it on and they look like painted dolls.'

'Well, come on, don't just sit there after me rushing round like mad.' Lily reached behind the couch for the bag with her dancing shoes in. 'I've got a key, Mam, if yer want to go to bed before I get home.'

'I'll come to the door with yer.' Nellie was delighted with the turn of events. She'd be able to tell Molly that tonight had been one step forward. 'Enjoy yerselves.'

'We will, Mrs Mac.' Archie gave her a cheeky grin. 'And you be careful yer don't put too much strain on yer husband's back.'

'Chance would be a fine thing, lad!' Nellie closed the door thinking she didn't half like him. If she was able to pick a husband for her daughter, Archie would definitely be first in line. 'Well, what d'yer say, love?' she asked when she was back in the living room. 'D'yer think there's romance in the air?'

'I'd like to think so, 'cos Lily couldn't do any better for herself.' There was tenderness in George's eyes when he looked at his wife. He knew she'd been unhappy about Lily's friendship with Len; he had been himself. But as a mother, it had been harder for Nellie. She wanted the best for her only daughter. 'But it isn't up to us, is it, love? It's up to Lily. All we can do is wait, watch and hope.'

'And keep me fingers crossed!' The mischief shining in his wife's eyes told George she was going to come out with something that would send a shiver down his spine if they had company. But seeing as they were alone, he waited with anticipation. 'I was going to say I'd cross me legs as well, for good measure, like, but I wouldn't do that to yer, love.'

George's head fell back and he roared with laughter. He must be one of the luckiest men in the world to have a wife who kept their marriage alive with her humour, warmth and passion.

The band struck up with a tango, and Archie held out his hand. 'Are yer going to try it?'

'Ye're a sucker for punishment, Archie, 'cos yer know I'm hopeless at a tango! Why don't yer ask another girl, 'cos I know it's one of yer favourites? I don't mind sitting it out.'

'I don't want to ask another girl, I want to dance with you! Anyway, ye're not *that* bad at it. Just take a look at some of them on the floor, they haven't got a clue!'

Lily took his hand and allowed him to lead her on to the dance floor. 'On your own head be it, Archie, if I make a mistake.'

'No, Lily, if yer make a mistake it'll be me feet that get it, not me head.'

'Unless I trip yer up and yer fall backwards. Then, if I carry on dancing on me own, it will be yer head that gets it.'

Archie was eight inches taller than Lily, so he had to hold her away from him to look down into her face. 'Yer sounded just like yer mam then.'

'Ooh, I've got a long way to go to catch up with me mam. She's so quick-witted she leave me spellbound at times. I wish I was more like her though, 'cos she's a smasher.'

'She is that! And you're more like her than yer realise.' Archie dared a quick squeeze of her waist before dancing on.

Lily flatly refused to try the rumba, saying she wanted to master the other dances first. But she was secretly pleased that she'd come on so well over the last few weeks; she was able now to follow Archie without looking down at her feet or feeling nervous. He was a good dancer and it hadn't escaped her that he was receiving admiring glances from some of the girls standing on the fringe of the dance floor. She could understand that because he really was tall, dark and handsome, and he stood out in the crowd. And he was good company, with his quick wit and ready smile. An ideal companion for an enjoyable night out.

On the way home, Lily took his arm. 'Thanks for taking me, Archie, I really enjoyed meself. I've learned a lot from yer, too, and am more confident on the floor. In another couple of weeks I'll be trying out all those intricate steps and spins.'

'Wouldn't yer prefer to go to the pictures one night, just for a change?'

Lily didn't answer straight away. It was one thing going to a dance, but sitting in the intimacy of a darkened cinema was something entirely different. She and Len used to go to the pictures nearly every night, and in the darkness he would hold her hand, or steal a kiss as sweethearts do. She didn't pine for Len any more, he'd hurt her so much it had killed any feelings she had for him. Even if he came crawling for forgiveness, she would never take him back. But she still thought of him. After all, you can't put two years out of your mind as though they'd never been.

Archie squeezed her arm. 'Yer haven't gone asleep on me, have yer?'

'No, I was miles away,' Lily lied. 'I was seeing meself waltzing around that dance floor like a real professional, and everyone else leaving the floor to gaze in admiration at me grace and nimble footwork.'

'Well, do yer mind coming down to earth again and telling me whether yer'd like to go to the pictures one night? We could see if Fred Astaire and Ginger Rogers are on anywhere, and yer could watch their twinkle toes.'

'I don't think so, Archie, if yer don't mind. Yer see, me and Len went to the pictures nearly every night 'cos there was nowhere else to go. He would never spend more than five minutes in our house, I never went to his, so it was Hobson's choice, I'm afraid. And I really did get a bit fed-up with it.' Lily's eyes slid sideways. Whenever they went out, Archie and Paul paid for her ticket between them, even though she'd wanted to pay for herself. But tonight the cost had fallen on Archie's shoulders and there'd almost been an argument when she'd tried to buy her own ticket. But she couldn't keep imposing on him, it wasn't fair. It wasn't as though they were courting or anything. 'I hope yer don't mind, Archie – about going to the pictures, I mean?'

'No, of course I don't mind.' He kept his voice light, even though he was bitterly disappointed. And hearing her talking of her ex-boyfriend hadn't helped. 'I enjoy dancing, so it suits me.'

'Well, the next time we go I'm paying for meself. I can't expect you to be forking out for me all the time.'

'That'll be the day, when I take a girl out and she pays for herself! I've never done it before and I'm not about to start now. I'd feel a right heel.'

I've insulted him now, Lily thought, and I didn't mean to. So she tried to put things right. 'Why don't we stay in tomorrow night and have a game of cards with me mam and dad? It'll be a change and we'd have a good laugh.'

That lifted Archie's spirits. Perhaps he was expecting too much, too soon. She needed time to get to know him, and what better place to do that than in her own home? 'That sounds good to me. But will you tell Paul in the morning in case he's expecting to come dancing with us?'

'Yeah, I'll do that.'

'Where was he off to tonight, by the way? I didn't see him with anyone special last night, did you?'

Lily shook her head. 'Not that I noticed. But nothing our Paul did would surprise me.'

Where Paul had taken himself off to that night would have certainly surprised his sister. The boy who was a wizard on the dance floor and didn't need any dancing lessons, had gone to Connie Millington's dancing school. And if anyone had asked him why, he would have had a problem trying to tell them something he couldn't understand himself.

Phoebe Corkhill was dancing with a new beginner and trying to keep her feet from getting under his, when she saw Paul walk through the door. The sight of him threw her into a state of confusion and she lost control of her feet. The lad she was dancing with, Danny, thought it was his fault and began to apologise. 'I'm sorry, I missed me footing. The way I'm shaping, yer feet will be black and blue tomorrow.'

'It was my fault, not yours.' Phoebe glared over to where Paul was grinning and waving to her. What the heck was *he* doing here? She wasn't going to be able to dance properly with him watching, he'd put her off completely. 'Don't worry, we've all got to learn. I was worse than you when I first started.'

343

At the end of the dance she walked over to join her friend, cursing the blushes that she knew would be colouring her face. She didn't even have time to sit down before Paul was upon them.

'Hiya! I thought I'd come and see for meself what is so good about this place that yer come a few times a week. Yer never know, I might learn something.'

Phoebe was tight-lipped. 'What are yer doing here, Paul McDonough?'

'The same as you, Phoebe Corkhill, to learn something. I could do with brushing up on me fox-trot. And now, why don't yer introduce me to yer friend?'

'Nancy, this is Paul.' The introduction was begrudged by Phoebe but welcomed by her workmate, who nearly swooned and thought she'd never seen anyone as gorgeous as the boy grinning down at her with a merry twinkle in his eye.

'So, are yer both going to take pity on me, seeing as it's me first time here? I'll have the next dance with Phoebe and the one after with you, eh, Nancy?'

Nancy looked so pleased it was as if someone had given her an unexpected birthday present. 'Oh yeah, I'd like that.'

'I've promised to have the next dance with Danny, 'cos he's just learning and is very shy. And the dance after I'm having with the boy I dance with every week. But Nancy will be happy to have yer for a partner, Paul, so yer won't feel left out.' Phoebe had set herself a target and she wasn't going to be thrown off-course. She'd dreamed of having her first dance with Paul at the wedding, when she was all dressed up in her beautiful bridesmaid's dress, and she wasn't about to let him spoil her dreams. So all night she found an excuse not to dance with him, and he was kept at arm's length. And when the night was over, she refused to let him walk her and Nancy home, much to her friend's dismay and Paul's bewilderment. He couldn't understand it; no girl had ever turned him down before.

Chapter Twenty-Five

'I didn't get a wink of sleep last night,' Molly said as she and Nellie walked to the shops. It was the Tuesday before the wedding and the excitement was mounting for both women. 'If it keeps up like that I'm going to look like a wet rag come Saturday.'

'I know, girl, I didn't get much sleep meself. And my feller gets on me flaming nerves 'cos he sleeps like a log, without a care in the world. Snores his ruddy head off, he does.'

'Jack's the same, sleeps like a baby. But it's just as well the men do sleep because they've got to go out to work.' Molly gave her friend a dig. 'Ay, don't men have an easy life, sunshine? I've got that many things to think about for this wedding, I don't know whether I'm on me head or me heels.'

'Yer must be on yer heels, girl, 'cos if yer were on yer head I'd be talking to yer knickers right now. And people would think I'd gone doolally.'

'Before I forget, Nellie, I've got something to tell yer that ye're not going to like. But before I tell yer, I want yer to remember that your family are part of this wedding, too! So are yer ready to hear the news without biting me head off?'

'Go on, girl, me shoulders are strong, I can take it.'

Molly pulled her arm from her mate's and put a space between them. 'Ye're going to have to have our table in your house on Saturday.'

'What! Holy suffering ducks, girl, not again! I've got that ruddy table more than you have! In fact, it spends so much time in our house, it takes its shoes off and makes itself at home!'

'I think yer've had that table four times in twenty-five years, sunshine, so don't you be exaggerating. And why have yer had it anyway? Have yer never thought of that? Well, I'll tell yer, shall I? I've asked yer to mind the table every time we've had a party and wanted more room. And why, pray, was I having parties? Because you, sunshine, were too ruddy mean, that's why.'

'All right, girl, there's no need to tell the whole ruddy street! I'll have the flaming table to stop yer moaning, but I'll be black and blue with bumping into it.'

'There's no need for it to go in yer living room, it can go in the yard. With the weather the way it is, it won't come to no harm.'

Nellie thought about that, then narrowed her eyes. 'Why can't it go in your yard?'

'Because when the reception is over, a few people might be coming back to the house. And I don't want the table in the yard in case someone who's had one too many decides to go to the lavvy and bumps into it. Now, does that satisfy yer?'

'I thought we were staying in the hall after the reception, and having a party there. So why d'yer say a few people might come back to yours? I hope yer not thinking of sloping off on the quiet without letting on to yer best mate?'

'Now, as if I'd do that to you! No, we've got the hall until eleven o'clock and most people will have had enough by then. Jack's brother and his wife have written to say they'll have to leave about eight 'cos it's a long drive back. And Lizzie Corkhill and Miss Clegg won't last much after that 'cos they'll be worn out. So I'm just thinking of asking our close family and friends if they want to come back for a cuppa, to finish the day off, like.'

'That's nice of yer, girl, and I accept yer invitation on behalf of me family and Mr Archibald Higgins.'

'I hadn't forgotten Archie, sunshine, not for a second. He's one of me favourite people. And I'm hoping romance will bloom between him and Lily so we can keep him in the family. D'yer think he's in with a chance?'

'If I told yer what I thought, yer'd say I'd gone stark, staring bonkers. She's in a world of her own, that's what yer'd say. Or, as my George tells me, it's wishful thinking.'

'Go on, tell us, I'm all ears.'

'If I do, will yer promise not to say a dickie bird to anyone? I don't want to be a laughing stock if I'm proved wrong.'

'Me lips are sealed, sunshine, cross my heart and hope to die.'

'I've got a feeling that on Saturday, all me three children's lives will be mapped out for them. And if it turns out that way, I'm going to get blind drunk with happiness, even though my George can't stand drunken women. Common as muck, he calls them.'

'Will yer get straight to the point, Nellie, instead of going all around the houses? What does this feeling that yer have tell yer?'

'Well, we know our Steve's sorted out, don't we? He's got the girl he always wanted and, please God, they'll both live happy ever after. And as far as our Lily's concerned, I think I know what's going on inside of her better than she does herself. I can see her getting closer to Archie, liking him more every day, but she's either as thick as two short planks or as stubborn as a ruddy mule 'cos she can't see what I can. Anyway, whether she's thick or

346

just stubborn, I'm pinning me hopes on her coming to her senses on Saturday.'

'I've told yer, ye're expecting too much of her. She's neither thick nor stubborn, Nellie, she's just a girl who's been badly let down and needs time to get over it. And now tell us who yer've got yer eyes on for your Paul? This I can't wait to hear, 'cos your Paul definitely has a mind of his own and if he thought yer were matchmaking for him, he'd tell yer in no uncertain terms to get lost.'

'I'm not telling yer nothing about him 'cos yer'd say I had a screw loose. Perhaps I am imagining things – it wouldn't be the first time. But if I get legless on Saturday, yer'll know it's because I'm in me seventh heaven and not as daft as yer think.'

'But your Paul hasn't even got a steady girlfriend! I've never even seen him with a girl, and he's never brought one to the house, has he?'

'I'm saying nowt.' Nellie's shake of the head meant that was an end to the matter. 'Ay, girl, are we going to the butcher's?'

'No, we got today's dinner in yesterday. Why, what made yer ask?'

'Because Ellen is waving her hand off to attract our attention. I think she wants us to go over there.'

Molly grabbed hold of her mate's arm as Nellie stepped off the pavement and almost into the path of an on-coming bus. 'In the name of God, Nellie, are yer trying to get us both killed! How many times do I have to tell yer to look *both* ways before crossing? Even a five-year-old's got more road sense than you.'

'Keep yer hair on, girl, ye're still in one piece, aren't yer? And if yer must know, I saw the ruddy bus coming before you did, so there was no need to pull me arm out of its socket.'

'You fibber! Now tell the truth, Nellie McDonough, yer never saw the bus, did yer?'

'Yes, I did, so there!' Nellie's eyes twinkled as her body shook with laughter. 'I saw it as it went past, didn't I?'

Molly tutted as she looked both ways, saw it was clear and took hold of her friend's arm before stepping into the road. 'What am I going to do with yer? Yer'll have me in an early grave, you will.'

Tony and Ellen had been watching the palaver through the shop window, and they were both grinning when the women entered the shop. 'Worse than a child, isn't she, Molly?'

'You ain't kidding, Tony! Our Ruthie had more road sense at five than Tilly Mint here's got. She'd have walked straight into that bus if I hadn't pulled her back.'

Nellie pulled on Molly's coat and put on the petulant expression of a spoilt child. 'Mam, can I have a lollipop, please? A pink one?'

347

Molly decided to go along with her. 'No, yer can't, yer mam's got no money.'

'Ah, ray, Mam!' The lips pouted and trembled. 'That big bad bus nearly ran over me.'

Taking her purse from her pocket, Molly rooted out a penny. 'Here yer are, go and ask the nice man in the sweetshop for a lollipop. And don't forget me ha'penny change.'

'Sod off, Molly Bennett!' Nellie held the penny in her open palm and showed it to the butcher. 'I don't suppose I could have a nice juicy pork chop for this, could I?'

'Ye're right, Nellie, yer couldn't. Even if yer had a handful yer couldn't, 'cos I haven't got a pork chop in the shop!' Tony chuckled. 'But I know the nice man in the sweetshop's got plenty of lollipops, all pretty colours.'

'You can sod off, as well!' Nellie dropped the coin in her pocket. 'I'll get a pennyworth of mint imperials with it, and I'll eat them all meself, for spite.'

'I doubt that, sunshine,' Molly said. 'Yer see, it's a foreign coin.'

Nellie delved into her pocket and brought out the coin. She looked puzzled as she examined it both sides. 'It looks all right to me. Same as any other penny.'

Molly laughed softly. 'Have yer ever been had, sunshine?'

The little woman didn't turn a hair. 'Yes, I have actually. Just this minute.' A slow smile crossed Nellie's face. 'Ay, did yer hear that? "Yes, I have actually." Didn't I sound proper posh? I'll have to remember to talk like that when I've got me posh hat on.'

'I can't wait to see this hat, it sounds out of this world,' Ellen said. She had been given Saturday off by Tony, who was bringing in his wife to help in the shop. 'I'll probably look like a poor relation.'

'I wouldn't advise yer to come to the wedding in a beret, Ellen, girl, 'cos yer would look like a poor relation then. Yer want to see the hat me mate's got! Talk about Hollywood here I come, isn't in it. She'll look like a real film star, honest!'

Molly shook her head. The way Nellie was going on, the whole neighbourhood would be coming out just to see her hat! 'Take no notice of her, Ellen, yer know what she's like for exaggerating. Anyway, did yer want us for anything?'

'Maisie nipped down before to tell me Corker had rung her to ask if she'd let me know he'll be home around lunch-time tomorrow.'

'Oh, that's the gear! Everything's falling into place, just like Jack said it would. The reception's paid for, the cars are booked, the flowers and drink ordered and Phil's sorted a photographer out. And now we know for certain that Corker will be here. I know he said he would be, but anything can happen, can't it? I mean, ships can break down like anything else, and the wedding wouldn't seem right without Corker there. But, God's in His heaven and all's well with the world.'

'Yer've had a lot on yer plate, Molly,' Tony said. 'Organising a double wedding takes some doing. I hope it all goes well and yer have a lovely day.'

'We will, Tony, we will.' Molly put her arm across Nellie's shoulder and smiled down at her. 'For me and my best mate, it's going to be one of the happiest days of our lives.'

Molly was as happy as Larry as she gazed around her family that night. 'I'm feeling dead chuffed with me little self now I know Corker's coming home. That was the one worry I had left. Now I've got everything worked out to a fine art. Tommy, you'll help yer dad to carry this table up to the McDonoughs' yard first thing Saturday morning. Then yer can take yerself round to me ma's out of the way. I don't want yer to think ye're getting thrown out, son, but with two brides and five bridesmaids getting ready here, we won't be able to turn around, it'll be chaotic. Anyway, there's a wedding car picking yer up from there to take yer to the church with me ma, da and Rosie.'

'How many cars are there, love?' Jack asked.

'Only two! There was no point in the boys ordering more when it's only a matter of minutes from here to Saint Anthony's, and the two cars can make a few trips. For instance, the car that picks Tommy and me family up, can come straight back for Lizzie Corkhill and Miss Clegg. I was worried about the two old dears, and I know Phil was, but Archie's mam volunteered to go in the car with them and make sure they were all right.' Molly was wishing she'd written it all down 'cos there was a lot to remember. 'Most of the guests are making their own way to the church, so that's a blessing. The second pick-up for the cars will be the two grooms with their best man in one, and Nellie, George and Archie in the other. Then they'll take the bridesmaids next, and they'll need the two cars for that. Otherwise the dresses will get creased to blazes.'

'They better hadn't be, Mam, or I'll go mad.' Doreen thought of all the hours she'd put in making those dresses. It was a labour of love, but a labour nonetheless. 'We want our wedding to be perfect, don't we, kid? Not a crease to be seen nor a hair out of place.'

'I wouldn't notice it anyway, 'cos I'll be too nervous.' Jill went weak when she even thought about walking down the aisle with all eyes on her. She had to keep telling herself not to be stupid, and reminding herself that when she got to the bottom of the aisle, Steve would be waiting for her. 'I bet all brides are nervous, aren't they, Mam?'

'Of course they are, sunshine! And d'yer think no one else will be nervous? I bet yer dad will be quaking in his shoes. Even Corker and Paul, who look as though nothing in the world would make them afraid, I bet they'll be nervous, too. It's a serious job being best man, yer know, not just a case of making sure the groom gets to the church on time. There's the ring to worry about, where to stand in church, make sure they're handy in case the groom faints, and after all that they've got to make a speech at the reception.'

That brought a smile to Jill's pretty face. 'I don't think Steve will faint. If anyone passes out, it will be me. I'll go mad if I make a fool of meself.'

'You won't, Sis,' Tommy said. 'You and Doreen are going to knock 'em dead in the aisles, I promise.' His eyes went to Ruthie, who was taking it all in. 'And I bet no one has ever had prettier bridesmaids.'

'Molly, I've been thinking,' Jack said. 'How are you getting to the church?'

'Erm, er . . .' Molly looked surprised by the question. Then she slapped a hand on her forehead. 'Oh my God, I'd forgotten about meself! It serves me right for bragging about how good I am. I've been patting meself on the back for being so well organised, and I've forgotten meself. It's the price of me!'

'You should be there the same time as Nellie and George. Yer'll have to get in the car with them – there'll be plenty of room.'

'Or yer could walk round to me nan's and come with us,' Tommy suggested. 'There'll be plenty of room in the car 'cos they hold about six.'

'What? Walk round to me ma's in the hat Nellie's told everyone about? I'm expecting the whole street out! In fact, it wouldn't surprise me if she's sold tickets.'

'Well, go in either Nellie's car or Miss Clegg's,' Jack said. 'Just make sure yer get to the church before I arrive with the brides.' He suddenly had a thought. 'Ay, I haven't seen this creation yet, where are yer hiding it?'

'In Lizzie Corkhill's, along with the brides' and bridesmaids' dresses. Nobody is going to see it until I'm dressed up in all me glory.'

'I can't wait.'

When Jack gave her that special, loving look that never failed to make her heart beat faster and her legs turn to jelly, Molly could feel herself blush. So to cover her confusion she said briskly,

'Right, that's it, yer all know where we're up to now so we'll bring the meeting to a close.'

When Corker called at the Bennetts' the following night, he found all the family there to greet him. Bridie and Bob had walked round with Rosie, and Steve and Phil were there. For he was a man who was not just liked, but loved by each and every one of them. 'Well, this is nice!' his loud voice boomed as the smile on his weatherbeaten face covered everyone in the room. He had good mates on the ship, but no one could come up to these friends he'd known for so many years. He noted Bridie and Bob sitting next to each other holding hands. They'd been married for nearly fifty years, but were still sweethearts. And next to them sat Tommy, with Rosie perched on his knee with a welcoming smile on her lovely face that would warm the cockles of the coldest of hearts. 'Ye're looking well, Bridie and Bob. It's easy to see where the Bennett girls get their good looks from.'

'Away with yer, Corker, sure it's yerself that's kissed the blarney stone more than once, so it is.'

'Not at all, Auntie Bridget,' Rosie said. 'Uncle Corker's right, so he is. The girls do get their good looks from you. And when me mammy comes over from Ireland for me wedding, yer'll see right enough that it's from her I get *my* good looks.'

There were hoots of laughter, the loudest of which came from Tommy. 'There's nothing like blowing yer own trumpet, Rosie! But what if we all think yer mam is as ugly as sin?'

'Tommy Bennett, is it an eejit yer think I am? Sure, if I was as ugly as sin, yer'd not be having me sitting on yer knee right now! And yer'd not be counting the days until we get married next year.'

'That's put you in yer place, son,' Jack laughed. 'I've never yet heard yer get the last word in with Rosie.'

Corker was laughing as he lifted Molly off her feet and gazed up into her face. 'Still the best-looking woman in the street, Molly, me darlin'.'

'Put me down, yer silly nit, I'm showing everything I've got.' But Molly was happy inside. Apart from Jack, this was the one man she cared for deeply. It wasn't the love of a woman for a man, but the love of a dear friend for a man who was always there when needed and always knew the right thing to do. A man you could trust with your life. 'I expected yer to call this afternoon.'

'I had a message to do, me darlin', and I got it out of the way so I'd be free to do any running around that needs doing. Oh, and while I was out, I dropped that tin of ham off at the cake-shop to save you lugging it.'

351

'Ye're an angel, Corker, and I don't know what we'd do without yer.'

'From what Ellen tells me, yer've got everything under control. But at least I'm here if yer want me, and the one thing I can do is make sure the drink is at the hall first thing Saturday morning.' He looked to where the two future brides were sitting on the knees of their husbands-to-be. 'I'll need a bit of tuition, lads, 'cos I've never been a best man before. So what exactly do I have to do?'

'I need some tuition meself, Mr Corker,' Phil grinned. 'Yer see, I've never been a groom before. But I do know that we have to be at the church at least fifteen minutes before the bride. And from what the priest told me, you and me sit on the front pew. When the organ starts to play, we stand up while the bride walks down the aisle and is handed over by her father. Then you stay at my side, with the ring ready to hand over. The priest will lead us after that, so there'll be no problem. I'm sure yer'll make a very good best man.'

'It's me that should be worrying,' Steve said. 'Every time I try to tell our Paul what he's got to do, he just waves a hand and says everything will be hunky-dory! I'm holding on to the ring meself, 'cos I wouldn't trust him not to lose it.'

'He won't let yer down, Steve,' Jill said. 'I bet he'll be as cool as a cucumber and do everything he's supposed to.'

'Can I suggest me and Jack taking the two grooms out for a pint?' Corker needed to talk to the lads on their own, and this was the only way he knew how. 'I could do with a good pint of bitter to whet me whistle, and the lads can fill me in with what they want me to do. I mean with regard to who they want to give the toasts at the reception, and who is going to make a speech. I think better when I've had a pint.'

'Don't go without George, or there'll be blue murder,' Molly said. 'Nellie wants to know everything, right down to the last detail.'

'We'll give a knock for George, don't worry. And I won't keep yer sweethearts out long, girls, just the one pint.' He raised his brows at Bob. 'D'yer feel like coming with us, Bob?'

Bob shook his head. 'I don't drink much these days. But I'm going to make an exception on Saturday when me two grand-daughters get wed. It'll be a special day for me and the wife.'

'Don't you be getting me boyfriend drunk, Uncle Corker,' Doreen said. 'I'm not waiting until we're married to put me foot down.'

'Me neither!' Jill didn't want to be parted from her loved one for even a minute. 'If Steve isn't back within an hour, I'll be waiting for him with the rolling pin.'

Corker's smile was tender for the girl who had always been special to him. 'If I was Steve, princess, I wouldn't leave you for any longer than was absolutely necessary. He'll be back within the hour, I promise yer.'

Jack pulled the door closed behind him. 'I'll give George a knock.'

Corker bent his head to whisper, 'I want to talk to the boys on their own for about fifteen minutes, Jack, so will yer hold back that long?'

'I'll have a cigarette with George before we come up.' Jack was curious but didn't like to ask. He'd be told eventually, anyway. 'You go ahead.'

Corker ordered three pints at the bar, then carried them over to a corner table. 'I've got something to tell yer that's got to be kept secret. Except for Jill and Doreen – they'll have to know.' He delved into his pocket and brought out a piece of white paper. 'This is my wedding present to yer, and I hope it meets with your approval.' He passed the paper over and picked up his pint.

Steve and Phil looked down at the paper which had *The Adelphi Hotel* printed at the top. It was a receipt for two double rooms at the hotel, for one night's bed and breakfast, and the date was for Saturday night. The cost of the two rooms came to more than the two boys earned between them for a week's work. They looked at Corker as though they didn't believe what they were seeing.

'I don't understand, Uncle Corker,' Steve said. 'What does this mean, and why would you do it?'

'To save the girls a lot of embarrassment.' The big man wiped some beer from his moustache. 'At any wedding there's always some smart Alec who'll make sly remarks about it being the first night – that sort of thing. They only say it for a laugh, no harm meant, but I don't think Jill or Doreen would find it funny. Nor you, either. Now I'm talking to yer man to man, and I hope yer don't take this the wrong way. Jill would have the embarrassment of coming downstairs on Sunday morning and facing my mother. Me ma wouldn't think anything of it, but Jill wouldn't know what to do with herself. The same goes for Doreen. Yer don't have to go along with it if yer don't want to, but my suggestion is that yer don't mention the Adelphi to anyone. Leave the reception at about eight o'clock, saying the girls want to change out of their wedding dresses. That way yer'll avoid all the cat-calls and smutty jokes. Get changed and take a taxi down to the hotel. When I think yer've had time to get away, I'll tell everyone where yer've gone and take the blame.' Corker took a swig of beer before going

353

on. 'Take it from me, a few stupid remarks could spoil the whole day for the girls. Me and Ellen were in our forties when we got married, and I took her to a hotel for the first night because she was terrified of looking anyone in the eye.'

'I know what yer mean, Uncle Corker, and I've been worried about Jill 'cos she's so shy and wouldn't think a smutty joke was funny.'

'I could do without it meself,' Phil said. 'I think it's a marvellous idea, but it would mean Aunt Vickie being in the house on her own all night.'

'No it wouldn't, son, 'cos I'll get one of the boys to sleep on her couch. No harm would come to her, I promise.'

Steve was looking down at the piece of paper in his hand. 'It's cost yer a small fortune, Uncle Corker. The Adelphi is the poshest hotel in Liverpool.'

'Only the best is good enough for my two princesses. They might never be able to go there again, so let me spoil them on their wedding night, please?'

'I can't find the right words to thank you enough,' Steve said. 'It's a marvellous present and very thoughtful. Jill will be over the moon and I'm pretty happy meself.'

Phil sighed. 'I'm having trouble finding the right words, too. It is clearly one hell of a wedding present. But then, you are one hell of a man, Uncle Corker. The girls will thank you themselves, but you have mine, and Steve's gratitude for the best wedding present anybody ever had.'

Corker's eyes were on the door. 'Here's Jack and George. Put that receipt away and don't say a word.'

Steve and Phil left the pub after the one pint. They couldn't wait to tell the girls the news, so when they got back to the Bennetts' house, Steve said, 'Let's go for a walk, it's too nice to be indoors.'

'Good idea,' Molly said. 'Go and blow the cobwebs away.'

'I'm not putting a coat on,' Doreen said. 'I might as well show me figure off.'

'We won't be long, Mam.' Jill kissed her mother's forehead. 'About half-an-hour.'

'I'll come to the door with yer.' Molly stood on the step and watched the youngsters walking down the street, their arms across each other's waists. In three days' time they'll be married, she thought. Then she shook her head. Don't think about it or you'll end up bawling your eyes out. There'll be time enough for tears after Saturday.

They turned the corner into the main road and Steve said, 'Let's stand in the Maypole doorway. Me and Phil have got something to show yer and a lot to tell yer.'

Doreen was the first to recover. 'Oh, my God, the Adelphi! I've always promised meself that I'd go in there one day, but I never thought I really would!' She was dancing up and down and clapping her hands with joy. 'Oh, that's marvellous!'

'Trust Uncle Corker to be so thoughtful,' Jill said, thrilled at the news. She had been dreading more smutty jokes like the ones she'd heard from the girls in work. They'd thought it was funny, but she didn't and was really embarrassed. 'When I see him I'm going to hug him to death.'

'It's a secret, love,' Steve told her. 'We mustn't even tell our parents, or the whole exercise will have been a waste of time.' He bent to kiss her lips. 'Just think, our wedding night in the Adelphi Hotel. Who'd have thought it?'

There were plenty of people walking past, out for a stroll on a beautiful summer's evening. And many curious glances were directed at the doorway of the Maypole, where two pretty girls, who looked like twins, were being held aloft by two strapping lads and twirled around. Their laughter told of their happiness, and it was contagious. Many passers-by looked and smiled, before walking on with a fresh spring in their step.

Chapter Twenty-Six

Jack took one look at his brother and the years seemed to roll away until they were young boys again. As they were shaking hands and patting each other on the back, he said, 'It's good to see yer, Bill, it's been a long time.'

'Too long!' Bill felt quite emotional as he too was recalling years gone by. 'I was made up when I got yer daughter's letter.'

Molly gave her sister-in-law, Annie, a big hug and kiss. 'It's lovely to see yer. But yer'll have to excuse the place, it's upside down. And I haven't pawned the table, in case yer think we're poverty-stricken. It's up at me mate's, to give us a bit of room.' She stood back and smiled. 'I've got to say yer look very smart, Annie, and the picture of health. The years have been kind to yer.'

'It's all the fresh air I get, Molly. We've got a small farm and me and Bill manage it between us. The kids help out, but they've got jobs and farm-life isn't their cup of tea. It's a very healthy life and I enjoy it.'

'Well, sit down and I'll put the kettle on. And will you let Bill sit down, Jack, instead of gawping at him?'

'I'm counting the white hairs in his head, love, and he's got hundreds more than me.'

'I can give yer a few years, that's why.' Bill dropped on to the couch and ran a finger down the creases in his trousers. He and Jack were alike in looks, and both had an even temperament. 'Is Nellie Mac still yer mate, Molly?'

'She certainly is, and the best mate anyone could ask for. Yer'll be seeing her soon, 'cos when yer've had a cuppa, I'll be chasing yer up there. Ye're going in the wedding car with them.' That had been a hasty arrangement because Molly wasn't as organised as she thought and had completely forgotten that it was only proper that Jack's brother and his wife should go in the wedding cars. She, herself, was now going with Miss Clegg and company. 'I don't want yer to think that after all these years, ye're getting chased from yer brother's house. But upstairs I've got two brides in one bedroom, and five bridesmaids in the other. And they're determined that no one is going to see them before they arrive at the church.'

'Five bridesmaids!' Annie looked stunned. 'It's going to be some wedding, isn't it?'

'Two weddings really, Annie, don't forget,' Jack said. 'Me and Molly are losing two of our daughters today.'

'Don't start me off, Jack Bennett,' Molly said, heading for the kitchen. 'I don't want to arrive at the church with me eyes red raw. I'll make a pot of tea, then when they've had a drink I'll take Bill and Annie up to Nellie's.'

Molly stood in front of her husband and did a little twirl. 'How do I look, love?'

Jack's eyes started at her shoes, moved up her still-shapely legs until he reached her hat. 'Nellie was right, yer do look like a film star. I'm very proud of yer and the girls will be. And I love yer to bits, Molly Bennett.'

'And you look very handsome in yer new suit with the red rose in yer lapel, Jack Bennett. If I wasn't already crazy about yer, I'd certainly fall for yer now.'

They heard footsteps on the stairs and their eyes were on the door when Doreen came in. She was clad in an old wrap-around pinny of Molly's, and grinned when she saw the shock on the faces of her parents. 'The bridesmaids are coming down now, Mam, so yer can see them before yer go over the road. But me and Jill are not coming down until everyone has left. We want yer to see us for the first time in our dresses at the church. Yer don't mind, do yer, Mam?'

'No, sunshine, I don't mind. But aren't you cutting it a bit fine for time?'

'I've only got to put me dress on. Me face is made-up and me hair's been brushed until me scalp is sore. It'll only take me a quarter of an hour to get ready.' Doreen wasn't a crier, and she tried to keep the catch out of her voice when she said, 'Mam, yer look really beautiful. I am so proud that you're my mother.' With that she turned tail and fled up the stairs.

Molly was wiping a tear away when Ruthie led the bridesmaids into the room. 'How do we look, Mam? Dad?'

'Yer look lovely, sunshine, all of yer.' Maureen and Lily were the same height and they stood together. Then came Phoebe and Dorothy, with Ruthie, the smallest, in the front. 'I'm trying not to cry, but I have never seen such a pretty picture as you five make. The dresses are really beautiful, and the flowers in the hair-bands look beautiful. But it is the beauty of the faces that completes the picture.'

'Thank you, Mrs B.,' Maureen said. She had known the family since she was fourteen and had started work in Johnson's the same day as Doreen. 'And if we're giving compliments, I'd like to say you look stunning.'

'You certainly do!' Lily said. 'The dress is perfect on you and the hat very eyecatching.'

For Phoebe and Dorothy it was the most exciting day of their lives and they were loving every minute of it. They'd had little to say for themselves, being too nervous, but now Phoebe ventured to say, 'Yer look lovely, Mrs Bennett.'

Dorothy wasn't going to be left out. 'Yes, yer look smashing.'

Ruthie, who thought her mother always looked lovely, said, 'I love you, Mam!'

'And I love you, sunshine.' Molly decided it was time to leave before things got too emotional. 'The posies are in the kitchen when ye're ready. I'll have to scarper now because the car is due at Miss Clegg's any minute. I'll see you all at the church.' She glanced at her husband, and knowing what this day meant to him, said softly, 'Good luck, love.'

Steve and Paul were sitting in the front pew at one side of the church, with Nellie sitting at the end of the pew behind. Next to her were George, his sister Ethel with her husband Johnny, and Archie. Nellie looked splendid in the dress and jacket Doreen had made for her, and the hat was such a huge success she was feeling on top of the world. Not one swearword had left her lips since she'd put the feathered creation on her head. George, God love him, thought his wife had got a bargain with her thirty-bob hat from TJ's. Nellie would tell him the truth one day, when he was reading the newspaper and not really listening. I mean, it was no good asking for trouble if it could be avoided.

On the opposite side of the aisle sat Phil and Corker. And behind them were Molly, Miss Clegg, Lizzie Corkhill, Archie's mother, Ida, and Jack's brother and his wife. The row behind was occupied by Bridie and Bob, Tommy and Rosie.

There was no sign of the priest, and being nosy, Molly wanted to see if any of their neighbours were there. She stood up and glanced around the church. The first familiar face she saw was Tommy's friend, Ginger, with his girlfriend. As she waved, she thought the lad hadn't changed much over the years. His hair was still bright ginger and his face covered with freckles. But he was a really nice lad and Molly was very fond of him. Then, near the back of the church she spied Mary and Harry Watson, with their daughter Bella. And beside them sat Ellen, with her two sons. They shouldn't be sitting back there, they were guests! Ellen's two daughters were bridesmaids, so she should be right down here at the front of the church. And so should the Watsons – they'd been invited as guests. Bella had been Ruthie's friend since they were toddlers and Ruthie spent more time in the Watsons' than she did in her own house. So Molly waved them forward to sit with family and friends.

Then she glanced across the aisle to where Nellie was sitting. I've never known her be so quiet, Molly thought. It must be that hat – it's literally gone to her head. I'll have a word with her. 'The church is filling up, Nellie, have yer noticed?' She spotted Maureen's boyfriend, Sammy, and waved. 'I think everyone from our street is here, and a few other streets.'

'I haven't looked, girl, 'cos I've found that if I turn me head, me hat doesn't turn with it. So I'd end up with me facing one way, and me hat the other!'

Molly put a hand across her mouth to stifle her laughter. Trust her mate to put humour into a serious occasion like this! 'I'm going back to me seat, Nellie, or folk will think I'm laughing 'cos I'm getting rid of two of me daughters.'

Corker looked around when she sat down. 'What's Nellie up to now?'

She beckoned him closer and repeated in a whisper what Nellie had said. She wasn't to know that Corker was of the opinion that churches should be places of joy, as well as sadness. And when his loud guffaw rang out, she knelt down and lowered her head as though in prayer.

'I'm going to tell Phil that little gem.' Corker's whisper was almost like the roar of a lion. 'He needs something to take his mind off the wait, he's getting nervous.'

'He's not the only one,' Steve said, walking on tiptoe across the aisle. 'I need something to take me mind off things. This is the longest quarter of an hour I've ever known.'

And so it was, when the organ struck up with the *Wedding March*, that thanks to Nellie's hat, the two grooms had broad smiles on their faces.

No father had ever been more proud than Jack Bennett was as he began the walk down the aisle with a daughter on each arm. There were gasps and smiles of admiration from the congregation for the two sisters who wore beautiful matching dresses of ivory silk which rustled with each step they took. And the ivory veils covering their faces were held in place with a band of flowers which matched those in their bouquets.

'Oh, my God, they're beautiful!' Molly clutched at her handkerchief but willed herself not to cry and spoil something so perfect. What she was seeing now, her beloved husband looking so proud and walking tall, with an angel on each arm, was a picture that would stay in her mind for ever. She looked behind to see her mother and father crying, and knew it was the same pride and happiness she felt.

Corker moved to stand at the side of Phil, while at the same time, Paul closed in on Steve. And the four men turned to see a sight that left them breathless. Behind the visions in ivory silk, came the five lovely bridesmaids. Maureen and Lily came first as chief bridesmaids, then Phoebe and Dorothy, followed by a happy, smiling Ruthie. It truly was a sight to behold.

His voice choked, Steve said, 'She's the most beautiful dream I've ever had.'

'Ye're a very lucky bloke, our kid,' Paul said, and meant it.

Phil was too full of emotion to speak. Everything became a blur, and when the priest asked who was giving the brides away, his voice seemed to come through a long tunnel. The brides' bouquets were passed to someone, but he didn't know who. He began to worry that he'd faint, or wouldn't be able to repeat the vows after the priest. Then he felt his hand being squeezed and he saw Doreen smiling at him through her veil. She felt so happy she wasn't nervous at all, and with the touch of her hand she passed her confidence over to Phil.

Nellie stepped from the pew and touched Lily on the arm. 'Yer all look lovely, girl. I'm proud of yer.'

Lily smiled and let her eyes go along the pew to where Archie was staring at her with his admiration clear for all to see. She gave him a broad wink before turning back to listen to the priest and to carry out her role as chief bridesmaid to Jill.

Molly and Nellie managed to keep their emotions under control until the brides lifted their veils and their beauty was exposed. Then the tears started, but even as Molly was dabbing at her eyes, she couldn't help a thought entering her head. Had Nellie managed to get the man's hankie out of the pocket of her knickers?

The service was longer than a usual marriage ceremony because the priest had to ask each couple to repeat the vows. But eventually he declared them man and wife and said the grooms could kiss the brides. Then the foursome were led through a door at the side of the altar where a registrar was waiting to complete their marriage certificates. Corker and Paul were asked to accompany them as they were acting as witnesses for both couples, also Molly and Jack, and Nellie and George.

'Where is everyone?' Corker was surprised to see the church empty except for the bridesmaids and several people sitting at the back. 'The church was packed before.'

'They've all gone outside so they can see us coming out,' Lily told him. 'We'll probably get pelted with confetti and rice.' She grinned. 'And perhaps a few old boots for luck.'

'I'm going outside then,' Molly said. 'I don't want to miss anything. Come on, Jack, the boys have taken over from yer now.'

'Wait for me and George, girl, we're coming with yer.'

'Don't get mixed up in the crowd, Mam,' Steve warned. 'The photographer will be taking pictures when we get outside.'

'Yer don't think I'd miss getting me picture took in this hat, do yer, son? Not ruddy likely I won't!' Nellie hurried to catch up with her mate, leaving Jack and George to follow.

'Jack, I've never seen anything like it in me life,' George said. 'Everything was perfect, yer couldn't fault it.'

'Yes, Molly and the girls did a good job. It was worth all the worry.'

The mass of people outside the church frightened Molly. 'In the name of God, they'll never be able to take photographs here!'

But Nellie had seen the photographer with his camera and she took charge. As she was to say later, what was the good of wearing a posh hat if you couldn't take charge? So she pushed her way through the crowd. 'Yer'll have to move some of these people out on to the pavement, lad, or yer'll never stand a chance.'

The photographer, whose name was Sam, eyed her up and down and decided she was a woman who could take care of herself. 'Will yer give me a hand?'

'Of course I will, lad! Only too happy to help.' Nellie's eyes moved over the mass of people until she saw a few near neighbours. 'Mrs Robinson, Mrs Cleary, will yer try and get some of these good folk to stand outside? They'll still be able to see through the railings. But if they don't move, there'll be no wedding photographs.'

About six voices answered. 'OK, Nellie, consider it done.' And, 'Leave it to us, queen, and you go and get yer photy took.'

Ida Higgins elbowed her way towards Molly. 'I'm worried about the two old dears, Molly, they'll get killed in the crush. Lizzie's not so bad, but Miss Clegg can't stand all these people.'

'Bring them back into the church, will yer, Ida? They can sit down and just be brought out to go on the photographs. The first car is for the brides and grooms, so they'll be at the hall first to welcome the guests. But I'll make sure Victoria and Lizzie are in the second car.'

The next half-hour was a flurry of activity, with the newlyweds being photographed as a foursome and separately. Then each with their best man, and then the bridesmaids. After that it was immediate family, then friends. No one noticed that on each of the group photos, Archie managed to be standing close to Lily, and Paul as near to Phoebe as she would allow. It would probably be noticed when the photographs were developed in a week's time, but by then a lot of water would have flowed under the bridge.

Molly and Nellie stood inside the door of the reception room over Hanley's cake-shop. They both had their hands laced in front of them and looked the picture of pride and contentment. Edna Hanley had certainly lived up to her promise because the room looked lovely. The seating arrangement had been made for the top table to take the newlyweds, bridesmaids, best men and immediate family. Then a long table ran down from each side to cater for the guests. The three-tier wedding cake stood proud in the centre, and there were three vases of flowers on each table. The glasses standing by each place setting were gleaming, as was the cutlery, and the paper serviettes had *Congratulations* printed in each corner.

'Yer couldn't fall out with it, could yer, sunshine?' Molly asked. 'Edna has certainly done us proud.'

'Ye're not kidding.' Nellie turned her head to look up at her friend but her hat didn't bother moving. 'If yer were rolling in money yer couldn't have done any better.'

Molly silently agreed as her eyes roamed the room. Jack was in animated conversation with his brother and his wife, and she knew he was asking them to come for dinner one Saturday, so they could really have a good talk about the old days, and how they'd fared in the years since they'd last met. 'I'm glad your George is looking after his sister and her husband. It's hard when there's so many people, to make sure no one is left out.'

'Lizzie and Victoria seem to be enjoying themselves, girl, so yer don't have to worry about them. Ida's keeping them amused, and the Watsons, too.'

'Have yer noticed anything else, sunshine?'

'Yes, I have girl, I'm not blind! Archie's never left our Lily's side since we came out of the church. She's not exactly falling over him, but she's not chasing him away, either. So I'm keeping me fingers crossed.'

'Is that all yer've noticed?'

Once again Nellie's hat stayed put. There was no point in trying to keep up with a head that was always swivelling around. 'No, I've noticed young Phoebe putting our Paul in his place. It's about time someone did, 'cos he thinks he's God's gift to women. It'll be interesting to see if he stays the course, 'cos he's not used to running after a girl; it's usually the other way around.'

Molly saw Ginger and his girlfriend coming up the stairs.

'Here's the last of the stragglers, so I'll get Corker to sit everyone down now. He's got a plan of the tables and knows where everyone is sitting.'

But Corker had no intention of doing it alone. There was another best man beside himself, and at this very moment, that man was trying very hard, using every trick in the book, to make an impression on Phoebe. The lad was having very little luck, much to Corker's amusement. His daughter was the shyest, most gentle person he knew, and she'd never had a boyfriend. There were times when he worried about her, and wished she was more outgoing, like Dorothy, because he wanted to see her enjoying herself. But right now he was seeing a different side to her and knew his fears were groundless. Phoebe could take care of herself, all right – no doubt about that. She was being very aloof with Paul and had him running around in circles. A surefire way of fanning the flames of the lad's interest.

'Paul, come and give us a hand.' Corker handed him a piece of paper. 'There's a plan of where everyone is sitting. So if you'll see them to their places, I'll get George to help me fill the glasses for a toast. Can yer manage that, son?'

'Of course I can, Uncle Corker.' Paul's eyes were devouring the names and seating plan. When he looked up, there was a gleam in his eyes which very much resembled that in Nellie's eyes, when she was up to mischief. 'Leave it to me, I'll have everything under control in no time. Have no fear, Paul is here.'

Chapter Twenty-Seven

And so it came to pass that even though Archie's name wasn't down for the top table, he was delighted to find himself seated next to Lily. And of course, wasn't Paul clever enough to wangle a seat next to Phoebe. This was no surprise to the girl; in fact, she'd have been really put out if he hadn't been next to her. Not that she would have admitted it, though.

Molly was puzzled when she saw Paul move a chair and place-setting from the side table to the top one. Why was he doing that? She'd spent hours getting the names and numbers right! Then she saw Archie slip on to the mysterious chair which had miraculously appeared next to Lily. The crafty beggars! Then Molly smiled. Wasn't all fair in love and war? And did it really matter if they all had to move their chairs up a bit to make room? In her book, romance came before comfort every time.

Corker had been asked to act as toastmaster before the meal was served, then later there would be speeches. So when everyone had a full glass in front of them, he rose to his feet. 'I would like to propose a toast to the newlyweds. May they have a long and happy life and may their love never dim. So raise your glasses to the beautiful brides and their grooms.'

'Hang on, hang on!' Glasses were lowered when Nellie's voice rang out. 'Why is it beautiful brides, but not handsome grooms? Let's be fair, now. I think my Steve and Phil look very handsome indeed!'

Molly looked along the table to where her friend was standing. Here was the opening for which she'd waited weeks. 'All right, sunshine, don't be losing yer equilibrium.'

The look on Nellie's face brought forth hoots of laughter. She narrowed her eyes, held on to her hat so it moved with her head, and glared at Molly. 'I don't know what it is yer think I'm losing, girl, but if it's an insult, that hat what makes yer look like a film star will be rammed down over yer ears.' Her narrowed eyes gazed around. 'Is there anyone in the room clever enough to know what that word means, before I clock her one?'

'I'll tell yer, sunshine,' Molly said. 'It means don't be losing yer rag!'

'Is that all? Yer don't half waste a lot of breath, Molly Bennett!' Nellie smiled sweetly at Corker. 'Can we have the toast now, but proper this time?'

The big man was chuckling as he raised his glass. 'To the beautiful brides and their *very handsome* husbands.'

Edna Hanley and her daughter waited for the guests to sit down, then working in harmony and with speed, they served plates of salad with bread and butter to go with the ham, tomato ketchup and salad cream. Then mother and daughter quietly withdrew to wait outside until the meal was finished. They could hear the talking and laughter and wished they were inside. Especially when Nellie was telling the guests how she managed to get her husband's hankie out of the pocket in her knickers. The laughter was so loud they knew she must be showing them how she did it – and they were right. Nellie wasn't going to miss an opportunity to make people laugh. Especially as it was her eldest son's wedding day.

When the meal was over, Emily cleared the plates while Edna brought in cake-stands filled with a wide variety of cakes, jelly creams and trifles. And once again the glasses were replenished. Jack had said he didn't want to make a speech because he didn't think he'd get the words past the lump in his throat. He was going to leave it to Corker and Paul, and of course the two grooms. But now the time had come, he felt he must say something, even if he made a fool of himself. So, taking a deep breath, he pushed his chair back. 'I only want to say a few words, then I'll leave the speechmaking to others.' He felt Molly grip his hand and grinned down at her. 'I don't think any man has ever felt as proud as I did today walking my beautiful, beloved daughters down the aisle. I didn't want to give them away, me and Molly don't want to lose them. But I did so in the knowledge I was handing them over to two fine men, who will love and take good care of them. We've haven't lost two daughters today, we've gained two sons.'

Tommy was sitting at the top of one of the side tables with his nan, granda and Rosie. He hadn't intended saying anything, either, but they were his two sisters and they were the grand-daughters of Bridie and Bob, who were shedding a few tears. He couldn't let the occasion pass without a word. So after kissing Bridie and Rosie, he got to his feet. 'This will be short and sweet and it comes from me nan and granda, as well as Rosie and meself. I'm so proud of me two big sisters, always have been. Today they look more beautiful because they've married the men they love. And I want them to know that me nan, granda, Rosie

366

and meself, love them very much. They'll be missed at home, but thank God they'll still be living down our street. We wish them, and Steve and Phil, all the luck in the world.'

'Oh dear,' Lily whispered to Archie. 'If they keep this up, I'll be crying me eyes out.'

'I'll lend yer me hankie.'

'Well, I certainly wouldn't borrow me mam's, not after knowing where it's been.' Lily turned to look straight into Archie's eyes. It was at that moment she felt a stirring in her heart, and she turned away quickly to hide her blushes.

A few seats away, Paul was getting nowhere fast with Phoebe. So he decided if he didn't take the plunge now, he might never get another chance. And she looked good enough to eat in her bridesmaid's dress. 'Will yer come dancing with me one night? Or to the flicks, whichever yer want?'

Phoebe lowered her lashes. Her heart was beating like mad because she'd dreamt of hearing him say this so often. But she wasn't about to let him know that. She wasn't going to run after him like other girls did. 'Yer'll have to ask me dad.'

'Ask yer dad?' Paul's voice was high with surprise. 'Why would I ask yer dad? It's not him I want to take out.'

'If yer want to take me out, yer'll have to ask him.' Phoebe lifted her hand. 'Hush, he's just got to his feet.'

It would have been difficult for anyone else to have stood up and, as Phil's best man, give a speech about a groom who had not one single relative in his life. Apart from the woman he called Auntie Vickie, and adored, he was alone in the world. But Corker didn't find it a problem. 'Phil came into our lives six years ago, and all our lives have been enriched because of him. He brought love and companionship to Miss Clegg, who gave him a home and idolises him. He joined the army before being called up, and he fought on the beaches at Dunkirk. A man to be proud of. Victoria Clegg looks on him as a grandson, I look on him as my son. He fell in love with Doreen at first sight, and although there was a time they had a short falling-out, they've been in love ever since. It does my heart good to see them now as man and wife, and I know they'll be good for each other.'

When Corker had finished, Molly dabbed at her eyes and whispered to Jack, 'I know every woman cries at a wedding, but I've never stopped!'

'Yer can't help it, love, it's so emotional. But I think all the sad bits are over now.'

It was Paul's turn next as his brother's best man. And there were many people in that room who blessed him for starting off by making them laugh. 'I've known me brother a long time.' The laughter perked him up and made him less nervous. 'Well, ever since the day I was born, really. And we've always got on, except when I borrow one of his shirts or something without asking. But one thing he'd never let me borrow was his girlfriend. He wouldn't let me push her go-chair, even though I offered him me best ollie! I thought it was a bit mean, really, 'cos brothers are supposed to share. But looking at her now, I know *I* wouldn't have parted with her for a bag of ollies, never mind one. They've waited so long for this day, and nobody is happier than I am that it has finally come at last. And what a perfect day it's been.' Paul glanced down at Phoebe and winked. Then he leaned forward and looked along the row. 'Uncle Corker, would yer like to come to a dance with me one night?'

After a second's stunned silence, Nellie said, 'Ay, things are not that bad, are they, Paul? Can't yer get yerself a girl? That's what boys are supposed to do, yer know.'

'I'm sorry, lad,' Corker said, 'but I don't think the missus would like it.' He knew Paul's humour was very like his mother's, they both loved slapstick comedy. 'But why ask?'

'Phoebe told me to! I asked her to come out with me one night and she said to ask you! I told her I didn't fancy yer, but she would have me ask.'

Corker chuckled as he looked across at his wife. 'What d'yer think, Ellen?'

Ellen was delighted. Never a word had ever been said, but as a mother, she knew where her eldest daughter's heart lay. 'It's all right with me, but it's up to Phoebe.'

Paul sat down looking pleased with himself. 'There yer are! Yer made me walk the plank and I did. Now will yer come out with me?'

'We'll see. Ask me later.' Little did he know Phoebe had it all planned in her head. It was part of her dream. She wanted to be dancing with him when he asked.

Glasses were refilled so the two grooms could thank Molly and Jack for giving them such a marvellous day, and also for having given them their two daughters. Steve praised his parents for the love they'd given him over the years, while an emotional Phil thanked his Aunt Vickie for giving him a home and someone to call his own. Then they both gave thanks for the presents and cards that had been delivered to the Bennetts' house over the last few days.

When the speeches were finished, Edna and Emily came in to clear the tables and push them back to make room for dancing. 'We'll bring the pies and sausage rolls up about eight, Molly,' Edna said. 'They'll be getting peckish by then.'

'I'm very grateful to yer, Edna, everything's been perfect. We'll have to ask yer to do the same for Tommy, next year.'

'Are yer dancing, Lily?' Archie asked, holding out his hand.

'Are yer asking, Archie?'

'I'm asking, Lily.'

'Then I'm dancing, Archie.' Lily slipped into his arms and they danced to the strains of a waltz. Then, almost shyly, she said, 'Fred Astaire and Ginger Rogers are on the Broadway next week, did yer know?'

'I'd go and see them if you'd come with me. Will yer do that, Lily?' When she nodded, he asked, 'Will yer be my girl?'

'Yes, Archie, I'll be your girl.'

'My God, Molly,' Nellie said. 'Look at the way Archie's spinning our Lily around! She'll get dizzy if she's not careful.'

'If the look on their faces is anything to go by, sunshine, I'd say he's asked and she's said yes.'

'Ooh, er! Now that would make my day complete.'

Paul was behaving in a very gentlemanly manner. 'Will yer dance with me, Phoebe?'

'Yes, Paul, I'd like that.' This was part of Phoebe's dream coming true. And as she knew they would, they danced beautifully together. All it needed now were the right words for her dream to be complete.

'Yer look very pretty, Phoebe, and I really do like yer.'

'I bet yer say that to all the girls!'

'I've never said it to a girl yet! I dance with them, that's all. Scout's honour, I've never told any girl that they were pretty and I liked them. So say yer'll come out with me one night, please? Then I'll be able to sleep tonight.'

'Oh well, I can't have yer losing any sleep over me, can I?' Everything Phoebe had hoped for in her dreams had come true, and her heart and tummy were doing somersaults. 'So if yer like yer can call for me on Monday night. Does that suit yer?'

'Oh my God, girl, there's our Paul at it now!' Nellie's hat stood still but her chins moved with her shaking head. 'They'll trip over if they're not careful.'

'If yer look closely, sunshine, yer'll see they've got the same soppy look on their faces as Lily and Archie have.'

'Go 'way!' Nellie looked very smug. 'I thought our Paul had taken a shine to Phoebe, but I didn't tell yer in case yer thought I was crazy. But I've watched him the last week or so, and he waits until he hears the Corkhills' door bang, then he's out like a shot.'

'It's not bad going, sunshine, two of yer kids starting courting in one night.'

'Oh, er, d'yer think so, girl? I'd better put this hat away carefully then, 'cos there's a few weddings in the offing.'

'Nellie, Phoebe is only seventeen!'

'It's a good hat, girl – it'll keep. And in the meantime I'll train it to turn when I do.'

'Gordon, are yer going to dance with me?' Ruthie pleaded. 'We can just walk around, we don't have to dance.'

'I can't dance.' Gordon's voice was breaking and at the moment it was gruff. 'We'd look right nits walking round.'

'Your Dorothy said she'd dance with Peter, so we could all look like nits together.' She pulled on his hand. 'Come on, Gordon, don't be mean. I'll never have another long dress like this again in me life. I just want to feel what it's like to twirl around in it.'

Peter, at thirteen years of age, wasn't as shy as his older brother. 'I'll have a go, our Dorothy. I don't care if people think I'm daft.'

Ruthie watched them walking on to the floor swinging their hands between them as they tried a few side steps. 'Ye're dead mean you are, Gordon.'

'Oh, all right! But don't say I didn't warn yer. If I see one person laugh I'm sitting down again, and staying put.' Gordon's voice was now at a high squeaking pitch. 'Come on, before I change me mind.'

Ruthie held her dress a couple of inches from the floor as she'd seen them do in the pictures, and she felt like a million dollars.

Nellie gave Molly a dig. 'Ay, girl, when did yer say your Tommy was getting married?'

'Next summer, so he says.'

'And what about your Ruthie?'

'Our Ruthie? In the name of God, Nellie, she doesn't leave school for another year!'

'I'm only asking, girl, 'cos she's spinning around now with young Gordon. She's not half starting young.'

Molly was about to tell her to stop acting the goat when she saw Maureen approaching with her boyfriend, Sammy. 'Are yer enjoying yerself, sunshine?'

'It's been a wonderful day, Mrs B.' Maureen was holding her boyfriend's hand. 'Me and Sammy have got something to tell yer, but we'd rather yer kept it to yerself for now because today belongs to Jill and Doreen.' She held her hand in front of Molly's face and wagged her fingers. 'See, we got engaged last week.'

'Oh, I'm so happy for yer, sunshine – and you, Sammy. That's a lovely ring.' Molly was thinking of the years she'd seen the hunger in Maureen's eyes every time she looked at Phil. But her eyes were clear now, no sadness or regret. 'We'll have a party for yer when we've got over this.'

'Yeah, we'll come up and see yer, Mrs B.' Sammy pulled on Maureen's arm, eager to get on to the dance floor and hold her in his arms. 'And thanks for today, it's been great.'

The couple had just walked away when Tommy's friend Ginger came up with his girlfriend. 'Don't tell me ye're going to say yer've got engaged, Ginger, 'cos I've had enough surprises to last me for a while.'

The freckled face broke into a smile. 'This is Rita, Mrs B. and we're getting engaged next week. But I won't tell yer now, I don't want to overload yer with surprises.'

While Molly was hugging him, she was thinking how quickly time passes. It seemed no time at all since this boy was a little nipper, always getting into scrapes and taking Tommy along with him. He'd been a good mate to her son, and they'd never had a falling-out.

When the couple left, Nellie gave Molly a sharp dig in the ribs. 'It must be something in the water, girl! Whatever it is, it's bloodywell catching. Oh, to be twenty-one again.'

'Nellie, yer were married at twenty-one.'

'Was I, girl? It's that long ago I'd forgotten.'

'Come on, let's mingle with the guests, sunshine. I'll go and sit with Victoria for a while. I'm surprised she's stayed the course till now, she must be getting tired. You have a natter with Lizzie and Ida, spread yerself around.'

Jill and Steve weren't dancers, but they took to the floor so they could hold each other and steal kisses. 'Don't blush, sweetheart, we're allowed to hold each other and kiss in public, now we're man and wife.'

'I'm getting worried about leaving and not telling me mam the truth,' Jill told him. 'She's been so good, and done so much, it seems a lousy thing to do. And I love the bones of her and me dad.'

'She'll understand, love, and she'll be pleased for yer, I bet.' They were dancing near Doreen and Phil, who were excellent dancers, and he beckoned them over and spoke softly about Jill's misgivings. 'What d'yer think?'

'It's been on my mind, as well,' Doreen said. 'I vote that when we say we're going home to change, we ask me mam to come down the stairs with us. What d'yer reckon, Jill?'

'I would feel better,' Jill admitted. 'And I think we should spend a bit of time now with me nan and granda.'

Phil nodded. 'You three go, I want to sit with Aunt Vickie for a while. And I haven't had much chance to talk to the bloke I work with, Jimmy and his wife.'

Doreen hesitated. 'Yer won't be long, will yer?'

'Ten minutes, love, that's all.'

'It's been a grand day, sweethearts, so it has,' Bridie said. 'Sure, it was better than I ever could have imagined. Me and Bob have shed a few tears, haven't we, me darlin'?'

'A few?' Bob laughed. 'I've shed a bucketful. I was so proud of you I thought me poor old heart would stop.'

'As Auntie Bridget said, it's been a grand day, right enough.' Rosie had been dancing with Tommy and their faces were red with the exertion. 'I've been telling meself that God said we mustn't envy others, but sure hasn't the divil himself been working on me? Try as I might, I have to admit to a little envy. But I'll not be telling me mammy that when I write home.'

'Wait until next year, love, then these two will be old married women,' Tommy said, with his arms across the shoulders of his two sisters. 'And you'll be the blushing bride.'

'Oh, that'll be the day, right enough!' Bridie said. 'Getting married to her beloved with her mammy and daddy here to see it. Sure, she'll be the happiest girl alive.'

'Yer'll make a lovely bride, Rosie, and we'll all be happy for yer,' Steve said. 'And I can't wait to meet yer mammy and hear all these sayings she has.'

Just talking of her parents was enough to put a smile of happiness on Rosie's beautiful face. 'As me mammy would say, Steve, patience is a virtue, and that's what we'll have to have for a whole year.'

'We'll be going home to get changed soon, Nan, so we'd better have a word with Uncle Bill and Auntie Annie 'cos they're leaving about eight.' Doreen bent down and gave her grandmother a hug and kiss, then her granda. 'I love yer both very much.'

Jill followed suit, then hurried away before the tears started. Phil joined them then, and they had a word with everyone in the hall before Corker whispered that it was time they left. Steve took him to one side and explained the girls couldn't face leaving without telling their mam what was happening. And the big man understood and thought himself that Molly deserved that. So when the newlyweds called that they were going home to change, the girls kissed their father and asked their mother if she'd mind carrying the bouquets down the stairs for them.

Steve felt a pang of guilt and ran back to kiss his mother. 'Ye're the best, bar none, Mam. I'll see yer!'

'Why do you have to go 'cos the girls are getting changed? Or do they need you and Phil to help them?'

Steve was halfway across the room and pretended not to hear. He could imagine the cheeky grin on his mother's face and smiled. He could take the ribbing, but knew Jill would have been sick with embarrassment. And the evening was just beginning; the jokes would start getting worse as more drink was consumed. Thank God for Uncle Corker!

When Steve reached the bottom of the stairs, Molly was being smothered with kisses. She'd been told what Corker had done, and although she was weepy, she was happy for the girls. Sniffing up, she said, 'The Adelphi, no less! We're certainly coming up in the world.'

'Will yer explain to everyone, Mam, and thank them?' Jill asked. 'Especially Mrs Corkhill, 'cos she's expecting us there tonight.'

'And me dad,' Doreen said. 'I hope he won't be upset.'

'Nobody will be upset, they'll be made up for yer. And before yer ask, Phil, I'll make sure Victoria is looked after.' Molly waved them away. 'Poppy off and enjoy the Adelphi. And take a good look around 'cos I'll want to know all about it. I've always longed to know how the other half live.'

Molly composed herself before walking back up the stairs. She'd give them time to get away before telling anyone. Except Jack, she'd have to tell him.

The dancing had stopped and everyone was watching Nellie. She was standing at the top of the room and asked for everyone's attention. 'My mate, Molly Bennett, says I can't walk in a straight line. And tonight, after a few drinks, I'm about to prove her wrong. So just watch this.' With her arms out balancing herself, she began to walk down the room. She looked like a tightrope walker with her arms out, and there was much laughter. When she reached the bottom of the room, she turned, her face split into a wide grin. 'How about that, then?'

Molly wasn't having any of that! 'Hang on, sunshine, tell it like it is. Corker, will you stand in the centre of the floor, at the top? And if me and Nellie start here, that should be a straight line. Right?'

Corker hopped to it. 'OK, Molly, walk down in a straight line, and yer'll bump into me.'

Molly bent her arm. 'Link me, sunshine, like yer always do.'

They began to walk, with Nellie's hips swaying. They'd only covered a few feet before Corker could see what was happening

373

and he bent double with laughter. But the friends carried on, and before they'd covered half the distance, they were rubbing knees with the people sitting on chairs at the side of the room. Molly spread out her hands. 'See what I mean?'

'You cheated, girl!' Nellie said. 'Yer pulled me over there.'

'Me pull you! Me and whose army, sunshine?'

Nellie put on the spoilt little girl look. 'I'm not playing that game no more 'cos I don't like it.'

Molly bent until their noses were touching. 'Ah, shall I pick yer dummy up for yer?'

'Sod off, Molly Bennett! I'll wait for me new daughter-in-law, she can pick me dummy up.'

This is it, thought Molly, putting her arm across Nellie's shoulder and pulling her close. 'I've some news for yer, sunshine, and for everyone. The newlyweds won't be coming back. Yer see, Corker gave them a wonderful wedding present. And just about now, they'll be stepping out of a taxi in front of the Adelphi Hotel, where they'll be spending the night. Thanks to their Uncle Corker.'

There were gasps as family and friends digested the news. Then the young ones started to clap and cheer. Nellie lost her voice for a while, then she squared her shoulders and thrust her bosom out. 'Did yer hear that, George? Our son sleeping in the Adelphi Hotel?' She took off her hat and flicked imaginary dust from the brim before settling it back firmly on her head. 'It's a good job we bought posh hats, girl, we wouldn't want to let the side down.'

'I don't know how yer make that out, sunshine, but I'll agree with yer for a quiet life. But isn't it wonderful for the kids to start their married life in style? I think Corker deserves a round of applause for what he's done.'

That was right up Nellie's street. 'Come on, folks, how about thanking Corker for what he did for the kids. Hip-hip-hurrah for Corker. Hip-hip-hurrah!' The room rang with laughter and cheering. And after waiting for the noise to die down, Nellie said, 'Me and my mate are now going to sing a song to match the occasion. Get yer hat on, girl!'

'I'm not singing in front of all these people!'

'Oh, yes you are!' Nellie marched over to the table where Molly had left her hat and returned to plonk it on her head. 'Now, follow me, Molly Bennett.' Pretending to be walking with a cane, and twirling it every few seconds, the little woman began to sing:

> 'As I walk along the Bois Bou-long
> With an independent air,
> You can hear the girls declare,
> He must be a millionaire . . .'

Ida ran to join in, followed by Maisie from the corner shop. And pretty soon the whole room was ringing to the sounds of 'The Man Who Broke the Bank at Monte Carlo'.

Jack was sitting next to George and they both gave a sigh of contentment. 'It's been a good day, Jack – the best I've ever had. Thanks to you and Molly, our kids have had a wedding day they'll remember all their lives. It did my heart good to see our Steve so happy.'

'I'm happy that both my girls have married good men, George. And right now, watching Molly and Nellie, I'm delighted the two families have been joined together. It's what they've always wanted. Mates for twenty-five years, and they love the bones of each other. We're lucky with our wives, George, we couldn't have picked better.'

'I'll say Amen to that, Jack! Just look at the pair of them now, they're ruddy heroes.'

'Put yer hat down, girl,' Nellie was saying. 'Yer don't need it 'cos the next song is about tramps.'

'I'm not singing another song!' Molly huffed. 'Get someone else up.'

'Ye're me best mate, Molly Bennett, and yer'll sing with me if I have to sit on yer.' Nellie turned her mate sideways and put a hand on her shoulder. She wouldn't have cared if she knew the elastic in one of her knicker legs was loose and everyone could see her best pale-blue bloomers. They were clean, weren't they, what more did they want? 'OK, let's go, girl!'

Nellie and Molly sang 'Underneath the Arches' with all their hearts. The room was filled with warmth, love and laughter. A perfect end to a perfect day. And a few miles away, in the Adelphi Hotel, four shy young lovers were discovering the joys of marriages that were made in heaven.

375